with **surprising twists and turns** that keep you rooting for
Nora and Charlie every step of the way'
TIA WILLIAMS, author of *Seven Days in June*

'A **rom-com lover's dream** of a book. **Razor-sharp** and modern,
featuring a **fierce heroine** who does not apologize for her ambition.
Emily Henry never fails to deliver **great banter** and a **romance
to swoon over,** but this may just be **her best yet**'
TAYLOR JENKINS REID, author of *Malibu Rising*

'I **loved every page, every line.** It's **so smart, so funny** and **so sexy**'
BETH O'LEARY, author of *The Flatshare*

'**Utterly one of a kind.** I've loved every single one of her
books more than the previous, to the point that
I cannot wait to see what her next title will do to me!'
ALI HAZELWOOD, author of *The Love Hypothesis*

'*Book Lovers* is **every bit as addictive** as *Beach Read*! Emily has that
gift for making you laugh and cry within the space of a few sentences.
Not to mention the **sizzling chemistry**! Her characters fizz like
good champagne. They **leap off the page and into your heart**'
JOSIE SILVER, author of *One Day in December*

'Emily Henry is my newest **automatic-buy author**'
JODI PICOULT, author of *Small Great Things*

'The **most phenomenal portrayal of enemies to lovers I have
ever read.** I don't understand how Emily Henry can **KEEP
getting better and better** when her books are already so good!

A ⟶ ... Tod ... ⟩ ...e'
LAUR... ... ...be

'Emily He... ...hron'
SOP...

TITLES BY EMILY HENRY

Book Lovers
You and Me on Vacation
Beach Read

BOOK LOVERS

~

EMILY HENRY

PENGUIN BOOKS

PENGUIN BOOKS

UK | USA | Canada | Ireland | Australia
India | New Zealand | South Africa

Penguin Books is part of the Penguin Random House group of companies
whose addresses can be found at global.penguinrandomhouse.com.

First published in the United States of America by Berkley 2022
First published in Great Britain by Penguin Books 2022
001

Printed and bound in Great Britain by Clays Ltd, Elcograf S.p.A.

The authorized representative in the EEA is Penguin Random House Ireland,
Morrison Chambers, 32 Nassau Street, Dublin D02 YH68

A CIP catalogue record for this book is available from the British Library

ISBN: 978–0–241–99534–1

www.greenpenguin.co.uk

MIX
Paper from
responsible sources
FSC® C018179

Penguin Random House is committed to a
sustainable future for our business, our readers
and our planet. This book is made from Forest
Stewardship Council® certified paper.

Noosha, this book isn't for you.
I already know which one will be for you, so you have to wait.

This book is for Amanda, Dache', Danielle, Jessica,
Sareer, and Taylor. This book would not exist without you.
And if somehow it did, then no one would be reading it.
Thank you, thank you, thank you.

PROLOGUE

WHEN BOOKS ARE your life—or in my case, your job—
you get pretty good at guessing where a story is going. The
tropes, the archetypes, the common plot twists all start to organize
themselves into a catalogue inside your brain, divided by category
and genre.

The husband is the killer.

The nerd gets a makeover, and without her glasses, she's smoking hot.

The guy gets the girl—or the other girl does.

Someone explains a complicated scientific concept, and someone
else says, "Um, in English, *please*?"

The details may change from book to book, but there's nothing
truly new under the sun.

Take, for example, the small-town love story.

The kind where a cynical hotshot from New York or Los Angeles gets shipped off to Smalltown, USA—to, like, run a family-owned

Christmas tree farm out of business to make room for a soulless corporation.

But while said City Person is in town, things don't go to plan. Because, *of course*, the Christmas tree farm—or bakery, or whatever the hero's been sent to destroy—is owned and operated by someone ridiculously attractive and suitably available for wooing.

Back in the city, the lead *has* a romantic partner. Someone ruthless who encourages him to do what he's set out to do and ruin some lives in exchange for that big promotion. He fields calls from her, during which she interrupts him, barking heartless advice from the seat of her Peloton bike.

You can tell she's evil because her hair is an unnatural blond, slicked back à la Sharon Stone in *Basic Instinct*, and also, she hates Christmas decorations.

As the hero spends more time with the charming baker/seamstress/tree farm . . . *person*, things change for him. He learns the true meaning of life!

He returns home, *transformed* by the love of a good woman. There he asks his ice-queen girlfriend to take a walk with him. She gapes, says something like, *In* these *Manolos?*

It will be fun, he tells her. On the walk, he might ask her to look up at the stars.

She snaps, *You* know *I can't look up right now! I just got Botox!*

And then he realizes: he can't go back to his old life. He doesn't want to! He ends his cold, unsatisfying relationship and proposes to his new sweetheart. (Who needs dating?)

At this point, you find yourself screaming at the book, *You don't even know her! What's her middle name, bitch?* From across the room, your sister, Libby, hushes you, throws popcorn at your head without lifting her gaze from her own crinkly-covered library book.

And that's why I'm running late to this lunch meeting.

Because that's my life. The trope that governs my days. The archetype over which my details are superimposed.

I'm the city person. Not the one who meets the hot farmer. The *other* one.

The uptight, manicured literary agent, reading manuscripts from atop her Peloton while a serene beach scene screen saver drifts, unnoticed, across her computer screen.

I'm the one who gets dumped.

I've read this story, and lived it, enough to know it's happening again right now, as I'm weaving through late-afternoon foot traffic in Midtown, my phone clutched to my ear.

He hasn't said it yet, but the hairs on the back of my neck are rising, the pit opening in my stomach as he maneuvers the conversation toward a cartoon-style drop off a cliff.

Grant was only supposed to be in Texas for two weeks, just long enough to help close a deal between his company and the boutique hotel they were trying to acquire outside San Antonio. Having already experienced two post–work trip breakups, I reacted to the news of his trip as if he'd announced he'd joined the navy and was shipping out in the morning.

Libby tried to convince me I was overreacting, but I wasn't surprised when Grant missed our nightly phone call three times in a row, or when he cut two others short. I knew how this ended.

And then, three days ago, hours before his return flight, it happened.

A force majeure intervened to keep him in San Antonio longer than planned. His appendix burst.

Theoretically, I could've booked a flight right then, met him at the hospital. But I was in the middle of a huge sale and needed to be glued to my phone with stable Wi-Fi access. My client was counting on me. This was a life-changing chance for her. And besides, Grant pointed out that an appendectomy was a routine procedure. His exact words were "no big deal."

So I stayed, and deep down, I knew I was releasing Grant to the small-town-romance-novel gods to do with what they do best.

Now, three days later, as I'm practically sprinting to lunch in my Good Luck heels, my knuckles white against my phone, the reverberation of the nail in my relationship's coffin rattles through me in the form of Grant's voice.

"Say that again." I mean to say it as a question. It comes out as an order.

Grant sighs. "I'm not coming back, Nora. Things have changed for me this past week." He chuckles. "I've changed."

A thud goes through my cold, city-person heart. "Is she a baker?" I ask.

He's silent for a beat. "What?"

"Is she a *baker*?" I say, like that's a perfectly reasonable first question to ask when your boyfriend dumps you over the phone. "The woman you're leaving me for."

After a brief silence, he gives in: "She's the daughter of the couple who own the hotel. They've decided not to sell. I'm going to stay on, help them run it."

I can't help it: I laugh. That's always been my reaction to bad news. It's probably how I won the role of Evil Villainess in my own life, but what else am I supposed to do? Melt into a crying puddle on this packed sidewalk? What good would that do?

I stop outside the restaurant and gently knead at my eyes. "So, to be clear," I say, "you're giving up your amazing job, your amazing apartment, *and me*, and you're moving to Texas. To be with someone whose career can best be described as *the daughter of the couple who own the hotel*?"

"There's more important things in life than money and a fancy career, Nora," he spits.

I laugh again. "I can't tell if you think you're being serious."

Grant is the son of a billionaire hotel mogul. "Raised with a silver spoon" doesn't even begin to cover it. He probably had gold-leaf toilet paper.

For Grant, college was a formality. Internships were a formality. Hell, wearing *pants* was a formality! He got his job through sheer nepotism.

Which is precisely what makes his last comment so rich, both figuratively and literally.

I must say this last part aloud, because he demands, "What's that supposed to mean?"

I peer through the window of the restaurant, then check the time on my phone. I'm late—I'm *never* late. Not the first impression I was aiming for.

"Grant, you're a thirty-four-year-old heir. For most of us, our jobs are tied directly to our ability to eat."

"See?" he says. "This is the kind of worldview I'm done with. You can be so cold sometimes, Nora. Chastity and I want to—"

It's not intentional—I'm not trying to be cutting—when I cackle out her name. It's just that, when hilariously bad things happen, I leave my body. I watch them happen from outside myself and think, *Really? This is what the universe has chosen to do? A bit on the nose, isn't it?*

In this case, it's chosen to guide my boyfriend into the arms of a woman named after the ability to keep a hymen intact. I mean, it *is* funny.

He huffs on the other end of the line. "These people are good people, Nora. They're salt of the earth. That's the kind of person I want to be. Look, Nora, don't act upset—"

"Who's acting?"

"You've never needed me—"

"Of course I don't!" I've worked hard to build a life that's my own, that no one else could pull a plug on to send me swirling down a cosmic drain.

"You've never even stayed over at my place—" he says.

"My mattress is objectively better!" I researched it for nine and a half months before buying it. Of course, that's also pretty much how I date, and still, I end up here.

"—so don't pretend you're heartbroken," Grant says. "I'm not sure you're even capable of *being* heartbroken."

Again, I have to laugh.

Because on this, he's wrong. It's just that once you've had your heart *truly* shattered, a phone call like this is nothing. A heart-twinge, maybe a murmur. Certainly not a break.

Grant's on a roll now: "I've never even seen you cry."

You're welcome, I consider saying. How many times had Mom told us, laughing through her tears, that her latest beau had told her she was too emotional?

That's the thing about women. There's no good way to be one. Wear your emotions on your sleeve and you're hysterical. Keep them tucked away where your boyfriend doesn't have to tend to them and you're a heartless bitch.

"I've got to go, Grant," I say.

"Of course you do," he replies.

Apparently my following through with prior commitments is just more proof that I am a frigid, evil robot who sleeps in a bed of hundred-dollar bills and raw diamonds. (If only.)

I hang up without a goodbye and tuck myself beneath the restaurant's awning. As I take a steadying breath, I wait to see if the tears will come. They don't. They never do. I'm okay with that.

I have a job to do, and unlike Grant, I'm going to do it, for myself and everyone else at Nguyen Literary Agency.

I smooth my hair, square my shoulders, and head inside, the blast of air-conditioning scrubbing goose bumps over my arms.

It's late in the day for lunch, so the crowd is thin, and I spot Charlie Lastra near the back, dressed in all black like publishing's own metropolitan vampire.

We've never met in person, but I double-checked the *Publishers Weekly* announcement about his promotion to executive editor at Wharton House Books and committed his photograph to memory: the stern, dark brows; the light brown eyes; the slight crease in his chin beneath his full lips. He has the kind of dark mole on one cheek that, if he were a woman, would definitely be considered a beauty mark.

He can't be much past his midthirties, with the kind of face you might describe as boyish, if not for how tired he looks and the gray that thoroughly peppers his black hair.

Also, he's scowling. Or pouting. His mouth is pouting. His forehead is scowling. Powling.

He glances at his watch.

Not a good sign. Right before I left the office, my boss, Amy, warned me Charlie is famously testy, but I wasn't worried. I'm always punctual.

Except when I'm getting dumped over the phone. Then I'm six and a half minutes late, apparently.

"Hi!" I stick out my hand to shake his as I approach. "Nora Stephens. So nice to meet you in person, finally."

He stands, his chair scraping over the floor. His black clothes, dark features, and general demeanor have the approximate effect on the room of a black hole, sucking all the light out of it and swallowing it entirely.

Most people wear black as a form of lazy professionalism, but he makes it look like a capital-c Choice, the combination of his relaxed merino sweater, trousers, and brogues giving him the air of a celebrity caught on the street by a paparazzo. I catch myself calculating how many American dollars he's wearing. Libby calls it my "disturbing middle-class party trick," but really it's just that I love pretty things and often online window-shop to self-soothe after a stressful day.

I'd put Charlie's outfit at somewhere between eight hundred and a thousand. Right in the range of mine, frankly, though everything I'm wearing except my shoes was purchased secondhand.

He examines my outstretched palm for two long seconds before shaking it. "You're late." He sits without bothering to meet my gaze.

Is there anything worse than a man who thinks he's above the laws of the social contract just because he was born with a decent face and a fat wallet? Grant has burned through my daily tolerance for self-important assholes. Still, I have to play this game, for my authors' sakes.

"I know," I say, beaming apologetically but not actually apologizing. "Thank you for waiting for me. My train got stopped on the tracks. You know how it is."

His eyes lift to mine. They look darker now, so dark I'm not sure there are irises around those pupils. His expression says he does *not* know how it is, re: trains stopping on the tracks for reasons both grisly and mundane.

Probably, he doesn't take the subway.

Probably, he goes everywhere in a shiny black limo, or a Gothic carriage pulled by a team of Clydesdales.

I shuck off my blazer (herringbone, Isabel Marant) and take the seat across from him. "Have you ordered?"

"No," he says. Nothing else.

My hopes sink lower.

We'd scheduled this get-to-know-you lunch weeks ago. But last Friday, I'd sent him a new manuscript from one of my oldest clients, Dusty Fielding. Now I'm second-guessing whether I could subject one of my authors to this man.

I pick up my menu. "They have a goat cheese salad that's phenomenal."

Charlie closes his menu and regards me. "Before we go any further," he says, thick black brows furrowing, his voice low and innately hoarse, "I should just tell you, I found Fielding's new book unreadable."

My jaw drops. I'm not sure what to say. For one thing, I hadn't planned on bringing the book up. If Charlie wanted to reject it, he could've just done so in an email. And without using the word *unreadable*.

But even aside from that, any decent person would at least wait until there was some bread on the table before throwing out insults.

I close my own menu and fold my hands on the table. "I think it's her best yet."

Dusty's already published three others, each of them fantastic, though none sold well. Her last publisher wasn't willing to take another chance on her, so she's back in the water, looking for a new home for her next novel.

And okay, maybe it's not *my* favorite of hers, but it has immense commercial appeal. With the right editor, I know what this book can be.

Charlie sits back, the heavy, discerning quality of his gaze sending a prickling down my backbone. It feels like he's looking right through me, past the shiny politeness to the jagged edges underneath. His look says, *Wipe that frozen smile off your face. You're not that nice.*

He turns his water glass in place. "Her best is *The Glory of Small Things*," he says, like three seconds of eye contact was enough to read my innermost thoughts and he knows he's speaking for both of us.

Frankly, *Glory* was one of my favorite books in the last decade, but that doesn't make this one chopped liver.

I say, "This book is every bit as good. It's just different—less subdued, maybe, but that gives it a cinematic edge."

"Less subdued?" Charlie squints. At least the golden brown has seeped back into his eyes so I feel less like they're going to burn holes in me. "That's like saying Charles Manson was a lifestyle guru. It might be true, but it's hardly the point. This book feels like someone watched that Sarah McLachlan commercial for animal cruelty prevention and thought, *But what if all the puppies died on camera?*"

An irritable laugh lurches out of me. "Fine. It's not your cup of tea. But maybe it would be helpful," I fume, "if you told me what you *liked* about the book. Then I know what to send you in the future."

Liar, my brain says. *You're not sending him more books.*

Liar, Charlie's unsettling, owlish eyes say. *You're not sending me more books.*

This lunch—this potential working relationship—is dead in the water.

Charlie doesn't want to work with me, and I don't want to work with him, but I guess he hasn't entirely abandoned the social contract, because he considers my question.

"It's overly sentimental for my taste," he says eventually. "And the cast is caricatured—"

"*Quirky*," I disagree. "We could scale them back, but it's a large cast—their quirks help distinguish them."

"And the setting—"

"What's wrong with the setting?" The setting in *Once in a Lifetime* sells the whole book. "Sunshine Falls is charming."

Charlie scoffs, literally rolls his eyes. "It's completely unrealistic."

"It's a real place," I counter. Dusty had made the little mountain town sound so idyllic I'd actually googled it. Sunshine Falls, North Carolina, sits just a little ways outside Asheville.

Charlie shakes his head. He seems irritable. Well, that makes two of us.

I do not like him. If I'm the archetypical City Person, he is the Dour, Unappeasable Stick-in-the-Mud. He's the Growly Misanthrope, Oscar the Grouch, second-act Heathcliff, the worst parts of Mr. Knightley.

Which is a shame, because he's also got a reputation for having a magic touch. Several of my agent friends call him Midas. As in, "Everything he touches turns to gold." (Though admittedly, some others refer to him as the Storm Cloud. As in, "He makes it rain money, but at what cost?")

The point is, Charlie Lastra picks winners. And he isn't picking *Once in a Lifetime*. Determined to bolster my confidence, if not his, I cross my arms over my chest. "I'm telling you, no matter how contrived you found it, Sunshine Falls is real."

"It might exist," Charlie says, "but *I'm* telling *you* Dusty Fielding has never been there."

"Why does that matter?" I ask, no longer feigning politeness.

Charlie's mouth twitches in reaction to my outburst. "You wanted to know what I disliked about the book—"

"What you *liked*," I correct him.

"—and I disliked the setting."

The sting of anger races down my windpipe, rooting through my lungs. "So how about you just tell me what kind of books you *do* want, Mr. Lastra?"

He relaxes until he's leaned back, languid and sprawling like some jungle cat toying with its prey. He turns his water glass again.

I'd thought it was a nervous tic, but maybe it's a low-grade torture tactic. I want to knock it off the table.

"I want," Charlie says, "*early* Fielding. *The Glory of Small Things*."

"That book didn't sell."

"Because her publisher didn't know how to sell it," Charlie says. "Wharton House could. I could."

My eyebrow arches, and I do my best to school it back into place.

Just then, the server approaches our table. "Can I get you anything while you're perusing the menu?" she asks sweetly.

"Goat cheese salad for me," Charlie says, without looking at either of us.

Probably he's looking forward to pronouncing my favorite salad in the city *inedible*.

"And for you, ma'am?" the server asks.

I stifle the shiver that runs down my spine whenever a twenty-something calls me *ma'am*. This must be how ghosts feel when people walk over their graves.

"I'll have that too," I say, and then, because this has been one hell of a day and there is no one here to impress—and because I'm trapped here for at least forty more minutes with a man I have no intention of *ever* working with—I say, "And a gin martini. Dirty."

Charlie's brow just barely lifts. It's three p.m. on a Thursday, not exactly happy hour, but given that publishing shuts down in the summer and most people take Fridays off, it's practically the weekend.

"Bad day," I say under my breath as the server disappears with our order.

"Not as bad as mine," Charlie replies. The rest hangs in the air, unsaid: *I read eighty pages of* Once in a Lifetime, *then sat down with* you.

I scoff. "You really didn't like the setting?"

"I can hardly imagine anywhere I'd less enjoy spending four hundred pages."

"You know," I say, "you're every bit as pleasant as I was told you would be."

"I can't control how I feel," he says coolly.

I bristle. "That's like Charles Manson saying he's not the one who committed the murders. It might be true on a technical level, but it's hardly the point."

The server drops off my martini, and Charlie grumbles, "Could I get one of those too?"

~

Later that night, my phone pings with an email.

Hi, Nora,

Feel free to keep me in mind for Dusty's future projects.

-Charlie

I can't help rolling my eyes. No *Nice meeting you*. No *Hope you're well*. He couldn't even be bothered with basic niceties. Gritting my teeth, I type back, mimicking his style.

Charlie,

If she writes anything about lifestyle guru Charlie Manson, you'll be the first to know.

-Nora

I tuck my phone into my sweatpants' pocket and nudge open my bathroom door to start my ten-step skin care routine (also known as the best forty-five minutes of my day). My phone vibrates and I pull it out.

N,

Joke's on you: very much want to read that.

-C

Hell-bent on having the last word, I write, Night.

(*Good* night is decidedly not what I mean.)

Best, Charlie writes back, like he's signing an email that doesn't exist.

If there's one thing I hate more than shoes with no heels, it's losing. I write back, x.

No reply. Checkmate. After a day from hell, this small victory makes me feel like all is right in the world. I finish my skin care routine. I read five blissful chapters of a grisly mystery novel, and I drift off on my perfect mattress, without a thought to spare for Grant or his new life in Texas. I sleep like a baby.

Or an ice queen.

1

~

TWO YEARS LATER

THE CITY IS baking. The asphalt sizzles. The trash on the sidewalk reeks. The families we pass carry ice pops that shrink with every step, melting down their fingers. Sunlight glances off buildings like a laser-based security system in an out-of-date heist movie, and I feel like a glazed donut that's been left out in the heat for four days.

Meanwhile, even five months pregnant and despite the temperature, Libby looks like the star of a shampoo commercial.

"Three times." She sounds awed. "How does a person get dumped in a full lifestyle-swap *three times*?"

"Just lucky, I guess," I say. Really, it's four, but I never could bring myself to tell her the whole story about Jakob. It's been years and I can still barely tell *myself* that story.

Libby sighs and loops her arm through mine. My skin is sticky from the heat and humidity of midsummer, but my baby sister's is miraculously dry and silky.

I might've gotten Mom's five feet and eleven inches of height, but the rest of her features all funneled down to my sister, from the strawberry gold hair to the wide, Mediterranean Sea–blue eyes and the splash of freckles across her nose. Her short, curvy stature must've come from Dad's gene pool—not that we would know; he left when I was three and Libby was months from being born. When it's natural, my hair is a dull, ashy blond, and my eyes' shade of blue is less idyllic-vacation-water and more last-thing-you-see-before-the-ice-freezes-over-and-you-drown.

She's the Marianne to my Elinor, the Meg Ryan to my Parker Posey.

She is also my absolute favorite person on the planet.

"Oh, Nora." Libby squeezes me to her as we come to a crosswalk, and I bask in the closeness. No matter how hectic life and work sometimes get, it's always felt like there were some internal metronomes keeping us in sync. I'd pick up my phone to call her, and it would already be ringing, or she'd text me about grabbing lunch and we'd realize we were already in the same part of the city. The last few months, though, we've been ships passing in the night. Actually, more like a submarine and a paddleboat in entirely separate lakes.

I miss her calls while I'm in meetings, and she's already asleep by the time I call back. She finally invites me to dinner on a night I've promised to take a client out. Worse than that is the faint, uncanny *off* feeling when we're actually together. Like she's only halfway here. Like those metronomes have fallen into different rhythms, and even when we're right next to each other, they never manage to match up.

At first I'd chalked it up to stress about the new baby, but as time has worn on, my sister's seemed *more* distant rather than closer. We're fundamentally out of sync in a way I can't seem to name, and not even my dream mattress and a cloud of diffused lavender oil are enough to keep me from lying awake, turning over our last few conversations like I'm looking for faint cracks.

The sign has changed to *WALK*, but a slew of drivers rushes through the newly red light. When a guy in a nice suit strides into the street, Libby pulls me along after him.

It's a truth universally acknowledged that cabdrivers won't clip people who look like this guy. His outfit says, *I am a man with a lawyer.* Or possibly just *I am a lawyer.*

"I thought you and Andrew were good together," Libby says, seamlessly reentering the conversation. As long as you're willing to overlook that my ex's name was Aaron, not Andrew. "I don't understand what went wrong. Was it work stuff?"

Her eyes flicker toward me on the words *work stuff,* and it triggers another memory: me slipping back into the apartment during Bea's fourth birthday party and Libby giving me a look like an injured Pixar puppy as she guessed, *Work call?*

When I apologized, she brushed it off, but now I find myself wondering if *that* was the moment I'd started to lose her, the exact second when our diverging paths pulled just a little too far from each other and the seams started splitting.

"What went wrong," I say, recovering my place in the conversation, "is that, in a past life, I betrayed a very powerful witch, and she's put a curse on my love life. He's moving to Prince Edward Island."

We pause at the next cross street, waiting for traffic to slow. It's a Saturday in mid-July and absolutely everyone is out, wearing as few clothes as legally possible, eating dripping ice cream cones from Big Gay or artisanal ice pops filled with things that have no business being anywhere near a dessert.

"Do you know what's on Prince Edward Island?" I ask.

"Anne of Green Gables?" Libby says.

"Anne of Green Gables would be dead by now," I say.

"Wow," she says. *"Spoiler."*

"How does a person go from living *here* to moving to a place where the hottest destination is the Canadian Potato Museum? I would immediately die of boredom."

Libby sighs. "I don't know. I'd take a little boredom right about now."

I glance sidelong at her, and my heart trips over its next beat. Her hair is still perfect and her skin is prettily flushed, but now new details jump out at me, signs I missed at first.

The drawn corners of her mouth. The subtle thinning of her cheeks. She looks tired, older than usual.

"Sorry," she says, almost to herself. "I don't mean to be Sad, Droopy Mom—I just . . . I *really* need some sleep."

My mind is already spinning, searching for places I could pick up the slack. Brendan and Libby's evergreen concern is money, but they've refused help in that department for years, so I've had to find creative ways of supporting them.

Actually, the phone call she may or may not be peeved about was a Birthday Present Trojan Horse. A "client" "canceled" "a trip" and "the room at the St. Regis" was "nonrefundable" so "it only made sense" to have a midweek slumber party with the girls there.

"You're not Sad, Droopy Mom," I say now, squeezing her arm again. "You're Supermom. You're the regulation hottie in the jumpsuit at the Brooklyn Flea, carrying her five hundred beautiful children, a giant bouquet of wildflowers, and a basket full of lumpy tomatoes. It's okay to get tired, Lib."

She squints at me. "When was the last time you counted my kids, Sissy? Because there are two."

"Not to make you feel like a terrible parent," I say, poking her belly, "but I'm eighty percent sure there's another one in there."

"Fine, two and a half." Her eyes dart toward mine, cautious. "So how are you, really? About the breakup, I mean."

"We were only together four months. It wasn't serious."

"*Serious* is the nature of how you date," she says. "If someone makes it to a third dinner with you, then he's already met four hundred and fifty separate criteria. It's not casual dating if you know the other person's blood type."

"I do *not* know my dates' blood types," I say. "All I need from them is a full credit report, a psych eval, and a blood oath."

Libby throws her head back, cackling. As ever, making my sister laugh is a shot of serotonin straight into my heart. Or brain? Probably brain. Serotonin in your heart is probably not a good a thing. The point is, Libby's laugh makes me feel like the world is under my thumb, like I'm in complete control of The Situation.

Maybe that makes me a narcissist, or maybe it just makes me a thirty-two-year-old woman who remembers full weeks when she couldn't coax her grieving sister out of bed.

"Hey," Libby says, slowing as she realizes where we are, what we've been subconsciously moving toward. "Look."

If we got blindfolded and air-dropped into the city, we'd probably still end up here: gazing wistfully at Freeman Books, the West Village shop we used to live over. The tiny apartment where Mom spun us through the kitchen, all three of us singing the Supremes' "Baby Love" into kitchen utensils. The place where we spent countless nights curled up on a pink-and-cream floral couch watching Katharine Hepburn movies with a smorgasbord of junk food spread across the coffee table she'd found on the street, its busted leg replaced by a stack of hardcovers.

In books and movies, characters like me always live in cement-floored lofts with bleak modern art and four-foot vases filled with, like, scraggly black twigs, for some inexplicable reason.

But in real life, I chose my current apartment because it looks so much like this one: old wooden floors and soft wallpaper, a hissing radiator in one corner and built-in bookshelves stuffed to the brim with secondhand paperbacks. Its crown molding has been painted over so many times it's lost its crisp edges, and time has warped its high, narrow windows.

This little bookstore and its upstairs apartment are my favorite places on earth.

Even if it's also where our lives were torn in half twelve years ago, I love this place.

"Oh my gosh!" Libby grips my forearm, waving at the display in the bookstore's window: a pyramid of Dusty Fielding's runaway hit, *Once in a Lifetime*, with its new movie tie-in cover.

She pulls out her phone. "We have to take a picture!"

There is no one who loves Dusty's book as much as my sister. And that's saying something, since, in six months, it's sold a million copies already. People are calling it *the* book of the year. *A Man Called Ove* meets *A Little Life*.

Take that, Charlie Lastra, I think, as I do every so often when I remember that fateful lunch. Or whenever I pass his shut-tight office door (all the sweeter since he moved to work at the publishing house that put out *Once*, where he's now surrounded by constant reminders of my success).

Fine, I think *Take that, Charlie Lastra* a lot. One never really forgets the first time a colleague drove her to extreme unprofessionalism.

"I'm going to see this movie five hundred times," Libby tells me. "Consecutively."

"Wear a diaper," I advise.

"Not necessary," she says. "I'll be crying too much. There won't be any pee in my body."

"I had no idea you had such a . . . comprehensive understanding of science," I say.

"The last time I read it, I cried so hard I pulled a muscle in my back."

"You should consider exercising more."

"Rude." She waves at her pregnant belly, then starts us toward the juice bar again. "Anyway, back to your love life. You just need to get back out there."

"Libby," I say. "I understand that you met the love of your life when you were twenty years old, and thus have never truly dated. But imagine for a moment, if you will, a world in which thirty percent of your dates end with the revelation that the man across the table from you has a foot, elbow, or kneecap fetish."

It was the shock of my life when my whimsical, romantic sister fell in love with a nine-years-older-than-her accountant who is *very* into reading about trains, but Brendan's also the most solid man I've ever met in my life, and I've long since accepted that somehow, against all odds, he and my sister are soul mates.

"Thirty percent?!" she cries. "What the hell kind of dating apps are you on, Nora?"

"The normal ones!" I say.

In the interest of full discretion, *yes*, I outright inquire about fetishes up front. It's not that thirty percent of men announce their kinks twenty minutes after meeting, but that's my point. The last time my boss, Amy, went home with an un-vetted woman, she turned out to have a room that was entirely dolls. Floor-to-ceiling ceramic dolls.

How inconvenient would it be to fall in love with a person only to find out they had a doll room? The answer is "very."

"Can we sit for a second?" Libby asks, a little out of breath, and we sidestep a group of German tourists to perch on the edge of a coffee shop's windowsill.

"Are you okay?" I ask. "Can I get you something? Water?"

She shakes her head, brushes her hair behind her ears. "I'm just tired. I need a break."

"Maybe we should have a spa day," I suggest. "I have a gift certificate—"

"First of all," she says, "you're lying, and I can tell. And second of all . . ." Her teeth worry over her pink-glossed lip. "I had something else in mind."

"*Two* spa days?" I guess.

She cracks a tentative smile. "You know how you're always complaining about how publishing pretty much shuts down in August and you have nothing to do?"

"I have *plenty* to do," I argue.

"Nothing that requires you to be in the city," she amends. "So what if we went somewhere? Got away for a few weeks and just *relaxed*? I can go a day without getting anyone else's bodily fluids on me, and *you* can forget about what happened with Aaron, and we can just . . . take a break from being the Tired Supermom and Fancy Career Lady we have to be the other eleven months out of the year. Maybe you can even take a page out of your exes' books and have a whirlwind romance with a local . . . lobster hunter?"

I stare at her, trying to parse out how serious she is.

"Fisher? Lobster fisher?" she says. "Fisherman?"

"But we never go anywhere," I point out.

"*Exactly*," she says, a ragged edge creeping into her voice. She grabs for my hand, and I note the way her nails are bitten down. I try to swallow, but it's like my esophagus is inside a vise. Because, right then, I'm suddenly sure there's more going on with Libby than run-of-the-mill money problems, lack of sleep, or irritation with my work schedule.

Six months ago, I'd have known exactly what was going on. I wouldn't have even had to ask. She would've stopped by my apartment, unannounced, and flopped onto my couch dramatically and said, *"You know what's bothering me lately, Sissy?"* and I would pull her head into my lap and tease my fingers through her hair while she poured out her worries over a glass of crisp white wine. Things are different now.

"This is our chance, Nora," she says quietly, urgently. "Let's take a trip. Just the two of us. The last time we did that was California."

My stomach plummets, then rebounds. That trip—like my relationship with Jakob—is part of the time in my life I do my best not to revisit.

Pretty much everything I do, actually, is to ensure Libby and I never find ourselves back in that dark place we were in after Mom died. But the undeniable truth is I haven't seen her look like this, like she's at her breaking point, since then.

I swallow hard. "Can you get away right now?"

"Brendan's parents will help with the girls." She squeezes my hands, her wide blue eyes practically burning with hope. "When this baby gets here, I'm going to be an empty shell of a person for a while, and before that happens, I really, really want to spend time with you, like it used to be. And also I'm like three sleepless nights away from snapping and pulling a *Where'd You Go, Bernadette*, if not the full *Gone Girl*. I need this."

My chest squeezes. An image of a heart in a too-small metal cage flashes over my mind. I've always been incapable of saying no to her. Not when she was five and wanted the last bite of Junior's cheesecake, or when she was fifteen and wanted to borrow my favorite jeans (the seat of which never recovered from her superior curves), or when she was sixteen and she said through tears, *I just want to not be here*, and I swept her off to Los Angeles.

She never actually asked for any of those things, but she's asking now, her palms pressed together and her lower lip jutted, and it makes me feel panicky and breathless, even more out of control than the thought of leaving the city. *"Please."*

Her fatigue has made her look insubstantial, faded, like if I tried to brush her hair away from her brow, my fingers might pass through her. I didn't know it was possible to miss a person this much while she was sitting right next to you, so badly everything in you aches.

She's right here, I tell myself, *and she's okay. Whatever it is, you'll fix it.*

I swallow every excuse, complaint, and argument bubbling up in me. "Let's take a trip."

Libby's lips split into a grin. She shifts on the windowsill to wriggle something out of her back pocket. "Okay, good. Because I already bought these and I'm not sure they're refundable." She slaps the printed plane tickets in my lap, and it's like the moment never happened. Like in the matter of point five seconds, I got my carefree baby sister back, and I'd trade any number of organs to cement us both into this moment, to live here always where she's shining bright. My chest loosens. My next breath comes easy.

"Aren't you even going to look where we're going?" Libby asks, amused.

I tear my gaze from her and read the ticket. "Asheville, North Carolina?"

She shakes her head. "It's the airport closest to Sunshine Falls. This is going to be a . . . *once-in-a-lifetime* trip."

I groan and she throws her arms around me, laughing. "We're going to have so much fun, Sissy! And you're going to fall in love with a lumberjack."

"If there's one thing that makes me horny," I say, "it's deforestation."

"An ethical, sustainable, organic, gluten-free lumberjack," Libby amends.

2

ON THE AIRPLANE, Libby insists we order Bloody Marys. Actually, she tries to pressure me into taking shots, but she settles for a Bloody Mary (and a plain tomato juice for herself). I'm not a big drinker myself, and morning alcohol has *never* been my thing. But this is my first vacation in a decade, and I'm so anxious I chug the drink in the first twenty minutes of our flight.

I don't like traveling, I don't like time off work, and I don't like leaving my clients in the lurch. Or, in this case, one rather indispensable client: I spent the forty-eight hours pre-takeoff alternating between trying to talk Dusty down and pump her up.

We've already bumped the deadline for her next book back six months, and if she can't start getting her editor pages this week, the whole publishing schedule will be thrown off.

She's so superstitious about the drafting process that we don't even know what she's working on, but I fire off another encouraging *you-can-do-it* email on my phone anyway.

Libby shoots me a pointed look, brow arched. I set my phone down and hold up my hands, hoping to signal *I'm present*.

"So," she says, appeased, and drags her cartoonishly large purse onto the folding tray table, "I figure now is as good a time as any to go over the plan." She fishes out an actual, full-sized folder and flops it open.

"Oh my god, what is that?" I say. "Are you planning a bank robbery?"

"*Heist*, Sissy. *Robbery* sounds so déclassé, and we're going to be wearing three-piece suits the whole time," she says, not missing a beat as she pulls out two identical laminated sheets with the typed heading **LIFE-CHANGING VACATION LIST**.

"Who are you and where did you bury my sister?" I ask.

"I know how much you love a checklist," she says brightly. "So I took the liberty of crafting one to create our perfect small-town adventure."

I reach for one of the sheets. "I hope number one is 'dance atop a Coyote Ugly bar.' Though I'm not sure any manager worth her salt will allow that in your condition."

She feigns offense. "Am I showing much?"

"Noooo," I coo. "Not at all."

"You're so bad at lying. It looks like your face muscles are being controlled by a half dozen amateur puppeteers. Now, back to the bucket list."

"Bucket list? Which of us is dying?"

She looks up, eyes sparkling. I'd say it's the glint of mischief, but her eyes are pretty much always sparkly. "Birth is a kind of death," she says, rubbing her tummy. "Death of the self. Death of sleep. Death of your ability not to pee yourself a little when you laugh. But I guess it's more like a *small-town romance novel experience* list than a bucket list. It's how we're both going to be *transformed* via small-town magic into more relaxed versions of ourselves."

I eye the list again. Before Libby got pregnant the first time, she briefly worked for a top-tier events planner (among many, many, many other things), so despite her natural tendency toward spontaneity (read: chaos), she'd made some strides in organization, even premotherhood. But this level of planning is so extremely . . . *me*, and I'm weirdly touched she's put so much thought into this.

Also shocked to discover the first item on the list is *Wear a flannel shirt*. "I don't own a flannel shirt," I say.

Libby shrugs. "Me neither. We'll have to thrift some—maybe we can find some cowgirl boots too."

When we were teenagers, we'd spend hours sorting through junk for gems at our favorite Goodwill. I'd go for the sleek designer pieces and she'd beeline toward anything with color, fringe, or rhinestones.

Again I feel that heart-pinch sensation, like I'm missing her, like all our best moments are behind us. That, I remind myself, is why I'm doing this. By the time we get back to the city, whatever little gaps have cropped up between us will be stitched closed again.

"Flannel," I say. "Got it." The second item on the list is *Bake something*. Continuing the trend of us being polar opposites, my sister *loves* cooking, but since she's usually beholden to the taste buds of a four- and three-year-old, she's always saved her more adventurous recipes for our nights in together. My eyes skim down the list.

3. General makeover (let hair down/get bangs?)
4. Build something (literal, not figurative)

The first four items almost directly correlate to Libby's Graveyard of Abandoned Potential Careers. Before her event-planning job, she'd briefly run an online vintage store that curated thrift store finds; and before that, she'd wanted to be a baker; and before that, a hairstylist; and for one very brief summer, she'd decided she wanted to be a carpenter because there weren't "enough women in that field." She was eight.

So everything so far makes sense—at least as much as this entire thing makes sense (which is to say, *only in Libby's brain*)—but then my gaze catches on number five. "Ummm, what is *this*?"

"Go on at least two dates with locals," she reads, visibly excited. "That one's not for me." She lifts her copy of the list, on which number five is struck through.

"Well, that doesn't seem fair," I say.

"You'll recall that I'm married," she says, "and five trillion weeks pregnant."

"And I'm a career woman with a weekly housekeeping service, a spare bedroom I turned into a shoe closet, and a Sephora credit card. I don't imagine my dream man is a lobster hunter."

Libby lights up and scooches forward in her seat. "Exactly!" she says. "Look, Nora, you know I love your beautiful, Dewey-decimal-organized brain, but you date like you're shopping for cars."

"Thank you," I say.

"And it *always* ends badly."

"Oh, thank god." I clutch my chest. "I was worried that wouldn't come up soon."

She tries to turn in her seat and grabs my hands on the armrest between us. "I'm just saying, you keep dating these guys who are exactly like you, with all the same priorities."

"You can really shorten that sentence if you just say 'men I'm compatible with.'"

"Sometimes opposites attract," she says. "Think about all your exes. Think about Jakob and his cowgirl wife!"

Something cold lances through me at the mention of him; Libby doesn't notice.

"The whole point of this trip is to step outside our comfort zones," she insists. "To get a chance to . . . to be someone different! Besides, who knows? Maybe if you branch out a little, you'll find your own *life-changing* love story instead of another walking checklist of a boyfriend."

"I *like* dating checklists, thank you very much," I say. "Checklists keep things simple. I mean, think about Mom, Lib." She was constantly falling in love, and never with men who made any sense for her. It always came crashing down spectacularly, usually leaving her so broken she'd miss work or auditions, or do so badly at either that she'd get fired or cut.

"You're nothing like Mom." She says it flippantly, but it still stings. I'm well aware how little I take after our mother. I felt those shortcomings every second of every day after we lost her, when I was trying to keep us afloat.

And I know that's not what Libby's saying, but it still doesn't feel all too different from every breakup I can remember: a long-winded monologue ending with something along the lines of **FOR ALL I KNOW, YOU DON'T EVEN HAVE FEELINGS.**

"I mean, how often do you get to just *let loose* and not worry about how it fits into your perfect little plan?" Libby goes on. "You deserve to have some low-pressure fun, and frankly, *I* deserve to live vicariously through you. Ergo, the dates."

"So am I allowed to take the earpiece out after dinner, or . . ."

Libby throws up her hands. "You know what, fine, forget number five! Even though it would be good for you. Even though I basically designed this whole trip for you to have your small-town romance novel experience, I guess—"

"Okay, okay!" I cry. "I'll do the lumberjack dates, but they'd better look like Robert Redford."

She squeals excitedly. "Young or old?"

I stare at her.

"Right," she says. "Got it. So, moving on. Number six: *Go skinny-dipping in a natural body of water.*"

"What if there are bacteria that affect the baby or something?" I ask.

"Damn it," she grumbles, frowning. "I really didn't think all of this through as well as I thought."

"Nonsense," I say. "It's an amazing list."

"You'll just have to go skinny-dipping without me," she says, distracted.

"A lone thirty-two-year-old woman, naked in the local swimming hole. Sounds like a good way to get arrested."

"Seven," she reads. "*Sleep under the stars.* Eight: *Attend a town function—i.e. local wedding or festival of some kind.*"

I find a Sharpie in my bag and add *funeral, bris, ladies' night at the local roller rink.*

"Trying to meet a hot ER doctor, are we?" Libby says, and I scratch out the part about the roller rink. Then I notice number nine.

Ride a horse.

"Again." I wave vaguely toward Libby's stomach. I cross out *ride* and change it to *pet,* and she gives a resigned sigh.

    10. Start a fire (controlled)
    11. Hike???? (Worth it???)

When she was sixteen, Libby had announced she'd be following her boyfriend out to work at Yellowstone for the summer, and Mom and I had howled with laughter. If there was one thing all Stephens girls had in common—aside from our love of books, vitamin-C serums, and pretty clothes—it was our avoidance of the great outdoors.

The closest we ever came to hiking was a brisk walk in Central Park's Ramble, and even then, there were usually paper bowls filled with food truck waffles and ice cream involved. Not exactly roughing it.

Needless to say, Libby dumped that guy two weeks before she was supposed to leave.

I tap the final line on the list: *Save a local business.* "You do realize we're only here for a month." Three weeks of just the two of us, and then Brendan and the girls will join. We've gotten a steep discount by staying so long, though how I'll make it past week one, I have no idea.

The last time I traveled, I went home after two days. Even letting my mind wander toward that trip with Jakob is a mistake. I jerk my focus back to the present. This won't be like that. I won't let it. I can do this, for Libby.

"They always save a local business in small-town romances," she's saying. "We literally have no choice. I'm hoping for a down-on-its-luck goat farm."

"Ooh," I say. "Maybe we can get the ritualistic sacrifice community to band together in dramatic fashion to save the goats. For now, I mean. Eventually, they'll have to die on the altar."

"Well, of course." Libby takes a swig of tomato juice. "That's the biz, baby."

~

Our taxi driver looks like Santa Claus, down to the red T-shirt and the suspenders holding his faded jeans up. But he drives like the cigar-smoking cabbie from Bill Murray's *Scrooged*.

Little squeaks keep sneaking out of Libby when he takes a corner too fast, and at one point, I catch her whispering promises of safety to her belly.

"Sunshine Falls, eh?" the driver asks. He has to shout, because he's made the unilateral decision to roll all four windows down. My hair is flapping so violently across my face I can barely see his watery eyes in the rearview mirror when I look up from my phone.

In the time that we were deplaning and collecting our luggage—a full hour, despite the fact that our flight was the *only* arrival in the dinky airport—the number of messages in my inbox has doubled. It looks like I just got back from an eight-week stranding on a desert island.

Nothing makes a coterie of already neurotic authors quite so neurotic as publishing's annual slow season. Every delayed reply they get seems to trigger an avalanche of *DOES MY EDITOR HATE ME??????* DO YOU HATE ME?? DOES EVERYONE HATE ME???

"Yep!" I shout back to our driver. Libby has her head between her knees now.

"You must have family in town," he screams over the wind.

Maybe it's the New Yorker in me, or maybe it's the woman, but I'm not about to announce that we don't know *anyone* here, so I just say, "What makes you say that?"

"Why else would you come here?" He laughs, whipping around a corner.

When we slow to a stop a few minutes later, it's all I can do to keep from bursting into applause like someone whose plane just made an emergency landing.

Libby sits up woozily, smoothing her gleaming (miraculously un-tangled) hair.

"Where . . . where are we?" I ask, looking around.

There's nothing but shaggy, sun-blanched grass on either side of the narrow dirt road. Ahead, it ends abruptly, and a meadow slopes upward, riddled with sprays of yellow and purple wildflowers. A dead end.

Which begs the question: are we about to be murdered?

The driver ducks his head to peer up the slope. "Goode's Lily Cottage, just over that hill."

Libby and I duck our heads too, trying to get a better look. Halfway up the hill, a staircase appears out of nowhere. Maybe *staircase* is too generous a word. Wooden slats cut a path into the grassy hillside, like a series of small retaining walls.

Libby grimaces. "The listing *did* note it wasn't wheelchair accessible."

"Did it also mention we'd need a ski lift?"

Santa has already gotten out of the car to wrestle our luggage from the trunk. I clamber out after him into the brilliant sunlight, the heat instantly making my all-black travel uniform feel stiflingly thick. Where the dirt road ends, there's a black mailbox, *Goode's Lily Cottage* painted in curly white on it.

"There isn't another way?" I ask. "A road that goes all the way up? My sister's . . ."

I swear Libby sucks in, trying to look as un-pregnant as possible. "I'm *fine*," she insists.

I briefly consider waving toward my four-inch suede heels next, but I don't want to give the universe the satisfaction of leaning into the cliché.

"'Fraid I can't get you any closer," he replies as he climbs back into the car. "An acre or two back is Sally's place. That's the second-closest road, but still a good ways further." He holds his business card out the window. "If you need another ride, use this number."

Libby accepts the scrap of paper, and over her shoulder, I read: *Hardy Weatherbee, Taxi Services and Unofficial* Once in a Lifetime

Tours. Her bark of laughter is lost beneath the roar of Hardy Weatherbee's car reversing down the road like a bat out of hell.

"Well." She winces, hunching her shoulders. "Maybe you should
take your shoes off?"

With all our luggage, it's going to take more than one trip, especially because there's no way Libby's carrying anything heavier than
my heels.

The climb is steep, the heat sweltering, but when we crest the hill
and see it, it is perfect: a winding path through shaggy, overgrown
gardens to a small white cottage, its peaked roof a lovely burnt si-
enna. Its windows are ancient, single-paneled, and shutterless, and
the only accent on the wall visible to us is a pale green arc of vines
painted over the first-floor window. At the back of the house, gnarled
trees press close, forest extending as far as I can see, and off to the left,
in the meadow, a gazebo twined with wild grape stands within a
smaller copse of trees. Sparkling glass-shard wind chimes and cutesy
bird feeders sway in the branches, and the path cuts past a row of
flowering bushes, curving onto a footbridge and then disappearing
into the woods on the far side.

It's like something out of a storybook.

No, it's like something out of *Once in a Lifetime*. Charming.
Quaint. Perfect.

"Oh my gosh." Libby juts her chin toward the next few steps. "Do
I *have* to keep going?"

I shake my head, still catching my breath. "I could tie a bedsheet
around your ankle and drag you up."

"What do I get if I make it to the top?"

"To make me dinner?" I say.

She laughs and loops her arm through mine, and we start up the
final steps, inhaling the softly sweet smell of warm grass. My heart

swells. Things already feel better than they have in months. It feels more *us*, before things amped up with my career and Libby's family and we fell into separate rhythms.

In my purse, I hear my phone chime with an email and resist the urge to check it.

"Look at you," Libby teases, "stopping to smell the literal roses."

"I'm not City Nora anymore," I say, "I'm laid-back, go-with-the-flow N—"

My phone chimes again, and I glance toward my purse, still keeping pace. It chimes twice more in quick succession, and then a third time.

I can't take it. I stop, drop our bags, and start digging through my purse.

Libby gives me a look of wordless disapproval.

"Tomorrow," I tell her, "I'll start on being that other Nora."

⌇

As different as we are, the second we start unpacking, it could not be more obvious that we're cut from the same cloth: books, skin care products, and very fancy underwear. The Stephens Women Trifecta of Luxury, as passed down from Mom.

"Some things never change," Libby sighs, a wistfully happy sound that folds over me like sunshine.

Mom's theory was that youthful skin would make a woman more money (true in both acting and waitressing), good underwear would make her more confident (so far, so true), and good books would make her happy (universal truth), and we've clearly both packed with this theory in mind.

Within twenty minutes, I've settled in, washed my face, changed into fresh clothes, and booted up my laptop. Meanwhile, Libby put half her stuff away, then passed out on the king bed we're sharing, her dog-eared copy of *Once in a Lifetime* facedown beside her on the quilt.

By then I'm desperately hungry, and it takes six more minutes of googling (the Wi-Fi is so slow, I have to use my phone as a hot spot) to confirm that the only place that delivers here is a pizza parlor.

Cooking isn't an option. Back home, I eat fifty percent of my meals out, and another forty percent come from a mix of takeout and delivery.

Mom used to say New York was a great place to have no money. There's so much free art and beauty, so much incredible, cheap food. *But having money in New York,* I remember her saying one winter as we window-shopped on the Upper East Side, Libby and I hanging on to her gloved hands, *now* that *would be magical.*

She never said it with bitterness, but instead with wonder, like, *If things are already this good, then how must they be when you don't have to worry about electric bills?*

Not that she was in the acting business for the money (she was optimistic, not deluded). Most of her income came from waitressing tips at the diner, where she'd set me and Libby up with books or crayons for the length of her shift, or the occasional nannying job lax enough to let her tote us along until I was about eleven and she trusted me to stay home or at Freeman Books with Libby, under Mrs. Freeman's watch.

Even without money, the three of us had been so happy in those days, wandering the city with street cart falafel or dollar pizza slices as big as our heads, dreaming up grand futures.

Thanks to the success of *Once in a Lifetime*, my life has started to resemble that imagined future.

But here, we can't even get an order of pad thai brought to the door. We'll have to walk the two miles into town.

When I try to shake Libby awake, she literally cusses me out in her sleep.

"I'm hungry, Lib." I jog her shoulder and she falls onto her side, burying her face in a pillow.

"Bring me something back," she grumbles.

"Don't you want to see your *favorite little hamlet?*" I say, trying to sound enticing. "Don't you want to see the apothecary where Old Man Whittaker almost overdoses?"

Without looking up, she flips me off.

"Fine," I say. "I'll bring you something back."

Hair scrubbed into a blunt little ponytail, sneakers on, I take off back down the sunny hillside toward the dirt road hemmed in by scraggly trees.

When the narrow lane finally T-bones into a proper street, I turn left, following the curving road downward.

As with the cottage, the town comes into view all at once.

One instant, I'm on a crumbling road on the side of a mountain, and the next, Sunshine Falls is spread out beneath me like the set from an old Western, tree-covered ridges jutting up at its back and an endless blue sky domed over it.

It's a little grayer and shabbier than it looked in pictures, but at least I spot the stone church from *Once*, along with the green-and-white-striped awning over the general store and the lemon-yellow umbrellas outside the soda fountain.

There are a few people out, walking their dogs. An old man sits on a green metal bench reading a newspaper. A woman waters the flower boxes outside a hardware store, through whose window I see exactly zero customers.

Ahead, I spot an old white stone building on the corner, perfectly matched to the description of Mrs. Wilder's old lending library in *Once*, my favorite setting in the book because it reminds me of rainy

Saturday mornings when Mom parked me and Libby in front of a shelf of middle grade books at Freeman's before hurrying across town for an audition.

When she got back, she'd take us for ice cream or for glazed pecans in Washington Square Park. We'd walk up and down the paths, reading the plaques on the benches, making up stories about who might've donated them.

Can you imagine *living anywhere else?* Mom used to say.

I couldn't.

Once, in college, a group of my transplant friends had unanimously agreed they "could never raise kids in the city," and I was shocked. It isn't just that I loved growing up in the city—it's that every time I see kids sleepily shuffling along en masse at the Met, or setting their boom box down on the train to break-dance for tips, or standing in awe in front of a world-class violinist playing beneath Rockefeller Center, I think, *How amazing it is to be a part of this, to get to share this place with all these people.*

And I love taking Bea and Tala to explore the city too, watching what mesmerizes a four-and-a-half-year-old and a newly three-year-old and which trappings of the city they walk right past, accepting as commonplace.

Mom came to New York hoping for the set of a Nora Ephron movie (my namesake), but the real New York is so much better. Because every kind of person is there, coexisting, sharing space and life.

Still, my love for New York doesn't preclude me from being charmed by Sunshine Falls.

In fact, I'm buzzing with excitement as I near the lending library. When I peer into the dark windows, the buzzing cuts out. The white stone facade of the building is exactly how Dusty described it, but inside, there's nothing but flickering TVs and neon beer signs.

It's not like I expected the widowed Mrs. Wilder to be an actual person, but Dusty made the lending library so vivid I was sure it was a real place.

The excitement sours, and when I think of Libby, it curdles entirely. This is *not* what she's expecting, and I'm already trying to figure out how to manage her expectations, or at least present her with a fun consolation prize.

I pass a few empty storefronts before I reach the awning of the general store. One glance at the windows tells me there are no racks of fresh bread or barrels of old-fashioned candy waiting inside.

The glass panes are grimy with dust, and beyond them, what I see can only be described as *random shit*. Shelves and shelves of junk. Old computers, vacuum cleaners, box fans, dolls with ratty hair. It's a pawnshop. And not a well-kept one.

Before I can make eye contact with the bespectacled man hunched at the desk, I push on until I come even with the yellow-umbrellaed patio on the far side of the street.

At least there are signs of life there, people milling in and out, a couple chatting with cups of coffee at one of the tables. That's promising. Ish.

I check both ways for traffic (none) before running across the street. The gold-embossed sign over the doors reads *MUG + SHOT*, and there are people waiting inside at a counter.

I cup my hands around my eyes, trying to see through the glare on the glass door, just as the man on the far side of it starts to swing it open.

3

T HE MAN'S EMERALD green eyes go wide. "Sorry!" he cries
as I swiftly sidestep the door without any damage.

It's not often that I'm stunned into silence.

Now, though, I'm staring, silent and agog, at the most gorgeous
man I've ever seen.

Golden-blond hair, a square jaw, and a beard that manages to be
rugged without looking unruly. He's brawny—the word pops into my
head, supplied by a lifetime of picking over Mom's old Harlequin
paperbacks—his (flannel) shirt snug, the sleeves rolled up his tan forearms.

With a sheepish smile, he steps aside, holding the door for me.

I should say something.

Anything.

Oh, no, my fault! I was in the way.

I'd even settle for a strangled *Hello, good sir.*

Unfortunately, it's not happening, so I cut my losses, force a smile, and slip past him through the door, hoping I look like I know where I am and have definitely come here on purpose.

I never loved Mom's small-town romance novels the way Libby does, but I've enjoyed enough that it shouldn't surprise me that my next thought is, *He smells like evergreens and impending rain.*

Except it does, because men don't smell like that.

They smell like sweat, bar soap, or a little too much cologne.

But this man is mythic, the too-shiny lead in a rom-com that has you shouting, *NO DAIRY FARMER HAS THOSE ABS.*

And he's smiling at me.

Is this how it happens? Pick a small town, take a walk, meet an impossibly good-looking stranger? Were my exes onto something?

His smile deepens (matching dimples; of course) as he nods and releases the door.

And then I'm watching him through the window as he walks away, my heart whirring like an overheated laptop.

When the stars in my eyes fade, I find myself not atop Mount Olympus but in a coffee shop with exposed brick walls and old wooden floors, the smell of espresso thick in the air. At the back of the shop, a door opens onto a patio. The light streaming in hits a glass display case of pastries and plastic-wrapped sandwiches, and I basically hear angels singing.

I get into line and scope out the crowd, a mix of hip, outdoorsy types in strappy hiking sandals and people in worn-out jeans and mesh-backed hats. Toward the front of the line, though, there's yet *another* good-looking man.

Two in my first hour here. An exceptional ratio.

He's not as striking as the door-holding Adonis, but good-looking in the way of a mere mortal, with coarse, dark hair and a lean elegance. He's around my height, maybe a hair taller or shorter, dressed in a black sweatshirt whose sleeves are pushed up and olive trousers with black shoes I have no choice but to describe as sexy. I can only see his face in profile, but it's a nice profile. Full lips, slightly jutted chin, sharp nose, eyebrows halfway between Cary Grant and Groucho Marx.

Actually, he kind of looks like Charlie Lastra.

Like, a *lot* like him.

The man glances sidelong at the display case, and the thought pops across my brain like a series of bottle rockets: *It's him. It's him. It's him.*

My stomach feels like someone tied it to a brick and threw it over a bridge.

There's no way. It's weird enough that *I'm* here—there's no way he is too.

And yet.

The longer I study him, the more unsure I am. Like when you think you spot a celebrity in person but the longer you gawk, the more sure you become that you've never actually *looked* at Matthew Broderick's nose before, and for all you can remember, he might not have one at all.

Or when you try to draw a car during a game of Pictionary and find out you have no idea what cars look like.

The person at the front of the line pays, and the queue shifts forward, but I duck out, tucking myself on the far side of a bookshelf filled with board games.

If it really is Charlie, it would be mortifying for him to see me hiding here—like seeing your stodgiest teacher outside a teens-only club while wearing a crop top and fake belly button ring (not that I had that experience [I did])—but if it's not, I can put this to rest easily. Maybe.

I get out my phone and open my email app, searching his name.

Aside from our first heated email exchange, there's only one more recent message from him, the mass email he sent with his new contact information when he moved from Wharton House to become an editor-at-large at Loggia six months back. I tap out a quick email to the new address.

Charlie,

New MS in the works. Trying to recall: how do you feel about talking animals?

Nora

It's not like I expect an out-of-office reply to detail where he's traveling, or what precise coffee shop he's likely to be in, but at least I'll know if he's away from work.

But my phone doesn't beep with an auto-reply.

I peer around the shelf. The man who may or may not be my professional nemesis slides his phone from his pocket, head bowing and lips thinning into an unimpressed line. Only they're still too full, so basically he's pouting. He types for a minute, then puts his phone away.

An honest-to-god chill slithers down my spine when my phone buzzes in my hand.

It's a coincidence. It has to be.

I open the reply.

Nora,

Terrified.

Charlie

The queue moves forward again. He's next up to order. I don't have long to make my escape without being seen, with even less time to confirm or dispel my fears.

Charlie,

What about Bigfoot erotica? Have some queries in my slush pile. Good fit for you?

Nora

As soon as I hit send, I snap to my senses. Why, of all the words available to me, is *this* what I said? Maybe my brain is organized by the Dewey decimal system, but right now all the shelves seem to be on fire. Embarrassment courses through my veins at the sudden image of Charlie opening that email and instantly gaining the professional high ground.

The man pulls his phone out. The teenage boy in front of him has just finished paying. The barista summons Maybe Charlie forward with a cheery smile, but he mumbles something and steps out of line.

He's halfway facing me now. He gives his head a firm shake, the corner of his mouth twisting into a grimace. It's *got* to be him. I'm sure of it now, but if I run for the door, I'll only draw his eye.

What could he possibly be doing here? My middle-class party trick tallies him up from head to toe: five hundred dollars of neutral tones, but if he was going for camouflage, it's not working. He might as well be standing under a movie-theater marquee advertising *THE OUT-OF-TOWNER* with an arrow pointed straight at his peppery hair.

I face the bookshelf, putting my back to him and pretending to peruse the games.

Considering how short, not to mention asinine, my message was, he takes a surprisingly long time to reply.

Of course, he could be reading any number of emails other than mine.

I nearly drop my phone in my frenzy to open the next message.

> No firm opinions as of yet, but extreme curiosity. Feel
> free to forward to me.

I check over my shoulder. Charlie has rejoined the queue.

How many times can I keep making him get out of line? I wonder with a thrill. I understand being glued to your phone when it comes to important work-related things, but I'm surprised the instinct runs so deep that he thinks a message about Bigfoot erotica requires an immediate response.

I do actually have a Bigfoot erotica submission in my inbox. Sometimes when my boss is having a rocky day, I'll do a dramatic reading from *Bigfoot's Big Feet* to cheer her up.

It would be unethical to share the manuscript outside the agency.

But the author actually included a link to his website, where a handful of self-published novellas are available for purchase. I copy the link to one and send it to Charlie without context.

I glance back to see him scowling down at his phone. A reply buzzes in.

> This costs 99 cents. . . . .

I reply, I know—such a bargain! If my professionalism is a gel manicure, then Charlie Lastra is apparently the industrial-grade acetone capable of burning right through it.

I search his name on Venmo and send him ninety-nine cents.

Another email comes in a second later. He's sent the dollar back to me, with the note, *I'm a grown man, Nora. I can buy my own Bigfoot erotica, thank you very much.*

The cashier greets him again, and this time he shoves his phone into his pocket and steps up to order. While he's distracted, I take my chance.

I am famished.

I am desperate to know what he's doing here.

And I am half running toward the door.

~

"No freaking way!" Libby cries. We're sitting at the rough-hewn wooden table in the cottage, devouring the breadsticks and salads we ordered from Antonio's Pizza. I had to trek back down to the mail-box to collect the order when the delivery guy said he wasn't allowed to climb the stairs "for insurance reasons."

Sounds made-up, but okay.

"The guy who was so rude about Dusty's book?" Libby clarifies.

I nod and stab a surprisingly juicy tomato in the salad, popping it into my mouth.

"What's he doing here?" she asks.

"I don't know."

"Ohmygosh," she says, "what if he's a *Once in a Lifetime* superfan?"

I snort. "I think that's the one possibility we can rule out."

"Maybe he's like Old Man Whittaker in *Once*. Just afraid to show his true feelings. Secretly, he loves this town. And the book. And the widowed Mrs. Wilder."

I'm actually unbearably curious, but we're not going to solve the mystery by guessing. "What do you want to do tonight?"

"Shall we consult the list?" She digs the sheet out of her bag and smooths it on the table. "Okay, I'm too tired for any of this."

"Too tired?" I say. "To pet a horse and save a local business? Even after your nap?"

"You think forty minutes is enough to make up for the three weeks of Bea crawling into bed with us after a nightmare?"

I wince. Those girls must have an internal body temperature of at least three hundred degrees. You can't sleep next to them without waking up drenched in sweat, with a tiny, adorable foot digging into your rib cage.

"You need a bigger bed," I tell Libby, pulling my phone out to start the search.

"Oh, please," Libby says. "We can't *fit* a bigger bed in that room. Not if we plan on ever opening our dresser drawers."

I feel a spark of relief right then. Because the change in Libby— the fatigue; the strange, intangible distance—suddenly makes sense. It has a cause, which means it has a solution.

"You need a bigger place." Especially with Baby Number Three on the way. One bathroom, for a family of five, is my idea of purgatory.

"We couldn't afford a bigger place if it were parked on top of a trash barge forty-five minutes into Jersey," Libby says. "Last time I looked at apartment listings, everything was like, *One-bedroom, zero-bath crawl space inside a serial killer's wall; utilities included but you provide the victims!* And even *that* was outside our price range."

I wave a hand. "Don't worry about the money. I can help out."

She rolls her eyes. "I don't need your help. I am a whole adult woman. All I need is a night in, followed by a month of rest and relaxation, okay?"

She's always hated taking money from me, but the whole reason to *have* money is to take care of us. If she won't accept another loan, then I'll just have to find her an apartment she can afford. Problem halfway solved.

"Fine," I say. "We'll stay in. Hepburn night?"

She gives a genuine grin. "Hepburn night."

Whenever Mom was stressed or heartbroken, she used to allow herself one night to lean into that feeling.

She'd call it a Hepburn night. She loved Hepburn. Katharine, not Audrey, not that she had anything against Audrey. That's how I wound up with the name Nora Katharine Stephens, while Libby got Elizabeth Baby Stephens, the "Baby" part being after the leopard in *Bringing Up Baby*.

On Hepburn nights, the three of us would each pick out one of Mom's over-the-top vintage robes and curl up in front of the TV with a root beer float and a pizza, or decaf and chocolate pie, and watch an old black-and-white movie.

Mom would cry during her favorite scenes, and when Libby or I caught her, she'd laugh, wiping away her tears with the back of one hand, and say, *I'm such a softy*.

I loved those nights. They taught me that heartbreak, like most things, was a solvable puzzle. A checklist could guide a person through mourning. There was an actionable plan for moving on. Mom mastered that, but never quite got to the next step: weeding out the assholes.

Married men. Men who didn't want to be stepfathers. Men who had absolutely no money, or who had lots of money and family members all too willing to whisper *gold digger*.

Men who didn't understand her aspirations to be on stage, and men who were too insecure to share the spotlight.

She was saddled with kids when she was little more than one herself, but even after everything she went through, she kept her heart open. She was an optimist and a romantic, just like Libby. I expected my sister to fall in love a dozen times over, be swept off her feet over and over again for decades, but instead she fell in love with Brendan at twenty and settled down.

I, meanwhile, had approximately one romantic bone in my body, and once it shattered and I pinned myself back together, I developed a rigorous vetting process for dating. So neither Libby nor I have need for our old-fashioned Hepburn nights. Now they're an excuse to be lazy, and a way to feel close to Mom.

It's only six o'clock, but we change into our pajamas—including our silk robes. We drag the blankets off the bed in the loft and down the iron spiral staircase to the couch and pop in the first DVD from the Best of Katharine Hepburn box set Libby brought with her.

I find two speckled blue mugs in the cabinet and put the kettle on for tea, and then we sink into the couch to watch *Philadelphia Story*, matching charcoal sheet masks plastered to our faces. My sister's head drops against my shoulder, and she heaves a happy sigh. "This was a good idea," she says.

My heart twinges. In a few hours, when I'm lying in an unfamiliar bed, sleep nowhere to be found—or tomorrow, when Libby sees the lackluster town square for the first time—my feelings might change, but right now, all is right in the world.

Anything broken can be fixed. Any problem can be solved.

When she drifts off, I pull my phone from my robe and type out an email, bcc'ing every real estate agent, landlord, and building manager I know.

You are in control, I tell myself. *You won't let anything bad happen to her ever again.*

My phone chirps with a new email around ten p.m.

Ever since Libby shuffled up to bed an hour ago, I've been sitting on the back deck, willing myself to feel tired and nursing a glass of the velvety pinot Sally Goode, the cottage's owner, left for us.

At home I'm a night owl. When I'm away, I'm more like an insomniac who just mixed a bunch of cocaine into some Red Bull and took a spin on a mechanical bull. I tried to work, but the Wi-Fi's so bad that my laptop is a glorified paperweight, so instead I've been staring into the dark woods beyond the deck, watching fireflies pop in and out of view.

I'm hoping to find a message from one of the real estate agents I reached out to. Instead **CHARLIE LASTRA** is bolded at the top of my inbox. I tap the message open and barely avoid a spit take.

> I would have preferred to go my whole life without knowing this book existed, Stephens.

Even to my own ears, my cackle sounds like an evil stepmother. You bought the Bigfoot erotica?

Charlie replies, Business expense.

Please tell me you charged it to a Loggia credit card.

This one takes place at Christmas, he writes. There's one for every holiday.

I take another sip, contemplating my reply. Possibly something like *Drink any interesting coffee lately?*

Maybe Libby's right: Maybe Charlie Lastra was secretly as charmed as the rest of America by Dusty's portrayal of Sunshine Falls and planned a visit during publishing's annual late-summer hibernation. I can't bring myself to broach the subject.

Instead, I write, What page are you on?

Three, he says. And I already need an exorcism.

Yes, but that has nothing to do with the book. Again, as soon as I've sent it, I have to marvel-slash-panic at my own unprofessionalism. Over the years, I've developed a finely tuned filter—with pretty much everyone except Libby—but Charlie always manages to disarm it, to press the exact right button to open the gate and let my thoughts charge out like velociraptors.

For example, when Charlie replies, I'll admit it's a master class in pacing. Otherwise I remain unimpressed, my instant reaction is to type, "Otherwise I remain unimpressed" is what they'll put on your headstone.

I don't even have the thought *I shouldn't send this* until I already have.

On yours, he replies, they'll put "Here lies Nora Stephens, whose taste was often exceptional and occasionally disturbing."

Don't judge me based on the Christmas novella, I reply. I haven't read it.

Would never judge you on Bigfoot porn, Charlie says. Would entirely judge you for preferring *Once in a Lifetime* to *The Glory of Small Things*.

The wine has slipped one Jenga piece too many loose from my brain: I write, IT'S NOT A BAD BOOK!

"IT'S NOT A BAD BOOK." —Nora Stephens, Charlie replies. I think I remember seeing that endorsement on the cover.

Admit you don't think it's bad, I demand.

Only if you admit you don't think it's her best either, he says.

I stare at the screen's harsh glow. Moths keep darting in front of it, and in the woods, I can hear cicadas humming, an owl hooting. The air is sticky and hot, even this long after the sun has sunk behind the trees.

Dusty is so ridiculously talented, I type. She's incapable of writing a bad book. I think for a moment before continuing: I've worked with her for years, and she does best with positive reinforcement. I don't concern myself with what's not working in her books. I focus on what she's great at. Which is how Dusty's editor was able to take *Once* from good to outrageously unputdownable. That's the thing that makes working on a book exciting: seeing its raw potential, knowing what it's trying to become.

Charlie replies, Says the woman they call the Shark.

I scoff. No one calls me that. I don't think.

Says the man they call the Storm Cloud.

Do they? he asks.

Sometimes, I write. Of course, I would never. I'm far too polite.

Of course, he says. That's what sharks are known for: manners.

I'm too curious to let it go. Do they really call me that?

Editors, he writes back, are terrified of you.

Not so scared they won't buy my authors' books, I counter.

So scared they wouldn't if the books were any less fucking fantastic.

My cheeks warm with pride. It's not like I wrote the books he's talking about—all I do is recognize them. And make editorial suggestions. And figure out which editors to send them to. And negotiate the contract so the author gets the best deal possible. And hold the author's hand when they get edit letters the size of Tolstoy novels, and talk them down when they call me crying. Et cetera.

Do you think, I type back, it has anything to do with my tiny eyes and gigantic gray head? Then I shoot off another email clarifying, The nickname, I mean.

Pretty sure it's your bloodlust, he says.

I huff. I wouldn't call it bloodlust. I don't revel in exsanguination. I do it for my clients.

Sure, I have some clients who are sharks themselves—eager to fire off accusatory emails when they feel neglected by their publishers—but most of them are more likely to get steamrolled, or to keep their complaints to themselves until their resentment boils over and they self-destruct in spectacular fashion.

This might be the first I'm hearing of my nickname, but Amy, my boss, calls my agenting approach *smiling with knives*, so it's not a total shock.

They're lucky to have you, Charlie writes. Dusty especially. Anyone who'd go to bat for a "not bad" book is a saint.

Indignation flames through me. And anyone who'd miss that book's obvious potential is arguably incompetent.

For the first time, he doesn't respond right away. I tip my head back, groaning at the (alarmingly starry; is this the first time I've looked up?) sky as I try to figure out how—or whether—to backtrack.

A prick draws my gaze to my thigh, and I slap away a mosquito, only to catch two more landing on my arm. Gross. I fold up my laptop and carry it inside, along with my books, phone, and mostly empty wineglass.

As I'm tidying up, my phone pings with Charlie's reply.

It wasn't personal, he says, then another message comes in. I've been known to be too blunt. Apparently I don't make the best first impression.

And I, I reply, am actually known to be very punctual. You caught me on a bad day.

What do you mean? he asks.

That lunch, I say. That was how it all started, wasn't it? I was late, so he was rude, so I was rude back, so he hated me, so I hated him, and so on and so forth.

He doesn't need to know I'd just gotten dumped in a four-minute phone call, but it seems worth mentioning those were extenuating circumstances. I'd just gotten some bad news. That's why I was late.

He doesn't reply for a full five minutes. Which is annoying, because I'm not in the habit of having real-time conversations over email, and of *course* he could just stop replying at any moment and go to bed, while I'll still be here, staring at a wall, wide awake.

If I had my Peloton, I could burn off some of this energy.

I didn't care that you were late, he says finally.

You looked at your watch. Pointedly, I write back. And said, if I recall, "You're late."

I was trying to figure out if I could catch a flight, Charlie replies.

Did you make it? I ask.

No, he says. Got distracted by two gin martinis and a platinum blond shark who wanted me dead.

Not dead, I say. Lightly mauled, maybe, but I would've stayed away from your face.

Didn't realize you were a fan, he writes.

A zing goes down my spine and right back up it, like my top vertebrae just touched a live wire. Is he *flirting*? Am *I*? I'm bored, yes, but not *that* bored. Never that bored.

I deflect with, Just trying to watch out for your eyebrows. If anything happened to those things, it would change your entire stormy scowl, and you'd need a new nickname.

If I lost my eyebrows, he says, somehow I think there would be no shortage of new nicknames available to me. I'm guessing you'd have some suggestions.

I'd need time to think, I say. Wouldn't want to make any rash decisions.

No, of course not, he replies. Seconds later, another line follows. I'll let you get back to your night.

And you to your Bigfoot novella, I type, then backspace and force myself to leave the message unanswered.

I shake my head, trying to clear the image of growly Charlie Lastra scowling at his e-reader in a hotel somewhere nearby, his frown deepening whenever he reaches something salacious.

But that image, it seems, is all my brain wants to dwell on. Tonight when I'm lying in bed, wide awake and trying to convince myself the world won't end if I drift off, this is what I'll come back to, my own mental happy place.

4

I WAKE, HEART RACING, skin cold and damp. My eyes snap open on a dark room, jumping from an unfamiliar door to the outline of a window to the snoring lump beside me.

Libby. The relief is intense and immediate, an ice bucket dumped over me all at once. The whirring of my heart starts its signature post-nightmare cooldown.

Libby is here. Everything must be okay.

I piece together my surroundings.

Goode's Lily Cottage, Sunshine Falls, North Carolina.

It was only the nightmare.

Maybe *nightmare* isn't the right word. The dream itself is nice, until the end.

It starts with me and Libby coming into the old apartment, setting down keys and bags. Sometimes Bea and Tala are with us, or Brendan, smiling good-naturedly while we fill up every gap with frantic chatter.

This time, it's just the two of us.

We're laughing about something—a play we just saw. *Newsies*, maybe. From dream to dream, those details change, and as soon as I sit up, breathing hard in the dark of this unfamiliar room, they fritter off like petals on a breeze.

What remains is the deep ache, the yawning canyon.

The dream goes like this:

Libby tosses her keys into the bowl by the door. Mom looks up from the table in the kitchenette, legs curled under her, nightgown pulled over them.

"Hey, Mama," Libby says, walking right past her toward our room, the one we shared when we were kids.

"My sweet girls!" Mom cries, and I bend to sweep a kiss across her cheek on my way to the fridge. I make it all the way there before the chill sets in. The feeling of wrongness.

I turn and look at her, my beautiful mother. She's gone back to reading, but when she catches me staring, she breaks into a puzzled smile. "What?"

I feel tears in my eyes. That should be the first sign that I'm dreaming—I never cry in real life—but I never notice this incongruity.

She looks the same, not a day older. Like springtime incarnate, the kind of warmth your skin gulps down after a long winter.

She doesn't seem surprised to see us, only amused, and then concerned. "Nora?"

I go toward her, wrap my arms around her, and hold tight. She circles me in hers too, her lemon-lavender scent settling over me like a blanket. Her glossy strawberry waves fall across my shoulders as she runs a hand over the back of my head.

"Hey, sweet girl," she says. "What's wrong? Let it out."

She doesn't remember that she's gone.

I'm the only one who knows she doesn't belong. We walked in the door, and she was there, and it felt so right, so natural, that none of us noticed it right away.

"I'll make tea," Mom says, wiping my tears away. She stands and walks past me, and I know before I turn that when I do, she won't be there anymore.

I let her out of my sight, and now she's gone. I can never stop myself from looking. From turning to the quiet, still room, feeling that painful emptiness in my chest like she's been carved out of me.

And that's when I wake up. Like if she can't be there, there's no point in dreaming at all.

I check the alarm clock on the bedside table. It's not quite six, and I didn't fall asleep until after three. Even with my sister's snores shivering through the bed, the house was too quiet. Crickets chirped and cicadas sang in a steady rhythm, but I missed the one-off honk of an annoyed cabdriver, or the sirens of a fire truck rushing past. Even the drunk guys shouting from opposite sides of the street as they headed home after a night of barhopping.

Eventually, I downloaded an app that plays cityscape sounds and set it in the windowsill, turning it up slowly so it wouldn't jar Libby awake. Only once I'd reached full volume did I drift off.

But I'm wide awake now.

My pang of homesickness for my mother rapidly shape-shifts into longing for my Peloton.

I am a parody of myself.

I pull on a sports bra and leggings and trip downstairs, then tug on my sneakers and step out into the cool darkness of morning.

Mist hovers across the meadow, and in the distance, through the trees, the first sprays of purply pinks stretch along the horizon. As I cross the dewy grass toward the footbridge, I lift my arms over my head, stretching to each side before picking up my pace.

On the far side of the footbridge, the path winds into the woods, and I break into an easy jog, the air's moisture pooling in all my creases. Gradually, the post-dream ache starts to ease.

Sometimes, it feels like no matter how many years pass, when I first wake up, I'm newly orphaned.

Technically, I guess we're not orphans. When Libby got pregnant the first time, she and Brendan hired a private investigator to find our father. When he did, Libby mailed dear old Dad a baby shower invitation. She never heard back, of course. I don't know what she expected from a man who couldn't be bothered to show up to his *own* kid's birth.

He left Mom when she was pregnant with Libby, without so much as a note.

Sure, he also left a ten-thousand-dollar check, but to hear Mom tell it, he came from so much money that that was his idea of petty change.

They'd been high school sweethearts. She was a sheltered, home-schooled girl with no money and dreams of moving to New York to become an actress; he was the wealthy prep school boy who impregnated her at seventeen. His parents wanted Mom to terminate the pregnancy; hers wanted them to get married. They compromised by doing neither. When they moved in together, both sets of parents cut them off, but his turned over his inheritance as a parting gift, a sliver of which he'd bequeathed to us on his way out the door.

She used the nest egg to move us from Philly to New York and never looked back.

I push the thoughts away and lose myself in the delicious burn of my muscles, the thudding of my feet against pine-needle-dusted earth. The only two ways I've ever managed to get out of my head are through reading and rigorous exercise. With either, I can slip out of my mind and drift in this bodiless dark.

The trail curves down a forested hillside, then turns to follow a split-rail fence, beyond which a pasture stretches out, glowing in the first spears of light, the horses dotting the field backlit, their tails swishing at the gnats and flies that float and glimmer in the air like gold dust.

There's a man out there too. When he sees me, he lifts a hand in greeting.

I squint against the fierce light, my stomach rising as I place him as the coffee shop Adonis. The small-town leading man.

Do I slow down?

Is he going to come over here?

Should I call out and introduce myself?

Instead I choose a fourth option: I trip over a root and go sprawling in the mud, my hand landing squarely in something that appears to be poop. A lot of it. Like, maybe a whole family of deer has specifically marked this spot as their shit palace.

I clamber onto my feet, gaze snapping toward Romance Novel Hero to find that he's missed my dramatic performance. He's looking at (talking to?) one of the horses.

For a second, I contemplate calling out to him. I play the fantasy out to its logical conclusion, this gloriously handsome man reaching to shake my hand, only to find my palm thoroughly smeared with deer pellets.

I shudder and turn down the path, picking up my jog.

If, eventually, I meet the exceptionally handsome horse whisperer, then great, maybe I can make progress on the list and check off number five. If not . . . well, at least I have my dignity.

I brush a strand of hair out of my face, only to realize I've used the scat-hand.

Scratch that part about dignity.

～

"I forgot how peaceful it is grocery shopping without a four-year-old, like, lying on the ground and licking the tile," Libby sighs, moseying down the toiletries aisle like an aristocrat taking a turn about the garden in Regency-era England.

"And all the space—the *space*," I say, far more enthusiastically than I feel. I've been able to forestall Libby seeing the droopy city center of Sunshine Falls by insisting on having Hardy drive us to the Publix a few towns over, but I'm still in preemptive damage-control mode, as evidenced by the fifteen minutes I spent pointing out various trees on the ride over.

Libby stops in front of the boxed dyes, a brilliant smile overtaking her face. "Hey, we should choose each other's makeover looks! Like hair color and cut, I mean."

"I'm not cutting my hair," I say.

"Of course you're not," she says. "I am."

"Actually, you're not."

She frowns. "It's on the list, Sissy," she says. "How else are we supposed to transform via montage into our new selves? It'll be fine. I cut the girls' hair all the time."

"That explains Tala's Dorothy Hamill phase."

Libby smacks me in the boob, which is completely unfair, because you can't hit a pregnant lady's boob, even if she's your little sister.

"Do you really have the emotional resilience to leave a checklist *unchecked*?" she says.

Something in me twitches.

I really do fucking love a checklist.

She pokes me in the ribs. "Come on! Live a little! This will be fun! It's why we're here."

It is decidedly *not* why *I'm* here. But the reason *I'm* here is standing right in front of me, a melodramatic lower lip jutted out, and all

I can think about is the month ahead of us, marooned in a town that's nothing like the one she's expecting.

And even aside from that, historically, Libby's crises can be tracked by dramatic changes in appearance. As a kid, she never changed her hair color—Mom made a big deal about how rare and striking Lib's strawberry blond waves were—but Libby showed up to her own wedding with a pixie cut she hadn't had the night before. A couple days later, she finally opened up to me about it, admitted she'd had a burst of cold-feet-bordering-on-terror and needed to make another dramatic (though less permanent) decision to work through it.

I personally would've gone with a color-coded pro-con list, but to each her own.

The point is, Libby's clearly reckoning with the arrival of this new baby and what it will mean for her and Brendan's already strained finances and tight quarters. If I push her to talk about it now, she'll clam up. But if I ride it out with her, she'll talk about it when she's ready. That aching, pulsing space between us will be sealed shut, a phantom limb made whole again.

That's why I'm here. *That's* what I want. Badly enough that I'll shave my head if that's what it takes (then order a very expensive wig).

"Okay," I relent. "Let's get made over."

Libby lets out a squeal of happiness and pushes up on her tiptoes to kiss my forehead. "I know *exactly* what color you're getting," she says. "Now turn around, and don't peek."

I make a mental note to schedule a hair appointment for the day I fly home to New York.

By the time we return to the cottage that afternoon, the sun is high in the cloudless blue sky, and as we hike the hillside, sweat gathers in every inconvenient place, but Libby chatters along, unbothered. "I'm *so* curious what color you picked for me," she says.

"No color," I reply. "We're just going to shave your head."

She squints through the light, her freckled nose wrinkling. "When will you learn that you're *so* bad at lying that it's not worth even trying?"

Inside, she sits me down in a kitchen chair and slathers my hair in dye. Then I do the same, neither of us showing our hand. At the time, I felt so confident in my choice, but seeing how eye-burningly vibrant the color looks caked over her head, I'm less sure.

Once our timers are set, Libby starts on brunch.

She's been a vegetarian since she was little, and after Mom died, I became one too, by default. Financially, it didn't make sense to buy two different versions of everything. Also, meat's expensive. From a purely mathematical standpoint, vegetarianism made sense for two newly orphaned girls of twenty and sixteen.

Even after Libby moved in with Brendan, it stuck. During her aspiring-chef phase, she won him over to a plant-based diet. So while it's tempeh frying in the pan beside the eggs she's scrambling for us, it smells like bacon. Or at least enough like bacon to appeal to someone who hasn't had the real thing in ten years.

When the timer goes off, Libby shoos me off to rinse, warning me not to look in the mirror "or else."

Because I'm so bad at lying, I follow her orders, then take over the job of transferring brunch into the oven to keep warm while she rinses *her* dye.

With her hair wrapped in a towel, she takes me onto the deck to trim mine. Every few seconds, she makes an inauspicious "huh" sound.

"Really instilling confidence in me, Libby," I say.

She snips some more at the front of my face. "It's going to be fine."

It sounds a little too much like she's giving herself a pep talk for my liking. After I've chopped her hair into a long bob—most of it air-dried by now—we go inside for the big reveal.

After matching deep breaths, preparing our egos for a humbling, we step in front of the bathroom mirror together and take it in.

She's given me feathery bangs somewhere between fringe and curtain, and somehow they make the ash-brown color read more Laurel Canyon free spirit than dirty dishwater.

"You really are sickeningly good at everything, you know that, right?" I say.

Libby doesn't reply, and when my gaze cuts toward hers, a weight plummets through me. She's staring at the reflection of her Pepto-Bismol-pink waves with tears welling in her eyes.

Shit. A huge and obvious misfire. Libby may generally favor a bold look, but I forgot to factor in how pregnancy tends to affect her self-image.

"It'll start rinsing out in a few washes!" I say. "Or we can go back to the store and get a different color? Or find a good salon in Asheville—my treat. *Really*, this is an easy fix, Lib."

The tears are reaching their breaking point now, ready to fall.

"I just remembered you begging Mom to let you get pink hair when you were in ninth grade," I go on. "Remember? She wouldn't let you, and you went on that hunger strike until she said you could do dip-dye?"

Libby turns to me, lip quivering. I have a split second to wonder if she's about to attack me before her arms fling around my neck, her face burying into the side of my head. "I love it, Sissy," she says, her sweet lemon-lavender scent engulfing me.

The roaring panic-storm settles in me. The tension dissolves from my shoulders. "I'm so glad," I say, hugging her back. "And you really did an amazing job. I mean, I'm not sure what would ever possess a person to choose this color, but you made it work."

She pulls back, frowning. "It's as close to your natural color as I could find. I always loved your hair when we were kids."

My heart squeezes tight, the back of my nose tingling like there's too much of something building in my skull and it's starting to seep out.

"Oh no," she says, looking back into the mirror. "It just occurred to me: what am I supposed to say when Bea and Tala ask to dye theirs into unicorn tails? Or shave their heads entirely?"

"You say no," I say. "And then, the next time I'm babysitting, I'll hand over the dye and clippers. Afterward I'll teach them how to roll a joint, like the sexy, cool, fun aunt I am."

Libby snorts. "You *wish* you knew how to roll a joint. God, I miss weed. The maternity books never prepare you for how badly you're going to miss weed."

"Sounds like there's a hole in the market," I say. "I'll keep an eye out."

"*The Pothead's Guide to Pregnancy*," Libby says.

"*Marijuana Mommy*," I reply.

"And its companion, *Doobie Daddies*."

"You know," I say, "if you ever need to complain about your lack of weed, or pregnancy—or anything else—I'm here. Always."

"Yep," she says, eyes back on her reflection, fingers back in her hair. "I know."

5

My PHONE BUZZES with an incoming email, and Charlie's name is bolded across the screen. The words *distracted by two gin martinis and a platinum blond shark* flash across my mind like a casino's neon sign, part thrill, part warning.

> I don't want my work email to get flagged, but there are so many excerpts of this book I can't unread. I'm in a horror movie and I won't be freed of this curse until I've inflicted it on someone else.

Technically, Charlie already has my phone number from my email signature; the question is whether to invite him to use it.

Pro: Maybe there'd be a natural opening to mention I'm in Sunshine Falls, thus lowering the risk of an awkward run-in.

Con: Do I really want my professional nemesis texting me Bigfoot erotica?

Pro: Yes I do. I'm curious by nature, and at least this way, the exchange of information is happening over private channels rather than professional ones.

I type out my phone number and hit send.

By then it's time for my check-in call with Dusty, a twenty-minute conversation that might as well just be me playing jock jams and running circles around her, chanting her name. I throw the word *genius* out a half dozen times, and by the time we hang up, I've convinced her to turn in the first chunk of her next book—even if it's rough—so her editor, Sharon, can get started while Dusty finishes writing.

Afterward, I rejoin Libby where she's primping in the bathroom, curling her freshly pink hair into soft ringlets. "Let's walk to dinner," she says. "My neck is sore from that last cab ride. Also it made me pee myself."

"I remember," I say. "It made you pee me too."

She glances over my outfit. "You sure you want to wear those shoes?"

I've paired my black backless sheath with black mules, my widest heels. She's in a daisy-print sundress from the nineties and white sandals.

"If you offer to lend me your Crocs again, I'm going to sue you for emotional damages."

She balks. "After that comment, you don't *deserve* my Crocs."

On the hike down the hillside, I attempt to hide my struggle, but based on Libby's gleeful smirk, she definitely notices that my heels keep puncturing the grass and spiking me into place.

The sun has gone down, but it's still oppressively hot, and the mosquito population is raging. I'm used to rats—most run away at the sight of a person, and the rest basically just hold out tiny hats to beg for bits of pizza. Mosquitoes are worse. I've got six new red welts by the time we reach the edge of the town square.

Libby hasn't gotten bitten once. She bats her lashes. "I must be too sweet for them."

"Or maybe you're pregnant with the Antichrist and they recognize you as their queen."

She nods thoughtfully. "I could use the excitement, I guess." She pauses at the very empty crosswalk and scans the equally desolate city center, her mouth shrinking as she considers it. "Huh," she says finally. "It's . . . sleepier than I expected."

"Sleepy is good, right?" I say, a bit too eagerly. "Sleepy means *relaxing*."

"Right." She sort of shakes herself, and her smile returns. "Exactly. That's why we're here." She looks more quizzical than devastated when we pass the general-store-turned-pawnshop, and I make a big deal of pointing out Mug + Shot to distract her.

"It smelled *amazing*," I insist. "We'll have to go tomorrow."

She brightens further, like she's on a dimmer switch powered by my optimism. And if that's the case, I'm prepared to be optimistic as hell.

Next, we pass a beauty parlor. ("Okay, definitely should've just gotten our hair cut here," Libby says, though I silently disagree, based on the dripping-blood-style letters on the sign and the fact that they spell out *Curl Up N Dye*.) After a couple more empty storefronts, there's a greasy-spoon diner, another dive bar, and a bookshop (which we pledge to return to, despite its dusty and lackluster window display). At the end of the block, there's a big wooden building with rusty metal letters reading, mysteriously, *POPPA SQUAT*.

By then, Libby's distracted by her phone, texting Brendan as she shuffles along beside me. She's still smiling, but it's a rigid expression, and it almost looks like she's on the verge of tears. Her stomach is growling and her face is pink from the heat, and I can imagine her texts are something along the lines of *Maybe this whole thing was a mistake*, and a sudden desperation swells in me. I need to turn this around, fast, starting with finding food.

I stop abruptly beside the wooden building and peer into its tinted windows. Without looking up from her phone, Libby asks, "Are you spying on someone?"

"I'm looking into the window of Poppa Squat's."

Her eyes lift slowly. "What . . . the hell . . . is a poppa squat?"

"Well . . ." I point up at the sign. "It's either a very large public bathroom *or* a bar and grill."

"WHY?" Libby screams in a mix of delight and dismay, any remnant of her disappointment vanishing. "Why does that exist?!" She plasters herself against the dark window, trying to see in.

"I have no answers for you, Libby." I sidestep to haul one of the heavy wooden doors open. "Sometimes the world is a cruel, mysterious place. Sometimes people become warped, twisted, so ill at a soul level that they would name a dining establishment—"

"Welcome to Poppa Squat!" a curly-haired waif of a hostess says. "How many are in your party?"

"Two, but we're eating for five," Libby says.

"Oh, congratulations!" the hostess says brightly, eyeing each of our stomachs whilst trying to perform an invisible math problem.

"I don't even know this woman," I say, tipping my head toward Libby. "She's just been following me for three blocks."

"Okay, rude," my sister says. "It's been much more than three blocks—it's like you don't even *see* me."

The hostess seems uncertain.

I cough. "Two, please."

She hesitantly waves toward the bar. "Well, our bar is full-service, but if you'd like a table . . ."

"The bar's fine," Libby assures her. The hostess hands us each a menu that's about . . . oh, forty pages too long, and we slide onto pleather-topped stools, setting our purses on the sticky bar and scanning our surroundings in a silence driven by either shock or awe.

This place looks like a Cracker Barrel had a baby with a honky-tonk, and now that baby is a teenager who doesn't shower enough and chews on his sweatshirt sleeves.

The floors and walls alike are dark, mismatched wooden planks, and the ceiling is corrugated metal. Pictures of local sports teams are framed alongside *HOME IS WHERE THE FOOD IS* needlepoints and glowing *Coors* signs. The bar runs along the left side of the restaurant, and in one corner a couple of pool tables are gathered, while in the corner opposite, a jukebox sits beside a shallow stage. There are more people in this one building than I've seen in the rest of Sunshine Falls combined, but still, the place manages to look desolate.

I flip open the menu and start to peruse. Easily thirty percent of the listed items are just various deep-fried things. You name it, Poppa Squat can fry it.

The bartender, a preternaturally gorgeous woman with thick, dark waves and a handful of constellation tattoos on her arms comes to stand in front of me, her hands braced against the bar. "What can I get you?"

Like the coffee shop/horse farm guy, she looks less like a bartender than like someone who would *play* a bartender on a sexy soap opera.

What's in the water here?

"Dirty martini," I tell her. "Gin."

"Soda water and lime, please," Libby says.

The bartender moves off, and I go back to skimming page five of the menu. I've made it to salads. Or at least that's what they're calling them, though if you put ranch dressing and Doritos on a bed of lettuce, I think you're taking liberties with the word.

When the bartender returns, I try to order the Greek.

She winces. "You sure?"

"Not anymore."

"We're not known for our salads," she explains.

"What are you known for?"

She waves a hand toward the glowing *Coors Light* sign behind her shoulder.

"What are you known for, with regard to food?" I clarify.

She says, "To be known isn't necessarily to be admired."

"What do you recommend," Libby tries, "*other* than Coors?"

"The fries are good," she says. "Burger's okay."

"Veggie burger?" I ask.

She purses her lips. "It won't kill you."

"Sounds perfect," I say. "I'll have one of those, and some fries."

"Same," Libby adds.

Despite her insistence that the burger won't kill us, the bartender's shrug reads, *Your funeral, bitches!*

Libby seems totally fine, happy even, but there's still a kernel of anxiety in my gut, and I accidentally drink my entire martini before our food arrives. I'm tipsy enough that everything's taking me longer than it should. Libby scarfs her burger down and hops up to use the bathroom before I've made a dent in mine.

My phone vibrates on the sticky counter, and I'm one hundred percent expecting it to be Charlie.

It's a zillion times better.

Dusty has *finally* turned in part of her manuscript, and not a minute too soon—her editor goes out on maternity leave in a month.

> Thank you all so much for your patience—I know this schedule hasn't been ideal for you, but it means so much that you trust me enough to let me work in the way that serves me best. I have a complete first draft, but have only had a chance to clean and tighten this first bit. I hope to have several more chapters to you within the week, but hopefully this gives you an idea of what to expect.

I tap open the attached document, titled *Frigid 1.0*.

It starts with *Chapter One*. Always a good sign that an author hasn't gone full Jack-Torrance-locked-up-with-his-typewriter-in-the-Overlook. I resist the urge to scroll through to the end, a tic I've had since I was a kid, when I realized there were too many books in the world and not enough time. I've always used it as a litmus test for whether I want to read a book or not, but given that this is a client's work, I'm going be reading the whole thing no matter what.

So instead my eyes skim over the first line, and it hits like a gut punch.

They called her the Shark.

"What the fuck," I say. An older man at the end of the bar jerks his head up from his watery soup and scowls. "Sorry," I grumble, and train my eyes on the screen again.

> *They called her the Shark, but she didn't mind. The name fit. For one thing, sharks could only swim forward. As a rule, Nadine Winters never looked back. Her life was predicated on rules, many of which served to ease her conscience.*

If she looked back, she'd see the trail of blood. Moving
forward, all there was to think about was hunger.
And Nadine Winters was hungry.

For a minute I'm actually hoping to discover that Nadine Winters is a literal shark. That Dusty has written the talking-animal story of Charlie Lastra's nightmares. But four lines down, a word jumps out as if, rather than Times New Roman, it's written in *Curl Up N Dye*'s bloodcurdling font.

AGENT.

Dusty's main character, the Shark, is an agent.

I backtrack to the word right before it. *Film.*

Film agent. Not literary agent. The differentiation does nothing to loosen the knot in my chest, or to quiet the rush of blood in my ears.

Unlike me, Nadine Winters has jet-black hair and blunt bangs.

Like me, she only skips heels when she's working out.

Unlike me, she takes Krav Maga every morning instead of virtual classes on her Peloton.

Like me, she orders a salad with goat cheese every time she eats out with a client and drinks her gin martinis dirty—never more than one. She hates any loss of control.

Like me, she never leaves the house without a full face of makeup and gets bimonthly manicures.

Like me, she sleeps with her phone next to her bed, sound turned to full volume.

Like me, she often forgets to say hello at the start of her conversations and skips goodbye at the end.

Like me, she has money but doesn't enjoy spending it and would rather scroll through Net-A-Porter, filling up her cart for hours, then leave it that way until everything sells out.

Nadine didn't enjoy most things, Dusty writes. *Enjoyment was beside the point of life. As far as she could tell, staying alive was the point, and that required money and survival instincts.*

My face burns hotter with every page.

The chapter ends with Nadine walking into the office right in time to see her two assistants giddily celebrating something. With a cutting glare, she says, "What?"

Her assistant announces she's pregnant.

Nadine smiles like the shark she is, says congratulations, then goes into her office, where she starts thinking through all the reasons she should fire Stacey the pregnant assistant. She doesn't approve of distractions, and that's what pregnancy is.

Nadine doesn't deviate from plans. She doesn't make exceptions to rules. She lives life by a strict code, and there's no room for anyone who doesn't meet it.

In short, she is a puppy-kicking, kitten-hating, money-driven robot. (The puppy-kicking is implied, but give it a few more chapters, and it might become canon.)

As soon as I finish reading, I start over, trying to convince myself that Nadine—a woman who makes Miranda Priestly look like Snow White—isn't me.

The third read through is the worst of all. Because this is when I accept that it's *good*.

One chapter, ten pages, but it works.

I stand woozily and head toward the dark nook where the bathrooms are, rereading as I go. I need Libby *now*. I need someone who knows me, who loves me, to tell me this is all wrong.

I should've been looking where I was going.

I shouldn't have worn such high heels, or had a martini on an empty stomach, or been reading a book that's giving me a surreal out-of-body experience.

Because some combination of those poor decisions leads to me barreling into someone. And we're not talking a casual *Oh, I clipped you on the shoulder—how adorably clumsy I am!* We're talking *"Holy shit! My nose!"*

Which is what I hear in the moment that my ankles wobble, my balance is thrown off, and my gaze snaps up to a face belonging to none other than Charlie Lastra.

Right as I go down like a sack of potatoes.

6

~

CHARLIE CATCHES MY forearms before I can tumble all the way down, steadying me as the words "What the hell?" fly out of him.

After the pain and shock comes recognition, followed swiftly by confusion.

"Nora Stephens." My name sounds like a swear.

He gapes at me; I gape back.

I blurt, "I'm on vacation!"

His confusion deepens.

"I just . . . I'm not stalking you."

His eyebrows furrow. "Okay?"

"I'm not."

He releases my forearms. "More convincing every time you say it."

"My sister wanted to take a trip here," I say, "because she loves *Once in a Lifetime*."

Something flutters behind his eyes. He snorts.

I cross my arms. "One has to wonder why *you'd* be here."

"Oh," he says dryly, "I'm stalking you." At my eye bulge, he says, "I'm *from* here, Stephens."

I gawk at him in shock for so long that he waves a hand in front of my face. "Hello? Are you broken?"

"You . . . are from . . . *here*? Like *here* here?"

"I wasn't born on the bar of this unfortunate establishment," he says, lip curled, "if that's what you mean, but yes, nearby."

It's not computing. Partly because he's dressed like he just stepped out of a Tom Ford spread in *GQ*, and partly because I'm not convinced this place isn't a movie set that production abandoned halfway through construction. "Charlie Lastra is from Sunshine Falls."

His gaze narrows. "Did my nose go directly into your brain?"

"You are from Sunshine Falls, North Carolina," I say. "A place with one gas station and a restaurant named *Poppa Squat*."

"Yes."

My brain skips over several more relevant questions to: "Is Poppa Squat a person?"

Charlie laughs, a surprised sound so rough I feel it as a scrape against my rib cage. "No?"

"What, then," I say, "is a Poppa Squat?"

The corner of his mouth ticks downward. "I don't know—a state of mind?"

"And what's wrong with the Greek salad here?"

"You tried to order a salad?" he says. "Did the townspeople circle you with pitchforks?"

"Not an answer."

"It's shredded iceberg lettuce with nothing else on it," he says. "Except when the cook is drunk and covers the whole thing in cubed ham."

"Why?" I ask.

"I imagine he's unhappy at home," Charlie replies, deadpan.

"Might have something to do with the kinds of thwarted dreams that lead a person to working here."

"Not *why does the cook drink*," I say. "Why would anyone cover a salad in cubed ham?"

"If I knew the answer to that, Stephens," he says, "I'd have ascended to a higher plane."

At this point, he notices something on the ground and ducks sideways, picking it up. "This yours?" He hands me my phone. "Wow," he says, reading my reaction. "What did this phone do to you?"

"It's not the phone so much as the sociopathic super-bitch who lives inside it."

Charlie says, "Most people just call her Siri."

I shove my phone back to him, Dusty's pages still pulled up. The furrow in his brow re-forms, and immediately, I think, *What am I doing?*

I reach for the phone, but he spins away from me, the crease beneath his full bottom lip deepening as he reads. He swipes down the screen impossibly fast, his pout shifting into a smirk.

Why did I hand this over to him? Is the culprit here the martini, the recent head injury, or sheer desperation?

"It's good," Charlie says finally, pressing my phone into my hand.

"That's all you have to say?" I demand. "Nothing else you care to comment on?"

"Fine, it's exceptional," he says.

"It's *humiliating*," I parry.

He glances toward the bar, then meets my eyes again. "Look, Stephens. This is the end of a particularly shitty day, inside a particularly shitty restaurant. If we're going to have this conversation, can I at least get a Coors?"

"You don't strike me as a Coors guy," I say.

"I'm not," he says, "but I find the merciless mockery from the bartender here dampens my enjoyment of a Manhattan."

I look toward the sexy TV bartender. "Another enemy of yours?"

His eyes darken, his mouth doing that grimace-twitch. "Is that what we are? Do you send all your enemies Bigfoot erotica, or just the special ones?"

"Oh no," I say, feigning pity. "Did I hurt your feelings, Charlie?"

"You seem pretty pleased with yourself," he says, "for a woman who just found out she was the inspiration for Cruella de Vil."

I scowl at him. Charlie rolls his eyes. "Come on. I'll buy you a martini. Or a puppy coat."

A martini. Exactly what Nadine Winters drinks, whenever she doesn't have easy access to virgin's blood.

For some reason, my ex-boyfriend Jakob flits into my mind. I picture him drinking beer from a can on his back porch, his wife curled under his arm, swigging on her own.

Even four kids in, she's laid-back and absurdly gorgeous, yet somehow "one of the guys."

The Anti-Nora.

They always are, the women I get dumped for. Pretty hard to learn to be "one of the guys" when your entire experience with men growing up was either 1) them making your mother cry or 2) your mother's dancer friends teaching you how to step-ball-change. I can be one of the guys, as long as the guys in question have a favorite song from *Les Mis*. Otherwise I'm hopeless.

"I'll have a beer," I say as I pass Charlie, "and you're buying."

"Like . . . I said?" he murmurs, following me to the peanut-shell-strewn bar.

As he's exchanging pleasantries with the bartender (definitely not enemies; there's a *vibe*, by which I mean he's fifteen percent less rude than usual), I glance back toward the bathroom, but Libby still hasn't emerged.

I don't even realize I've gone back to rereading the chapters until Charlie tugs my phone from my hands. "Stop obsessing."

"I'm not obsessing."

He studies me with that black-hole gaze, the one that makes me want to scrabble for purchase. "I'm surprised this is such a problem for you."

"And I'm shocked your artificial intelligence chip allows you to feel surprise."

"Well, *hello*." I flinch toward Libby's voice and find her smiling like a cartoon cat whose mouth is stuffed with multiple canaries.

"Libby," I say. "This is—"

Before I can introduce Charlie, she pipes up, "Just wanted to let you know, I called a cab. I'm not feeling well."

"What's wrong?" I start to rise but she pushes my shoulder back down, hard.

"Just exhausted!" She sounds anything but. "You should stay—you're not even done with your burger."

"Lib, I'm not going to just let you—"

"Oh!" She looks at her phone. "Hardy's here—you don't mind getting the bill, do you, Nora?"

I'm not traditionally a blusher, but my face is on fire because I've just realized what's going on, which means Charlie likely has too, and Libby's already retreating, leaving me with half a veggie burger, an unpaid bill, and a deep desire for the earth to swallow me whole.

She throws a look over her shoulder and calls loudly, "Good luck checking off number five, Sissy!"

"Number five?" Charlie asks as the door swings shut, vanishing my sister into the night.

I really don't like the idea of her hiking up those steps alone. I snatch my phone back up and text her, LET ME KNOW THE SECOND YOU MAKE IT UP TO THE COTTAGE OR ELSE!!!!

Libby replies, Let me know the second you make it to third base with Mr. Hottman.

Over my shoulder, Charlie snorts. I turn my phone away, squaring my shoulders. "That was my sister, Libby," I say. "Ignore everything she says. She's always horny when she's pregnant. Which is always."

His (truly miraculous) eyebrows lift, his heavy-lidded gaze homing in. "There is . . . so much to unpack in that sentence."

"And so little time." I bite into my burger just to focus on something other than his face. "I should get back to her."

"So no time for that beer." He says it like a challenge, like *I knew it*. His brow is arched, the tiniest shred of a smirk hiding in one corner of his mouth. Somehow this doesn't totally extinguish his pout. It just makes it a smout.

The bartender returns with our sweating glass bottles then, and Charlie thanks her. For the first time, I see her staggeringly incandescent smile. "Of course," she says. "If you need anything, just say the word."

As she turns away, Charlie faces me, taking a long sip.

"Why do *you* get a smile?" I demand. "I'm a thirty-percent-minimum tipper."

"Yeah, well, you should try almost marrying her and see if that helps," he replies, leaving me so stunned I'm back to gawping.

"Speaking of sentences with a lot to unpack."

"I know you're a busy woman," he says. "I'll let you get back to sharpening your knives and organizing your poison cabinet, Nadine Winters."

He says everything so evenly, it's easy to miss the joke in it. But this time the unmistakably cajoling note in his voice back-combs over me until I feel like a dog with its hackles up.

"First of all," I say, "it's a pantry, not a cabinet. And second of all, the beer's already here, and it's after work hours, so I might as well drink it."

Because I am *not* Nadine Winters. I grab my bottle and chug, feeling Charlie's owlish eyes heavy on me.

He says, "It's fucking good, right?" For once, he lets a little excitement into his voice. His eyes flash like lightning just crackled through the inside of his skull.

"If you're into cat pee and gasoline."

"The *chapter*, Nora."

My jaw tightens as I nod.

As far as I've seen, Charlie's eyebrows have three modes: brooding, scowling, and portraying something that's either concern or confusion. That's what they're up to now. "But you're still upset about it."

"Upset?" I cry. "Just because my oldest client thinks I'd fire someone for getting pregnant? Don't be silly."

Charlie tucks one foot on the rung of his stool, his knee bumping mine. "She doesn't think that." He tips his head back for another swig. A bead of beer sneaks down his neck, and for a moment, I'm hypnotized, watching it cut a trail toward the collar of his shirt.

"And even if she does," Charlie says, "that doesn't make it true."

"If she wrote a whole book about it," I say, "it might make *other* people think it's true."

"Who cares?"

"This guy." I point to my chest. "The person who needs people to work with her in order to have a job."

"How long have you been representing Dusty?" he asks.

"Seven years."

"She wouldn't be working with you, after seven years, if you weren't a great agent."

"I *know* I'm a great agent." That's not the problem. The problem is, I'm embarrassed, ashamed, and a little hurt. Because, as it turns out, I do have feelings. "It's fine. I'm fine."

Charlie studies me.

"I'm fine!" I say again.

"Clearly."

"You're laughing now, but—"

"I'm not laughing," he interjects. "When did I laugh?"

"Good point. I'm sure that's never happened. But just you wait until one of your authors turns in a book about an amber-eyed asshole editor."

"Amber-eyed?" he says.

"I notice you didn't question the *asshole* part of that sentence," I say, and chug some more. Clearly, the filter has melted away again, but at least that's proof I'm not the woman in those pages.

"I'm used to people thinking I'm an asshole," he says stiffly. "Less used to them describing my eyes as 'amber.'"

"That's what color they are," I say. "It's objective. I'm not complimenting you."

"In that case, I'll abstain from being flattered. What color are yours?" He leans in without any hint of embarrassment, only curiosity, his warm breath feathering over my jaw. That's pretty much when I realize I think he's hot.

I mean, I know I thought he was hot in Mug + Shot when I thought he was someone else, but *this* is when I realize I think *he*—specifically Charlie Lastra, not just someone who looks like him—is *hot*.

I take another sip. "Red."

"Really brings out the color of your forked tail and horns."

"You're too sweet."

"Now that," he says, "is something I've never been accused of."

"I can't imagine why not."

He arches a brow, that honey-gold ring around his black-hole pupils glinting. "And I'm sure people line up to recite sonnets about *your* sweetness?"

I scoff. "My sister's the sweet one. If she pees outside, flower gardens burst up from it."

"You know," he says, "Sunshine Falls might not be the big city, but you should let your sister know, we *do* have indoor plumbing. Pretty much the only thing Dusty got right."

"Shoot!" I grab my phone. *Dusty.* She's in a vulnerable place, and she's used to me being one hundred percent accessible. Whether this book makes me look like the Countess Báthory or not, I owe it to her to do my job. I start typing a reply, using an uncharacteristic excess of exclamation points.

Charlie checks his watch. "Nine o'clock, on vacation, in a bar, and you're still working. Nadine Winters would be proud."

"You're one to judge," I say. "I happen to know *your* Loggia Publishing email account has had plenty of action this week."

"Yes, but I have no problem with Nadine Winters," he says. "In fact, I find her fascinating."

My eyes catch on the word I'm typing. "Oh? What's so interesting about a sociopath?"

"Patricia Highsmith might have something to say about that," he replies. "But more importantly, Nora, don't you think you're judging this character a little too harshly? It's ten pages."

I sign the message, hit send, and swivel back to him, my knees locking into place between his. "Because as we all know, reviewers are notoriously kind to female characters."

"Well, I like her. Who the fuck cares whether anyone else does, as long as they want to read about her?"

"People also slow down to gawk at car wrecks, Charlie. Are you calling me a car wreck?"

"I'm not talking about you at all," he says. "I'm talking about Nadine Winters. My fictional crush."

A feeling like a scorching-hot Slinky drops through me. "Big fan of jet-black hair and Krav Maga, huh?"

Charlie leans forward, face serious, voice low. "It's more about the blood dripping from her fangs."

I'm unsure how to respond. Not because it's gross, but because I'm pretty sure he's making a reference to *the Shark* of it all, and that feels dangerously close to flirting.

And I should definitely *not* be flirting with him. For all I know, he has a partner—or a doll room—and then there's the fact that publishing is a small pond, and one wrong move could easily pollute it.

God, even my internal dialogue sounds like Nadine. I clear my throat, take a sip of beer, and force myself not to overthink the way I'm sitting tucked between his thighs, or how my eyes keep zeroing in on that crease beneath his lip. I don't need to overthink. I don't *need* to be in complete control.

"So tell me about this place," I say. "What's interesting here?"

"Do you like grass?" Charlie asks.

"Big fan."

"We've got lots."

"What else?" I ask.

"We made a BuzzFeed list of the 'Top 10 Most Repulsively Named Restaurants in America.'"

"Been there." I wave to our general surroundings. "Done that."

He tips his chin toward me. "You tell me, Nora. Do *you* think this place is interesting?"

"It's certainly . . ." I search for the word. "Peaceful."

He laughs, a husky, jagged sound, one that belongs in a crammed Brooklyn bar, the streetlights beyond the rain-streaked window tinting his golden skin reddish. Not here.

"Is that a question?" he says.

"It's peaceful," I say more confidently.

"So you just don't like 'peaceful.'" He's smirking through his pout. Smirting. "You'd rather be somewhere loud and crowded, where just existing feels like a competition."

I've always considered myself an introvert, but the truth is I'm used to having people on all sides of me. You adapt to living life with a constant audience. It becomes comforting.

Mom used to say she became a New Yorker the day she openly wept on the subway. She'd gotten cut in the final round of an audition, and an old lady across the train car had handed her a tissue without even looking up from her book.

The way my mind keeps springing back to New York seems to prove his point. Once again, I'm unnerved by the feeling that Charlie Lastra sees right through my carefully pressed outermost layers.

"I'm perfectly happy with peace and quiet," I insist.

"Maybe." Charlie twists to grab his beer, the movement pressing his outside knee into mine just long enough for him to take another sip before he faces me again. "Or maybe, Nora Stephens, I can read you like a book."

I scoff. "Because you're so socially intelligent."

"Because you're like me."

A zing shoots up from where his knee brushes mine. "We're nothing alike."

"You're telling me," Charlie says, "that from the moment you stepped off the airplane, you haven't been itching to get back to New

York? Feeling like . . . like you're an astronaut out in space, while the world's just turning at a normal speed, and by the time you get back, you'll have missed your whole life? Like New York will never need you like you need it?"

Exactly, I think, stunned for the forty-fifth time in as many minutes.

I smooth my hair, like I can tuck any exposed secrets back into place. "Actually, the last couple of days have been a refreshing break from all the surly, monochromatic New York literary types."

Charlie's head tilts, his lids heavy. "Do you *know* you do that?"

"Do what?" I say.

His fingers brush the right corner of my mouth. "Get a divot here, when you lie."

I slap his hand out of the air, but not before all the blood in my body rushes to meet his fingertips. "That's not my Lying Divot," I lie. "It's my Annoyed Divot."

"On that note," he says dryly, "how about a game of high-stakes poker?"

"Fine!" I take another slug of beer. "It's my Lying Divot. Sue me. I miss New York, and it's too quiet here for me to sleep, and I'm *very* disappointed that the general store is actually a pawnshop. Is that what you want to hear, Charlie? That my vacation is not off to an auspicious start?"

"I'm always a fan of the truth," he says.

"No one's *always* a fan of the truth," I say. "Sometimes the truth sucks."

"It's *always* better to have the truth up front than to be misled."

"There's still something to be said for social niceties."

"Ah." He nods, eyes glinting knowingly. "For example, waiting until *after* lunch to tell someone you hate their client's book?"

"It wouldn't have killed you," I say.

"It might've," he says. "As we learned from Old Man Whittaker, secrets can be toxic."

I straighten as something occurs to me. "*That's* why you hated it. Because you're from here."

Now *he* shifts uncomfortably. I've found a weakness; I've seen through one of Charlie Lastra's outermost layers, and the scales tip ever so slightly in my favor. Big fan—*huge*.

"Let me guess." I jut out my bottom lip. "Bad memories."

"Or maybe," he drawls, leaning in, "it has something to do with the fact that Dusty Fielding clearly hasn't even googled Sunshine Falls in the last twenty years, let alone visited."

Of course, he has a point, but as I study the irritable rigidity of his jaw and the strangely sensual though distinctly grim set of his lips, I know my smile's sharpening. Because I see it: the half-truth of his words. *I* can read *him* too, and it feels like I've discovered a latent superpower.

"Come on, Charlie," I prod. "I thought you were *always a fan of the truth*. Let it out."

He scowls (still pouting, so *scowting*?). "So I'm not this place's biggest fan."

"Wooooow," I sing. "All this time I thought you hated the book, but really, you just had a deep, dark secret that made you close off from love and joy and laughter and—oh my god, you *are* Old Man Whittaker!"

"Okay, maestro." Charlie plucks the beer bottle I'd been gesticulating with from my hand, setting it safely on the bar. "Chill. I've just never liked those 'everything is better in small towns' narratives. My 'darkest secret' is that I believed in Santa Claus until I was twelve."

"You say that like it *isn't* incredible blackmail."

"Mutually assured destruction." He taps my phone, an allusion to the *Frigid* document. "I'm just evening the field for you after those pages."

"How noble. Now tell me why *your* day was so bad."

He studies me for a moment, then shakes his head. "No . . . I don't think I will. Not until you tell me why you're really here."

"I already told you," I say. "Vacation."

He leans in again, his hand catching my chin, his thumb landing squarely on the divot at the corner of my lips. My breath catches. His voice is low and raspy: *"Liar."*

His fingertips fall away and he gestures to the bartender for two more beers.

I don't stop him.

Because I am *not* Nadine Winters.

7

◡

HOW ABOUT," CHARLIE says, "a game of pool. If I win, you tell me why you're really here, and if you do, I'll tell you about my day."

I snort and look away, hiding my lying dimple as I tuck my phone into my bag, having confirmed Libby made it home safely. "I don't play."

Or I haven't since college, when my roommate and I used to shark frat boys weekly.

"Darts?" Charlie suggests.

I arch a brow. "You want to hand me a weapon after the turn my night has taken?"

He leans close, eyes shining in the dim bar lighting. "I'll play left-handed."

"Maybe *I* don't want to hand *you* a weapon either," I say.

His eye roll is subtle, more of a twitch of some key face muscles. "Left-handed pool, then."

I study him. Neither of us blinks. We're basically having a

sixth-grade-style staring contest, and the longer it goes on, the more the air seems to thrum with some metaphysical buildup of energy.

I slink off my stool and drain my second beer. "Fine."

We make our way back to the only open table. It's darker on this side of the restaurant, the floor stickier with spilled booze, and the smell of beer emanates from the walls. Charlie grabs a pool cue and a rack and starts gathering the balls in the center of the felt table. "You know the rules?" he asks, peering up at me as he leans across the green surface.

"One of us is stripes and one of us is solids?" I say.

He takes the blue chalk cube from the edge of the table and works it over the pool cue. "You want to go first?"

"You're going to teach me, right?" I'm trying to look innocent, to look like Libby batting her eyelashes.

Charlie stares at me. "I really wonder what you think your face is doing right now, Stephens."

I narrow my eyes; he narrows his back exaggeratedly.

"Why do you care why I'm here?" I ask.

"Morbid curiosity. Why do you care about my bad day?"

"Always helpful to know your opponent's weaknesses."

He holds the cue out. "You first."

I take the stick, flop it onto the edge of the table, and look over my shoulder. "Isn't now the part where you're supposed to put your arms around me and show me how to do it?"

His mouth curves. "That depends. Are you carrying any weapons?"

"The sharpest thing on me is my teeth." I settle over the cue, holding it like I've not only never played pool before but have quite possibly only just discovered my own hands.

Charlie's smell—warm and uncannily familiar—invades my nose as he positions himself behind me, barely touching. I can feel the front of his sweater graze my bare spine, my skin tingling at the friction, and his arms fold around mine as his mouth drops beside my ear.

"Loosen your grip." His low voice vibrates through me, his breath warm on my jaw as he pries my fingers from the cue and readjusts them. "The front hand's for aiming. You're not going to move it. The momentum"—his palm scrapes down my elbow until he catches my wrist and drags it back along the cue toward my hip—"will come from here. You just want to keep the stick straight when you're starting out. And aim as if you're lining up perfectly with the ball you want to sink."

"Got it," I say.

His hands slide clear of me, and I will the goose bumps on my skin to settle as I line up my shot. "One thing I forgot to mention"—I snap the stick into the cue ball, sending the solid blue one across the table into the pocket—"is that I did *used* to play."

I walk past Charlie to line up my next shot.

"And here I thought I was just a really good teacher," he says flatly.

I pocket the green ball next, and then miss the burgundy one. When I chance a glance at him, he looks not only unsurprised but downright smug. Like I've proven a point.

He pulls the cue from my hands and circles the table, eyeing several options for his first shot before choosing the green-striped ball and getting into position. "And I guess I should've mentioned"—he taps the cue ball, which sends the green-striped ball into a pocket, the purple-striped ball sinking right behind it—"I'm left-handed."

I jam my mouth closed when he looks at me on his way to line up his next shot. This time, he pockets the orange-striped ball, then the burgundy one, before finally missing on his next turn.

He sticks his lip out like I did when I teased him about bad memories. "Would it help the sting if I bought you another beer?"

I yank the stick from his hand. "Make it a martini, and get yourself one too. You're going to need it."

~

Charlie wins the first game, so one game becomes two. I win that one, and he's unwilling to tie, so we play a third. When he wins, he pulls the cue out of my reach before I can demand a fourth match.

"*Nora*," he says, "we had a deal."

"I never agreed to it."

"You played," he says.

I tip my head back, groaning.

"If it helps," he says with his signature dryness, "I'm willing to sign an NDA before you tell me about whatever deep, dark, twisted fantasy brought you here."

I slit my eyes.

He moves my glass off the cocktail napkin and feels around in his pockets until he finds a Pilot G2, admittedly my own pen of choice, though I always use black ink and he's got the traditional editor red. He leans over and scribbles:

I, Charles Lastra, of sound mind, do swear I will keep Nora Stephens's dark, dirty, twisted secret under penalty of law or five million dollars, whichever comes first.

"Okay, you've absolutely never seen a contract," I say. "Maybe never been in the same room as one."

He finishes signing and drops the pen. "That's a fine fucking contract."

"Poor uninformed book editors, with their whimsical notions of how agreements are made." I pat his head.

He swats my arm away. "What could possibly be so bad, Nora? Are you on the run? Did you rob a bank?" In the dark, the gold of his eyes looks strangely light against his oversized pupils. "Did you fire your pregnant assistant?" he teases, voice low. The allusion is a shock to my system, a jolt of electricity from head to toe.

Miraculously, I'd forgotten about Dusty's pages. Now here Nadine is again, taunting me.

"What's so wrong with being in control anyway?" I demand, of the universe at large.

"Beats me."

"And what, just because I don't want kids, I would supposedly punish a pregnant woman for making a different decision than me? My favorite person's a pregnant woman! And I'm obsessed with my nieces. Not every decision a woman makes is some grand indictment on other women's lives."

"Nora," Charlie says. "It's a novel. Fiction."

"You don't get it, because you're . . . *you*." I wave a hand at him.

"Me?" he says.

"You can afford to be all surly and sharp and people will admire you for it. The rules are different for women. You have to strike this perfect balance to be taken seriously but not seen as bitchy. It's a constant effort. People don't want to work with sharky women—"

"I do," he says.

"And even men exactly *like* us don't want to be *with* us. I mean, sure, some of them think they do, but next thing you know, they're dumping you in a four-minute phone call because they've never seen you cry and moving across the country to marry a Christmas tree heiress!"

Charlie's full lips press into a knot, his eyes squinting. ". . . What?"

"Nothing," I grumble.

"A very specific 'nothing.'"

"Forget it."

"Not likely," he says. "I'm going to be up all night making diagrams and charts, trying to figure out what you just said."

"I'm cursed," I say. "That's all."

"Oh," he says. "Sure. Got it."

"I am," I insist.

"I'm an editor, Stephens," he says. "I'm going to need more details to buy into this narrative."

"It's my literary stock character," I say. "I'm the cold-blooded, overly ambitious city slicker who exists as a foil to the Good Woman. I'm the one who gets dumped for the girl who's prettier without makeup and loves barbecue and somehow makes destroying a karaoke standard seem adorable!"

And for some reason (my low alcohol tolerance), it doesn't stop there. It comes spilling out. Like I'm just puking up embarrassing history onto the peanut-shell-littered floor for everyone to see.

Aaron dumping me for Prince Edward Island (and, confirmed via light social media stalking, a redhead named Adeline). Grant breaking up with me for Chastity and her parents' little inn. Luca and his wife and their cherry farm in Michigan.

When I reach patient zero, Jakob the novelist-turned-rancher, I cut myself off. What happened between him and me doesn't belong at the end of a list; it belongs where I left it, in the smoking crater that changed my life forever. "You get the idea."

His eyes slit, an amused tilt to his lips. ". . . Do I though?"

"Tropes and clichés have to come from somewhere, right?" I say. "Women like me have clearly always existed. So it's either a very specific kind of self-sabotage or an ancient curse. Come to think of it, maybe it started with Lilith. Too weird to be coincidence."

"You know," Charlie says, "I'd say Dusty writing a whole-ass book about my hometown and then me running into her agent in said town is too weird to be a coincidence, but as we've already established, you're 'not stalking me,' so coincidences do occasionally happen, Nora."

"But this? Four relationships ending because my boyfriends decided to walk off into the wilderness and never come back?"

He's fighting a smirk but losing the battle.

"I'm not ridiculous!" I say, laughing despite myself. Okay, *because* of myself.

"Exactly what a not-ridiculous person would say," Charlie allows with a nod. "Look, I'm still trying to figure out how your shitty Jack London—wannabe ex-boyfriends factor in to why you're here."

"My sister's . . ." I consider for a moment, then settle on, "Things have been kind of off between us for the last few months, and she wanted to get away for a while. Plus she reads too many small-town romance novels and is convinced the answer to our problems is having our own transformative experiences, like my exes did. In a place like this."

"Your exes," he says bluntly. "Who gave up their careers and moved to the wilderness."

"Yes, those ones."

"So, what?" he says. "You're supposed to find happiness here and ditch New York? Quit publishing?"

"Of course not," I say. "She just wants to have fun, before the baby comes. Take a break from our usual lives and do something new. We have a list."

"A list?"

"A bunch of things from the books." And this is why I don't drink two martinis. Because even at five eleven, my body is incapable of processing alcohol, as evidenced by the fact that I start listing, "Wear flannel, bake something from scratch, get small-town makeovers, build something, date some locals—"

Charlie laughs brusquely. "She's trying to marry you off to a pig farmer, Stephens."

"She is not."

"You said she's trying to give you your own small-town romance novel," he says wryly. "You know how those books end, don't you, Nora? With a big wedding inside of a barn, or an epilogue involving babies."

I scoff. Of course I know how they end. Not only have I watched my exes *live* them, but when Libby and I still shared an apartment, I'd read the final pages of her books almost compulsively. That never really tempted me to turn back to page one.

"Look, Lastra," I say. "My sister and I are here to spend time together. You probably didn't learn this in whatever lab spawned you, but vacations are a fairly typical way for loved ones to bond and relax."

"Yes, because if anything's going to relax a person like you," he says, "it's spending time in a town conveniently situated between two equidistant Dressbarns."

"You know, I'm not as much of an uptight control freak as either you or Dusty seem to think. I could have a perfectly nice time on a date with a pig farmer. And you know what? Maybe it's a good idea. It's not like I've had any luck with New Yorkers. Maybe I *have* been fishing in the wrong pond. Or, like, the wrong stream of nuclear waste runoff."

"You," he says, "are so much weirder than I thought."

"Well, for what it's worth, before tonight, I assumed you went into a broom closet and entered power saving mode whenever you weren't at work, so I guess we're both surprised."

"Now *you're* being ridiculous," he says. "When I'm not at work, I'm in my coffin in the basement of an old Victorian mansion."

I snort into my glass, which makes him crack a real, human smile. *It lives,* I think.

"Stephens," he says, tone dry once more, "if you're the villain in someone else's love story, then I'm the devil."

"You said it, not me," I reply.

He lifts a brow. "You're scrappy tonight."

"I'm always scrappy," I say. "Tonight I'm just not bothering to hide it."

"Good." He leans in, dropping his voice, and an electric current charges through me. "I've always preferred to have things out in the open. Though the pig farmers of Sunshine Falls might not feel the same way."

His gaze flicks sidelong toward mine, his scent vaguely spicy and familiar. An unwelcome heaviness settles between my thighs. I really hope my chin divot hasn't found a way to announce that I'm turned on.

"I already told you," I say. "I'm here for my sister."

And as much anxiety as I feel being away from home, the truth is, I spend the length of Libby's pregnancies in a low-grade panic anyway. At least this way I can keep an eye on her.

I never dreamed of having my own kids, but the way I felt during Libby's first pregnancy really sealed the deal. There are just too many things that can go wrong, too many ways to fail.

I pitch myself onto a stool at the corner of the bar and almost fall over in the process.

Charlie catches my arms and steadies me. "How about some water?" he says, sliding onto the empty stool beside mine, that suppressed smirk/pout/what-even-is-this tugging his full lips slightly to one side as he signals to the bartender.

I square my shoulders, trying for dignified. "You're not going to distract me."

His brow lifts. "From?"

"I won one of those games. You owe *me* information." Especially given the horrifying amount I just blurted out.

His head tilts, and he peers down his face at me. "What do you want to know?"

Our lunch two years ago pops into my head, Charlie's irritated glance at his watch. "You said you were trying to catch a flight the day we met. Why?"

He scratches at his collar, his brow furrowing, jaw etched with tension. "The same reason I'm here now."

"Intriguing."

"I promise it's not." Waters have appeared on the bar. He turns one in place, his jaw tensing. "My dad had a stroke. One back then, and another a few months ago. I'm here to help."

"Shit. I—wow." Immediately, my vision clears and sharpens on him, my buzz burning off. "You were so . . . together."

"I made a commitment to be there," he says, with a defensive edge, "and I didn't see how talking about it would be productive."

"I wasn't saying—look, I'd gotten dumped like forty-six seconds earlier, and I still sat down for a martini and a salad with a perfect stranger, so I get it."

Charlie's eyes snag on mine, so intense I have to look away for a second.

"Was he—is your dad okay?"

He turns his glass again. "When we had lunch, I already knew he wasn't in danger. My sister had just told me about the stroke, but it actually happened weeks earlier." His face hardens. "He decided I didn't need to know, and that was that." He shifts on his stool—the discomfort of someone who's just decided he's overshared.

Even factoring in the gin and beer sloshing around in my body, I'm shocked to hear myself blurt, "Our dad left us when my mom was pregnant. I don't really remember him. After that, it was pretty much a parade of loser boyfriends, so I'm not really an expert on dads."

Charlie's brows pinch, his fingers stilling on his damp glass. "Sounds terrible."

"It wasn't too bad," I say. "She never let most of them meet us. She was good about that." I reach for my glass, trying his tic, turning it in a ring of its own sweat. "But one day, she'd be floating on a cloud, singing her favorite *Hello, Dolly!* songs and fluffing embroidered thrift-store pillows like Snow White in New York, and the next—"

I don't trail off so much as just outright cut myself off.

I'm not ashamed of my upbringing, but the more you tell a person about yourself, the more power you hand over. And I particularly avoid sharing Mom with strangers, like the memory of her is a newspaper clipping and every time I take it out, she fades and creases a little more.

Charlie's thumb slides over my wrist absently. "Stephens?"

"I don't need you to feel sorry for me."

His pupils dilate. "I wouldn't dare." A dare is *exactly* what his voice sounds like.

At some point, we've drawn together, my legs tucked between his again, an endless, buzzing feedback loop everywhere we're touching. His eyes are heavy on me, his pupils almost blotting out his irises, a lustrous ring of honey around a deep, dark pit.

Heat gathers between my thighs, and I uncross and recross my legs. Charlie's eyes drop to follow the motion, and his water glass hitches against his bottom lip, like he's forgotten what he was doing. In that moment, he is one hundred percent legible to me.

I might as well be looking into a mirror.

I could lean into him.

I could let my knees slide further into the pocket between his, or touch his arm, or tip my chin up, and in any of those hypothetical scenarios, we end up kissing. I may not like him all that much, but a not insignificant part of me is dying to know what his bottom lip feels like, how that hand on my wrist would touch me.

Just then it starts to rain—*pour*—and the corrugated metal roof erupts into a feverish rattle. I jerk my arm out from under Charlie's and stand. "I should get home."

"Share a cab?" he asks, his voice low, gravelly.

The odds of finding *two* cabs at this hour, in this town, aren't great. The odds of finding one that isn't driven by Hardy are terrible. "I think I'll walk."

"In this rain?" he says. "And *those* shoes?"

I grab my bag. "I won't melt." Probably.

Charlie stands. "We can share my umbrella."

8

~

WE MAKE OUR way out of Poppa Squat's huddled under Charlie's umbrella. (I'd called it *fortuitous*, but it turns out he checks a weather app obsessively, so apparently I've found someone even more predictable than I am.) The smell of grass and wildflowers is thick in the damp air, and it's cooled considerably.

He asks, "Where are you staying?"

"It's called Goode's Lily Cottage," I say.

He says, almost to himself, "Bizarre."

Heat creeps up my neck from where his breath hits it. "What, I couldn't possibly be happy anywhere that isn't a black marble penthouse with a crystal chandelier?"

"Exactly what I meant." He casts a look my way as we pass under a bar of streetlight, the rain sparkling like silver confetti. "And also it's my parents' rental property."

My cheeks flush. "You're—Sally Goode's your mom? You grew up next to a horse farm?"

"What," he says, "I couldn't possibly have been raised anywhere but a black marble penthouse with a crystal chandelier?"

"Just hard to imagine you belonging anywhere in this town, let alone so close to a manure pyramid."

"*Belonging* might be overstating things," he says acidly.

"So where are you staying?"

"Well, I usually stay at the cottage," he says. Another sidelong glance at me through the dark. "But that wasn't an option."

His smell is so uncannily familiar, but I still can't place it. Warm, with a slightly spicy edge, faint enough that I keep catching myself trying to inhale a lungful of it. "Then where?" I ask. "Your child-hood bedroom?"

We pause at the dead-end street the cottage sits on, and Charlie sighs. "I'm sleeping in a race car bed, Nora. Are you happy?"

Happy doesn't begin to cover it. The image of stern-browed, highly polished Charlie tucked into a plastic Corvette and scowling at his Kindle makes me laugh so hard it's a struggle to stay upright. He's probably the last person I could picture in a race car bed, aside from myself.

Charlie hooks an arm around my waist as I keel over. "Little re-minder," he says, keeping me moving down the gravel lane. "*That* is far from the most embarrassing thing one of us has said tonight."

I get out, "Were you, like, a NASCAR kid?"

"No," he says, "but my dad never stopped trying."

I devolve into another fit of laughter that threatens to tip me over. Charlie pulls me against his side. "One foot in front of the other, Stephens."

"Mutually assured destruction indeed," I cry.

He starts to lead me up the hillside, and immediately my heel sinks into the mud, pinning me to the ground. I take another step and the other heel punctures the mud too. An indignant half shriek rises out of me.

Charlie stops, sighing heavily as he eyes my shoes. "Am I going to have to carry you?"

"I am *not* letting you give me a piggyback ride, Lastra," I say.

"And I," he replies, "am not letting you destroy those poor, innocent shoes. I'm not that kind of man."

I look at my mules, and a miserably petulant sound squeaks out of me. *"Fine."*

"You're *welcome.*" He turns and hunches as I hike up my dress and say a fond farewell to the last remnants of my dignity, then hook my arms over his shoulders and hop onto his back.

"All good?" he says.

"I'm getting a piggyback ride," I reply, adjusting the umbrella over us. "Does that answer your question?"

"Poor Nora," he teases, his hands settling against my thighs as he starts up the steps. "I can only imagine what you're going through."

A realization clangs through me, chaotic and emphatic as church bells: the reason his smell is so familiar. It's the same subtle gender-neutral cologne I wear. A cedarwood and amber blend called BOOK, meant to summon images of sunbathed shelves and worn pages. When I found out the company was going under, I put in a bulk order so I could stockpile it.

I would've placed it sooner, but it smells different on him, the way Mom's signature lemon-lavender scent hits different on Libby, a note of vanilla drawn out that was never there before. Charlie's rendition of BOOK is spicier, warmer than mine.

"Awfully quiet back there, Stephens," he says. "Anything I can do to make your journey more comfortable? A neck pillow? Some of those tiny Delta cookies?"

"I'd take some spurs and a riding crop," I say.

"Should've seen that coming," he grumbles.

"I'd also accept a sworn affidavit that we'll never speak of this again."

"After the way you disparaged my last contract? I don't think so."

When we reach the front steps, I slide off Charlie's back and try to pull my dress back into place, which is a struggle because I didn't do an *amazing* job of keeping the umbrella over us, and we're both fairly drenched, my dress plastered to my thighs and bangs stuck to my eyes.

Charlie reaches out to brush them away. "Nice haircut, by the way."

"Straight men love bangs," I say. "They make women approachable."

"Nothing more intimidating than a forehead," he says. "Although I sort of miss the blond."

And there it is: that mushroom cloud of want low in my belly, a twinge between my thighs. "It's not natural," I announce.

"Didn't think it was," he says, "but it suits you."

"Because it looks vaguely evil?" I guess.

He splits into a rare, full grin, but only for a second. Just long enough to send my stomach flipping. "I've been thinking."

"I'll call a news crew immediately."

"You should scratch number five."

"Number five?"

"On the list."

I palm my face. "Why did I tell you about that?"

"Because you wanted someone to stop you from going through with it," he says. "The last thing you need is to get mixed up with someone who lives here."

I drop my hand and narrow my eyes at him. "Do they eat outsiders?"

"Worse," he says. "They keep them here forever."

I scoff. "Lasting commitment. How terrible."

"Nora," he says, tone low and chiding. "You and I both know you don't want that epilogue. Someone like you—in shoes like *that*—could never be happy here. Don't get some poor pig farmer's hopes up for nothing."

"Okay, rude," I say.

"Rude?" He steps in closer, the searing fluorescent light over the door casting him in stark relief, etching out the hollows beneath his cheekbones and making his eyes gleam. "*Rude* is declaring the entire dating pool of New York City tainted just because you managed to pick four assholes in a row."

My throat warms, a lump of lava sliding down it. "Don't tell me I hurt your feelings," I murmur.

"You of all people should know," he says, gaze dropping to my mouth, "we 'surly, monochromatic literary types' don't have those."

In my head, Nadine Winters's voice is screaming, *Abort, abort! This fits into no plan!* But there's a lot of rushing blood and tingling skin for the words to compete with.

I don't remember doing it, but my fingers are pressed against his stomach, his muscles tightening under them.

Bad idea, I think in the split second before Charlie tugs my hips flush to his. The words break apart like alphabet soup, letters splintering off in every direction, utterly meaningless now. His mouth catches mine roughly as he eases me back into the cottage door, covering my body with his.

I half moan at the pressure. His hands tighten on my waist. My lips part for his tongue, the tang of beer and the herbal edge of gin tangling pleasantly in my mouth.

It feels like my outline is dissolving, like I'm turning to liquid. His mouth skates down my jaw, over my throat. My hands scrape through his coarse, rain-soaked hair, and he lets out a low groan, his hand trailing to my chest, fingers brushing over my nipple.

At some point, the umbrella has clattered to the ground. Charlie's shirt is plastered to him. He palms me through my damp dress, making me arch. Our mouths slip together.

The last dregs of beer and gin evaporate from my bloodstream, and everything is happening in high definition. My hands skim up the back of his shirt, fingernails sinking into his smooth, warm skin, urging him closer, and his palm moves to the hem of my dress, shucking it up my thigh. His fingers glide higher, sending chills rippling over my skin, and something like *Wait* just barely, half-heartedly slips out of me.

I'm not even sure how he heard it, but Charlie jerks back, looking like a man freshly out of a trance, hair mussed, lips bee-stung, dark eyes blinking rapidly. "Shit!" he says, hoarse, stepping back. "I didn't mean to . . ."

Clarity hits me with a cold-water shock.

Shit is right!

As in, I don't shit where I eat. Or kiss where I work. It's bad enough that in a year and a half, everyone I work with is going to think of me as Nadine Winters—I don't need to add any more potential fuel to my reputation's funeral pyre.

He says, "I can't really get involved—"

"I don't need an explanation!" I cut him off, yanking the hem of my dress back down my thighs. "It was a mistake!"

"I know!" Charlie says, sounding vaguely offended.

"Well, I know too!"

"Fine!" he says. "Then we agree!"

"Fine!" I cry, continuing recorded history's strangest and least-productive argument.

Charlie hasn't moved. Neither of us has. His eyes are still inky dark and hungry, and thanks to the light bulb over the door, his hard-on might as well be in a display case at a particularly lascivious museum.

I take a breath. "Let's just act like—"

At the same time, he says, "We should pretend it never happened."

I nod.

He nods.

It's settled.

He grabs his umbrella off the ground, and neither of us bothers with "good night." He just nods again stiffly and turns and walks away.

It never happened, I think with some force.

Which is good, because my reckless decisions *always* have disastrous consequences.

9

~

WHEN I WAS twelve, my mother was cast in a crime procedural. She hit it off with the showrunner. Before long, she was seeing him nightly.

Four episodes into filming, he reconciled with his estranged wife. Mom's plucky young detective character was swiftly killed off, her body discovered in a meat locker.

I'd never seen Mom quite so distraught. We avoided whole swaths of the city afterward, dodging anyplace she might run into him, or be reminded of him, or of the job she'd lost.

After that, it was an easy decision for me to never fall in love.

For years, I stuck by it. Then I met Jakob.

He made the world open up around me, like there were colors I'd never seen, new levels of happiness I couldn't have imagined.

Mom was ecstatic when I told her I was moving in with him. After everything she'd been through, she was still a romantic.

He's going to take such good care of you, sweet girl, she said. He was

a couple of years older than me and had a well-paying bartending job
and a tiny apartment uptown.

A week later, I hugged Mom and Libby goodbye and schlepped
my stuff to his place. Two weeks after that, Mom was gone.

The bills came due all at once. Rent, utilities, a credit card we'd
opened in my name when things got particularly tight. Mom's credit
was shot, and I wanted to help pull my weight.

I'd been working at Freeman Books since I was sixteen, but I
made minimum wage and could only manage part-time while I was
in college, and someday, the student loans I'd taken out would come
back to haunt me.

Mom's actor friends did a fundraiser for us, announcing after the
funeral that they'd raised over fifteen thousand dollars, and Libby
cried happy tears, because she had no idea how little of a dent that
would make.

She'd been on a fashion design kick and wanted to go to Parsons,
and I debated dropping out of my English program to fund her tu-
ition, though I'd already sunk tens of thousands into mine.

I moved out of Jakob's place and back in with Libby.

I budgeted.

Scoured the internet for the cheapest, most filling meals.

Took on other jobs: tutoring, waitressing, outright writing class-
mates' papers.

Jakob found out he'd gotten accepted into the Wyoming writing
residency and left, and then there was the breakup, the utter desola-
tion, the reminder of why the promise I'd made to myself years ago
still mattered.

I stopped dating, mostly. First dates were allowed (dinner only),
and though I'd never tell anyone, the reason was that I'd have one
less meal to pay for. Two if I ordered enough to bring Libby leftovers.

Second dates were a no-go. That's when the guilt kicked in—or the feelings did.

Libby playfully heckled me about how no one was good enough for a second date.

I let her. It would destroy me to hear what she thought of the truth.

She worked too. Without Mom's income, we had to tighten our purse strings, but Libby never wanted to spend money on herself anyway.

Sometimes, after complaining to her about a particularly bad date, though, I'd come home from classes or a tutoring shift to find her already asleep in her room (I'd moved out into the living room, where Mom used to sleep, so she could have the bedroom to herself) and a bundle of sunflowers sitting in a vase beside the pullout couch.

If I were normal, I might've cried. Instead I'd sit there, clutching the vase, and just fucking *shake*. Like there were emotions deep in me, but too many layers of ash lay over them, deadening them to nothing but a tectonic murmur.

There is a spot in my foot I can't feel. I stepped on a piece of glass and the nerves there are dead now. The doctor said they'd grow back, but it's been years and that place is still numb.

That was how my heart had felt for years. Like all the cracks callused over.

That enabled me to focus on what mattered. I built a life for me and Libby, a home that no bank or ex-boyfriend could ever take from us.

I watched my friends in relationships make compromise after compromise, shrinking into themselves until they were nothing but a piece of a whole, until all their stories came from the past, and their career aspirations, their friends, and their apartments were replaced by *our* aspirations, *our* friends, *our* apartment. Half lives that could be taken from them without any warning.

By then I'd had all the practice in first dates that a person could get. I knew which red flags to watch for, the questions to ask. I'd seen my friends, coworkers, colleagues get ghosted, cheated on, bored in their relationships, and rudely awakened when partners turned out to be married or have gambling problems or be chronically unemployed. I saw casual hookups turn into miserably complicated half relationships.

I had standards and a life, and I wasn't about to let some man destroy it like it was merely the paper banner he was meant to crash through as he entered the field.

So only once my career was on track did I start dating again, and this time I did it right. With caution, checklists, and carefully weighed decisions.

I did not kiss colleagues. I did not kiss people I knew next to nothing about. I did not kiss men I had no intention of dating, or men I was incompatible with. I didn't let random bouts of lust call the shots.

Until Charlie Lastra.

It never happened.

～

I expected Libby to be giddy about my slipup. Instead, she's as disapproving as *I* am.

"Your Professional Nemesis from New York does *not* count for number five, Sissy," she says. "Couldn't you have made out with, like, a rodeo clown with a heart of gold?"

"I was wearing entirely the wrong shoes for that," I say.

"You could kiss a million Charlies back in the city. You're supposed to be trying new things here. We both are." She brandishes the eggy spatula in my direction. Growing up, our apartment was a yogurt-or-granola-bar-breakfast home, but now Libby's a full English breakfast kind of gal, and there are already pancakes and veggie sausages stacked next to the egg pan.

I fell out of bed at nine after another restless night, took a run followed by a quick shower, then came down for breakfast. Libby's been up for hours already. She loves morning now even more than she loved sleeping as a teenager. Even on weekends, she never sleeps past seven. Partly, I'm sure, because she can hear Bea's high-pitched squeal or Tala's little pounding feet from three miles and a dose of morphine away.

She always says the two of them are us, but body swapped.

Bea, the oldest, is sweet as cherry pie like Libby, but with my lankiness and ash-brown hair. Tala has her mother's strawberry-gold hair and is destined to be no taller than five four, but like her Aunt Nono, she's a brute: opinionated and determined to never follow any command without a thorough explanation.

"You're the one who Parent-Trapped me with him," I point out, pulling the spatula from Libby's hand and ushering her toward a chair. "It never would've happened if you hadn't ditched me."

"Look, Nora, sometimes even mommies need alone time," she says slowly. "Anyway, I thought you *hated* that guy."

"I don't hate him," I say. "We're just, like, opposing magnets, or something."

"Opposing magnets are the ones that draw together."

"Okay, then we're magnets with the same polarity."

"Two magnets with the same polarity would never make out against a door."

"Unlike other magnets, which would definitely do that." I carry over our loaded plates, flopping into the chair across from her. It's already hellishly hot. We've got the windows open and the fans on, but it's as misty as a low-rent sauna.

"It was a moment of weakness." The memory of Charlie's hands on my waist, his chest flattening me into the door, sears through me.

Libby arches an eyebrow. With her blunt pink bob, she's closer to mastering my own Evil Eye, but her cheeks are still, ultimately, too soft to get the job done. "Lest you forget, Sissy, *that* type of man has not worked out for you in the past."

Personally, I wouldn't lump Charlie in with my exes. For one thing, none of them ever tried to ravage me outside. Also, they never lurched out of a kiss like I'd shoved a hot fire poker down their pants.

"I'm proud of you for going off book—I just wouldn't have chosen a hard-core groping by Count von Lastra as The Move."

I drop my face into my forearm, newly mortified. "This is all Nadine Winters's fault."

Libby's brow pinches. "Who?"

"Oh, that's right." I lift my head. "In your desperation to see me barefoot and pregnant, you ran out before I could tell you." I unlock my phone and open the email from Dusty, sliding it into Libby's field of vision. She hunches as she reads, and I shovel food into my mouth as fast as I can so I can get my workday started.

Libby's not a startlingly fast reader. She absorbs books like they're bubble baths, whereas my job has forced me to treat them more like hot-and-fast showers.

Her mouth shrinks, tightening into a knot as she reads, until finally, she bursts into laughter. "Oh my god!" she cries. "It's Nora Stephens fan fiction!"

"Can it really be called fan fiction if the author clearly isn't a fan?" I say.

"Has she sent you more? Does it get smutty? Lots of fan fiction gets smutty."

"Again," I say, "not fan fiction."

Libby cackles. "Maybe Dusty's got a crush."

"Or maybe she's hiring a hit man as we speak."

"I *hope* it gets smutty," she says.

"Libby, if you had your way, every book would end with an earth-shattering orgasm."

"Hey, why wait until the end?" she says. "Oh, right, because that's where *you* start reading." She pretends to dry heave at the thought.

I stand to rinse my plate. "Well, it's been fun, but I'm off to track down Wi-Fi that doesn't make me want to put my head through a wall."

"I'll meet you later," she says. "First, I'm going to spend a few hours walking around naked, shouting cuss words. Then I'll probably call home—want me to tell Brendan you say hi?"

"Who?"

Libby flips me off. I loudly kiss the side of her head on my way to the door with my laptop bag. "Don't go anywhere from *Once in a Lifetime* without me!" she screams.

I cut myself off before *Not sure those places even exist* can spew out of me. For the first time in months, *we* feel like the *us* of a different time—fully connected, fully present—and the last thing I want is some uncontrollable variable messing things up. "Promise," I say.

10

~

AFTER PAYING FOR my iced Americano at Mug + Shot, I ask the chipper barista with the septum piercing for the Wi-Fi password.

"Oh!" She gestures to a wooden sign behind her reading, *Let's unplug!* "No Wi-Fi here. Sorry."

"Wait," I say, "really?"

She beams. "Yep."

I glance around. No laptops in sight. Everyone here looks like they came straight from climbing Everest or doing drugs in a Coachella yurt.

"Is there a library or something?" I ask.

She nods. "A few blocks down. No Wi-Fi there yet either—supposed to get it in the fall. For now they've got desktops you can use."

"Is there *anywhere* in town with Wi-Fi?" I ask.

"The bookstore just got it," she admits, quietly, like she's hoping the words don't trigger a stampede of coffee drinkers who would very much like to be un-unplugged.

I thank her and emerge into the sticky heat, sweat gathering in my armpits and cleavage as I trek toward the bookstore. When I step inside, it feels like I've just wandered into a maze, all the breezes, wind chimes, and bird chatter going quiet at once, that warm cedar-and-sunned-paper smell folding around me.

I sip my ice-cold drink and bask in the double-barreled serotonin coursing through me. Is there anything better than iced coffee and a bookstore on a sunny day? I mean, aside from hot coffee and a bookstore on a rainy day.

The shelves are built at wild angles that make me feel like I'm sliding off the edge of the planet. As a kid, I would've loved the whimsy of it—a fun house made of books. As an adult, I'm mostly concerned with staying upright.

On the left, a low, rounded doorway is cut into one of the shelves, its frame carved with the words *Children's Books*.

I bend to peer through it to a soft blue-green mural, like something out of *Madeline*, words swirling across it: *Discover new worlds!* Off the other side of the main room, an average-sized doorway leads to the *Used and Rare Book Room*.

This main room isn't exactly brimming with crisp new spines. As far as I can tell, there's very little method to this store's organization. New books mixed with old, paperbacks with hardcovers, and fantasy next to nonfiction, a not-so-fine layer of dust laid over most of it.

Once, I bet this place was a town jewel where people shopped for holiday presents and preteens gossiped over Frappuccinos. Now it's another small-business graveyard.

I follow the labyrinthine shelves deeper into the store, past a doorway to the world's most depressing "café" (a couple of card tables and some folding chairs), and around a corner, and I freeze for a millisecond, midstep, one foot hovering in the air.

Seeing the man hunched over his laptop behind the register, an unimpressed furrow in his brow, is like waking up from a nightmare where you're falling off a cliff, only to realize your house has been scooped up by a tornado while you slept.

This is the problem with small towns: one minor lapse in judgment and you can't go a mile without running into it.

All I want to do is turn and hightail it, but I can't let myself do it. I won't let one slipup, or any man, start governing my decisions. The whole reason to avoid workplace entanglements is to protect against *this* scenario. Besides, the entanglement *was* avoided. Mostly.

I square my shoulders and rise my chin. In that moment, for the very first time, I wonder if I might have a guardian angel, because directly across from me, on the local bestsellers shelf, sits a face-out stack of *Once in a Lifetime*.

I grab a copy and march up to the counter.

Charlie's gaze doesn't lift from his laptop until I've smacked the book onto the gouged mahogany.

His golden-brown eyes slowly rise. "Well. If it isn't the woman who 'isn't stalking me.'"

I grind out, "If it isn't the man who 'didn't try to ravish me in the middle of a hurricane.'"

His sip of coffee goes spewing back into his mug, and he glances toward the tragic café. "I certainly hope my high school principal was ready to hear that."

I lean sideways to peer through the doorway. At one of the card tables, a stooped, gray-haired woman is watching *The Sopranos* on a tablet with only one earbud in. "Another one of your exes?"

That downward tick in the corner of his mouth. "I can tell you're pleased with yourself when your eyes go all predatory like that."

"And I can tell you are when you do that lip-twitch thing."

"It's called a smile, Stephens. They're common here."

"And by 'here,' you must mean Sunshine Falls, because you definitely aren't referring to the five-foot radius of your electric fence."

"Have to keep the locals away somehow." His eyes drop to the book. "Finally biting the bullet and reading the whole thing?" he says dryly.

"You know . . ." I grab the book and hold it in front of my chest. "I found this on the *bestsellers* shelf."

"I know. It's shelved right next to the *Guide to North Carolina's Bike Trails* my old dentist self-published last year," he says. "Did you want one of those too?"

"This book has sold more than one million copies," I tell him.

"I'm aware." He picks up the book. "But now I'm wondering how many of those *you* bought."

I scowl. He rewards me with an almost grin, and for the first time, I know exactly what my boss means when she describes my "smile with knives."

I look away from his face, which really just means my eyes skate down his golden throat and over his pristine white T-shirt to his arms. They're good arms. Not in a ripped way, just an attractively lean way.

Okay, they're just arms. Chill, Nora. Straight men have it too easy. A heterosexual woman can see a very normal-looking, nonsexual appendage, and biology's like, *Step aside, last four thousand years of evolution, it's time to contribute to the continuation of the human race.*

He brushes his laptop aside and starts rearranging the pens, pamphlets, and other office supplies on the desk. Maybe I'm not horny for *him* so much as his clothes and his organizational skills. "I was actually just emailing you."

I jolt back to the conversation, vibrating like a snapped rubber band. "Oh?"

He nods, his jaw set, his eyes dark and intense. "Have you heard from Sharon yet?"

"Dusty's editor?"

He nods. "She's out on leave—had her baby."

And just like that, all the lean arms, nice fingers, and perfectly organized jars of pens and highlighters in the world aren't enough to hold my attention.

"But she's not due for another month," I say, panicked. "We have another *month* to get Dusty edits."

Another small tick. "Would you like me to call her and tell her that? Maybe something can be done—wait, do you have any connections at Mount Sinai Hospital?"

"Are you done?" I ask. "Or is there a second punch line to this *hilarious* joke?"

Charlie's hands brace against the counter and he leans forward, voice going raspy, eyes crackling with that strange internal lightning. "I want it."

I feel like I missed a step. "Wh-what?"

"Dusty's book. *Frigid*. I want to work on it."

Oh, thank God. I wasn't sure where that was going. And also: no way in hell.

"If we want to keep the release date," Charlie goes on, "Sharon won't be back in time to edit. Loggia needs someone to step in, and I've asked to do it."

My mind feels less like it's spinning than like it's spinning fifteen plates that are on fire. "This is Dusty we're talking about. Shy, gentle Dusty, who's used to Sharon's soothing, optimistic demeanor. And you, who—no offense—are about as delicate as an antique pickax."

His jaw muscles flex. "I know I don't have the best bedside manner. But I'm good at my job. I can do this. And you can get Dusty on board. The publisher doesn't want to bump back the release date. We need to push this thing through, no delays."

"It's not my decision."

"Dusty will listen to you," Charlie says. "You could sell snake oil to a snake oil salesman."

"I'm not sure that's how the saying goes."

"I had to revise it to accurately reflect how good you are at your job."

My cheeks are on fire, less from the compliment than from a sudden vivid memory of Charlie's mouth. The part where he staggered back from me like I'd shot him quickly follows.

I swallow. "I'll talk to her. That's all I can do." By habit, I've unthinkingly flipped to the last page of *Once*. Now I thumb to the acknowledgments, letting my muscles relax at the sight of my name. It's proof—that I *am* good at my job, that even if I can't control everything, there's a lot I can strong-arm into shape.

I clear my throat. "What are you doing here anyway, and how long do you have until the sunlight makes you burst into flames?"

Charlie folds his forearms on the counter. "Can you keep a secret, Stephens?"

"Ask me who shot JFK," I say, adopting his own deadpan tone.

His eyes narrow. "Far more interested in how you got that information."

"That one Stephen King book," I reply. "Now, who are we keeping secrets from?"

He considers, teeth running over his full bottom lip. It's borderline lewd, but no worse than what's happening in *my* body right now.

"Loggia Publishing," he replies.

"Okay." I consider. "I can keep a secret from Loggia, if you make it juicy."

He leans in closer. I follow suit. His whisper is so quiet I almost have to press my ear to his mouth to hear it: *"I work here."*

"You . . . work . . . here?" I straighten up, blinking clear of the haze of his warm scent.

"I work here," he repeats, turning his laptop to reveal a PDF of a manuscript, "while I'm technically working *there*."

"Is that legal?" I ask. Two full-time jobs happening simultaneously seems like it might actually add up to two part-time jobs.

Charlie drags a hand down his face as he sighs exhaustedly. "It's inadvisable. But my parents own this place, and they needed help, so I've been running the shop for a few months while editing remotely."

He swipes the book off the counter. "You really buying this?"

"I like to support local businesses."

"Goode Books isn't so much a local business as it is a financial sinkhole, but I'm sure the tunnel inside the earth appreciates your money."

"Excuse me," I say, "did you just say this place is called Goode Books? As in your mother's last name, but also *good book*?"

"City people," he tuts. "Never stop to smell the roses, *or* look up to see the very prominently displayed signs over local businesses."

I wave a hand. "Oh, I have the time. It's just that the Botox in my neck makes it hard to get my chin that high."

"I've never met someone who is both so vain and so practical," he says, sounding just barely awed.

"Which will be what actually goes on my headstone."

"What a shame," he says, "to waste all *that* on a pig farmer."

"You're really hung up on the pig farmer," I say. "Whereas Libby won't be satisfied with me dating anyone but a widowed single father who rejected a country music career to run a bed-and-breakfast."

He says, "So you've met Randy."

I burst out laughing, and the corner of his mouth ticks.

Oh, shit. It *is* a smile. He's pleased to have made me laugh. Which makes my blood feel like maple syrup. And I hate maple syrup.

I take a half step back, a physical boundary to accompany the mental one I'm trying to rebuild. "Anyway, I heard a rumor you're hoarding the entire city's internet here."

"You should never believe a small-town rumor, Nora," he chides. "So . . ."

"The password is *goodebooks*," he says. "All lowercase, all one word, with the *e* on *goode*." He jerks his chin toward the café, brow arched. "Tell Principal Schroeder hi."

My face prickles. I look over my shoulder toward a wooden chair at the end of an aisle instead. "On second thought, I'll just set up there."

He leans forward, dropping his voice again. *"Chicken."*

His voice, the challenge of it, sends goose bumps rippling down my backbone.

My competitive streak instantly activates, and I turn on my heel and march into the café, pausing beside the occupied table.

"You must be Principal Schroeder," I say, adding meaningfully, "Charlie's told me *so* much about you."

She seems flustered, almost knocking over her tea in her rush to shake my hand. "You must be his girlfriend?"

She absolutely heard my comment about the ravishing, and the hurricane.

"Oh, no," I say. "We just met yesterday. But you come up a *lot* with him."

I glance over my shoulder to see the look on Charlie's face and know: I win this round.

～

"I wouldn't call spending all day on your laptop ten feet from your New York nemesis 'trying new things.' " Libby is absolutely delighted by the dusty old shop, less so by its cashier. "The last thing you need is to spend this whole vacation immersed in your career."

I glance cautiously toward the doorway from the café (which sells only decaf and regular coffee) to the bookstore proper, making sure Charlie isn't within earshot. "I can't take a whole month off work. After five every day, I promise I'm yours."

"You'd better be," she says. "Because we have a list to get through, and that"—she tips her head in Charlie's general direction—"is a distraction."

"Since when am I distracted by men?" I whisper. "Have you *met* me? I'm here using the Wi-Fi, not giving out free lap dances."

"We'll see," she says tartly. (Like, give it twenty minutes, and I will, in fact, be doling out lap dances in the local independent bookstore?)

She surveys our surroundings again, sighing wistfully. "I hate seeing bookstores empty." Some of it might be the pregnancy hormones, but she's legitimately tearing up.

"It's expensive to keep shops like this up," I tell her. Especially when so many people are turning to Amazon and other places that can afford to sell at a massive markdown. This kind of store is always the result of someone's dream, and as with most dreams, it appears to be dying a slow, painful death.

"Hey," Libby says. "What about number twelve?" At my blank stare, she adds, eyes sparkling, "*Save a local business*. We should help this place!"

"And leave the sacrificial goats to fend for themselves?"

She swats me. "I'm serious."

I chance another glance in Charlie's general direction. "They might not need our help." Or want it.

She snorts. "I saw a copy of *Everyone Poops* shelved right next to a *1001 Chocolate Desserts* cookbook."

"Traumatizing," I agree with a shudder.

"It'll be fun," Libby says. "I already have ideas." She pulls a notebook from her purse and starts scribbling, teeth sunk into her bottom lip.

I'm not thrilled by the prospect of spending even more time within a ten-foot radius of Charlie after last night's humiliating blip, but if this is what Libby really wants to do, I'm not going to let one kiss—that allegedly "never happened" anyway—scare me off.

Just like I'm not going to let it keep me from getting some work done today. People always talk about compartmentalization like it's a bad thing, but I *love* the way that, when I work, everything else seems to get folded away neatly in drawers, the books I'm working on swelling to the forefront, immersing me every bit as wholly as reading my favorite chapter books did when I was a kid. Like there's nothing to worry over, plan, mourn, or figure out.

I'm so engrossed I don't even notice Libby's paused her brainstorming to slip away, until she comes back some time later with a fresh iced coffee from across the street and a three-foot stack of small-town romance novels she's culled from the Goode Books shelves.

"It's been months since I read more than five pages in a sitting," she says giddily. Unlike me, Libby does *not* read the last page first. She doesn't even read the jacket copy, preferring to go in without any preconceived notions. Probably why she's been known to throw books across the room.

"Once I tried to lock myself in the bathroom with a Rebekah Weatherspoon novel," she says. "Within minutes, Bea wet herself."

"You need a second bathroom."

"I need a second *me*." She opens her book, and I click over to a new browser, checking for new apartment listings. There's nothing in Libby and Brendan's price range that doesn't look like an *SVU* crime scene set.

An email comes in from Sharon then, and I tap over to it.

She's doing well, and so is the baby, though they both plan to be in the hospital for a bit, since he arrived prematurely. She's sent me some pictures of his tiny pink face in its tiny little knit cap. Honestly, all newborns look more or less the same to me, but knowing he came from someone I like is enough to make my heart swell.

It constricts again when I read on and get to the part of the email dedicated to raving about *Frigid*. For a second, I'd almost forgotten that, in just over a year, everyone I've ever worked with will read about Nadine Winters. It's that in-school-in-your-underwear night-mare times one hundred.

Even so, I feel a wash of pride when I read Sharon's confirmation of what I already knew: this is the *right* book. There's an unquantifi-able spark in these pages, a sense of clarity and purpose.

Some books just have that inevitability from the beginning, an eerie déjà vu. You don't know what's going to happen, but you're sure there's no avoiding it.

Much like the rest of Sharon's email:

> We'd like to bring in our very talented new editor-at-large Charlie Lastra to get Dusty through the first round of major edits. I'll send out another email making the introduction between them but wanted to mention to you first so you could prime the pump, so to speak.
>
> Charlie's fantastic at what he does. *Frigid* will be in excellent hands.

Flashes of Charlie's *excellent hands* sizzle across my mind. I exit the email with the ferocity of a teenager slamming a door and screaming, *You're not my real dad!*

If there's anything more embarrassing than having a thinly veiled novel about you published, it's probably having that book edited by a man who felt you up in a thunderstorm.

This is why the rules exist. To protect against this exact (okay, *approximate*) scenario.

There's only one way to handle this. *Be the shark, Nora.*

I stand, roll my shoulders back, and approach the register.

"Is she going to buy any of those," Charlie drawls, tipping his chin toward Libby's tower of books, "or just get coffee all over them?"

"Has anyone ever told you you're a natural at customer service?" I ask.

"No," he says.

"Good. I know how you feel about liars."

His lips part, but before he can retort, I say, "I'll get Dusty on board—but I have a stipulation."

Charlie's mouth jams shut, his eyes going flinty. "Let's hear it."

"Your notes go through me," I say. "Dusty's first publisher did a real number on her psyche, and she's *just* regaining her confidence. The last thing she needs is you bulldozing her self-esteem." He opens his mouth to object, and I add, "Trust me. This is the only way it can work. If it can work at all."

After a long moment of consideration, he stretches his hand across the desk. "Okay, Stephens, you've got yourself a deal."

I shake my head. I won't be making the mistake of touching Charlie Lastra again. "Nothing's settled until I talk to her."

He nods. "I'll have my cocktail napkin and pen waiting for your signature."

"Oh, Charlie," I say. "How adorable that you think I'd sign a contract with anyone else's pen."

The corner of his mouth hitches. "You're right," he says. "I should've guessed."

11

B UT SHE WASN'T due until next month," Dusty says.

"Trust me: I tried telling her that." I pick at a bit of peeling paint on the gazebo as I watch a plump bumblebee drunkenly spiral through the flower beds. The woods are thick with the creaking-door chirp of cicadas, and the sky's turning a bruised shade of purple, the heat thick as ever. "But Charlie's *really* excited about this book, and from what I hear, he's great at what he does."

Dusty says, "Didn't we submit *Once* to him? And he passed?"

I tuck my phone between my shoulder and ear, moving my frizzy bangs aside. "That's right, but even then, he was adamant that he would love to see your future projects."

A long pause. "But you've never worked with him. I mean, you don't know what his editorial tastes are like."

"Dusty, he's in love with these pages. I mean that. And looking at his other titles . . . I think *Frigid* makes sense for him."

She sighs. "I can't really say no, can I? I mean, not without seeming difficult."

"Look," I say. "We've pushed this deadline back before, and if we have to do it again, we will. But I think, timing wise, with the *Once* movie coming out, your release couldn't be positioned much better. And I'll be there every step of the way. I'll run interference—do whatever I have to do to make sure *you're* happy with how this book turns out. That's what matters most."

"That's the other thing," she says. "With *Once*, there was all this time. I had your notes before we sold the book, and—this is all happening so fast, and I knew with Sharon, we could make it work, but—I feel sort of panicked."

"If you want my notes, I'll get you notes," I promise. "We can fold them into Charlie's, so you'll have two sets of eyes on it. Whatever you need, Dusty, I've got you, okay?"

She lets out a breath. "Can I think about it? Just for a day or two?"

"Of course," I say. "Take your time."

If Charlie Lastra has to sweat, I won't complain.

~

Four of my clients have decided to have simultaneous meltdowns, about everything from overzealous line edits to lackluster marketing plans. Two more clients have sent me surprise manuscripts, mere weeks after I read their *last* books.

I do my best to honor my promise to Libby—to be fully present with her after five every day—but that just means I hardly come up for air during the workday.

As different as we are, my sister and I are both creatures of habit, and we fall into a rhythm almost immediately.

She wakes first, showers, then reads on the deck with a steaming cup of decaf. I get up and run until I can barely breathe, take a scorching shower, and meet her at the breakfast table as she's dishing up hash browns or ricotta pancakes or veggie-stuffed quiche.

The next fifteen minutes are devoted to a detailed description of Libby's dreams (famously grisly, disturbing, erotic, or all three). Afterward, we FaceTime with Bea and Tala at Brendan's mom's house, during which Bea recounts *her* dreams while Tala runs around, almost knocking things over and shrieking, *Look, Nono! I'm a dinosaur!*

From there, I head to Goode Books, leaving Libby to call Brendan and do whatever else she wants during her treasured alone time.

Charlie and I exchange sharp-edged pleasantries and I pay him for a cup of coffee and then settle into my spot in the café, where I refuse to give him the satisfaction of glancing his way no matter how often I feel his eyes on me.

By the third morning, he has my coffee waiting by the register. "What a surprise," he says. "Here at eight fifty-two, same as yesterday and the day before."

I grab the coffee and ignore the dig. "Dusty's giving me her answer tonight, by the way," I say. "A free coffee isn't going to change anything."

He drops his voice, leans across the counter. "Because you're holding out hope for a giant check?"

"No," I say. "It can be a normal-sized check, just needs a lot of zeroes."

"When I want something, Nora," he says, "I don't give up easily."

Externally, I'm unaffected. Internally, my heart lurches against my collarbone from his closeness or his voice or maybe what he just said. My phone buzzes with an email, and I take it out, grateful for the distraction. Until I see the message from Dusty: I'm in.

I resist an urge to clear my throat and instead meet his eyes coolly. "Looks like you can forget the check. You'll have pages by the end of the week."

Charlie's eyes flash with a borderline vicious excitement.

"Don't look so victorious," I say. "She's asked me to be involved every step of the way. Your edits go through me."

"Is that supposed to scare me?"

"It should. I'm scary."

He pitches forward over the desk, biceps tightening, mouth in a sultry pout. "Not with *those* bangs. You're extremely approachable."

~

Most days I don't see Libby until after work. Sometimes I even get back to the cottage before her, and she guards her alone time so jealously that every time I ask her how she spent those nine hours, she gives me an increasingly ridiculous answer (*hard drugs; torrid affair with a door-to-door vacuum salesman; started the paperwork to join a cult*). On Friday, though, she joins me around lunchtime with veggie sandwiches from Mug + Shot that are about eighty percent kale. With a full mouth, she says, "This sandwich tastes exceptionally unplugged."

"I just got a bite of pure dirt," I say.

"Lucky," Libby says. "I'm still only getting kale."

After we eat, I return to work and Libby turns her focus to a Mhairi McFarlane novel, gasping and laughing so regularly and loudly that, finally, Charlie's gruff voice calls from the other room, "Could you keep that down? Every time you gasp like that, you almost give me a heart attack."

"Well, your café chairs are giving me hemorrhoids, so I'd say we're even," Libby replies.

A minute later, Charlie appears and thrusts two velvet throw pillows at us. "Your majesties," he says, scowl/pouting before returning to his post.

Libby's eyes light up and she leans over to stage-whisper to me. "Did he just bring us butt pillows?"

"I believe he did," I agree.

"Count von Lastra has a beating heart," she says.

"I can hear you," he calls.

"The undead have famously heightened senses," I tell Libby.

Throughout the week, the rings around Libby's eyes have faded, her color returning and cheeks plumping so quickly that it feels like those strained months were a dream.

In direct contrast, every day darkens the circles around Charlie's eyes. I'd guess he's having trouble sleeping too—I have yet to fall asleep in our dead-silent, pitch-black cottage before three a.m., and most nights I startle awake, heart racing and skin cold, at least once.

At precisely five, I close my laptop, Libby puts her book away, and we head out.

My concerns about Sunshine Falls disappointing her have largely come to naught. Libby's more or less content to wander, popping into musty antique stores or pausing to watch an impressively brutal seniors' kickboxing class in the town square.

Every so often we pass a placard proclaiming to be the site of a pivotal scene from *Once*. Never mind that three separate buildings claim to be the site of the apothecary, including an empty space whose windows are plastered with posters reading, *RENT THE APOTHECARY FROM HIT NOVEL* ONCE IN A LIFETIME! *PRIMO LOCATION!*

"I haven't heard anyone say *primo* since the eighties," Libby says.

"You weren't alive in the eighties," I point out.

"Precisely."

Back at the cottage, she cooks a big dinner: sweet summer corn and creamy potato salad with crisp chives, a salad topped with shaved watermelon and toasted sesame, and grilled tempeh burgers on brioche buns, with thick slices of tomato and red onion, all smothered with avocado.

I chop whatever she tells me to, then watch her *re*chop it to her liking. It's a strange reversal, seeing the things my baby sister has mastered that I never got around to. It makes me proud, but also sort of sad. Maybe this is how parents feel when their kids grow up, like some piece of them has become fundamentally unknowable.

"Remember when you were going to be a chef?" I ask one night while I'm chopping basil and tomato for a pizza she's making.

She gives a noncommittal *hm* that could mean *of course* as easily as *not ringing any bells*.

She was always so smart, so creative. She could've done anything, and I *know* she loves being a mom, but I can also understand why she needed this so badly, the chance to be a lone person before she's got a newborn attached to her hip again.

Like every night so far, we eat dinner out on the deck, and afterward, once I've washed the dishes and put everything away, we scour the trunk full of board games and play dominoes out on the deck, the strands of globe lights our only illumination.

A little after ten, Libby shuffles to bed, and I go back to the kitchen table to hunt through apartment listings online. Soon I have to face the fact of the wonky internet and give up, but I'm not even close to tired, so I stuff my feet into Libby's Crocs and wander out into the meadow at the front of the cottage. The moonlight and stars are bright enough to turn the grass silvery, and the humidity holds the day's heat close, the sweet, grassy smell thick in the air.

Feeling so entirely alone is unnerving, in the same way as staring at the ocean at night, or watching thunderclouds form. In New York, it's impossible to escape the feeling of being one person among millions, as if you're all nerve endings in one vast organism. Here, it's easy to feel like the last person on earth.

Around one, I climb into bed and stare at the ceiling for an hour or so before I drift off.

On Saturday morning, we follow our usual schedule, but when I walk into the bookstore, I come up short.

"Hello there!" The tiny woman behind the register smiles as she stands, the scents of jasmine and weed wafting off her. "Can I help you?"

She looks like a woman who's spent her life outside, her olive skin permanently freckled, the sleeves of her denim shirt rolled up her dainty forearms. She has coarse, dark hair that falls to her shoulders; a pretty, round face; and dark eyes that crinkle at the corners to accommodate her smile. The crease beneath her lip is the giveaway.

Sally Goode, the owner of our cottage. Charlie's mother.

"Um," I say, hoping my smile is natural. I hate when I have to think about what my face is doing, especially because I'm never convinced it's translating. I wasn't planning to stay long, just an hour or so to work through some more email before meeting Libby for lunch, but now I feel guilty using the Wi-Fi for free.

I grab the first book I see, *The Great Family Marconi*, one of those books fated to be hurled across a room by my sister, then picked up by me. Unlike Libby, I loved the last page so much I read it a dozen times before flipping back to the front. "Just this!"

"My son edited this one," Sally Goode says proudly. "That's what he does, for a living."

"Oh." Someone get me a public speaking trophy, I'm on fire. Only speaking to Libby and Charlie for a week has clearly diminished my capacity to slip into Professional Nora.

Sally tells me my total, and when I hand over my card, her eyes slide across it. "Thought that might be you! Not often I don't recognize someone in here. I'm Sally—you're staying in my cottage."

"Oh, wow, hi!" I say, once again hoping I come across as a human, raised by other humans. "It's nice to meet you."

"You too—how's the place working out for you? You want a bag for the book?"

I shake my head and accept the book and card back. "Gorgeous! Great."

"It is, isn't it?" she says. "Been in my family as long as this shop. Four generations. If we hadn't had kids, we would've lived there forever. Lots of happy memories."

"Any ghosts?" I ask her.

"Not that I've ever seen, but if you meet any, tell them Sally says hi. And not to scare off my guests." She pats the counter. "You girls need anything up at the cottage? Firewood? Roasting stakes for marshmallows? I'll send my son over with some wood, just in case."

Oh, Lord. "That's okay."

"He's got nothing to do anyway."

Except his two full-time jobs, one of which she *just* mentioned.

"It's not necessary," I insist.

Then *she* insists, saying verbatim, "I insist."

"Well," I say, "thanks." After a few minutes of work in the café, I thank her again and slip out into the dazzlingly sunny street to cross over to Mug + Shot.

My phone gives a short, snappy vibration. A text from an unknown number.

Why is my mother texting me about how hot you are?

This can only be one person.

Weird, I write. Think it has anything to do with the fact that I just went to the bookstore in nothing but a patent leather trench coat?

Charlie replies with a screenshot of some texts between him and his mom.

Cottage guest is very pretty, Sally writes, then, separately, No ring.

Charlie replied: Oh? Thinking about leaving Dad?

She ignored his comment and instead said, Tall. You always liked tall girls.

What are you talking about, Charlie wrote back, no question mark.

Remember your homecoming date? Lilac Walter-Hixon? She was practically a giant.

That was the eighth-grade formal, he said. It was before my growth spurt.

Well this girl's very pretty and tall but not too tall.

I stifle a laugh.

Tall but not TOO tall, I tell Charlie, can also be added to my headstone.

He says, I'll make a note.

I say, She told me you would bring wood over to the cottage for me.

He says, Please swear to me you didn't make a "too late for that" joke.

No, but Principal Schroeder was in the café, and I've heard the gossip moves fast here, so it's only a matter of time.

Sally's going to be so disappointed in you, Charlie says.

Me? What about her SON, the Rake of Main Street?

The ship of her disappointment in me set sail a long time ago. I'd have to do something WAY sluttier to let her down now.

When she finds your stash of Bigfoot erotica under your race car bed, maybe the ship will circle back.

Outside Mug + Shot, I lean against the sun-warmed window, the trees lining the lane rustling in a gentle breeze that heightens the smell of espresso in the air.

Another message comes in. A page from the Bigfoot Christmas book, featuring a particularly egregious use of *decking the halls*, as well as a reference to a sex move called the Voracious Yeti, which doesn't sound remotely anatomically possible.

Libby walks into my periphery. "Already done with the Wi-Fi?"

"Thoroughly unplugged," I reply. "Have you ever heard of the Voracious Yeti?"

"That a children's book?"

"Sure."

"I'll have to look it up."

My phone vibrates with another message: I find the Voracious Yeti highly implausible.

I find myself smiling, possibly with knives. So disappointing. Really pulls the reader out of an otherwise stunning work of realism.

12

~

I SIT UP, GASPING, cold, panicked.

Libby.

Where is Libby?

My eyes zigzag across the room, searching for something grounding. The first rays of sunlight streaming through a window. The sound of pots and pans clanking. The smell of brewing coffee drifting through the door.

I'm in the cottage.

It's okay. She's here. She's okay.

At home, when I'm anxious, I cycle. When I need a boost of energy, I cycle. When I need to knock myself out, I cycle. When I can't focus, I cycle.

Here, running is my only option.

I dress quietly, pull on my muddy sneakers, and creep down the stairs to sneak out into the cool morning. I shiver as I cross the foggy meadow, picking up my pace at the woods.

I leap over a gnarled root, then thunder across the footbridge that arcs over the creek.

My throat starts to burn, but the fear is still chasing me. Maybe it's being here, feeling so far away from Mom, or maybe it's spending so much time with Libby, but something is bringing me back to all those things I try not to think about.

It feels like there's poison inside of me. No matter how hard I run, I can't burn through it. For once, I wish I could cry, but I can't. I haven't since the morning of the funeral.

I pick up my pace.

~

"I've found him!" Libby squeals, running into the bathroom as I'm trying to coax my curtain bangs into submission, against the express wishes of the unrelenting humidity.

She thrusts her phone toward me, and I squint at a headshot of an attractive man with short, chocolaty hair and gray eyes. He's wearing a down vest over a plaid shirt and gazing across a foggy lake. Over his picture is *BLAKE, 36.*

"Libby!" I shriek, realization dawning. "Why the hell are you on a dating app?"

"I'm not," she says. "*You* are."

"I am definitely not," I say.

"I made an account for you," she says. "It's a new app. Very marriage minded. I mean, it's called Marriage of Minds."

"MOM?" I say. "The acronym for the app is MOM? Sometimes I worry about the severe lack of warning bells in your brain, Libby."

"Blake's an avid fisherman who's unsure if he wants kids," she says. "He's a teacher, and a night owl—like you—and extremely physically active."

I snatch the phone and read for myself. "Libby. It says here he's looking for a down-to-earth woman who doesn't mind spending her Saturdays cheering on the Tar Heels."

"You don't need someone exactly like you, Sissy," Libby says gently. "You need someone who *appreciates* you. I mean, you obviously don't *need* anyone, period, but you *deserve* someone who understands how special you are! Or at least someone who can give you a low-pressure night out."

She's looking at me now with that hopeful Libby look of hers. It's halfway between the expression of a cat who's dropped a mouse at a person's feet and that of a kid handing over a Mother's Day drawing, blissfully unaware that Mommy's "snow hat" looks only and exactly like a giant penis.

Blake is the penis hat in this scenario.

"Couldn't we just have a low-pressure night out together?" I ask.

She glances away with an apologetic grimace. "Blake already thinks he's meeting you at Poppa Squat's for karaoke night."

"Nearly every part of that sentence is concerning."

She wilts. "I thought you *wanted* to switch things up, not be so . . ."

Nadine Winters, a voice in my mind says. It takes me a second to recognize it as the husky, teasing timbre of Charlie. I suppress a groan of resignation.

It's one night, and Libby's gone to a lot of trouble for this very weird gift.

"I guess I should google what a Tar Heel is beforehand," I say.

A grin breaks across her face. If Mom's smile was springtime, Libby's is full summer. She says, "No way. That's what we call a conversation starter."

~

Libby (acting as me) didn't tell Blake where we were staying, and instead suggested I (secretly *we*) meet him at Poppa Squat's around seven. In her flowy wrap dress with her hair perfectly tousled and pink gloss smudged across her lips, you'd think she had something better to do than nurse a soda and lime while watching me from across the bar, but she seems perfectly excited for the underwhelming night ahead.

Normally, I'd arrive to a date early, but we're operating on Libby's timeline and thus arrive ten minutes late. Outside the front doors, she stops me by the elbow. "We should go in separately. So he doesn't know we're together."

"Right," I say. "That will make it easier to knock him out and empty his pockets. What should our signal be?"

She rolls her eyes. "*I* will go in first. I'll scope him out and make sure he's not carrying a sword, or wearing a pin-striped vest, or doing close-up magic for strangers."

"Basically that he's none of the four horsemen of the apocalypse."

"I'll text you when it's safe to come in."

Forty seconds after she slips inside, she sends me a thumbs-up, and I follow.

It's hotter in Poppa Squat's than it is outside, probably because it's packed.

The crowd is drunkenly singing "Sweet Home Alabama" around and on the karaoke stage at the back of the room, and the whole place smells like sweat and spilled beer.

Blake, 36, is sitting at the first table, facing the door with his hands folded like he's here with Ruth from HR to fire me.

"Blake?" I outstretch a hand.

"Nora?" He doesn't get up.

"Yep."

"You look different than your picture," he replies.

"Haircut," I say, taking my seat, hand unshaken.

"You didn't say how tall you were in your profile," he says. This from a man who listed himself as six feet and an inch but can't be taller than five nine unless he's wearing stilts under this table.

So at least dating in Sunshine Falls is exactly the same as in New York.

"Didn't occur to me it would matter."

"How tall *are* you?" Blake asks.

"Um," I stall, hoping this will give him time to rethink his first-date strategy. No such luck. "Five eleven."

"Are you a model?" He says this hopefully, like the right answer could excuse a multitude of height-related sins.

There is, of course, the misconception that straight men universally love tall, thin women. Being such a woman, I can debunk this.

Many men are too insecure to date a tall woman. Many of those who *aren't* are assholes looking for a trophy. It has less to do with attraction than status. Which is only effective if the tall person is a model. If you're dating someone taller than you and she's a model, then you must be hot and interesting. If you're dating someone taller than you and she's a literary agent, cue the jokes about her wearing your balls on a silver necklace.

On the bright side, at least Blake, 36, isn't asking about—

"What size are your shoes?" His face is pinched as if in pain. Same, Blake. Same.

"What are you drinking?" I say. "Alcohol? Alcohol sounds good."

The waitress approaches, and before she can get a word out, I say, "Two very large gin martinis, please." She must see the familiar signs of first-date misery on me, because she skips her welcome speech, nods, and virtually sprints to put in our order.

"I don't drink," Blake says.

"No worries," I say, "I'll drink yours."

Back by the pool tables, Libby grins and flashes two thumbs up.

13

YOU WOULD THINK he'd be in a hurry to call this thing
what it is: dead in the water.

But Blake is not a casual MOM user. He's on the prowl for a wife,
and despite my hulking stature, giantess feet, and indulgence in gin,
he's not willing to let me go until he's individually clarified that I
don't know how to make any of his favorite foods.

"I *really* don't cook," I say, when we've made it through Super
Bowl finger foods and moved on to various fried fish.

"Not even tilapia?" he says.

I shake my head.

"Salmon?" he asks.

"No."

"Catfish?"

"Like the TV show?" I say.

He briefly pauses the inquest when the front doors swing open
and Charlie Lastra steps inside. I fight an urge to sink in my chair
and hide behind the menu, but it wouldn't matter. The second a

person walks through those doors they come face-to-face with our table, and Charlie's eyes snap right to me, his expression somersaulting through surprise to something like distaste and then wicked glee.

It really is like watching a storm building in a time-lapse video, culminating in that flash-crack of lightning.

He nods at me before beelining toward the bar, and Blake resumes his fish list. Just like that, I lose another fifteen minutes of my life.

Blake was handsome in his photographs, but I truly find this man heinous.

I pat the table and stand. "You need anything from the bar?"

"I don't drink," he reminds me, sounding awfully impatient for a man who's heard the sentence *I don't cook* seventeen times in the last thirty minutes without it making any lasting impression.

I can't *actually* order another drink. A third cocktail and I'd probably make Blake stand back-to-back with me while our waitress measured us. Or maybe I'd *actually* knock him out and steal his wallet.

Either way, I'm on a mission to find Libby rather than booze, but this place is jammed. I wedge myself against the bar and pull out my phone to find not one but two missed calls from Dusty, along with a text message apologizing for calling so late. I fire off a reply asking if she's all right and whether I can call her back in twenty minutes, then type out a message to Libby: WHERE ARE YOU? As I hit send, I push onto my tiptoes to scan the crowd.

"If you're looking for your dignity," someone says through the roar of conversation (and the girls screaming "Like a Virgin" at the back of the room), "you won't find it here."

Charlie sits around the corner of the bar with a glistening bottle of Coors.

"What's so undignified about karaoke night?" I ask. "I mean, *you're* here."

Someone steps between us to order. Charlie leans behind her to continue the conversation, and I do too. "Yes, but *I'm* not here with Blake Carlisle."

I glance over my shoulder. Blake is staring longingly at a brunette who looks about four foot six.

"Grow up together?" I guess.

"Very few people who are born here ever escape," he says sagely.

"Does the Sunshine Falls Tourism Bureau know about you?" I ask.

The woman standing between us clearly has no plans to leave, but we just keep talking around her, leaning in front of and then behind her depending on her posture.

"No, but I'm sure they'll want an endorsement from *you* once you've done your walk of shame from Blake's house. I've got it on good authority he has a carpeted bathroom."

"Joke's on you, because I haven't slept over at a man's apartment in like ten years."

Charlie's eyes glint, another lightning strike across the dark clouds of his face. "I am *desperate* for more information."

"I have an intense nighttime skin care routine. I don't like to miss it, and it doesn't all fit in a handbag." My mom used to say, *You can't control the passage of time, but you can soften its blow to your face.*

His head cocks to one side as he considers my half-truth of an answer. "So how'd you end up here with Blake? Throw a dart at a phone book?"

"Have you heard of MOM?"

"That woman who works at the bookstore?" Charlie deadpans. "I think so. Why?"

"The dating app." I smack the bar as the realization hits me. "Do you think that's why they named it that? So you could be like, *Mom set me up?*"

Charlie balks. "I would never go out with someone Sally set me up with."

"Your mom thinks I'm gorgeous," I remind him.

"I'm aware," he says.

"I guess we've already established that you wouldn't date me though," I say.

His brow lifts, tugging at one corner of his mouth. "Oh, we're going to do *this* now?" He fails to hide a pouty smirk behind his beer bottle. As he sips, the crease under his lip deepens, and my insides start fizzing.

"Do what?"

"The thing where we pretend I rejected you."

"You *exactly* rejected me," I say.

"You said *wait*," he challenges.

"Yes, and you apparently heard *I'm going to tase you in the crotch*."

"You said it was a mistake," he says. "Fervently."

"You said that first!" I say.

He snorts. "We both know"—the woman between us has *finally* left, and Charlie slides onto her abandoned seat—"all that was for you was a checked box on your extremely depressing list, and that's not a game I'm interested in playing, Nora."

"Oh, please. You don't even qualify for the list. You're as city-person as it gets." Immediately I regret saying it. I could've pretended the kiss was calculated; now he knows I just *wanted* it.

The way his beer bottle pauses against his parted lips, like I've caught him off guard, almost makes it worth it. Whatever game we *are* playing, I've won another round: the prize is his chagrined expression.

He sets his bottle down, scratches his eyebrow. "I'll let you get back to your date."

I check my phone. Libby has replied: *Headed home. I won't wait up for you.* She had the audacity to include a winky face.

I look up, and Charlie's watching me. "Is there a way out of here," I ask, "that *doesn't* take me past Blake?"

He studies me for a beat and says dryly, "Nora Stephens, MOM is *not* going to be happy with you." Then he holds his hand out. "Back door."

~

Charlie tugs me away through the crowd and behind the bar, and we duck through a narrow door into the kitchen, only to be immediately cut off.

"Hey! You can't—" the pretty bartender cries, throwing her arms out to her sides. She clocks Charlie and flushes. Somehow it makes her even prettier.

"Amaya," Charlie says. He's gone a little more rigid, like he's just remembered he has a body and every muscle in it has tightened reflexively.

I've been thinking of Amaya's smile—and her tone with Charlie—as flirty, but that was before I knew their history. Now when that smile makes an appearance, I parse out shades of hurt and hesitancy, a wispy beam of hope shining through it all.

Charlie clears his throat, his fingers twitching around mine. Amaya's gaze judders toward the motion, and just like that, *my* face is on fire too.

"We need the back door," Charlie says, apologetic. "Blake Carlisle thinks he's on a date with this woman."

Her eyes flicker between us again. After a moment of weighing her options, she sighs and steps aside. "Just this once. We're *really* not supposed to let anyone back here."

"Thanks." He nods, but doesn't move for a second. Probably too stunned by the return of her brilliant, hopeful, *I-still-love-you* smile. "Thanks," he says again, and leads the way through the door. Out in the alleyway, the air feels cool and dry, and with the sudden rush of oxygen to my brain, I remember to jerk my hand from his. "Well, that was awkward."

"What?"

I cut him a glance. "Your jilted lover and her X-ray vision."

"She wasn't jilted. And as far as I know, she has no superpowers."

"Well, maybe she wasn't jilted," I say, "but she's hung up."

"You're misinformed," he says.

"You're clueless," I say.

"Trust me," he says, leading me to the cross street. "The way things ended left no room for hang-ups."

"She looked *haunted*, Charlie."

"She heard Blake Carlisle's name," he replies. "How else was she supposed to look?"

"So Blake has a reputation."

"It's a small town," Charlie says. "Everyone has a reputation."

"What's yours?"

His gaze slices toward me, brow lifting and jaw muscles leaping. "Probably whatever you think it is."

I look away before those eyes can swallow me whole.

A few people are smoking in front of Poppa Squat's, a couple more shuffling toward an ivy-wrapped redbrick Italian restaurant, Giacomo's. Until now, I haven't seen it open.

Tonight, the windows are aglow, the awnings twinkling, servers in white dress shirts and black ties whizzing back and forth with trays of wineglasses and pastas.

I tip my chin toward Giacomo's. "I thought that place was closed down."

"It's only open on Saturday and Sunday nights," Charlie says. "The couple who run it retired a long time ago, but everyone talked them into keeping things going on the weekend."

"You mean the whole town banded together to save a beloved establishment?" I prod. "Exactly like the trope?"

"Sure," he says evenly, "or they showed up with pitchforks and demanded their weekly cacio e pepe."

"Is it good?" I ask.

"Actually, it's very good." He hesitates for a moment. "Are you hungry?"

My stomach grumbles, and his mouth twitches. "Would you like to have dinner with me, Nora?" He heads off my response with, "As *colleagues*. Ones who can't fulfill each other's checklists."

"I wasn't aware you *had* a checklist," I say.

"Of course I have a checklist." His eyes glint in the dark. "What am I, an animal?"

14

WELL, IF IT isn't young Charles Lastra!" An old woman with a pile of silvery-gray hair on top of her head and a dress whose neckline tops her chin comes toward us. "And you've brought a date! How lovely!"

Her hazel eyes twinkle as she gives Charlie and me both squeezes on the arm.

He looks downright adoring, by Charlie's standards. Even Amaya didn't get *this* smile. "How are you, Mrs. Struthers?"

She holds out her hands, gesturing to the bustling dining room. "Can't complain. Just the two of you?"

When he nods, she takes us to a white-clothed table tucked against a window lined with candles dripping wax down wicker-wrapped wine bottles.

"You two enjoy." She taps the table with a wink, then returns to the host stand.

The smell of fresh bread is thick and intoxicating, and within thirty seconds, a bottle of red wine appears on the table.

"Oh, we didn't order that," I tell the server, but he tips his head in Mrs. Struthers's direction and hurries away.

Charlie looks up from the glass of wine he's pouring for me. "She's the owner. Also my favorite former substitute teacher. Gave me an Octavia Butler book that changed my life."

My heart gives a strange flutter at the thought. I jut my chin toward the wine. "You have to drink all of that. I've already had two drinks, and I'm a lightweight."

"Oh, I remember," he teases, sliding my glass toward me, "but this is *wine*. It's the grape juice of alcohol."

I lean across the table, grabbing the bottle and tipping it over *his* glass until it's full to the brim. As deadpan as ever, he hunches and slurps from the glass without lifting it.

I burst into laughter against my will, and he's so visibly pleased it gives me a full-body twinge of pride. He *wants* to make me laugh.

"So how bad should I feel," I ask, "about ditching Blake?"

Charlie leans back in his chair, his legs stretching out, grazing mine. "Well," he says, "when we were in high school, he used to take my books out of my gym locker and put them in the toilet tank, so maybe a three out of ten?"

"Oh no." I try to stifle a giggle, but I'm slaphappy, high on adrenaline from my escape.

"How many dates are left?" he asks. "On your Life-Ruining Vacation List."

"Depends." I take a sip. "How many more high school bullies did you have?"

His laugh is low and hoarse. It makes me think of the satisfying *snap* sound of a tennis racket delivering a perfect return.

His voice, his laugh, has a texture; it scrapes. I take another sip of wine to dull the thought, then switch back to water.

"Does that mean you want to date my bullies, or to humiliate them?" He grabs some bread from the basket on the table, tears off a piece, and slips it between his lips.

I look away as the heat creeps up my neck. "That's all down to whether they ask how big my feet are within the first five minutes of meeting."

Charlie chokes over the bread. "Was it, like, a fetish thing?"

"I think it was more of a *Wow, did you have to fall in a pit of radio-active waste to get that tall?* kind of thing."

"Blake never did have the most secure sense of self," Charlie muses.

We're interrupted by a teenage waiter with an unfortunate bowl cut taking our order—two goat cheese salads and cacio e pepes.

As soon as he's out of earshot, I say, "Libby picked Blake. She's running an app for me."

"Right." His brows rise apprehensively. "MOM."

"Two dates on the list. Blake is the first."

Charlie's eyes do a bored allusion-to-an-eye-roll. "Save yourself the trouble and use this as number two."

"I already told you. You don't count."

"The words every man dreams of hearing."

"Consider yourself the grape juice of dates."

"So number five is go on two shitty dates with men you could never be into, in a town you couldn't stand to live in," Charlie says. "What's number six again? Voluntary lobotomy?"

I slide his mostly full wineglass toward him. "I'm still waiting on *your* secrets, Lastra."

He pushes the glass back toward the middle of the table. "You already know mine. I'm the uninvited prodigal son, here to run a rapidly dying bookstore while my dad's busy with physical therapy and my mom's trying to keep him from climbing on the roof to clean the gutters."

"That's . . . a lot," I say.

"It's fine." His tone makes it clear that sentence ends with a period.

"And Loggia's been good with letting you work remotely," I say.

"For now." When his gaze meets mine, it's startlingly dark. It feels like I've stumbled toward the edge of something dangerous. And worse, like I'm trapped there in viscous honey, incapable of stepping back from the ledge.

"Now, what does Libby have on you that you went out with Blake?" Charlie asks. "Did you sell state secrets? Commit a murder?"

"And here I thought you had a younger sister."

He relaxes back in his chair. "Carina. She's twenty-two."

Even though I've met his mother, it's hard to imagine Charlie with a family. He seems so . . . self-contained. Then again, that's probably what people say about me.

"And Carina can't compel you to do something simply by asking?" I say. Or by dodging you for months, keeping secrets, and consistently looking like she just got unhitched from being dragged behind a train.

Charlie hesitates. "Carina's why I'm here."

I lean into the table, its edge digging into my ribs. I've got that feeling of reading a mystery novel, knowing a reveal is coming up, and fighting the urge to skip ahead.

"She was planning to come back and run the bookstore after college," he says. "Then she decided last minute to just stay in Italy for a while. Florence. She's a painter."

"Wow," I say. "People really just do that? Move to Italy to paint?"

Charlie frowns, turns his water glass in place, then readjusts his silverware into a tidy row. It's satisfying to watch; feels like having someone scratch the spot right between my shoulder blades. "The women in my family do. My mom also went there to paint for a couple weeks when she was twenty and ended up staying for a year."

"The whimsical free spirit bringing magic into everyone's lives," I say. "I'm familiar with that trope."

"Some people call it magic," he says. "I prefer to think of it as 'raging stress hives.' Carina was living in an Airbnb owned by a literal drug dealer until I booked her another place."

I shudder. "That is exactly Libby in a parallel universe."

"Little sisters," he says, the twist of his mouth deepening the crease beneath his bottom lip.

I stare at it for a beat too long. My brain scrambles for purchase in the conversation. "What about your dad? What's he like?"

He tips his head back. "Quiet. Strong. A small-town contractor who swept my mom so thoroughly off her feet that she decided to put down roots."

At my self-satisfied look, he leans forward, matching my posture. "Fine, yes, they are the quintessential small-town love story," he admits, eyes sparking as our knees press together. Under the table we're playing a game of chicken: who will pull away first?

The seconds stretch on, thick and heavy as molasses, but we stay where we are, locked together by the challenge.

"All right, Stephens," he says finally. "Let's hear about *your* family. Where exactly do they fall in your catalogue of two-dimensional caricatures?"

"Easy," I say. "Libby's the chaotic, charming nineties rom-com heroine who's always running late and is windblown in a cute and sexy way. My dad's the deadbeat, absent father who 'wasn't ready to have kids' but now, according to a paid PI, takes his three sons and wife out in their boat on Lake Erie every weekend."

"What about your mom?" he asks.

"My mom . . ." I rearrange my own silverware, like they're words in my next sentence. "She was magic." I meet his eyes, expecting a sneer or a smirk or a storm cloud, but instead finding only a small crease inside his brows. "She was the struggling actress who chased her dreams to New York. We never had any money, but somehow, she made *everything* fun. She was my best friend. I mean, not just when we got older. As long as I can remember, she'd take us with her everywhere. And you know, for a lot of people who move to the city, it loses its glow in a couple years? But with Mom, it was like every single day was the first one.

"She felt so lucky to be there. And *everyone* fell in love with her. She was such a romantic. That's where Libby gets it from. She started reading Mom's old romance novels way too young."

"You were close with her," Charlie says quietly, halfway between observation and question. "Your mom?"

I nod. "She just made things better." I can still smell her lemon-lavender scent, feel her arms around me, hear her voice—*Let it out, sweet girl*. Just one look and those five words, and it would all come spilling out. I do my best for Libby, but I've never had that kind of tenderness that slips past defenses.

When I look up, Charlie isn't watching me so much as reading me, his eyes traveling back and forth over my face like he can translate each line and shadow into words. Like he can see me scrambling for a segue.

He clears his throat and hands me one. "I read some romance novels as a kid."

My relief at the topic change rapidly morphs into something else, and Charlie laughs. "You couldn't possibly look more evil right now, Stephens."

"This is my delighted face," I say. "Did they teach you anything helpful?"

He murmurs, "I could never share that information with a *colleague*."

I roll my eyes. "So that would be a no."

"Is that how you got into books? Your mom's love of romance?"

I shake my head. "For me, it was this shop. Freeman Books."

Charlie nods. "I know it."

"We lived over it," I explain. "Mrs. Freeman used to run all these programs, things that were free with the purchase of a book, and it made it easier for our mom to justify spending money. I was never stressed out there, you know? I'd forget about everything. It felt like I could go anywhere, do anything."

"A good bookstore," Charlie says, "is like an airport where you don't have to take your shoes off."

"In fact," I say, "it's discouraged."

"Sometimes I think Goode Books could use a sign about it," he replies. "It's the reason I never tell customers to *make themselves at home*."

"Right, because then the shoes and bras go flying, and the Marvin Gaye starts playing at top volume."

"For every kernel of information you offer, Stephens," he says, "there are a hundred new questions. And yet I *still* don't know how you got into agenting."

"Mrs. Freeman made these shelf-talker cards for us to fill out," I explain. "*Book Lovers Recommend*, they said—that's what she called us, her little book lovers. So I guess I started to think about books more critically."

The crevice under his lip turns into an outright crevasse. "So you started leaving scathing reviews?"

"I got super stingy with my recommendations," I reply. "And then I started just changing things as I read; fixing endings if Libby didn't like how they played out, or if all the main characters were boys, I'd add a girl with strawberry blond hair."

"So you were a child editor," Charlie says.

"That's what I wanted to do. I started working at the shop in high school and stayed there all through undergrad, saving up for Emerson's publishing program. Then my mom died, and I became Libby's legal guardian, so I had to put it off. A couple of years later, Mrs. Freeman passed away too, and her son had to cut half the staff to make ends meet. I managed to get an admin job at a literary agency, and the rest is history."

There was more to it, of course. The year of balancing two jobs, napping in the hours between shifts. The knack I discovered for talking down panicking authors when their agents were out of office. The eventual bestselling novels I'd pulled out of the slush pile and forwarded to my bosses.

The offer to come on as a junior agent, and the list of cons I wrote out: I'd have to leave my waitressing gig; working on commission was risky; there was a chance I'd land us in the exact hole I'd been digging us out of since Mom's death.

And then, in both the pro and con columns: now that I'd had a taste of working with books, how could I ever be happy with anything else?

"I gave myself three years," I tell Charlie, "and a dollar amount I'd need to make, and if I didn't reach it, I promised I'd quit and look for something salaried."

"How early did you make your deadline?"

I feel my smile curve involuntarily. "Eight months."

His lips curve too. *Smiling with knives.* "Of course you did," he murmurs. Our eyes lock for a beat. "What about editing?"

I feel the dent in my chin before I've even lied. The first few years, I checked job listings compulsively. Once I even went to an interview. But I was about to push through a huge sale, and I was terrified to be locked into a lower salary with an entry-level position. Three days before my second interview, I canceled it.

"I'm good at agenting," I reply. "What about you? How'd you end up in publishing?"

He scrubs one hand up the back of his salt-and-pepper curls. "I had a lot of problems in school when I was small," he says. "Couldn't focus. Things didn't click. Got held back."

I try to rein in my surprise.

"You don't have to do that," he says, amused.

"Do what?"

"The Shiny, Polite Nora thing," he says. "If you're *aghast* at my failure, then just be aghast. I can take it."

"It's not that," I say. "You just put off this . . . academic vibe. I would've expected you to be, like, a Rhodes scholar, with a tattoo of the Bodleian Library on your ass."

"Then where would my Garfield the cat tattoo go?" he asks so dryly that I have to spit my wine back into the glass. "One-one," he says with a faint smile.

"What's that?"

"Our spit take score."

I try to wipe my grin off, but it sticks. Charlie's commitment to the truth is contagious, apparently, and the truth is, I'm having fun. "So what then?" I say. "After you got held back?"

He sighs, straightens his silverware. "My mom was—well, you've met her. She's a free spirit. She wanted to just pull me out of school and call me helping tend her marijuana plants 'homeschooling.' My dad's the more . . . steady of the two of them." His smile is delicate, almost sweet.

"Anyway, he figured if I was bad at school, then he just needed to figure out what I was good at. What I *could* focus on. Tried a million hobbies out with me, then finally, when I was eight, he got me this CD player—probably hoping I'd turn out to be the next Jackson Browne or something. Instead I immediately took the CD player apart."

I nod soberly. "And that's how he discovered your passion for serial killing."

Charlie's eyes spark as he laughs. "It's how he realized I wanted to learn how to put things together. I thought the world made sense, and I wanted to find the sense. After that, my dad started asking me to help him work on this car he was fixing up. I got pretty into it."

"At *eight*?" I cry.

"As it turns out," he says, "I have incredible focus when I'm interested in something."

Despite the innocence of the comment, it feels like molten lava is rolling up my toes, my legs, engulfing me.

I shift my gaze to my glass. "So that's how you ended up with a race car bed?"

"Along with a ton of books about cars and restoration. The reading finally clicked, and I stopped caring about mechanics overnight."

"Did it crush him?" I ask.

Now Charlie's eyes drop, storm clouds rolling in across his brow. "He just wanted me to love something. He didn't care what."

Dads, as a concept, have always felt as irrelevant to my daily life as astronauts. I know they're out there, but I rarely think about them. Suddenly, though, I can almost imagine it. I can almost miss it, this thing I never had.

"That's really nice." It feels like not just an understatement, but a complete mistranslation for something vast and unruly.

"He's a sweet guy," Charlie says quietly. "Anyway, he let the car stuff go and started picking up paperbacks for me every time he stopped by a garage sale, or a new donation box came into Mom's shop. He has no idea how much erotica he's given me."

"And you actually read it."

Charlie turns his wineglass one hundred and eighty degrees, eyes boring into me. "I wanted to understand how things worked, remember?"

I arch a brow. "How'd that turn out for you?"

He sits forward. "I was slightly disappointed when my first serious girlfriend didn't have three consecutive orgasms, but otherwise okay."

A torrent of laughter rips through me.

"So I've found the key to Nora Stephens's joy," he says. "My sexual humiliation."

"It's not the humiliation so much as the sheer optimism."

His lips press together. "I'd say I'm a realist, but one who doesn't always understand when what he's seeing isn't realism."

"So why'd you run away to New York?"

"I didn't run," he says. "I moved."

"Is there a difference?" I ask.

"No one was chasing me?" he says. "Also, 'running' implies speed. I had to go to community college for a couple years here, work construction with my dad to save up so I could transfer in my junior year."

"You don't strike me as a hard hat guy."

"I'm not a hat guy, period," he says. "But I needed money to get to New York, and I thought all writers lived there."

"Ah," I say. "The truth comes out. You wanted to be a writer." My brain flips straight to Jakob, like a book whose spine is creased to land on a favorite page.

"I thought I did," Charlie says. "In college, I realized I liked workshopping other people's stories more. I like the puzzle of it. Looking at all the pieces and figuring out what something's trying to be, and how to get it there."

I feel a pang of longing. "That's my favorite part of the job too."

He studies me for a moment. "Then I think you might be in the wrong job."

Editing might've been the dream, but you can't eat, drink, or sleep on top of dreams. I landed the next best thing. Everyone has to give up their dreams eventually. "You know what *I* think?"

His eyes stay trained on me, his pupils growing like they're somehow absorbing all the shadows from the room. "No, but I'm desperate to find out," he deadpans.

"I think you *did* run away from this place."

He rolls his eyes and leans back in his chair, the posture of a jungle cat. "I left calmly. Whereas, in one week, you will run, screaming, for the city limits, begging every passing semitruck driver for a lift to the nearest bagel."

"Actually," I say, rising to the challenge in his voice, "I'm here for a month."

His lips press together. "Is that so?"

"It is," I say. "Libby and I have a *lot* of fun things planned. But you already know that. You've seen the list."

Because I am *not* Nadine. I'm capable of spontaneity, and flannel won't make me break out in a rash, and I'm *going* to finish that list.

His gaze narrows. "You're going to 'sleep under the stars'? Offer yourself to the mosquitoes?"

"There are body sprays for that."

"Ride a horse?" he says. "You said you're terrified of horses."

"When did I say that?"

"The other night, when you were three sheets to the wind. You said you were terrified of anything larger than a groundhog. And then you took it back and said even groundhogs make you uneasy, because they're unpredictable. You're not going to ride a horse."

We changed it to *Pet a horse*, but now I'm unwilling to back down. "Would you like to make a bet?"

"That you won't 'save a dying business' in a month?" he says. "Wouldn't call it a gamble."

"What will you give me, when I win?"

"What do you want?" he says. "A vital organ? My rent-stabilized apartment?"

I slap his hand on the table. "You have a rent-stabilized apartment?"

He tugs his hand back. "I've had it since college. Shared it with two other people until I could afford it on my own."

"How many bathrooms?" I ask.

"Two."

"Pictures?"

He pulls his phone out and scrolls for a beat, then hands it over. I was expecting photos where the apartment was incidental. These were obviously taken by a real estate photographer. It's a gorgeous, airy, tastefully minimalist apartment. Also, it's extremely clean, which: hot.

The bedrooms are small, but there are three of them, and the main bathroom has a gigantic double vanity. It's the stuff of New York dreams.

"Why do you just . . . have these?" I say. "Is this your version of porn?"

"A page covered in red ink is my version of porn," he says. "I have the pictures because I was considering subletting while I'm here."

"Libby and her family," I say. "When I win this bet, they get the apartment."

He scoffs. "You're not serious."

"I've done more unpleasant things for less of a reward. Remember Blake?"

He considers for a moment. "Okay, Nora. You do everything on that list, and the apartment is yours."

"Indefinitely?" I clarify. "You sublet it to them for as long as they want, and find somewhere else to live when you go back?"

He gives a kind of growly snort. "Sure," he says, "but it's not going to happen."

"Are you in your right mind right now?" I say. "Because if we shake on this, it *is* happening."

His gaze holds mine and he reaches across the table. When I take his hand, the friction feels like it could light a fire. A shiver races up between my shoulder blades.

I only remember to let go of his hand because, at that moment, the salad and cacio e pepe show up in a cloud of the most heavenly scent imaginable, carried by the bowl-cut server, and Charlie and I startle apart like we just got caught in flagrante on the table.

After that, we waste no time with small talk, instead shoveling handmade pasta into our mouths for ten minutes straight.

By the time we finish, most of the two-top tables have been dragged together for larger groups, their chairs rearranged so parties can combine, the laughter swelling to overtake the soft Italian music and clink of wineglasses, the smell of bread and buttery sauces denser than ever.

"I wonder where Blake is now," I say. "I hope he found happiness with that minuscule hostess."

"I hope he's been mistaken for a wanted criminal and picked up by the FBI," Charlie says.

"He'll be released in forty-eight hours," I add. "But until then, he will *not* have a great time." Charlie outright smiles, and I add, "I just hope his interrogator isn't as tall as me. That's a bridge too far."

"I think you should know something." Charlie's voice fades to a rasp as he leans across the table, goose bumps racing up my legs as his calf brushes mine.

I scoot forward too, our knees fitting together under us, like interlocking fingers this time: his, mine, his, mine.

He whispers, *"You're not that tall."*

I whisper back, "I'm as tall as you."

"*I'm* not that tall," he says.

What my body hears is, *Let's make out.*

"Yes, but for men," I say, "there's no such thing as *too* tall."

He holds my gaze far too seriously for this very unserious conversation. My skin buzzes, like my blood is made of iron fillings and his eyes are magnets sweeping over them.

"There isn't for women either. There's just tall women," he says, "and the men too insecure to date them."

15

⁓

WE AMBLE DOWN the dark road in near silence, but the air hums with an electric charge between us.

"You don't have to walk me all the way to the cottage," I finally say.

"It's on my way," Charlie says.

I cast him a disbelieving look.

His head tilts, streetlight lancing his face. I'm not sure anyone on the planet has nicer eyebrows than this man. Of course, I'm not sure I've ever *noticed* a man's eyebrows before, so it might just be that my general under-stimulation during publishing's slow season has forced me to find new interests. "Fine," he relents. "It's not far *out* of my way."

At the edge of town, the sidewalk gives way to a grassy shoulder, but tonight I'm wearing sensible shoes. On our right, a narrow footpath winds into the foliage. "What's through there?"

"Woods," he says.

"I got that much," I say. "Where does it go?"

He runs a hand over his face. "To the cottage."

"Wait, like a shortcut?"

"More or less."

"Is there a reason we're not taking it?"

He arches a brow. "I didn't take you for the hiking-in-the-dead-of-night type?"

I push past him.

"Stephens," he says. "You don't have to prove anything." His faintly spicy scent catches up to me before he does, so familiar and yet surprising, notes of cinnamon and orange that are much stronger on him than they are on me. "Let's just go back and follow the road." Overhead, an owl hoots, and he ducks his head and throws his arms over it protectively.

"Wait." I cut him a glance, stop. "Are you . . . afraid of the dark?"

"Of course not," he growls, starting down the path again. "I'm just surprised how far you're taking this small-town-transformation thing. And just so you know, those bangs do *not* make you more approachable. You just look like a hot assassin in an expensive wig."

"All I just heard," I say, "is *hot* and *expensive*."

"If I showed you a Rorschach blot, you'd find *hot* and *expensive* somewhere in there."

My gaze catches over his shoulder. Just beyond the trail, a stream funnels over a small waterfall, massive rocks jutting up like teeth on either side of it to form a swimming hole. A break in the tree cover lets moonlight pool on its center, turning the frothy water into a landscape of shimmering silver spirals.

"Number six," I exhale.

Charlie follows my gaze, his brow furrowing. "There is absolutely no way."

The urge to surprise him surges like a tidal wave. But there's something else too. In college, I was always the Party Mom, the one who made sure no one fell down stairs or drank anything they hadn't seen poured. With Libby, I'm the doting-slash-worrying older sister. For my clients, the hard-ass who argues and presses and negotiates.

Here, I realize abruptly, I'm none of those things. I don't have to be, not with obsessive, organized, responsible Charlie Lastra. So I step onto the nearest boulder and kick off my shoes.

"*Nora*," he groans. "You're not serious."

I peel my dress over my shoulders. "Why not? Are there alligators?"

I look back at him in time to catch his eyes cutting up from my underwear, instinctively snagging on my bra for a split second before launching to my face with a clench of his jaw.

"Sharks?" I ask.

"Only you," he says.

"Leeches? Nuclear waste?"

"Regular waste isn't bad enough?" he says.

"I'm not making *you* get in," I say.

"Not until you start drowning."

I sit on the rock, dangling my legs into the cool water. A shiver breaks across my shoulder blades. "I'm a very proficient swimmer." I slip into the stream, suppressing a yelp.

"Cold?" Charlie says, tone self-satisfied.

"Balmy," I reply, wading deeper until the water reaches my chest. "I would have to try *very* hard to drown in this."

He steps up to the ledge. "At least the bacterial infection will come easily."

"I would've thought this was some kind of Sunshine Falls rite of passage," I say.

"Do I seem like the kind of person who would honor local rites of passage?"

"Well, your boots are Sandro and I've seen you wear luxury cashmere at least thrice," I say, "so maybe not."

"Capsule wardrobe," he says, like this explains everything. "I only buy things that can be worn with everything else I already own, and that I know I like enough to wear for years. It's an investment."

"*Such* a city person," I sing.

He rolls his eyes. "You know this doesn't count for number six, right? Maybe in Manhattan they consider this skinny-dipping, but in Sunshine Falls we'd call that getup 'a glorified bathing suit.'"

Another challenge.

I'm a woman possessed. I sink beneath the water, unclasp my bra, and hurl it at him. It thwacks against his chest. "Closer," he allows, lifting the dainty black lace strap to examine it in the moonlight. "All this," he says seriously, "wasted on Blake Carlisle."

"I exclusively own pretty underwear," I say. "They're bound to be wasted occasionally."

"Spoken like a true lady of luxury."

I drift backward, knees bent, toes gliding along the smooth stone creek bed. "I think we've proven that, of the two of us, *you* are the aristocrat here. *I'm* skinny-dipping. In a local watering hole. Whereas you can't even swim."

He rolls his eyes. "I can swim."

"Charlie," I say. "It's okay. There's no shame in the truth."

"Remember when you used to pretend to be polite?"

"Do you miss it?"

"Not at all." He tugs his shirt over his head and discards it on the rocks. "You're way more fun this way." When his pants are halfway off, I remember to look away, and a moment later, when the water breaks, I spin to find him wincing at the cold slosh against his stomach.

"*Shit!*" he gasps. "Shit-fuck!"

"Such a way with words." I swim toward him. "It's not that bad."

"Is it possible you don't have any pain receptors?" he hisses.

"Not only possible but probable," I reply. "I've been told I feel nothing."

Charlie frowns. "Whoever said that clearly only met Professional Nora."

"Most people do."

"Poor assholes," he says, almost affectionately. The same voice in which he said *Of course you did* when I told him I met my agenting goals eight months early.

I stop close enough to see his skin prickling. The droplets on his throat and jaw catch the moonlight, and my chest and thighs tingle in response.

I drift backward as he wades toward me, maintaining the gap between us. "What other Sunshine Falls rites of passage did you ignore?"

The muscles along his jaw shadow as he thinks. "People are really into bouldering here."

"Let me guess," I say. "That's when you stand at the top of a mountain and wait for one of your enemies to walk by, then push a rock over the ledge."

"Close," he says. "It's when you climb boulders."

"For . . . what reason?"

"To get to the top, presumably."

"And then?"

His golden shoulder lifts in a shrug, water sluicing down his chest. "Probably there's another boulder, and then you climb to the top of that one. Human beings are a mysterious species, Nora. I once watched a bike courier get hit by a car, get up, and scream *I become God* at the top of his lungs before riding off in the opposite direction."

"What's mysterious about that?" I say. "He tested the limits of his own mortality and found they didn't exist."

Charlie's pouty mouth tugs to one side in a half smirk. "That's what I love about New York."

"So many bike couriers with god complexes."

"You're never the weirdest person in the room."

"There's always that person in silver body paint," I agree, "who asks for donations to repair his UFO."

"He's my Q train favorite," Charlie says.

My skin warms. I wonder how many times we've passed each other in our city of millions.

"I like that you're anonymous there," he continues. "You're whoever you decide to be. In places like this, you never shake off what people first thought about you."

I swim closer. He doesn't retreat. "And what did they think of you?"

"Not huge fans," he says.

"Mrs. Struthers is," I point out, "and—your ex is too." I shoot him a glance and sink lower in the water to hide the way my body lights up under his gaze.

I don't feel like Nadine Winters when he's this close. I feel like I'm sugar under a blowtorch, like he's caramelizing my blood.

"Mrs. Struthers liked me because I fucking loved school," he says. "I mean, once I figured out how to actually read. Didn't exactly make me a hit with other kids, though. In high school, things weren't as bad, and then eventually . . ."

"You got hot," I say somberly.

His laugh grates over my skin. "I was going to say 'I moved to New York.'"

We've stopped moving. Heat corkscrews through my rib cage, coiling tighter with each spiral.

I clear my throat enough to joke, "And *then* you got hot."

"Actually," he says, "that only happened four or five weeks ago.

There was this big meteor shower, and I made a wish and . . ." Charlie holds his arms out as he drifts closer.

My heart feels light and jittery in my chest, my limbs incongruently heavy. "So you're saying Amaya's expression was less about longing than outright shock over your new face."

"I didn't notice Amaya's expression," he says.

My mouth goes dry, heaviness gathering between my thighs. He catches a bead of water as it trickles over my cupid's bow. My lips part, the pad of his finger lingering on my bottom lip.

I'm acutely aware of how flimsy the space is between us now, slippery, finite, closable. Maybe this is why people take trips, for that feeling of your real life liquefying around you, like nothing you do will tug on any other strand of your carefully built world.

It's a feeling not unlike reading a really good book: all-consuming, worry-obliterating.

Usually I live like I'm trying to see four moves ahead in a chess game, but right now I can't seem to think past the next five minutes. It takes a lot of effort to say, "You probably want to get home."

He shakes his head. "But if you do . . ."

I shake my head.

For a moment, nothing happens. It feels like there's a silent negotiation happening between us. His hand catches mine under the water. After a beat, he draws me toward him, slowly—plenty of time for either of us to pull away.

My fingers brush his hip instead, and the chessboard in my mind disintegrates.

His other hand finds my waist, closing the gap between us. The feeling of being pressed against him is somewhere between bliss and torture. A small sound sighs out of me. He doesn't tease me for it. Instead his hands cut a slow path down my sides, tucking each inch of me against him: chest, stomach, hips flush, all my softest parts against all his hardest, my thighs settling loose around his hips. His thumbs catch on the curves of my hips, and a gravelly hum rumbles through him.

My nipples pinch against his skin, and his arms tighten across my back.

We're both silent, like any word could break the spell of the silver moonlight.

Our lips catch lightly once, then draw apart, slip together a little deeper. His hands follow the curve of my back lower, curling around me, squeezing me to him, rolling his hips into mine.

My mouth feels like it's melting under his, like I'm wax and he's the burning wick down my center. One of his hands curls around my jaw, the other sweeping up to cup my breast as my thighs wrap tight around him. My breath catches against his mouth when his thumb rolls across my nipple. He hitches me higher, everything to my belly button above the water now, exposed to the moonlight, and he's looking, touching, tasting his way across me.

My brain grapples for control of my short-circuiting body. "Should we think about this?"

"Think?" He says it like he's never heard the word. Another hungry, stomach-flipping kiss erases it from my vocabulary too. My hands twist into his hair. His mouth moves down the side of my throat, teeth sinking into my collarbone.

I'm trying to think my way through this, but it feels like I'm a passenger in a very willing body.

Charlie teases against my ear, "You should never wear clothes, Nora." My laugh dies in my throat as he pins me against one of the flat rocks at the edge of the water, my hips locking around his, sensation flaming through my thighs at the friction between us, at the push of his stomach and his erection shifting against me through our underwear.

Charlie kisses like no one I've ever been with. Like someone who takes the time to figure out how things work.

Every tilt of my hips, arch of my spine, shallow breath guides him, landmarks on a map he's making of my body.

He hums my name into my skin. It sounds as much like a swear as when I slammed into him at Poppa Squat's, his voice sizzling through me until I feel like a struck tuning fork.

His lips drag down my throat to my chest, his breath ragged as he draws me into his mouth. His fingers circle my wrists against the rock, our hips moving in a hungry rhythm.

"*Shit*," he hisses, but at least this time, he's not slingshotting away from me. His hands are still everywhere. His mouth hasn't left my skin. "I don't want to stop."

My mind's still half-heartedly warring for control. My body makes the unilateral decision to say, "Then don't."

"We have to talk about this first," he says. "Things are complicated for me right now." And yet we're still clamoring for each other. Charlie's hands raze over my thighs, squeezing so hard I might bruise. My nails are in his back, urging him close. His warm mouth skims over my shoulder, his tongue and teeth finding my pulse at the base of my throat.

I nod. "Then talk."

Another sharp kiss, his teeth hard against my lip, his hands hard against my ass. "It's hard to think in words right now, Nora."

His hands wind into my hair, his mouth slipping against the corner of mine, his breath shallow and frantic. I lift myself against him and one of his hands curls tight against my spine, his groan crackling through me like a dozen bolts of lightning heading straight to my center.

Everything else is briefly obliterated as I roll myself against him, and he returns the favor, the friction between us electric.

"God, Nora," he hisses.

Something like *I know* slips out of me, right into his mouth. His fingers dig under the lace at the sides of my hips, burrowing into my skin. I've never felt someone else's frustration so palpably; I've never been so frustrated. I'm seeing spots, everything lost behind a wall of need.

And then my phone rings from the rocks.

All at once, reality crashes in from all sides, a rock slide of thoughts my lust has been holding back. I push back from Charlie, gasping out, "Dusty!"

He blinks at me through the dark, chest heaving. "What?"

"Shit! No! No!" I swim for the rocks, the ringer echoing through the dark.

"What's wrong?" Charlie asks, close behind me.

"I was supposed to call Dusty. Hours ago." I haul myself out of the water and rush for the phone. I miss the last ring by seconds, and when I dial back, it goes straight to voicemail. "Shit!"

How could I do that? How could I just forget about my oldest, most sensitive, highest-earning client? How could I let myself get this distracted?

I dial again and get her voicemail message. "Hey, Dusty!" I say brightly after the beep. "Sorry about that. I had a . . ."

What could I possibly be busy with this late at night? No *respectable* meeting, certainly.

"Something came up," I say. "But I'm free now, so give me a call back!"

I hang up, then skim Libby's string of messages, increasingly frantic requests for me to confirm that Blake hasn't fed me to a wood chipper. My heart rockets into my throat, and hot, prickling shame rises to the surface of my skin. On my way home, I text Libby.

"Everything okay?"

I turn and find Charlie pulling on his pants, his shirt bundled in one hand. "What happened?" he asks.

I wasn't there, I think. *They needed me and I wasn't there. Just like*—I cut myself off before my mind can boomerang back there, say instead, "I don't do this."

Charlie's brow arches. "Do what?"

"Everything that just happened," I say. "All of it. This isn't how I operate."

He half laughs. "And what, you think this is a pattern for me?"

"No," I say. "I mean, maybe. That's the point! How would I even know?" His smile falls, and my chest stings in response. I shake my head. "It's this book, *Frigid*, and this trip—I started thinking I could just go with this, but . . ." I lift my phone at my side, like this explains everything. Libby's pre-baby crisis, Dusty's intense insecurity, not to mention all my other clients, everyone who's counting on me. "I can't afford a distraction right now."

"Distraction." He repeats the word emptily, like he's unfamiliar with the concept. Probably he is. For a solid decade, *I* was.

Prioritization. Compartmentalization. Qualification. These things have always worked for me in the past, but now just one sprinkle of recklessness has distracted me from both my sister and my prize client. After what happened with Jakob, I should've known I couldn't trust myself.

I force down the hard knot in my throat. "I need to be focused," I say. "I owe that to Dusty."

When I'm distracted, I miss things. When I miss things, bad things happen.

Charlie studies me for a long moment. "If that's what you want."

"It is," I say.

His brow slightly lifts, his eyes reading the obvious lie. It doesn't matter. *Want* is not a good way to make decisions.

"And besides," I add, "things are complicated for you anyway, right?"

After a beat, he sighs. "More every second."

Still, neither of us moves. We're in a silent standoff, waiting to see if the dam holds, the pressure building between us, my cells all still vibrating under his gaze.

Charlie looks away first. He rubs the side of his jaw. "You're right. I don't know why it's so hard for me to accept this can't be anything." He snatches my dress off the rock and holds it out.

My stomach sinks, but I accept the dress. "Thanks."

Without looking at me, he says dryly, "What are colleagues for?"

16

CRAWL OUT OF bed at nine, my head pounding and my stomach feeling like a half-wrecked boat lost at sea. Apparently I drank enough to poison myself, without even getting past tipsy. One of the many ways that being thirty-two absolutely rules.

Libby's already moving around downstairs, humming to herself. I'm not surprised—despite her panicky messages last night, she was already fast asleep and loudly snoring by the time I got home. Dusty had finally called me back, and I'd paced, damp, through the meadow for an hour, convincing her Part Two of *Frigid* couldn't possibly be as bad as she was convinced it was. Bleary-eyed, I check my phone, and sure enough, the new pages are waiting in my inbox.

I am *not* ready for that. After pulling on leggings and a sports bra, I stagger outside, rubbing heat into my arms as I cross the meadow. I shamble through the woods, clutching my stomach, until the nausea eases enough to jog.

Okay, I think. *This is going all right.* It's more of a positive affirmation than an observation. I follow the sloping path through the woods to the fence and make it three more paces before *This is going all right* becomes *Oh, god, no.* I pitch over my thighs and vomit into the mud just as a voice cuts through the morning: "You okay, ma'am?"

I whirl toward the fence, swiping the back of my hand across my mouth.

The blond demigod is leaning against the far side of the fence, no more than four feet away.

Of course he is.

"Fine," I force out. I clear my throat and grimace at the taste. "Just drank a bathtub's worth of alcohol last night."

He laughs. It's a great laugh. Probably his scream of terror is even fairly pleasant. "I've been there."

Wow, he's tall.

"I'm Shepherd," he says.

"Like the . . . job?" I ask.

"And my family owns the stable," he says. "Go ahead and laugh."

"I would never," I say. "I have a terrible sense of humor." I start to stretch out my hand, then remember where it's recently been (vomit) and drop it. "I'm Nora."

He laughs again, a clear silver-bell sound. "You staying at Goode's Lily?"

I nod. "My sister and I are visiting from New York."

"Ah, big-city folk," he jokes, eyes sparkling.

"I know, we're the worst," I play along. "But maybe Sunshine Falls will convert us."

The corners of his eyes crinkle. "It'll certainly do that."

"Are you from here originally?"

"All my life," he says, "minus a short stint in Chicago."

"City life wasn't for you?" I guess.

His huge shoulders lift. "Northern winters certainly weren't."

"Sure," I say. I'm personally pro-season—but it's a familiar complaint.

People basically leave New York because they're cold, claustrophobic, tired, or financially overwhelmed. Over the years, most of my college friends frittered off to Midwestern cities that are less expensive or suburbs with huge lawns and white picket fences, or else left in one of the mass exoduses to L.A. that comes every few winters.

There are easier places to live, but New York's a city filled with hungry people, their shared want a thrumming energy.

Shepherd pats the fence. "Well, I'll let you get back to your . . ." I swear he glances toward my vomit pile. ". . . run," he finishes diplomatically, turning to go. "But if you need a tour guide while you're here, Nora from New York, I'm happy to help."

I call after him. "How should I . . . get ahold of you?"

He looks back, grinning. "It's a small town. We'll run into each other."

I take it as the world's most gentle brush-off right up until the second he shoots me a wink, the first hot wink I've ever seen in real life.

∼

Ever since I finished recounting what happened, Libby's just been staring at me.

"What's happening inside your brain right now?" I ask.

"I'm trying to decide whether to be impressed you went skinnydipping, annoyed you went with Charlie, or just grovelingly sorry for setting you up on such a terrible date."

"Don't be so hard on yourself," I say. "I'm sure if I'd cut off the bottom six inches of my legs at the table, he would've been perfectly pleasant."

"I'm so sorry, Sissy," she cries. "I swear he seemed normal in his messages."

"Don't blame Blake. *I'm* the one with this giant flesh sack."

"Seriously, what an asshole!" Libby shakes her head. "God, I'm sorry. Let's just forget about number five. It was a bad idea."

"No!" I say quickly.

"No?" She seems confused.

After last night, I would *love* to throw the towel in, but there's also Charlie's apartment to think about. If I back out of our deal now, then everything that happened was for nothing. At least this way, something good can come out of it.

"I'm gonna stick with it," I say. "I mean, we have a *checklist*."

"Really?" Libby claps her hands together, beaming. "That's great! I'm so proud of you, Sissy, getting out of your shell—which reminds me! I spoke to Sally about number twelve, and she'd love help sprucing up Goode Books."

"When did you even talk to her?" I say.

"We've exchanged a few emails," she says with a shrug. "Did you know that she painted the mural in the children's section of the shop?"

Considering Libby bakes her gluten-intolerant mail carrier a special pie every December, I shouldn't be surprised she's also having in-depth email correspondence with our Airbnb host.

My pulse spikes at the buzz of my phone. Mercifully, the message isn't from Charlie.

It's from Brendan. Which is rare. When you scroll through our thread, it's a riveting back-and-forth of Happy birthday! interspersed with cute pictures of Bea and Tala.

Hi, Nora. Hope the trip is going well. Is Libby all right?

"What's this about?" I hold my phone out, and she leans forward to read, her lips tightening to a purse.

"Tell him I'll call him later."

"Yes, ma'am, and which calls *do* you want forwarded to your office?"

She rolls her eyes. "I don't want to go upstairs and get my phone right now. The world won't end if Brendan doesn't hear from me every twenty-five minutes."

The impatience in her voice catches me off guard. I've seen her and Brendan argue before, and it's basically like watching two people swing feathers in each other's general direction. *This* is real irritation.

Are they fighting? About the apartment, or the trip, maybe?

Or is this trip happening *because* they're fighting?

The thought instantly nauseates me. I try to put it out of my head—Libby and Brendan are obsessed with each other. I might've missed some things over the last few months, but I would've noticed something like *that*.

Besides, she's been calling him every day.

Except you've never seen her call him. I've just assumed that somewhere, in those nine hours we're apart each afternoon, she's been talking to him.

A cold sweat breaks along the back of my neck. My throat twists and tightens, but Libby doesn't seem to notice. She's smiling coolly as she hauls herself out of her Adirondack chair.

You're overthinking this. She just left her phone upstairs.

"Anyway, let's go," she says. "Goode Books isn't going to save itself. Goode Books *aren't* going to save *themselves*? Whatever. You get it."

I type out a quick reply to Brendan. Everything's good. She says she'll call you later. He answers immediately with a smiley face and a thumbs-up.

Everything's fine. I'm here. I'm focused. I'll fix it.

I would like to say that, having realized everything at stake on this trip, the spell of Charlie Lastra instantly lifted. Instead, every time his eyes cut from Libby to me, there's a flash in his irises that makes me wonder how long it would take to peel off my clothes.

"You want," he drawls, eyes back on my sister, "to give Goode Books a makeover?"

"We're giving it a head-to-toe *revitalization*." Libby's fingertips press together in excitement. Her skin is sun-kissed and the bags beneath her eyes are almost entirely gone. She looks not only rested but downright exhilarated by the opportunity to mop a dusty bookstore.

Charlie leans into the counter. "This is for the list?" His eyes tick toward mine, flashing again. My body reacts like he's touching me. Our gazes hold, the corner of his mouth curving like, *I know what you're thinking*.

"He knows about the list?" Libby asks, then, to Charlie, "You know about the list?"

He faces her again, rubs his jaw. "We don't have a budget for 'revitalization.'"

"All the furniture will be secondhand," she says. "I have the thrift-store magic touch. I was grown in a lab for this. Just point us in the direction of your cleaning supplies."

Charlie's eyes return to me, pupils flaring. If I were to look down, I'm confident I'd find my clothes reduced to a pile of ash at my feet. "You won't even know we're here," I manage.

"I doubt that," he says.

~

Another "universal truth" Austen could've started *Pride and Prejudice* with: When you tell yourself not to think about something, it will be all that you can think about.

Thusly, while Libby's running me ragged cleaning Goode Books, scrubbing scuff marks off the floor, I'm thinking about kissing Charlie. And while I'm reshelving biographies in the newly appointed nonfiction section, I'm actually counting how many times and where I catch him looking at me.

When I'm poring over the new portion of *Frigid* back in the café, tugging on its plot strings and nudging at its trapdoors, my mind invariably finds its way back to Charlie pinning me against a boulder, his rasp in my ear: *It's hard to think in words right now, Nora.*

It's hard to think, period, unless it's about the one thing I should *not* be thinking about.

Even now, walking back into town with Libby for the "secret surprise" she planned for us, I'm only two-thirds present. Determined to wrangle that last third into submission, I ask, "Am I dressed okay?"

Without breaking stride, Libby squeezes my arm. "*Perfect.* A goddess among mortals."

I look down at my jeans and yellow silk tank, trying to guess what they might be "perfect" for.

Out of the corner of my eye, I do another quick audit of her body language. I've been watching her closely since the weird text from Brendan, but nothing's seemed amiss.

When we were kids, she used to beg Mrs. Freeman to let her reshelve books, and now her efforts to update Goode Books have turned her into bizarro Belle, right down to singing the "provincial life" song into her broom handle while Charlie shoots me fiery *make-it-stop* glares.

"I can't help you," I finally told him. "I have no jurisdiction here."

To which Libby yelled from across the shop, "I'm a wild stallion, baby!"

When we finally left for the day, she forced me into Hardy's cab to scout furniture at every secondhand shop in greater Asheville. Whenever we *did* find something perfect for the Goode Books café, Libby insisted on 1) haggling and 2) talking to literally everyone, about literally anything.

The work has energized her, whereas I'm fervently hoping tonight's surprise excursion ends at Sunshine Falls's lone spa. Though it *is* called Spaaaahhh, which gives me pause. It's unclear whether that's meant to be read as a sigh or a scream. Either the same deranged person owns that, Mug + Shot, *and* Curl Up N Dye, or there's something extremely punny in the Sunshine Falls water supply.

Libby passes Spaaaahhh and we round the corner to a wide, pink-brick building with two-story arched windows, a gabled roof, and a bell tower. On one side sits a half-full parking lot, and on the other, a few kids with dirt-smeared knees play kickball in an overgrown baseball diamond with gnats swarming the fence behind home plate.

"Here for the big game?" I ask Libby.

She tugs me up the building's steps and into a musty lobby. A horde of teens in ballet tights runs past, shrieking and laughing, to race up the stairwell on our right. A half dozen younger kids in colorful leotards are sprawled on the floor wiping down blue gymnastics mats.

Libby says, "I think it's through there." We step over and around the tiny gymnasts and turn through another set of doors into a spacious room filled with echoing chatter and folding chairs. To my relief, no one is wearing a leotard, so probably we're not here for a pregnant gymnastics class, which definitely strikes me as something Libby would sign us up for.

I spot Sally near the front, grabbing an older blond man's shoulder as she laughs (and, I'm pretty sure, sucks on a vape pen). A few rows behind her are the hip Mug + Shot barista with the septum ring and Amaya, Charlie's Pretty Bartender Ex.

Libby pulls me into the last row, where we take two seats just as someone pounds a gavel at the front of the room.

There's a stage there, but the podium sits on the ground, level with the chairs. The woman behind it has the largest, reddest hair I've ever seen, the only lights on in the room shining on her like a diffused spotlight.

"Let's get started, people!" she barks, and the crowd quiets as piano music seeps down from upstairs.

I lean into Libby, hissing, "Did you bring me to a witch trial?"

"The first item we're considering," the redhead says, "is a complaint against the business at 1480 Main Street, currently known as Mug and Shot."

"Wait," I say. "Are we—"

Libby shushes me just as the barista leaps out of her seat, spinning to a balding man a few seats over. "We're not changing our name again, Dave!"

"It sounds," Dave booms, "like a place for vagabonds and criminals!"

"You weren't happy with *Bean to Be Wild*—"

"It's a weak pun," Dave reasons.

"You threw a *fit* when we were *Some Like It Hot*."

"It's practically pornographic!"

The redhead pounds the gavel. Amaya pulls the barista back into her seat. "We'll put it to a vote. All in favor of renaming Mug and Shot." A few hands go up, Dave's included. She pounds the gavel again. "Motion dismissed."

"There is absolutely no way any of this holds up in a court of law," I whisper, amazed.

"What'd I miss?"

I jump in my seat as Charlie slides into the chair beside me. "Not much. 'Dave' just filed a motion to rename every Peter in town to something less pornographic."

"Did anyone cry yet?" Charlie asks.

"People cry?" I whisper.

He drops his mouth beside my ear. "Next time try not to look so excited at the thought of misery. It'll help you blend in better."

"Considering we're in the hecklers-only section of the crowd, I'm not all that worried about blending in," I whisper back. "What are *you* doing here?"

"My civic duty."

I fix him with a look.

"There's a vote my mom's excited about. I'm nothing but a hand in the air. I'm glad I came now though—I finished the new pages. I've got notes."

I spin toward him, the end of my nose nearly brushing his in the dark. "Already?"

"I think we should try starting the book at Nadine's accident," he whispers.

I laugh. Several people in the row in front of us glare at me. Libby smacks me in the boob, and I smile apologetically. When our audience returns to watching the *new* argument at the front of the room, between a man and woman whose combined age must top two hundred, I face Charlie again, who smirks. "Guess you needed help blending in after all."

"The accident's fifty pages in," I hiss back. "We lose all context."

"I don't think we do." He shakes his head. "I'd like to at least suggest it to Dusty and see what she thinks."

I shake *my* head. "She'll think you hate the first fifty pages of the one hundred she's sent you."

"You know how badly I wanted this book," he says, "just based on those first ten. I simply want it to be its best version, same as you. *And* Dusty. By the way, what did you think about the cat?"

I worry at my lip and get a shot of pure, undiluted satisfaction at the way he watches the action. I let the pause go longer than is strictly natural. "I'm worried it feels too similar to the dog in *Once*."

Charlie blinks. I see the moment he finds his place in the conversation again. "My thoughts exactly."

"We'd have to see where she plans to take it," I say.

"We just mention the similarity and let her make the call," he agrees.

The redhead pounds her gavel, but the old man and woman at the front keep shouting at each other for twenty more seconds. When she finally gets them to stop, they—no joke—nod, take each other's hands, and head back to their seats together. "This is like something out of *Macbeth*," I marvel.

"You should see how holiday event planning goes," he says. "It's a bloodbath. Best day of the year."

I smother a laugh with the back of my hand. His face twitches, and my heart flutters at the extraordinarily pleased look on his face. In my mind I hear him saying, *You're way more fun this way.*

I turn away before the look can sink any deeper into my bloodstream.

"What did you make of Nadine's motivations?" he whispers, managing to make the words sound innately sexual. Four different points on my body start tingling.

Focus. "For which part?"

"Running across the street before the sign changed to *WALK*," he clarifies, the decision that lands Nadine in the hospital, when a bus clips her.

That's right: my proxy nearly dies fifty pages into the book. Or on page one, if Charlie has his way.

"I wonder if having her be in a legitimate rush undermines Dusty's argument," I whisper. "We're supposed to think this woman is a cold, selfish shark. Maybe she should be rushing for rushing's sake, because that's what she does."

I swear Charlie's eyes flash in the dark. "You would've made a good editor, Stephens."

"And by that," I say, "you mean you agree with me."

"I think we need to see Nadine exactly as the world sees her, before the curtain gets pulled back."

I study him. He's got a point. It's always a strange thing, working with only a chunk of a book, not knowing for certain what comes next—especially for someone who doesn't even like reading that way—but I know Dusty's writing like my own heartbeat, and I have a sense Charlie's right on this one.

"So," he whispers, "you'll tell her about the first fifty?"

"I'll ask her," I parry. Even when we're agreeing with each other, our conversations feel less like we're taking turns carrying the torch and more like we're playing table tennis while said table is on fire.

Charlie holds out his hand to shake on it. I hesitate before sliding my palm into his, this one careful touch unraveling pieces of the other night across my mind like film reels. His pupils expand, the golden wisps around them smoldering, and his pulse leaps at the base of his throat.

Being able to read each other so well is going to make this "business relationship" complicated.

Where his thigh *not quite* touches mine, it feels like a piping hot knife held against butter.

Someone near the front of the room gives a hacking stage cough that pops the bubble. All around us, arms are in the air—including Libby's. Sally is twisted around in her chair, coughing in our direction, her hand over her head.

Charlie jerks his hand free and thrusts it up. Sally's eyes cut to mine next, almost pleading. When I lift my hand, she grins and spins back around in her chair.

While the red-haired woman is counting the votes, I lean in to ask Libby, "What exactly are we voting on?"

"Weren't you listening? They're putting a statue in the town square!"

"Of what?"

Charlie snorts. Libby beams. "What else?" she says. "Old Man Whittaker and his dog!"

A literal *statue* to *Once in a Lifetime*.

I turn to Charlie, ready to taunt him, but he meets my gaze with a wicked smile. "Go ahead and try, Stephens; nothing is going to ruin my night."

My adrenaline spikes at the challenge, but this is too dangerous a game for me to play with him, when my grip on self-control is already so tenuous. Instead I force a placid, professional smile and turn back to face the front of the room.

I spend the rest of the meeting stuck in a worse game with myself: *Don't think about touching Charlie's hand. Don't think about the lightning strikes in Charlie's eyes. Don't think about any of it. Focus.*

17

~

T O MY SURPRISE, Dusty's on board with the cuts. Within an hour of promising to get her formal notes soon, Charlie sends me a five-page document on *Frigid*'s first act.

I examine it in the café while Libby's reorganizing the children's book room and singing an off-key rendition of "My Favorite Things," but replacing all of the listed *things* with her own preferences: *Books with no dog ears and shiny new covers, cleaning and shelving and reading 'bout lovers!*

I send Charlie's document back with sixty-four tracked changes, and he replies within minutes, as if we aren't twenty-five feet apart, with him at the register and me in the café.

You're absolutely vicious, Stephens.

I write back, I have a reputation to uphold.

I hear the low laugh in the next room as clearly as if his lips were pressed to my stomach.

In the used and rare book room, Libby's singing, *Shop-cats in windows and full-caf iced coffee.*

Isn't this praise a little overboard? Charlie emails me. Perhaps referring to the forty-odd compliments I inserted into his document.

You love the pages, I reply. I just added details.

It just seems inefficient and condescending to spend so much time talking about things she doesn't need to change.

If you tell Dusty to cut a bunch of stuff, but don't make it clear what's working, you risk losing the good stuff.

We volley the document back and forth until we're satisfied, then send it off. I don't expect to hear from Dusty for days. Her reply dings two hours later.

> So many great ideas here. A lot to think about, and I'll get
> to work on incorporating the changes. Only thing is, we
> need to keep the cat. In the meantime, I've finished
> cleaning the next hundred pages (attached).

She sends me a private email, its subject reading But seriously and the body reading can you just be my coeditor forever? I'm actually excited to get started. X

I feel like a lit-up light bulb, all hot and glowy with pride. Charlie sends me another message, and all that heat tightens, like one of those snakes-in-a-can gag gifts being reset for another go.

I think we might be good together, Stephens.

A very small star lodges itself in my diaphragm. I reply, yes, together we add up to one emotionally competent human, a real accomplishment, then listen for his gruff laugh.

But another sound draws my attention to the window—Libby's voice, muffled by the glass but still half shouting, obviously frustrated. I follow the maze of shelves toward the front of the store, where I can see her through the window out on the sidewalk, her phone pressed to her ear and one hand shielding her eyes against the sun.

Her posture is defensive, her shoulders lifted, elbows tucked in against her sides. She gives a frustrated huff, says something else, and hangs up. I start toward the front door to meet her, but she hitches her purse up her shoulder and takes off across the street, turning to the right and briskly marching off.

I freeze midstep, my stomach bottoming out.

What just happened?

My phone chirps, and I jump at the sound. It's a message from Libby. Had some errands to run! Should be home around eight.

I swallow a fist-sized glob of tension and write back, Anything I can help with? Not much work to do today after all. A blatant lie, but she's not here to see that in my face.

Nope! she says. Enjoying the Me Time—no offense. See you later!

I walk back to my computer in a daze. It feels like a sort of betrayal, but I don't know what else to do at this point, weeks into this trip and no closer to any answers. I text Brendan.

Hey, how are things back home? Did Libby ever get back to you?

He answers immediately. Things are good! Yep, we caught up! All good there?

I try fourteen different versions of *What's wrong with my sister* before accepting she'd *definitely* be furious with me if she found out I'd asked him. The rules that govern family dynamics are nonsensical, but they're also rigid. Mom knew exactly how to get us to open up, but I'm increasingly feeling like I'm in a booby-trapped cave, Libby's heart on a dais in the center. Every step I take risks making things worse.

All good! I write back to Brendan and turn my focus to work. Or try to.

The rest of the afternoon, customers come and go, but for the most part Charlie and I are the only two people in the shop, and I've never been less productive.

After a while, he texts from the desk, Where'd Julie Andrews go?

Back to the nunnery, I write. She gave up. She couldn't help you.

I have that effect, he says.

Not on Dusty, I write. She's loving you.

She's loving us, he corrects. Like I said, we're good together.

I cast around for a response and find none. The only thing I can really think about is the strained look on my sister's face and her sudden departure. Libby had some mysterious plans, I tell him.

He says, Must be the grand opening of the Dunkin' Donuts two towns over.

A minute later, he adds, you okay? Like even from separate rooms, with multiple screens between us, he is reading my mood. The thought sends a strange hollow ache out through my limbs. Something like loneliness. Something like Ebenezer Scrooge watching his nephew Fred's Christmas party through the frosty window. An *outsideness* made all the more stark by the revelation of *insideness*.

All I really want is to go perch on the edge of Charlie's desk and tell him everything, make him laugh, let him make *me* laugh until nothing feels quite so pressing.

Fine, I write back. Afterward, I catch myself refreshing my email a couple of times and force myself to click back over to the manuscript. I'm so distracted by *trying* to distract myself, it's eight minutes after five when I next look at the clock.

The shop is silent, and I pack with the care of one trying not to wake a pride of hungry lions. I sling my bag over my shoulder and run-walk from the café, still unsure whether Charlie is the lion in the scenario or if I am.

That's what I'm pondering when I make it through the doorway and almost collide with Charlie on the other side, which might explain why I shout, "LION!"

His eyes go wide. His hands fly in front of his face (maybe he thought I meant, *Here's a lion! Catch!*), and miracle of all miracles, we both screech to a halt, landing almost toe-to-toe on the sidewalk, but touching absolutely nowhere.

My heart thrums. My chest flushes.

"I didn't know you were still here," he says.

"I am," I say.

"You always leave at five." He shifts the watering can in his left hand to his right. Behind him, the flowers in the shop's window box glisten, plump droplets clinging to their orange and pink petals and sparkling in the afternoon light. "Exactly five," Charlie adds.

"Things got busy," I lie.

His eyes dart to my chin. My skin warms ten more degrees. Quietly, he begins, "Is everything okay? You haven't seemed like—"

"Hey! Charlie!" A low, smooth voice cuts him off. Across the street, an angelic giant of a man with twin dimples and gemstone eyes is climbing out of a muddy pickup truck.

"Shepherd," Charlie says, somewhat stiffly, his chin dipping in greeting. It's not like there are daggers in his eyes, but he doesn't seem *happy* to see Shepherd either. History, subtext, backstory—whatever you want to call it, these two people have it.

"Sally asked me to drop this by," Shepherd says, thrusting a tote bag in Charlie's direction as he crosses the street toward us.

Charlie thanks him, but Shepherd's facing me now, his smile widening. "Well, well, well, if it isn't Nora from New York," he says. "Told you we'd run into each other again."

I read once that sunflowers always orient themselves to face the sun. That's what being near Charlie Lastra is like for me. There could be a raging wildfire racing toward me from the west and I'd still be straining eastward toward his warmth.

So despite being eighty percent sure Shepherd's flirting with me, of course I look straight toward Charlie. Or rather, to the shop door swinging closed behind him.

"Hey," Shepherd says. "Any chance you're free right now? I could give you that tour we talked about?"

"Um." I check my phone, but there are still no new messages from Libby. For a beat, anxiety swells on every side of me, a hundred fists banging on the doors of my mind, demanding to run loose. I shove my phone back into my bag. *Focus on something you* can *control. The list. Number five.*

Resisting the urge to glance back at the shop window, I meet Shepherd's eyes, smile, and lie through my teeth: "A tour sounds perfect."

~

We drive with the windows down, the smells of pine and sweat and sunbaked dirt braided into the wind. I've never seen anything quite like the Blue Ridge Parkway, the way its easy curves are sliced into the side of the mountains so that shaggy treetops tower over us on one side and unfurl beneath us on the other. Shepherd's a rare sight too. He has the kind of forearms that authors could spend full pages on, thick with muscle and dusted with fine golden-blond hair. He hums along to the country song on the radio, fingers drumming on the steering wheel and the clutch.

After the initial thrill of doing something spontaneous, the nerves set in. It's been a long time since I've been out with an unvetted man. Setting aside the possibility that he's a rapist, murderer, or cannibal,

I also just don't know how to talk to a man I know nothing about and am *not* considering as a long-term partner.

You can do this, Nora. You're not Nadine to him. You can be anyone. Just say something.

He finally puts me out of my misery: "So, Nora, what you do?"

"I work in publishing," I say. "I'm a literary agent."

"No kidding!" His green eyes flash from the road to me. "So you already knew Charlie, before your visit?"

My stomach drops, then surges upward in my chest. "Not really," I say noncommittally.

Shepherd laughs, a clear, booming sound. "Uh-oh. I know that look—don't judge the rest of us based on him."

I feel a swell of protectiveness—or maybe it's empathy, an understanding that this might be how people talk about me. Simultaneously though, I'm annoyed that I literally got into a stranger's car like it was a deep-space escape pod, and somehow the specter of Charlie is still here.

"He's not as bad as he seems," Shepherd goes on. "I mean, coming back here to help Sal and Clint, when pretty much all he ever wanted was to get away from . . ." He waves his hand in a sweeping arc, gesturing toward the sun-dappled road ahead of us. He turns up a side street that winds further up the foothill we've been climbing.

"So what do you do?" I say.

"I'm in construction," he says. "And I do some carpentry on the side, when I have time."

"Of course you do," I accidentally say aloud.

"What's that?" he asks, eyes twinkling like well-lit emeralds.

"I just mean, you look like a carpenter."

"Oh."

I explain, "Carpenters are famously handsome."

His brow crinkles as he grins. "Are they?"

"I mean, carpenters are the love interests in a lot of books and movies. It's a common trope. It's how you show someone's down-to-earth and patient, and hot without being shallow."

He laughs. "That doesn't sound too bad, I guess."

"Sorry, it's been awhile since I've been . . ." I stop short of saying *on a date*—which this is definitely not—and finish with the far more tragic "anywhere."

He grins, like it hasn't even occurred to him that I might have recently escaped a doomsday hatch in the ground after years of little to no socialization. "Well then, Nora from New York, I know exactly where I'm taking you."

~

I'm not much of a gasper—dramatic, audible reactions are more Libby's terrain—but when I climb out of the truck, I can't help it.

"Bet you don't have views like *that* back in New York," Shepherd says proudly.

I don't have the heart to tell him I wasn't gasping about the view. Though it *is* gorgeous, I was actually stunned by the three-quarters-built house that sits on the ridge, overlooking the valley below us. At its far side, the sun sinks toward the horizon, coating everything in a honeycomb gold that might just be my new favorite color.

But the *house*—a massive modern ranch with a back wall made entirely of glass—is blazing in the fiery wash of the sunset. "Did you build this?" I look over my shoulder to find Shepherd pulling a cooler from the bed of his trunk, along with a blue moving blanket.

"*Am* building," he corrects, knocking the tailgate shut. "It's for me, so it's taking years, between paying jobs."

"It's incredible," I say.

He sets the cooler down and shakes out the blanket. "I've wanted to live up here since I was ten years old." He gestures for me to sit.

"Did you always want to be in construction?" I tuck my skirt against my thighs and lower myself to the ground, just as Shepherd pulls two canned beers from the cooler and drops down beside me.

"Structural engineer, actually," he says.

"Okay, no ten-year-old wants to be a structural engineer," I say. "They don't even know that's a thing. Frankly, *I* just found out it was a thing in this moment."

His low, pleasant laugh rumbles through the ground. I get that shot of adrenaline that making *anyone* laugh sends through me, but the drunken-butterflies-in-the-stomach feeling is obnoxiously absent. I adjust my legs so they're a little closer to his, let our fingers brush as I accept a beer from him. Nothing.

"No, you're right," he says. "When I was ten I wanted to build stadiums. But by the time I went to Cornell, I'd figured it out."

I choke on my beer, and not just because it's disgusting.

"You okay?" Shepherd asks, patting my back like I'm a spooked horse.

I nod. "Cornell," I say. "That's pretty fancy."

The corners of his eyes crinkle handsomely. "Are you surprised?"

"Yes," I say, "but only because I've never met a Cornell alum who waited so long to mention that he was a Cornell alum."

He drops his head back, laughing, and runs a hand over his beard. "Fair enough. I probably used to bring it up a little more before I moved home, but no matter where I went to college, people here are still more impressed by my years as the quarterback."

"The what now?" I say.

"Quarterback—it's a position in . . ." He trails off as he takes in my expression, a smile forming in the corner of his mouth. "You're joking."

"Sorry," I say. "Bad habit."

"Not *so* bad," he says, a flirtatious edge in his voice.

I nudge his knee with mine. "So how'd you end up back here? You said you lived in Chicago for a while?"

"Right out of school I got a job there," he says. "But I missed home too much. I didn't want to be away from all this."

I follow his gaze over the valley again, purples and pinks swarming across it as shadow unspools from the horizon. Trillions of gnats and mosquitoes dance in the dying light, nature's own sparkling ballet. "It's beautiful," I say.

Up here, the quiet seems more calming than eerie, and he wears the thick humidity so well I'm able to (somewhat) believe that I *also* don't look like a waterlogged papillon. The hot stickiness is almost pleasant, and the grassy scent is soothing. Nothing feels urgent.

In the back of my mind, a familiarly hoarse voice says, *You'd rather be somewhere loud and crowded, where just existing feels like a competition.*

I feel eyes on me, and when I glance sidelong, the surprise is disorienting. Like I'd fully expected someone else.

"So what brings *you* here?" Shepherd asks.

The sun is almost entirely gone now, the air finally cooling. "My sister."

He doesn't press for information, but he leaves space for me to go on. I try, but everything going on with Libby is so intangible, impossible to itemize for a near-perfect stranger.

"Wait here a sec," Shepherd says, jumping up. He walks back to his truck and digs around in the cab until country music crackles out of the speakers, a slow, crooning ballad with plenty of twang. He leaves the door ajar and returns to me, stretching his hand down with an almost shy grin. "Would you like to dance?"

Ordinarily, I could imagine nothing so mortifying, so maybe the small-town magic is real. Or maybe some combination of Nadine, Libby, and Charlie has knocked something loose in me, because without hesitating, I set my beer aside and take his hand.

18

~

I CAN SEE THE scene playing out like it's happening to someone else. Like I'm reading it, and in the back of my mind, I can't stop thinking, *This doesn't happen*.

Only, apparently it does. Tropes come from somewhere, and as it turns out, from time immemorial, women have been slow-dancing to staticky country music with hot architect-carpenters as deep shadows unfurl over picturesque valleys, crickets singing along like so many violins.

Shepherd smells how I remembered. Evergreen and leather and sunlight.

And everything feels *nice*. Like I'm letting loose in all the right ways and none of the ones that could come back to bite me.

Take that, Nadine. I'm present. I'm sweaty. I'm following someone else's lead, letting Shepherd spin me out, then twirl me in. I am not stiff, rigid, cold. He dips me low, and in the half-light he flashes that movie star smile before swinging me back onto my feet.

"So," he says, "is it working?"

"Is what working?" I ask.

"Are we winning you over?" he says. "To Sunshine Falls."

Someone like you—in shoes like that—could never be happy here. Don't get some poor pig farmer's hopes up for nothing.

I miss a step, but Shepherd's too graceful for it to matter. He catches my weight and moves me through a quarter turn, all trouble avoided except where my heels are concerned. They're caked in dirt, smeared with grass stains, and I am *furious* with myself for noticing.

For flashing back to Charlie carrying me up the hillside after our pool game.

From the outside, Shepherd and I still form that perfect, heart-squeezing scene, but I have that feeling of outsideness again. Like it's not really me, here in Shepherd's arms. Or like I'm still on the wrong side of the window.

The image is immediate, intense: *Our* old window. *Our* apartment. A sticky-floored kitchen and a waterlogged laminate counter-top. Me and Libby perched on it, Mom leaned up against it. A carton of strawberry ice cream and three spoons.

It hits me like a horror movie jump-scare. Like I rounded a corner and found a cliff.

I tighten my fingers through Shepherd's, let him draw me closer, my heart racing. I backtrack to his question and stammer out, "It's definitely making an impression."

If he's noticed the change in me, he gives no indication. He smiles sweetly and tucks a strand of hair behind my ear. *This is it,* I realize. I'm about to kiss a nice, handsome man on an unplanned date in an unfamiliar place. *This* is how the story's supposed to go, and it finally is.

His forehead lowers toward mine, and my phone chimes in my bag.

Instantly, another window glows bright in my mind. Another apartment. *Mine*.

The squashy floral couch, the endless stacks of books, my favorite Jo Malone candle burning on the mantel. Me lounging in an antique robe and a sheet mask with a shiny new manuscript, and on the far side of the couch, a man with a furrowed brow, mouth in a knot, book in hand.

Charlie, hitting my brain like an Alka-Seltzer tab, dispersing in every direction.

My face jerks sideways. Shepherd stops short, his mouth hovering an inch shy of my cheek. "I should be getting back to my sister!" It comes out unplanned and roughly sixty times louder than I meant for it to. But I can't go through with this. My brain feels too muddy.

Shepherd draws back, vaguely puzzled, and smiles good-naturedly. "Well, if you ever need a tour guide again . . ." He reaches into his shirt pocket and pulls out a scrap of paper and a blue Bic pen, scribbling against it in his palm. "Don't be a stranger." He hands me the number, then hesitates for a second before saying, "Or even if you don't need a tour guide."

"Yeah," I stammer. "I'll call you." Once I figure out what's going on in my head.

~

Charlie pushes my coffee across the counter. "Precisely on time," he says. "So I guess Shepherd didn't break your city-person curse."

For some reason, his confirmation that he *did* see me getting into the truck yesterday rankles. Like it's proof that he purposely invaded my thoughts.

I tuck my sunglasses atop my head and stop at the desk. "We had a very nice time. Thanks so much for asking." I'm mad at him. I'm mad at me. I'm just generally, irrationally mad.

Charlie's jaw muscles leap. "Where'd he take you? The Creamy Whip in the next town over? Or the Walmart parking lot for some truck-bed stargazing?"

"Careful, Charlie," I say. "That sounds like jealousy."

"It's relief," he says. "I expected you to show up here today in Daisy Dukes and pigtails, maybe a Ford tattoo on your tailbone."

I slide my forearms onto the desk and lean forward in such a way that I really might as well have brought a silver platter out and presented my cleavage to him *that* way. The lack of sleep is really getting to me. I feel haunted by him, and I'm determined to haunt him right back.

"I would be"—I drop my voice—"adorable in Daisy Dukes and pigtails."

His eyes snap back to my face, flashing; his mouth twitches through that grimacing pout, a pair as reliable as thunder and lightning. "Not the word *I'd* use."

Awareness sizzles down my backbone. I lean closer. "Charming?"

His eyes stay on my face. "Not that either."

"Sweet," I say.

"No."

"Comely?" I guess.

"*Comely?* What year is it, Stephens?"

"A real girl next door," I parry.

He snorts. "Whose door?"

I straighten. "It'll come to me."

"I doubt it," he says under his breath.

The self-satisfaction lasts about as long as it takes to set up in the café and pull up my checklist for today's tasks. There are proposals I didn't finish marking up yesterday, queries I need to send on delayed payments, and submissions lists I need to solidify before the slow season ends.

Once again my work needs my full attention, and once again I can't compartmentalize enough to make that happen. Last night's dinner with Libby keeps spiraling through my mind like flaming butterflies. She was effusively chipper, no sign of anything wrong, until I pressed her on her mysterious errands, at which point her energy flagged and her eyes hardened.

"Can't a grown woman have a little alone time?" she said. "I think I've earned the right to a little privacy." And that was that. We'd brushed the awkwardness aside, but the rest of the night, some of that distance had come back into her eyes, a secret looming between us like a glass wall or a block of ice, more or less invisible but decidedly material.

I open Dusty's pages and picture myself in a submarine, sinking into them, urging the world around me to dull. It's never taken effort—that's what made me fall in love with reading: the instant floating sensation, the dissolution of real-world problems, every worry suddenly safely on the other side of some metaphysical surface. Today is different.

The bells chime at the front of the shop, and a familiar, feminine purr of a voice greets Charlie. He responds warmly, and she gives a sexy laugh. I can't make out every word, but every few sentences are punctuated by that same gravelly sound.

Amaya, I realize, as she's saying something like, "Are we still on for Friday?"

Charlie says something like, "Still works for me."

And my brain says something like, *DOESN'T WORK FOR ME. NOT AT ALL.*

To which the career woman angel on my shoulder replies, *Shut up and mind your own business. He's not supposed to occupy any of your mental real estate anyway.*

I put on headphones and blast my cityscape sounds to make myself stop listening in, but not even the dulcet tones of New York City's finest cabdrivers cussing one another out is enough to soothe me.

Charlie said Amaya wasn't jilted, which more than likely means *she* broke up with *him*. I don't *want* to be following this thought out to its logical conclusion, but my brain is a runaway train, smashing through station after station with unrelenting speed.

Charlie didn't want the relationship to end.

Amaya regrets her decision now.

Things are complicated for Charlie. Whatever's going on between him and me "can't be anything."

Charlie's keeping the door open to something with his ex.

Amaya just asked him out.

I mean, that's only one possible through line, but that's how my brain works: it plots.

This is why crushes are terrible. You go from feeling like life is a flat path one needs only to cruise over to spending every second on an incline, or caught in a weightless, stomach-in-your-throat drop. It's Mom running out to catch a cab, hair curled and smiling lips painted, only to come home with streaks of mascara down her face. Highs and lows, and nothing in between.

When Libby finally shows up, I'm grateful for the number-twelve-related tasks she assigns me, even if they're all of the dusting/scrubbing/organizing variety.

Charlie mostly remains tucked in the office, and when he does come out to help customers, I avoid looking at him and somehow *still* always know right where he is.

After our lunch break, Libby sets out some *Book Lovers Recommend* cards by the register for customers to fill out, along with a decoupage shoebox drop-box to return the cards to. She hands me three cards "to get them started," and I wander the shop, searching for inspiration. I see the January Andrews circus book I bought my first weekend here, the one Sally told me Charlie had edited, and prop my card against the bookshelf to scribble a few lines. Next I choose an Alyssa Cole romance Libby loaned me last year, which I made the mistake of opening on my phone and ended up devouring in two and a half hours while standing in front of my fridge.

Next I duck into the children's book room and straighten to find myself nose to nose with Charlie. *Magnets,* I think. He catches my elbows, holding me back before we can collide, but you'd still think we were smashed up to each other from mouth to thigh based on the instant crush of heat that wells in me.

"I didn't know you were in here!" I say in a rush. Huge improvement over *LION!*

I see the spark in his burnt-sugar eyes the second the perfect response pops into his brain, and I feel the lurching drop of disappointment when he decides to say instead, "Inventory." He releases me and lifts the clipboard from the shelf. A whopping three point five inches separates us, and an electric charge leaps off him, buzzing through my veins. "I'll let you get back to . . ."

Still neither of us moves.

"So you and Amaya are hanging out." I add, almost involuntarily: "I wasn't eavesdropping—it's a quiet shop."

His eyebrow ticks. " 'Not eavesdropping,' " he teases in a low voice. " 'Not stalking.' I'm sensing a pattern here."

"*Not* jealous." I challenge, stepping closer. "*Not* adorable."

His eyes dip to my mouth and slightly dilate before rising. "Nora . . ." he murmurs, a heaviness in his voice, an apology or a half-hearted plea.

My throat squeezes as our stomachs brush, every nerve ending on high alert. "Hm?"

He sets his hands on my shoulders, his touch light and careful. "I need to go," he says quietly, avoiding my gaze. He sidesteps me and slips from the room.

~

On Friday another batch of *Frigid* pages hits our inboxes. I spend the first couple of hours reading and rereading, gathering my thoughts into a document and resisting the urge to live-text Charlie in the other room. Libby's only around from lunchtime to about three, at which point she leaves with the reminder that she has another surprise for me tonight.

I try to convince myself *that's* what her disappearance the other day was about, but I can't escape the thought that it had something to do with Brendan. I've suggested we video call him a few times, but she always has an excuse.

At five, I pack up and leave to meet her. Once again, Charlie's not at the register, and now I'm not only annoyed and frustrated, I'm *sad*.

I *miss* him, and I'm tired of us hiding from each other.

Steeling myself, I duck into the office. He looks up, startled, from where he's leaned against the bulky mahogany desk on the right side of the room, reading. His eyes, his posture, everything reads *jungle cat*. If by some strange, ancient curse, a jaguar was turned into a man, he would be Charlie Lastra. After a seconds-long staring contest, he remembers himself and says, "Did you need something?"

Last year, I would've thought he was being snotty. Now I realize he's cutting to the chase.

"We should schedule a time to talk through the next hundred pages."

His eyes bore into me until there's smoke lifting off my skin. I'm an ant beneath his sunlit magnifying glass. Finally, he looks away. "We can just do it over email. I know Libby's keeping you running."

"It needs to be in person." I can't take this tension between us anymore. Avoiding him is only making this worse, and I hate feeling like I'm hiding. With Libby, the way to get to the heart of things might be a slow, cautious obstacle course, but this is Charlie, and Charlie's like me. We need to bulldoze through the awkwardness. I *miss* him. His teasing, his challenges, his competitiveness, his care for my overpriced shoes, his smell, and—

Shit, I didn't expect the list to be so long. I'm in deeper than I realized. "Unless you're too busy!" I add.

He flashes his first smirk-pout of the week. "What could I possibly be busy with?"

His plans with Amaya surge to the front of my mind. I picture him sweeping her over a puddle to save her shoes, flicking open an umbrella to protect her blown-out hair.

"Maybe that Dunkin' Donuts grand opening," I say. "Or the divorce proceedings for that couple who fought at town hall."

"Oh, they'll never split up," he says seriously. "That's just the Cassidys' foreplay."

Foreplay. Not a word I would've chosen to introduce to this conversation.

"Does tomorrow work for you?" I ask. "Late morning?"

He studies me. "I'll reserve us a room." At my expression, he laughs. "At the *library*, Stephens. A *study room*. Get your mind out of the gutter."

Believe me, I think, *I've tried.*

19

LIBBY HOISTS ME out of Hardy's cab, toward the sound of chatter, and positions me for optimal drama. "Ta-da!"

I pull down the scarf-cum-blindfold she made me wear and blink against the pink and orange of dusk. I'm facing an elementary school's marquee.

TONIGHT, 7 P.M.

SUNSHINE FALLS COMMUNITY THEATER
PRESENTS:

ONCE IN A LIFETIME

"Oh," I say. "My. God."

She lets out a wordless shriek of excitement. "See? Local theater! Everything New York has, you can find right here too!"

"That is . . . quite the leap."

Libby giggles, hooking an arm around me. "Come on. The tickets are general admission, and I want to get popcorn *and* good seats."

I'm not sure there's such thing as "good seats" when you're choosing from rows of folding chairs in a school gymnasium. The stage is elevated, meaning we'll be craning our necks for the length of the play, but as soon as the house lights drop, it's clear the seating arrangement is the *least* of this production's issues.

"Oh my god," Libby whispers, gripping my arm as an actor shuffles out in front of the painted apothecary backdrop. He wanders to the prop counter and gazes wistfully at a framed picture there.

"*No,*" I whisper.

"*Yes!*" she hisses.

Old Man Whittaker is being played by a child.

"What about the drug abuse?!" Libby says.

"What about the overdose?!" I say.

"He can't even be thirteen, right?" Libby whispers.

"He has the voice of a ten-year-old choirboy!"

Someone harrumphs near us, and Libby and I sink in our chairs, chastened. At least until Mrs. Wilder—the owner of the lending library—comes onto the stage and I have to turn my bark of laughter into a cough.

Libby wheezes beside me. "Oh my god, oh my god, oh my god." She's not looking at the stage, just staring at her feet and trying not to explode.

I drop my voice next to her ear: "What do you think the age gap is between these actors? Sixty-eight years?"

She clears her throat to keep a handle on her would-be laughter.

The woman playing Mrs. Wilder could easily be Old Man Whittaker's grandmother.

Hell, maybe she is. "Maybe little Delilah Tyler will be played by the family Rottweiler," I whisper. Libby flings herself forward over her belly, hiding her face as her shoulders quake with silent laughter.

Another dirty look from the woman to our right. *Sorry,* I mouth. *Allergies.* She rolls her eyes, looks away.

Into Libby's ear, I whisper, "Uh-oh, Whittaker's mommy is mad."

She bites my shoulder, like she's trying not to scream. Onstage, Little Boy Whittaker grabs his back and winces out the F-word at the pain of his character's chronically pinched nerves.

Libby squeezes my hand so hard it feels like she might break it.

"It is very clear," she whispers haltingly, "that small, bearded child has yet to experience physical pain."

"That boy has yet to experience the dropping of his testicles," I reply.

As if to disprove this, his next line sends his voice lurching, cracking into a squeak that makes Libby scrunch her eyes shut and cross her legs. "I will *not* pee myself!"

We stare at our feet, erupting into silent shivers of laughter every few minutes. It's the most fun I've had in years.

Whatever else is happening, with Brendan, with the apartment, with my sister, right now, we're us, like we haven't been for a long time.

~

The second the play ends, Libby and I sprint out. We're both about to lose it and would rather do so privately. Halfway to the marquee, a cheery voice stops us.

"Nora! Libby?" Sally Goode cuts a trail toward us, alongside a blond behemoth of a man using a wheelchair. Her dimpled smile is Charlie-esque; the cloud of jasmine and marijuana in which she arrives is not. It's hard to imagine structured, sharp-edged Charlie being raised by this woodsy, freewheeling waif.

"Fancy seeing you here!" Libby sings.

"Small towns and all that," Sally says. "I don't think y'all have met my husband?"

"Clint," the man offers. "Pleasure to meet you."

"Nice to meet you," Libby and I say in unison.

He asks, "What'd you think of the play?"

Libby and I exchange a panicked look.

"Oh, don't make them answer that." Sally swats his arm, smiling. "At least not before the salon. You gotta come—we always have friends over for drinks and pie after a show."

"This is a regular occurrence?" My sister almost chokes over the words. We're still too slaphappy to be having this conversation.

"They do four shows a year," Sally says.

Clint's brow lifts. "Is that all? Seems like a lot more."

Libby swallows a laugh, but a squeak still makes it out of her throat.

"Please say you'll come," Sally pleads.

"Oh, we couldn't intrude—" I begin.

"Nonsense!" she cries. "There's no such thing as intruding in Sunshine Falls. Or did you not just watch the same play as us?"

"We definitely watched it," Libby mumbles.

Sally hands her purse to her husband and digs through it for a scrap of paper and a pen, then jots down an address. "We're just on the other side of the woods and up the path from you." She hands the paper to Libby. "But there's a street and driveway that runs right up to our house, if you don't feel like tromping through the dark."

She doesn't wait for an RSVP or even a reply. They're moving off, the crowd bottlenecking behind us.

"Oh, Boris did *wonderfully*," an older gentleman is saying. "And only eleven years old!"

Libby squeezes my hand, and we take off down the sidewalk, giggling like preteens high on Mountain Dew.

~

The Lastra-Goode home sits at the end of a long drive lined with mature oaks. It's far enough outside town that there's little light to interrupt the sparkling blanket of night sky overhead or the masses of fireflies blinking in the shrubs.

It's a two-story colonial, with white siding and freshly painted black shutters. In the oversized driveway, around ten cars are already parked, with another pulling in behind us as Hardy stops to let us out.

As we approach the front doors, Libby gazes up at the front of the cozy house and says dreamily, "I would pay a million dollars to be here on Christmas."

"I guess that explains why Brendan does the budgeting."

Libby's arm stiffens through mine. I glance over at her. She's paled a bit too. I can't tell if she looks stressed or sick, or both. Either way, the knot of dread gives a sharp pulse behind my rib cage, a reminder that even in those hours when it shrinks, it never vanishes.

I jog her arm. "Is everything okay, Lib?"

Her surprise melts into neutrality. "Of course! Why wouldn't it be?"

"I just mean, if you need anything," I say, "you know I'd always—"

"Hello, hello!" Sally calls, swinging the door open. "Come on in!" She has to shout to be heard as she ushers us through the jasmine-scented front hall toward the thunder-roll of laughter and hum of overlapping conversations at the back of the house. "Just so you know, we typically pretend everything was good."

"Excuse me?" I say.

Her smile deepens her crow's feet. She looks every bit like a woman in her sixties, and all the more striking for it, in a woodsy, sun-beaten way.

"The play," she clarifies. "Or when it's a ceramics show, or a craft market, or whatever else: We pretend it's good. At least until we've had a couple rounds." She pats our shoulders and moves off, calling, "Make yourselves at home!"

"I'm gonna need everyone to make it through a couple rounds *real* quick," Libby says.

"What I was saying outside, Lib—"

She squeezes my arms. "I'm good, Nora. I've just been off because I'm having this restless leg thing that interrupts my sleep. Stop worrying and just—enjoy our vacation, okay?"

The more she insists everything's fine, the more sure I am that it's not. But as has been the case for years, she's just shuttered at the first sign of worry.

This is how it is. She never asks for help, so I have to figure out what she needs and how to get it to her in a way she feels okay about accepting.

Even with her wedding dress, I had to pretend to track down a sample sale and get a damaged dress at a discount, when actually I put it on a card and smudged some concealer inside the bodice myself.

But with this—I don't even know where to start.

Oh god.

A sudden, terrifying clarity hits me like a sandbag to the stomach. *The list.* All these homages to Libby's almost-futures: building, baking, bookstore . . . marketing.

Is this all some foray back into the working world? Or a way to prove she could survive on her own if she needed to? *Three* weeks away from her husband. I should've thought that was strange. Especially with how strange she's been acting. *Especially* more than five months along in her pregnancy.

She loves *Brendan,* I remind myself. Even if they're going through something, buckling under the stress of a new baby, that can't have changed.

My clothes feel too tight, too hot. I look around, searching for something to focus on, to ground myself with. My gaze catches on Clint, standing with a walker across the crowded kitchen, then over to the equally tall, though far younger and brawnier man beside him.

"Wooow," Libby says, clocking Shepherd at the same time I do.

His green eyes find mine, and he murmurs something to Clint before extricating himself and sauntering our way.

"Oh my god," Libby says. "Is that archangel coming toward us right now?"

"Shepherd," I say, distracted by the hamster wheel of worries spinning inside my skull.

Libby asks, "Is that a shepherd coming toward us?"

"No, his name is—"

"Ohhhh. *Shepherd,*" she says, realization dawning, right as he stops in front of us.

"See," he says, beaming. "This is why you've gotta love small towns."

20

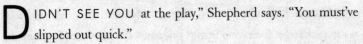

"**D**IDN'T SEE YOU at the play," Shepherd says. "You must've slipped out quick."

Libby gives me a look that reads: *You forgot to mention your date was Adonis?*

"My sister had to pee," I say, which only magnifies her put-out expression. "This is Libby. Libby, Shepherd."

Libby says only, "Wow."

"Nice to meet you, Libby," he replies.

She shakes his hand. "Strong grip. Always a great quality in a man, right, Nora?" She looks at me pointedly, simultaneously trying to be my wingwoman *and* to embarrass me.

"It seems to come in handy in James Bond movies," I agree. Shepherd smiles politely. No one says anything. I cough. "Because of all the people dangling off buildings . . ."

He nods. "Got it."

The temporary madness or magic of the other night has worn off. I have no idea how to interact with this man.

He says, "Can I grab either of you something? Beer? Seltzer?"

"I'd have wine," I say.

"You know what?" Libby grins. "This darn bladder! I *already* have to pee again."

Shepherd gestures down the hall. "Restroom's right down that way."

"I'll be back in a sec," Libby promises, and as Shepherd turns to pour me a glass of wine from an open bottle on the counter, she makes a break for it, mouthing over her shoulder, *NO I WON'T.*

Shepherd hands me the glass, and I tip my chin at the—approximately—fourteen thousand bottles of wine on the island. "You all *really* want to forget that play."

He laughs. "What do you mean?"

I take a big sip. "Just joking. About the wine."

He scratches the back of his head. "My aunt runs this informal wine exchange. Everyone brings one, and she puts numbers on the bottom. At the end, she raffles off whatever doesn't get drunk."

"Sounds like my kind of lady," I say. "Is she here?"

"Course," he says. "She wouldn't miss her own party."

I almost inhale my wine and have to cough to clear my lungs. "Sally? Sally's your aunt? Charlie Lastra's your cousin?"

"I know, right?" he says, chuckling. "Total opposites. Funny thing is, we were pretty close as kids. Grew apart as we got older, but his bark's worse than his bite. He's a good guy, underneath it all."

I need to either change the topic or scout out a fainting couch. "I promise I was going to call, by the way."

"No worries," he says, a bashful dimple appearing. "I'll be around."

I say, "So your family owns the horse farm?"

"Stables," he corrects me.

"Right." I have no clue what the difference is.

"It's my parents' place. When construction stuff is slow for me and my uncle, I still help them out sometimes."

Uncle. Construction. He works with Charlie's dad.

Shepherd's phone buzzes. He sighs as he reads the screen. "Didn't realize it had gotten so late. I've gotta head out."

"Oh," I say, still on a snappy dialogue hot streak.

"Hey," he says, brightening, "I hope this doesn't sound too pushy—because I understand if you're not interested—but if you want to go on a trail ride while you're here, I'd love to take you."

His warm, friendly expression is as dazzling as it was when I first bumped into him outside Mug + Shot. He is, I wholeheartedly believe, a truly nice man.

"Maybe so," I say, then renew my promise to call him. As his pine-and-leather scent retreats across the room, I stay rooted to the spot, caught in an endless loop of *Shepherd is Charlie's cousin. I almost kissed Charlie's cousin.*

It shouldn't matter, but it does. I can hear Charlie saying, *This can't be anything,* but I can't shake the feeling that it already is.

I feel vaguely sick. Libby still isn't back yet, and I'm too deep in my thoughts for small talk with strangers. Avoiding every attempt at eye contact, I wander through the crowd to the far end of the living room.

A series of three massive paintings hangs in a triptych. The walls are covered in paintings, actually, every color palette and size, giving the house a cozy, eclectic feeling mismatched to its old-fashioned exterior.

The paintings are definitely nudes, though abstracted: all pinks and tans and browns, purple curves and shadows. They remind me of the Matisse Cut-Outs, but whereas those always strike me as romantic, even erotic—all artful arches and curved, pretzeling legs—these feel casual, the kind of vulnerable nudity of walking around naked in your apartment, looking for your hairbrush.

The scent of weed hits me right before her voice, but I still flinch when Sally says, "Are you an artist?"

"Definitely not. But I'm an appreciator."

She lifts the wine bottle in her hand like it's a question. I nod and she tops off my glass.

"Who made them?" I ask.

Sally's lips tighten into an apple-cheeked smile. "I did. In another life."

"They're phenomenal." From a technical standpoint, I know very little about art, but these paintings are beautiful, calming in their earthy colors and organic shapes. They're decidedly *not* the kind of art that makes a person say, *My four-year-old niece could paint this.*

"I can't believe you made these." I shake my head. "It's so strange to see something like this and realize it just came from a normal person. Not that you're normal!"

"Oh, honey," she laughs. "There are far worse things to be. *Normal* is a badge I wear proudly."

"You could've been famous," I say. "I mean, that's how good these are."

She appraises the paintings. "Speaking of those 'worse things to be than normal.'"

"Fame comes with money," I point out. "Money's helpful."

"Fame also comes with people telling you whatever they think you want to hear."

"Hello there," Libby coos, slipping into place beside us. She gives me an indiscreet waggle of the eyebrows, and I'm grateful Sally misses it, so I don't have to explain the meaning behind it is *She wants*

*me to screw your nephew! Instead of your son! Which was also briefly on
the table!*

"Sally painted these," I say.

Libby looks to her for confirmation. "No freaking way!"

Sally laughs. "So shocked!"

"These are, like, professional, Sally," Libby says. "Have you ever
tried to sell any?"

"I used to." She looks displeased at the thought.

"Wuh-oh," Libby says. "There's clearly a story here. Come on,
Sal. Let it out."

"Not a very interesting one," she says.

"Lucky for you, we just saw a play that severely lowered our standards," I say.

Sally lets out a devilish snort and pats my arm. "Don't let Reverend Monica hear you say that. Old Man Whittaker is her godson."

"I hope he'll pose for the statue in the town square," I say.

"That statue could look like my mail carrier, Derek, for all I
care," Sally says. "Long as the plaque says *Whittaker*. We need the
business that sort of thing could bring in."

"Back to the story," Libby says. "You used to sell your paintings?"

She sighs. "Well, when I was a girl, I wanted to be a painter. So
when I was eighteen, I went to Florence to paint for a few weeks,
which turned into months—Clint and I broke up, of course—and
after a year, I came back to the States to try to break into the art scene
in New York."

"Get out!" Libby lightly thwacks Sally's arm. "Where'd you live?"

"Alphabet City," she says. "Long, long time ago. Stayed for the
next eleven years, working my ass off. Sold some paintings, applied
for shows constantly. Worked for three or four different artists and
spent every night trying to network in galleries. Worked myself to

the bone. Then, finally, when I'd been at it for eight years, I was part of this group show. And this guy walks in, picks out one of my paintings, and buys it. Turns out he's a renowned curator. My career takes off overnight."

"That's the dream!" Libby squeals.

"I thought so," Sally replies. "But I realized the truth pretty fast."

"That Clint was your true love?" Libby guesses.

"That it was all a game. My paintings hadn't changed, but suddenly all these places that had turned me down wanted me. People who'd never looked my way were all over me. Hardly mattered what I made. My work became a status symbol, nothing more, nothing less."

"*Or*," I say, "you were extremely talented, and it took one person with good taste to say so before the masses caught on."

"Maybe," Sally allows. "But by then I was tired. And homesick. And usually pretty hungry and broke, and the curator came on to me when I was just lonely enough to fall into bed with him. Not long after my father passed, we broke up, and I came home to be with my mother. While I was here, she asked Clint to come clean our gutters."

"The jokes just write themselves," I say.

"So *then* you realized he was your true love?" Libby says.

Sally smiles. "That time, yes. He was engaged by then. Didn't stop my mother's machinations. Her mantra was *It's not official until they're down the aisle*. Thank God she was right. As soon as I saw Clint again, I knew I'd made a huge mistake. Three weeks later, he was engaged to *me*."

"That's so romantic," Libby says.

"But didn't you miss it?" I say.

"Miss what?" Sally says, clearly not tracking.

"The city," I say. "The galleries in New York. All of it."

"Honestly, after all those years of toiling, it was a huge relief to come here and just . . ." She lets out a deep breath, her arms floating up at her sides. "Settle."

"No kidding," Libby says. "We moved to the city so our mom could try to make it as an actress—the most chronically exhausted person in the world."

"That's not fair." She was spread thin, sure, but she was also full of life, ecstatic to be chasing her dreams.

Libby shoots me a look. "Remember that time she was a nickel short at the bodega? Right after that *Producers* audition? The clerk told her to put a lime back, and she *broke down.*"

My heart squeezes. I had no idea Libby remembered that. She'd just turned six, and Mom wanted to bake Lib's favorite corn-lime cookies. When Mom started melting down at the register, I grabbed the extra lime in one hand and Libby's little fingers in my other and dragged her back to the produce, taking our time zigzagging back to Mom while she gathered herself.

If you could have any treat, from any book, I asked her, *what would you choose?*

She picked Turkish delight, like Edmund ate in Narnia. I picked frobscottle from *The BFG*, because it could make you fly. That night, the three of us watched *Willy Wonka* and cleaned out the remains of our Halloween candy.

It's a happy memory, the kind that almost sparkles. More proof that every problem could be solved with the right itinerary.

Everything turned out okay, I remember thinking. *As long as we're together, it always does.*

We were happy.

But that's not what Libby's telling Sally. She's saying, "Mom was broke, tired, and lonely. She put her career ahead of absolutely everything and was miserable because of it." She turns to Sally, conspiratorial. "Nora's the same way—worked to the bone. No time for a real life. She once refused a second date with a guy because he asked her to put her phone on Do Not Disturb during dinner. Work *always* comes first for her. That's why I dragged her here. This trip is basically an intervention."

She says it all like a joke, but there's something hard and thorny underneath, and her words land in my gut like a punch. The room has started to pulse and waver. My throat feels full, my clothes itchy against my skin, like something is swelling inside me. She's still talking, but her words are garbled.

Tired, lonely, no real life, work always comes first.

For weeks, I've worried how people will see me once *Frigid* hits shelves, but Libby—Libby's the only person who's ever really known me. And this is how she sees me.

Like a shark.

The shame hits hot and fast, a desperation to crawl out of my skin. To be anywhere else. To be *someone* else.

I break away, heading for the bathroom in the front hall, but it's locked, and I beeline toward the front door instead, only to find a handful of people crowding it. I double back, dizzy.

I want to be alone. I need to be somewhere I can vanish into a crowd, or at least where no one will acknowledge what's happening to me.

What *is* happening to me?

The stairs. I take them to the second floor. There's a bathroom at the end of the hall. I'm almost to it when a room on the right catches my eye. A wall of books is visible through the cracked-open door.

It's a beacon, a lighthouse on a far shore. I step inside and close the door behind me, the party receding to a muffle. My shoulders relax a little, the thud of my heart settling as I take in the cherry-red race car bed against the wall on my left.

Not a store-bought plastic monstrosity, but a homemade wooden frame, painted to glossy perfection. The sight of it sends a pang through me. As do the homemade bookshelves lining the far wall. There's so much care, not just in the construction but in the organization, Charlie's touch *and* Clint's as visible as inky fingerprints.

The books are meticulously ordered by genre and author, but not pretty. Not rows of leather-bound tomes, just paperbacks with creased spines and half-missing covers, books with five-cent thrift store stickers on them, and Dewey decimal indicators on the ones that came from library sales.

They're the kinds of books Mrs. Freeman used to give us, the ones she'd stick in the Take a Book, Leave a Book bin.

Libby and I used to joke that Freeman Books was our father. It helped raise us, made us feel safe, brought us little presents when we felt down.

Daily life was unpredictable, but the bookstore was a constant. In winter, when our apartment was too cold, or in summer, when the window unit couldn't keep up, we'd go downstairs and read in the shop's coveted window seat. Sometimes Mom would take us to the Museum of Natural History or the Met to cool down, and I'd bring my shredded copy of *From the Mixed-Up Files of Mrs. Basil E. Frankweiler* with me and think, *If we had to, we could live here, like the Kincaid siblings*. Between the three of us, we'd be fine. It'd be fun.

Magic. That's what those days felt like. Not how Libby made it sound.

Sure, there were problems, but what about all those days lying on our bellies in the Coney Island sand reading until the sun set? Or nights spent in a row on our sofa, eating junk food and watching old movies?

What about the Rockefeller Center tree lighting, hot cocoa keeping our hands warm?

Life with Mom, life in New York, was like being in a giant bookstore: all these trillions of paths and possibilities drawing dreamers into the city's beating heart, saying, *I make no promises but I offer many doors.*

You may chassé across a spotlit stage with the best of them, but you may also weep over an unbought lime.

Four days after the lime incident, Mom's friends came over with Cook's champagne and an envelope of cash they'd pooled to help us out.

Yes, New York is exhausting. Yes, there are millions of people all swimming upstream, but you're also in it together.

That's why I put my career first. Not because I have no life, but because I can't bear to let the one Mom wanted for us slip away. Because I need to know Libby and Brendan and the girls and I will all be okay no matter what, because I want to carve out a piece of the city and its magic, just for us. But carving turns you into a knife. Cold, hard, sharp, at least on the outside.

Inside, my chest feels bruised, tender.

It's one thing to accept that the person I love most is fundamentally unknowable to me; it's another to accept that she doesn't quite see me either. She doesn't *trust* me, not enough to share what's going on, not enough to lean on me or let me comfort her.

All those old feelings bubble up until I can't get a good breath, until I'm drowning.

"Nora?" A voice spears through the miasma, low and familiar. Light spills in from the hallway. Charlie stands in the doorway, the only fixed point in the swirl.

He says my name again, tentative, a question. "What happened?"

21

CHARLIE'S LAPTOP BAG slides to the floor as he comes toward me. "Nora?" he says one more time.

When I can't get any sound out, he pulls me toward him, cupping my jaw, thumbs moving in soothing strokes against my skin. "What happened?" he murmurs.

His hands root me through the floor, the room stilling. "Sorry. I just needed . . ."

His eyes search mine, thumbs still sweeping in that gentle rhythm. "A nap?" he teases softly, tentatively. "A fantasy novel? A competitively fast oil change?"

The block of ice in my chest cracks. "How do you do that?"

His brow furrows. "Do what?"

"Say the right thing."

The corner of his mouth quirks. "No one thinks that."

"I do."

His lashes splay across his cheeks as his gaze drops. "Maybe I just say the right thing for you."

"I felt like I was suffocating." My voice breaks on the word, and his hands slide into my hair, his eyes rising to mine again. "Like—like everyone was looking at me, and they could all see what's wrong with me. And I'm used to feeling like . . . like I'm the wrong kind of woman, but with Libby it's always been different. She's the only person I've ever really felt like myself with, since my mom died. But it turns out Dusty was right about me. That's who I am, even to my sister. The wrong kind of woman."

"Hey." He tips my face up to his. "Your sister loves you."

"She said I have no life."

"Nora." He just barely smiles. "You're in *books*. Of course you don't have a life. None of us do. There's always something too good to read."

A weak half laugh whisks out of me, but the feeling doesn't last. "She thinks I don't care about anything except my job. That's what everyone thinks. That I have no feelings. Maybe they're right." I laugh roughly. "I haven't cried in a fucking decade. That's not normal."

Charlie considers for a moment. His arms slide around my waist to lock against the small of my back, and the contact cannonballs directly into my thoughts, sending them zinging away from the impact. I don't remember doing it, but my arms are around him too, our stomachs flush, heat gathering between us. "You know what I think?"

Touching him feels so good, so strangely uncomplicated, like he's the exception to every rule. "What?"

"I think you love your job," he says softly. "I think you work that hard because you care ten times more than the average person."

"About *work*," I say.

"About *everything*." His arms tighten around me. "Your sister.

Your clients. Their books. You don't do anything you're not going to do one hundred percent. You don't start anything you can't finish.

"You're not the person who buys the stationary bike as part of a New Year's resolution, then uses it as a coatrack for three years. You're not the kind of woman who only works hard when it feels good, or only shows up when it's convenient. If someone insults one of your clients, those fancy kid gloves of yours come off, and you carry your own pen at all times, because if you're going to have to write anything, it might as well look good. You read the last page of books first—don't make that face, Stephens." He cracks a smile in one corner of his mouth. "I've *seen* you—even when you're shelving, you sometimes check the last page, like you're constantly looking for all the information, trying to make the absolute best decisions."

"And by you've *seen me*," I say, "you mean you've *watched me*."

"Of course I fucking do," he says in a low, rough voice. "I can't stop. I'm always aware of where you are, even if I don't look, but it's impossible not to. I want to see your face get stern when you're emailing a client's editor, being a hard-ass, and I want to see your legs when you're so excited about something you just read that you can't stop crossing and uncrossing them. And when someone pisses you off, you get these red splotches." His fingers brush my throat. "Right here."

My nipples pinch, my thighs squeezing and skin shivering. The tension in his hands makes his fingers curl against the curve in the small of my back, gathering the fabric there like he's talking himself out of ripping it.

"You're a fighter," he says. "When you care about something, you won't let anything fucking touch it. I've never met anyone who cares as much as you do. Do you know what most people would give to have someone like that in their life?" His eyes are dark, probing, his heartbeat fast. "Do you know how fucking lucky anyone you care about is? You know . . ."

He hesitates, teeth sinking into his lip, eyes low, fingers loosening but not removing themselves from my vertebrae. "When Carina and I were kids, my dad had to work a lot. We didn't have much money, and then my mom's mother passed, and—the bookstore started hemorrhaging money.

"My mom isn't a businessperson. She isn't even really a person who keeps a schedule. So the shop's hours were totally unpredictable. Some artist talk would get scheduled for the middle of the week in Georgia, and she'd take me and Carina out of school to go to it, without notice. Or she'd get caught up with a painting and not only miss the workday, but forget to pick us up from school. Carina was always more like my parents, laid-back, but I was anxious. Maybe because I'd had such a hard time when I first started school, or maybe just because I finally actually liked it, but I hated missing class, and on top of that—"

He draws a breath. My hands have been twisting into the back of his shirt, keeping him close, connected to me at all times.

"—people didn't approve of my family," he goes on. "My dad was already engaged when he and my mom got together, and she was already three months pregnant with me."

My mouth opens and closes. "Oh. Clint's not . . ."

He shakes his head. "My biological father's an art curator, back in New York, actually. We've exchanged a couple emails, and that was enough for us. As far as I'm concerned, Clint's the only dad I've ever had or needed, but as far back as I can remember, I knew I wasn't like him. Didn't look like him. Didn't like the same things as him."

The warm gold and inky dark of his eyes lift to mine again, and a painful wanting blooms behind my solar plexus. "I was in fifth grade when I found out the truth. From some kids at school."

The ragged edge of his voice knocks the wind out of me. I fight the impulse to rein in my shock, and then it all clicks, the bits of Charlie I've been collecting like puzzle pieces becoming a full picture. Not the Darcy trope. Not the self-important, dour academic I met for one very unpleasant lunch. A man who craves complete honesty, the realist who doesn't always understand when he's not seeing realism. Charlie, who wants to understand the world but has learned not to trust it.

"I'm so sorry, Charlie," I whisper.

He swallows. "I know he just didn't want me to think I was anything but his son," he says. "But it was a bad way to find out. Everyone in town was more or less nice to my parents' faces, but those first few years of school were hell. My mom's approach was to kill them with kindness, and it worked. She won the whole fucking town over. But I couldn't do it. I can't make small talk with people I *know* hate me. I can't play nice with people I think are assholes. Carina was in *third* grade the first time someone told her she was probably born with an STD because our mom was such a whore."

"Holy shit, Charlie." I unknot my arms from his back and take his face between my hands, feeling like my lungs are on fire, like there are feelings my vocabulary isn't advanced enough to put into words. I want to drape myself over him like chain mail, or swallow some gasoline, go downstairs, and spit it out as fire.

"I spent half of middle school in the library and the other half in the principal's office for getting into fights, and honestly those were the only two places I felt like I had any control over my life." He shakes his head, like he's clearing it. "My point is, being that 'magic free spirit' you think is this mythical perfect woman? It comes with its own problems. Just because not everyone gets you doesn't mean *you're* wrong. You're someone people can count on. Really count on. And that doesn't make you cold or boring. It makes you the most . . ."

He trails off, shakes his head. "You and your sister might have your differences, and she might not totally understand you, but you're never going to lose her, Nora. You don't have to worry about that."

"How can you be so sure?" I ask.

Now his eyes are all liquid caramel, his hands tender, moving back and forth over my hips, a tide that draws us together, apart, together, each brush more intense than the last.

"Because," he says quietly, "Libby's smart enough to know what she has."

I want to pull him down into the ridiculous car bed and wrap myself in the smell of his shampoo, to feel the pressure of his fingers grow frantic on me, for the warm, hard press of his stomach and our steady rocking together and drawing apart to mount.

"Until you got here," he rasps, "all this place had ever been was a reminder of the ways I was a disappointment, and now you're here, and—I don't know. I feel like I'm okay. So if you're the 'wrong kind of woman,' then I'm the wrong kind of man."

I can see all of the shades of him at once. Quiet, unfocused boy. Precocious, resentful preteen. Broody high schooler desperate to get out. Sharp-edged man trying to fit himself back into a place he never belonged to begin with.

That's the thing about being an adult standing beside your childhood race car bed. Time collapses, and instead of the version of you you've built from scratch, you're all the hackneyed drafts that came before, all at once.

"You're not a disappointment." It comes out faint. "You're not wrong."

Charlie's eyes sweep down my face. His fingers brush the smooth spot at the right corner of my mouth, his jaw tightening. When his eyes lift to mine again, they're blazing, a trick of the warm light coming from the bedside lamp, but I still I feel heat rising off of him.

"And all those people who made you feel like you were," he says huskily, "have fucking terrible taste." The affection in his voice rushes me like a warm tide, filling a million tiny tide pools in my chest.

We really are two opposing magnets, incapable of being in the same room without drawing together. I want to scrape my fingers through his hair and kiss him until he forgets where we are, and everything and everyone that ever made him feel like he was a disappointment. And he's looking at me like I could, like there's an ache in him only I could soothe.

I want to tell him, *You are someone who looks for a reason for everything.*

Or, *You are the person who pulls things apart and figures out how they work instead of simply accepting them. You're someone who would rather have the truth than a convenient lie.*

Or even, *You're the person who only has five outfits, but each of them is perfect, carefully chosen.*

"I think," I whisper, "you're one of the least disappointing people I've ever met."

The line beneath his bottom lip shadows as his lips part, and his warm, minty breath is light against my mouth. For a second, we're caught in a push and pull, tasting the space between us. It feels like there's no air left in the room, but what I really want anyway is to breathe *him* in.

All my reasons for keeping those walls up between us seem suddenly inconsequential. Because the wall *isn't* up. It's not. Charlie sees me. He's touching me. And for the first time in so long—maybe even since we lost Mom—I feel like I'm *not* outside the scene, watching through glass, longing so badly to find a way in.

My phone chirps, and all that warm heaviness evaporates as Charlie straightens, jolted back to reality, to his own reasons for trying to build a barricade between us.

He turns to face the shelves, and my throat goes dry when I realize he's adjusting himself.

Everything in me aches to touch him again, but I don't. My feelings may have changed, but there's still Charlie's end of things: *This can't be anything. Things are complicated.*

My mind goes straight to Amaya, and guilt, jealousy, and hurt wriggle together in the pit of my stomach.

Another message comes in from Libby, and another.

Where are you??

When you're done introverting in a dark corner, I found us a ride home.

HELLO? U alive????

"It's Libby."

Behind me, Charlie clears his throat, says hoarsely, "You should rescue her before the knitting club recruits her. They're the Sunshine Falls equivalent of the Mafia."

I nod. "I'll see you tomorrow."

"Good night, Stephens."

❧

I almost collide with Sally at the bottom of the stairs.

"I was just looking for your sister!" she says. "I dug up the number she asked for—could you pass it along?"

I accept the scrap of paper, and before I can ask for clarification, Sally's scurrying after a woman with very thoroughly sprayed bangs.

I text a picture of the phone number to Libby. From Sally. Also: where are you?

Out front, she says. Hurry! Gertie Park the Anarchist Barista is giving us a ride home!

Libby is acting normal, but in the back of Gertie's heavily

bumper-stickered hatchback, I sift through the last few weeks like it's all shredded paper.

What Libby said about Mom, about me. Brendan's strange texts, and Libby's reaction to them. The argument outside the bookstore, the list, the way she disappears and reappears mysteriously, how her fatigue and paleness seem to come and go.

I organize it all into piles, into solvable problems, into scenarios from which I can devise escape plans. I am back in the thick of it, gazing out across the chessboard and trying to mitigate whatever happens next.

But for a minute, upstairs, with Charlie's arms tight across my back, everything was okay.

I was okay.

Drifting in a comforting, bodiless dark, where nothing needed to be fixed and I could just—I think of Sally's arms lifting at her sides—*settle*.

22

THE LIBRARY AT the edge of town is hulking: three stories of pink brick and gabled peaks. While Libby's directing furniture deliveries to Goode Books, I'm meeting Charlie for an edit session in Study Room 3C, on the top floor.

All morning, things felt strained between Libby and me. We're caught in a feedback loop of vague bad feelings.

She's frustrated with how much I work, and that's creating distance. The distance has her keeping secrets. The secrets have me frustrated with her. It's a self-fulfilling prophecy, keeping us locked in an invisible, unspoken argument, wherein we both pretend nothing's wrong.

That hollow ache: *You're losing her, and then what was it all for?*

As soon as the library's automatic doors whoosh open, that delicious warm-paper smell folds around me like a hug, and my chest loosens a bit. On the right, some high schoolers lounge at a row of ancient desktop computers, their chatter muffled by the industrial blue carpet. I pass them and take the wide staircase to the second floor, and then the third.

I follow the row of windowed study rooms along the outside wall to 3C and find Charlie angled over his laptop, the overhead light off and diffused daylight pouring through the window to cast him in cool blues.

The room is tiny, with a steepled roof. A laminate table and four matching chairs take up the vast majority of the space.

For some reason—the quiet, maybe, or what happened last night—I feel shy as I hover in the doorway. "Am I late?"

He looks up, eyes darkly ringed. "I'm early." He clears the gruff sleepiness from his voice. "I edit here most Saturdays."

An enormous coffee from Mug + Shot sits in front of an open seat, waiting for me. I drop into the chair. "Thanks."

Charlie nods, but he's hyper-focused on his screen, one hand tugging at the hair behind his ear.

My phone vibrates with another message from Brendan: You girls still having fun?

Cords of anxiety slither over one another in my stomach. Libby texted me from the shop five minutes ago, so I *know* she has her phone. Which means he either didn't text her first or she just didn't respond.

Yep! I type back. Why? Everything okay?

Definitely!!! He's really selling it with those exclamation points.

Maybe it's time to resort to begging for answers.

For now, though, I fold that line of thought into a compartment at the back of my mind. It goes with surprising ease. "Did you need a minute?" I ask Charlie as I boot up my computer.

He startles, like he's forgotten I'm here. "No. No, sorry. I'm good." He runs his hand over his mouth, then stands and drags his chair around the corner, where he can look at my notes on-screen. His thigh bumps mine as he sits, and for a few moments after, there's some kind of avalanche happening behind my rib cage.

I ask, "Should we start with everything we liked?" Charlie stares for a beat too long; he absolutely missed the question. "Oh, come on, Charlie," I tease. "You can admit you like things. Dusty and I won't tell anyone."

He blinks a few times. It's like watching his consciousness swim toward the surface. "Obviously I like the book. I begged to work on it, remember?"

"I'll remember you begging until my last dying breath."

He looks abruptly to the screen, all business, and it feels like my heart is taking on water. "The pages are great," he says. "The perky physical therapist is a good foil to Nadine, but I think by the end of this section, she needs more depth."

"I wrote that too!" I'm immediately self-conscious about my teacher's pet I-just-aced-a-quiz voice when I see Charlie's face. *"What?"*

He squelches his smirk. "Nothing."

"Not 'nothing,'" I challenge. "That's a face."

"I've always had one, Stephens," he says. "Fairly disappointing you just noticed."

"Your *expression*."

He leans back in his chair, his red Pilot balanced over one knuckle and under two. "It's just that you're good at this."

"And that's a shock?"

"Of course not," he says. "Am I not allowed to enjoy seeing someone be good at their job?"

"Technically this is *your* job."

"It could be yours too, if you wanted."

"I interviewed for an editing job once," I tell him.

His brows flick up. "And you didn't take it?"

"I didn't do the second interview," I say. "Libby had just gotten pregnant."

"And?"

"And Brendan got laid off." My shoulders tighten, locking into defensive mode. "I was making good money on commission, and taking an entry-level job would've meant a pay cut."

He studies me until my skin starts to thrum, then looks away again; we're caught in an endless game of chicken, taking turns losing. "How did Libby feel about that?"

"I didn't tell her." I turn back to my notes. "Next up, we have Josephine."

After a beat, Charlie says, "Don't you think she'd be sad you gave up your dream job for her?"

"She doesn't exactly admire my devotion to my current job," I remind him. "Now, *Josephine*."

He sighs, giving in. "Love Jo."

"Is she different enough from Old Man Whittaker, you think? I mean, old, crotchety person with no family?"

"I think so. We get depth to her character quickly, and her backstory, with the ex who drove her out of Hollywood, doesn't ring any *Once* bells. Old Man Whittaker lost his family, but Josephine never had one to begin with. And besides, the discussion of how her being a woman dictated how the media and world treated her is kind of this book's whole deal."

"True," I say. "And I love that, but it does bring me to my next thought. Maybe we should pull back on the reveal about her connection to the film industry until later."

Charlie's eyes take on a Mac spinning-wheel quality, like his thoughts are loading. "I disagree," he says slowly. "What I'd prefer is if we didn't find out why *Nadine* never became an actress until later. I think there's opportunity for tension there. Like maybe when Nadine finds Jo's Oscar, it comes out that Nadine originally wanted to act and Jo asks what changed her mind, and we get some foreshadowing."

"Shit," I say.

"What?" Charlie says.

"You're right."

"My condolences," he says. "This has clearly been very hard on you."

I start typing the update into my notes.

"Nadine shouldn't have given up on acting," Charlie says.

The words float there for a minute, an obvious trap. "She makes a lot of money agenting," I reply.

"She doesn't enjoy her money," he reminds me.

I keep typing. "She likes agenting."

"She loved acting."

"I thought you were her biggest fan."

"I am," he says. "That's why I want her to get her happy ending."

"I don't think it's that kind of book, Charlie."

His shoulder shrugs in tandem with a flick of his full lips. "We'll see."

Despite my carefully organized document, the way we move through our edits feels more like those days wandering the Central Park Ramble with Mom and Libby.

The document balloons and then we pare it down, Charlie pulling my laptop over to him to reduce four sentences into one, me pulling it back to thread through more compliments, until, hours into the process, I realize we've switched roles. Now *he's* the one inserting praise and *I'm* the one trimming fat.

As he watches me, he murmurs, "I've just always wanted to see a shark attack up close. *So much blood.*"

Face warming, along with a few less innocuous places, I turn back to the document, overrun by tracked changes. "I like to see my progress."

"Nora," he says. "It's *all* progress at this point." He reaches out to select the whole document, then hovers the cursor over *Accept All Changes*, his elbow nestling against mine on the wood laminate table. He looks to me for approval.

I nod, but he doesn't move, and the light contact of his arm pulls all the nerves in my body toward that one spot.

Any second the walls will go back up, and I can't take that. I thought about how to broach the subject for hours as I lay awake last night, and somehow, what comes out is still just, "I forgot to mention, last night I ran into your *cousin.*"

I say the word purposefully. Charlie glances away as he scratches his jaw. "Was he rescuing a kitten from a tree, or helping an old lady across the street?"

"Neither," I say. "He was just shirtless and washing a car."

"I hope you tipped him for his trouble." His gaze comes back to mine, a crackle of electricity jumping the gap between us.

"Hey, buddy," I say, "here's a tip: put on a shirt. This is a family-friendly literary salon."

The corners of his Charlie's lips twitch as he stands and leans against the table, his eyes fixing on the window. "If you'd really said that, the ladies' knitting club would've run you out of town. Shirtless Shepherd is a Sunshine Falls staple."

I fight to keep my voice even. "I didn't know he was your cousin. Or I wouldn't have gone out with him."

He looks away. "You don't owe me anything, Nora."

"Oh, I know." I stand too. I can't dance around it any longer—

it's not working anyway. I can't do anything about the *Libby* piece of things, but this—this can be resolved. One way or another, the wall of tension is coming down today.

I take a breath and go on: "Especially if something's going on with you and your ex."

His eyes dart back to mine. "It's not."

"You saw her last night, didn't you?"

His jaw flexes. "I was working. She just stopped by."

I feel my gaze narrow skeptically. "For a planned visit?"

He shifts his weight. "Yes," he admits.

"To buy a book?" I say.

His jaw tightens again. "Not exactly."

"To hang out?"

"To *talk*."

"As ex-fiancés so often do."

"It's a small town," he says. "We can't avoid each other. We needed to clear the air."

"Ah," I say.

"Don't *ah*," he says, sounding frustrated now. "Nothing happened between us, and it's not going to."

"It's none of my business," I say.

"Exactly." Somehow this seems to make him more frustrated, which makes *me* more acutely, hungrily aware of the space shrinking between us. "Just like it's none of my business if you date my cousin."

"Whom I have no intention of seeing again," I say. "And with whom I wouldn't have gone out even once if I'd *known* he was your cousin."

"You didn't do anything wrong," Charlie insists.

"And you didn't either, by spending time with Amaya," I reply. We are either too good or too bad at fighting. We are *viciously* trading support for each other's romantic lives.

He one-ups me with, "Shepherd's a great guy. Most eligible bachelor in town. He's perfect for your list, checks all your boxes."

"What about Amaya?" I throw back. "How's she measure up to yours?"

"Doesn't make the cut," he says.

"Must be a pretty long list."

"One item," he replies. "Very specific."

The way he's looking at me wakes up my skin, my bloodstream, my want. "Too bad it's not going to work out for you guys," I say.

"And I'm sorry to hear about you and Shepherd." His eyes flash. "I thought you two had a nice time."

"Oh, I did," I say. "Just turns out a nice time isn't what I really want right now."

He stares at me, eyes blackening, and I hope I'm as legible to him now as ever, that he knows I'm done brushing off this thing between us. Scratchily, he says, "And what is it you want, Stephens?"

"I just . . ." *Now or never.* I feel like I'm readying myself for a skydive. "I want to be here with you and not worry about what comes next."

He steps closer, my heart whirring as he invades my space. "Nora," he says gently.

"It's okay if you don't want that," I say. "But I'm thinking about you way too much. And the more space I try to put between us, the worse it is."

His lips twist; his eyes glint. "So you're trying to get this out of your system?"

"Maybe," I admit. "But maybe I also just want something that's easy for once."

His brow lifts, teasing. "Now I'm easy?"

Yes, I think, *to me, you are the easiest person in the world.* But I say, "God, I hope."

Charlie laughs, but it fades quickly and his gaze drops to the side. "What if I already know this can't go anywhere," he says, "no matter how much we might end up wanting it to?"

"Is there someone else?"

His eyes lift, widened. "*No.* It's nothing like that. It's just that—"

"Charlie," I say. "I told you. I don't want to think about what comes next. I'm not even sure I could handle that right now."

He studies me, his jaw working. "Are you sure?"

"Completely," I say, and mean it. "If you want, I'll even sign a napkin."

I'm not sure which of us started it, but his mouth is on mine, warm and hungry, his hands running down my sides and back up my front, taking in as much of me as he can at once. No hesitancy, no politeness, only want. My fingers twine into his shirt as he hauls me against him, closing every gap we can find.

Within seconds, he's yanking my blouse out of my skirt and his hands are up the front of it, so perfectly rough and warm that the silk is unbearable by comparison. A desperate sound twists through me, and he spins us around, pushing me onto the table, hiking my skirt up my thighs so he can step in against me.

I pull him to me, arching into his touch. His fingers curl around the back of my neck and knot into my hair, his teeth on my throat.

"We can't do this in a library," I hiss into his mouth, though my hands are still moving, skimming up his back beneath his shirt, nails scraping his skin and leaving goose bumps.

He murmurs, tone chiding, "I thought you didn't want to worry about the rules."

"When it comes to public indecency, it's less of a rule and more of a federal law," I whisper.

His lips move down my throat, one hand sliding under me to tilt my hips against his, positioning his length against me. *Oh, god.* "That only counts," he says, "if we take our clothes off."

The sound I make couldn't be much less sexy or *more* dying-feral-animal. "And to be clear," I get out, "*you're* okay with the fact that we're working together?"

He kisses along my collarbone, his voice all gravel. "We both know you won't go easier on me for it."

"And what about you?" It's completely absurd that I'm keeping up the charade of having a totally normal conversation while my palms are flattening on the table behind me and my body is lifting unsubtly, making it easier for his mouth to brush under the collar of my shirt.

"I have no interest in going easy on you, Nora," he says.

My fingers snake into his hair, drag down his neck, his pulse humming under my touch. My mind feels like it went straight through a shredder and into a kaleidoscope. His fingers skim up the inside of my thigh until they can go no higher, his eyes watching the progress with an almost drunken sheen.

My knees fall open for him. His jaw tightens as he runs his hand over me, featherlight at first and then with more pressure. His fingers slip under the lace, my hips lifting into the motion, no sound in the room but our ragged breath.

"You have the red splotches, Nora," he teases, drawing his lips over my throat. "Are you mad at me?"

"Furious," I pant as his mouth drags lower, one of his hands working the top buttons of my blouse loose. He tugs my bra down until the cool air meets my skin.

"Tell me how I can make it up to you," he murmurs against my chest.

I arch back to give him more of me. "That's a start."

He draws me between his lips and I try not to cry out when a low groan rumbles through him. His hand is under my skirt again, his breath catching against my chest. "You fucking undo me," he says.

I pull him closer, needing more of him. We're more or less flat on the table now, the inside of my thigh against his hip. I bury my mouth against his throat to stifle the sounds he's drawing out of me.

I feel totally out of control, and what's more, I can see how much he likes seeing me like this, and it's only fanning the flame. I *want* to be out of control. I want him to see me like this and know he's the reason why. His hand roams down my side until it reaches the spike of my heel, hitching my leg higher, coiling it around his hips as we try to get closer.

If we had anywhere more private to go, we'd already be gone.

"I want to go down on you so badly," he rasps into my mouth, my heart spiking.

"I want go down on *you*," I tell him.

He gives a low laugh. "Everything's a competition with you."

I slip my hands beneath his waistband, all of my focus narrowing to the feeling of him, the sound of his breath turning jagged when my grip tightens, his hips shifting to let me have more of him.

I have never enjoyed this so much. I'm not sure I've ever enjoyed *this*, period, but I've also never seen Charlie so uninhibited and I'm drunk on the power.

"God," he says, "I need to be inside you."

Everything in me pulls taut. "Okay." I nod furiously, and he laughs again.

"No, you're right," he says. "Not here."

"We don't have many options," I point out.

"When we finally do this, Nora," he says, straightening away from me, his hands slipping my buttons back into buttonholes as easily as he undid them, "it's not going to be on a library table, and it's *not* going to be on a time crunch." He smooths my hair, tucks my blouse back into my skirt, then takes my hips in his hands and guides me off the table, catching me against him. "We're going to do this right. No shortcuts."

23

I LEAVE THE LIBRARY on shaky legs, heart racing like I'm forty minutes deep into spin class. I've gone hours without checking my phone, and the usual emails have accumulated—one from my boss, who rarely honors the concept of the weekend, and a slew from clients who feel similarly—along with a string of texts from Libby.

I squint against the sunlight to see the pictures she sent of the progress she made today. The Goode Books café now looks snug and cozy, and the window display of *SUMMER FAVORITES* is lined in twinkly lights. In most of the pictures, Sally stands off to one side, beaming, but in one wonky shot that includes a good portion of someone's thumb, Libby stands with arms flung wide and a huge smile on her face, silky pink bun lopsided atop her head.

Her heart-shaped face looks more or less the same as when she was fourteen years old and got accepted into the high school art show: proud, confident, capable. Even with all the weirdness between us, it makes me so happy to see her like that.

Looks amazing! I tell her. You're a wunderkind!! Can't even tell it's the same place!!!

Thanks! she replies. Everything all right? Not like you to be late.

I was supposed to meet her at Poppa Squat's ten minutes ago. I type back, All good. Be there in a minute.

I just have a call to make first. I stop at one of the green benches along the street, the metal hot from baking in the sun, and dig through my purse for the phone number Shepherd gave me. Maybe it's old-school of me to follow up with someone to let him know I'm *not* interested, but Shepherd's a nice guy. He deserves better than long-form ghosting.

The line rings three times before someone picks up, a woman's voice saying, "Dent, Hopkins, and Morrow. How may I help you?"

After a second of confusion, I say, "I'm looking for Shepherd?"

"I'm sorry," she says, "there's no one here by that name."

"Um, can I—who is this?" I say.

"This is Tyra," she says, "at the law offices of Dent, Hopkins, and Morrow."

"I must . . . have the wrong number." I hang up and feel around in my purse until I find a receipt with chicken-scratch numbers on it. *This* is the one Shepherd gave me. The number I just called . . . must've been the one Sally gave me. *For your sister. I dug up the number she asked for.*

I could use some food to soak up the gallon of coffee I drank today, but it's not *just* over-caffeination making my hands shake as I type the name of the law office into a Google search.

When the results appear, it's like someone injected ice into my veins.

Dent, Hopkins & Morrow: Family Law Attorneys

Libby asked Sally . . . for the number of a divorce lawyer? For an instant, the street, the stone walkway, the pale blue sky, the world feels like it's being shredded into ribbons. My lungs are overinflated, something large and heavy blocking anything from getting in or out.

I'm back in our old apartment, in those terrible weeks after Mom died, watching Libby fall apart, holding her tight while she sobs, until she can't breathe, until she's gagging.

I'm drowning in her pain, my own hardening, calcifying into my heart.

I don't want to be alone, she sometimes gasps, or else, *We're alone. We're all alone, Nora.*

I'm holding her tight, burying my mouth in her hair and promising she's wrong, that she'll *never* be alone.

I have you, I tell her. *I'll always have you.*

All those nights I jarred awake and found it all still there waiting for me: Mom gone. No money. Libby breaking.

Sometimes she cried in her sleep. Other times I woke while she was in the bathroom, and the cold spot in the bed beside me sent me into a panic.

In those days, pain waited like a shadowy monster, towering over our bed, and instead of shrinking night by night, it grew, feeding on us, getting fat with our grief.

Early one morning, we lay wrapped under the blankets and I smoothed my sister's strawberry hair, and she whispered, *I just don't want to be here anymore. I want it to stop.*

And that same cold panic grew too big for my body, swelling, throbbing angrily.

Without thinking about money or work or school or any of the millions of practicalities for which I'd become responsible, I said, *Then let's go somewhere.*

And we did.

Bought round-trip, middle-of-the-week, red-eye tickets to Los

Angeles. Checked into a seedy motel whose dead bolt didn't work and wedged the desk chair under the knob while we slept each night.

Every morning, we took a cab to the beach and stayed there until dinner, always something cheap and greasy. We took some of Mom's ashes and dumped them in the ocean when no one was looking, then ran away, shrieking and laughing, unsure whether we'd just broken a law.

Later, we'd split the rest of the ashes between the East River and the Hudson, bits of Mom on either side of our city, hemming us in, holding us. But we weren't ready to let go of that much of her yet.

For one whole week, Libby didn't cry, and then, on the plane home, during takeoff, she looked out the window, watching the water shrink beneath us, and whispered, *When will it stop hurting?*

I don't know, I told her, knowing she'd see I was lying. That I believed it would never stop, not ever.

She descended into ugly, wrenching sobs, and the other passengers shot tired glares in our direction. I ignored them, pulled Libby into my chest. *Let it out, sweet girl,* I murmured, just like Mom used to say to us.

A flight attendant either overestimated our ages or took pity on us, and discreetly dropped off two miniature liquor bottles.

Through her hiccups, Libby chose the Bailey's. I drank the gin.

Ever since that day, I couldn't so much as smell it without thinking about holding tight to my sister, about missing Mom so much that she felt closer than she had in weeks.

Maybe that's why it's the only thing I really drink. Feeling that hole in your heart is better than feeling nothing at all.

I blink clear of the memory, but the pain in my chest, the ache deep in my hands don't let up. I sink onto the hot metal of the bench and count out the seconds of my inhalations, matching them to my exhalations.

That was the last trip Libby and I took. It was the last trip I've taken, *period*, aside from that one ill-fated weekend in Wyoming with Jakob.

Once I got our debt under control, I started setting aside money here and there so I could take Libby somewhere amazing, like Milan or Paris, when she graduated from college. Once, she had all kinds of ambition, but after we lost Mom, it seemed like that all dried up. She stopped helping out at Freeman's and cycled through a few other potential career paths, but none of them held her attention.

I spent her college years over her shoulder, pushing her, reading her essays for her, making her flash cards. We fought more than before, our new roles chafing on us, her endless grief warping from anger to exhaustion and back again. Sometimes, even years later, she still cried in her sleep.

And then she met Brendan, and she decided not to finish school.

When she told me they were engaged, I wasn't surprised. All I could think about was that teenage girl, terrified of being alone.

I worried that she was too young, that she was making the decision more out of a need for security than because it was what she wanted deep down. But the truth is, she seemed happy. For the first time in years, I had my sister back.

Brendan settled her. I didn't like that she'd given up the event-planning job I'd pulled strings to get her, but the hunted look left my sister's eyes, and I could finally breathe.

For years, she was *finally* okay, and all the work—all the missed birthday parties, all the early-morning meetings, all the relationships that never got off the ground because of my schedule—it was all so fucking worth it.

She was *okay*.

Now she's dodging her husband's calls and talking to a divorce attorney. Spending *three weeks* away from him. And maybe that's why it suddenly matters so much that I'm a workaholic. Not because Libby doesn't approve but because she *needs* me. She needs me and I haven't been there.

Fear rips through me as violent as a wildfire, but ice-cold.

Hidden there, under my rigidly manufactured sense of control and my checklists and my steel exterior, there is *always* fear.

Libby was wrong when she told Sally I am just like Mom. Mom worked nonstop to chase something she wanted. For me, it's running endlessly trying to escape the past.

Fear of the money running out again. Of hunger. Of failure. Of wanting anything badly enough that it will destroy me when I can't have it. Of loving someone I can't hold on to, of watching my sister slip through my fingers like sand. Of watching something break that I don't know how to fix.

I am afraid, always, of the kind of pain I know we won't survive a second time.

I focus on the pressure of the ground beneath my soles, digging myself into place.

One by one, action items slide into a tidy column in my mind.

Find the best divorce lawyer money can buy.

Find Libby an apartment she can afford on her own, or else one we can share with the girls. (Could we all fit in Charlie's rent-stabilized place?)

Get a counselor to help her through this.

Possibly hire a hit man. Or maybe not a hit man, but at least someone who can exact minor revenge—drinks thrown in Brendan's face, keys dragged up the side of his car—depending on what exactly happened, hard as it is to imagine him doing *anything* but staring lovingly at Libby while rubbing her swollen feet.

And then the final item on the list and the most immediate: Bring Libby as much happiness as possible right now. Make her feel safe enough to open up to me.

My shoulders drop back into place. My lungs relax. Now that I know what's wrong, I can fix it.

~

"You know you can tell me anything," I say. "Right?"

Libby looks up from the mayo-ketchup mixture we've been dipping our Poppa Squat's fries in and snorts. "Dude," she says flatly. "Not *this* again. Focus on your own life, Sissy."

Rather than throwing a barb back, I let it go. "What's next on the list?"

She relaxes. "I'm glad you asked, because I have an amazing idea."

"How many times do I have to tell you?" I say. "A water park made out of alcohol is *not* a good idea."

"Agree to disagree." She swipes her hands together, dusting the salt off her fingertips. "But that's not what I'm talking about. I figured out how to save the bookstore."

"How many bronze statues can one town square *have*?"

"A *ball*," Libby says. "A Blue Moon Ball. Like in *Once*."

I feel my brow creasing. "Is there even a blue moon this month?"

"Not the point."

"Right, because the point is . . ."

"A huge fundraising opportunity!" she says. "Sally knows someone who owns an events company. He can get us a dance floor and a sound system, and then we get volunteers to decorate and bring pies for a bake sale. We do the whole thing out in the town square, just like in the book."

"This is a lot of work," I say hesitantly.

"We won't be doing it alone," she insists. "Sally already put out calls to everyone in her wine exchange, and Amaya will work the bar, and Gertie—"

"The anarchist barista?" I clarify.

"—offered to make flyers for us to spread around Asheville. Mug and Shot will turn into a pop-up soda fountain. Plus they already have a liquor license, so they can do a couple of hard soda drinks. Half the town's already on board." She snatches my hand against the sticky bar. "It'll be a piece of cake. A piece of *pie*, really. The only thing is . . ."

"Uh-oh," I say at her wince.

"It's fine if we can't make it happen!" she says quickly. "But Sally and I thought it would be cool to do a virtual Q and A with Dusty. And then maybe have some signed stock on hand, for her to promote. Only if she wouldn't mind! And only if you don't mind asking her."

She presses her palms together, begging or praying.

"This is how you want to spend the next two weeks?" I say, skeptical. "Not resting? Not reading and watching movies and lying out in the sun?"

"Desperately."

Whether it's a distraction or a way for her to exercise control or a chance to try a new life, this is what she wants, so this is what she gets.

"I'll ask Dusty."

Libby throws her arms around my neck, kissing my head a dozen times over. "We're doing it! We're saving a local business."

I'm not convinced, but she's happy, and Libby's happiness has always been my drug of choice.

24

OF COURSE, OF course!" Dusty says, in her Dusty way, at once a bit hyperactive and vaguely spacey. "I'd love to help, Nora. But . . . I've never actually *been* to Sunshine Falls. I just happened to drive through, years ago."

"Well, the people here *love* your book," I say. I glance back toward the side of the cottage, where Libby's stretched out on a picnic blanket, sunning herself whilst eavesdropping. She flashes me two encouraging thumbs up, and I clear my throat into the phone and go on. "The whole town has these plaques about different parts of the story. It's really cute."

"Really cute?" She repeats these words with awe. Probably because they sound like an ancient Latin curse coming out of my mouth.

My voice wrenches higher. "Yep!"

I feel out of sorts, asking a client for a favor, especially since it requires admitting *I* am *here*, working in person with Charlie.

Dusty is shocked to hear I've left the city, and when I explain I came here with my sister, she is nearly as shocked to learn I have a sibling.

As it turns out, all my longest-standing client really knows about me is I never leave New York and I'm always reachable by phone.

So after some backstory, I fill her in on the plight of Goode Books and lay out the plan for the fundraiser: an online book club with Dusty herself, open to any and all who order a book from the shop.

"It's an hour of my life," she says. "I think I can make it work. For the world's best agent."

"Have I told you lately you're my *favorite* client?" I say.

"You've never told me that," she replies. "But you *have* sent me some very expensive champagne over the years, so I figured."

"When edits for *Frigid* are done, I'm sending you a *swimming pool* of champagne."

Libby straightens up on her blanket and points a finger at me. *SEE? ALCOHOL WATER PARK*, she mouths victoriously, then pitches herself onto her feet and thunders inside to call Sally with the good news.

Yesterday I broke down and texted Brendan to ask if something was going on between them, and he simply *didn't* reply, but I'm trying not to focus on that.

"Can I ask you something, Dusty?" I say.

"Of course! Ask away," she says.

"Why Sunshine Falls?"

She stops and thinks. "I guess," she says, "it just seemed like the kind of place that might look one way on the outside, and be something totally different once you got to know it. Like if you had the patience to take the time to understand it, it might be something beautiful."

~

Sally, Gertie, Amaya, and a slew of other semi-familiar faces are in and out of the shop over the next few days, prepping for the ball. Finally I'm able to concentrate on my work. Libby, meanwhile, is at the center of the planning whirlwind, constantly coming and going, loudly taking phone calls until other customers' disgruntled looks send her into an apology tailspin on her way out the door.

Charlie and I mostly only work over email. If we're in the same room for too long, I'm positive that Libby—and maybe even Sally—will know exactly what's going on, and *complicated* will be here fast.

I've been taking Libby's disapproval of Charlie at her word, but now a part of me wonders if it's something else. If me using the dating apps was a sort of soft launch for her, just to see what's out there. Either way, I don't need to put this fling on display when she's dealing with her own relationship's implosion.

My stomach roils every time I let myself think about it, but honestly, Charlie's and my email correspondence is the picture of professionalism. Our texts are not, and sometimes I have to sneak out of Libby's pop-up war room in the café to read them someplace where no one can see me flush.

Half the time Charlie intercepts me, and we sneak around the shop, stealing seconds alone wherever we can get them. The bathroom hallway. The children's book room. The dead end in the nonfiction aisle. Places where we're out of sight, but still have to be nearly silent. Once he pulls me through the back door into the alleyway behind the shop, and we have our hands on each other before the door swings shut.

"You look like you haven't slept in years," I whisper.

His palms roam down to my ass, hoisting me against him, and he drops his mouth beside my ear. "I've had a lot on my mind." His hands range up me, testing each curve. "Let's go somewhere."

"Where?"

"Anywhere that my mother and your sister aren't within eyeshot," he says. "Or earshot."

I glance back at the door, in the general direction of Libby & Co.'s thousand-point whiteboard checklist.

All those little superglued cracks in my heart pulse with pain, a sensation like emotional brain freeze. I want this, *him*, but I can't forget what I'm doing here.

I look back into his honeycomb eyes, feeling like I'm sinking waist deep into them, like there's no hope of getting away, in part because I lack any motivation while his hands are on me. "Anywhere?" I ask.

"Name it."

~

Libby's so immersed in Work Mode, she doesn't insist on joining our Target run, and instead forks over the fundraiser's shopping list. Sally agrees to run the register if anyone comes in, and we set out in the old beat-up Buick Charlie's borrowing while he's in town.

The air-conditioning doesn't work, and the sun beats down on us hard, the blazing-hot, grass-scented wind ripping my hair free from its tie strand by strand. All of this just makes the cool blast of air and clean plasticky smell of Target more pleasant. I didn't think we'd been spending an inordinate amount of time outside, but in the surveillance cameras at the self-checkout, my skin looks browned, Libby-esque freckles are dappled across my nose, and the humidity has given my hair a slight wave.

Charlie catches me studying myself and teases, "Thinking about how 'hot and expensive' you look?"

"Actually . . ." I grab the receipt. "I'm daydreaming about how hard I'm about to work you."

His eyes spark. "I can take it."

We drive straight to the cottage, and as soon as we step into the cool quiet, I'm keenly aware that this is, realistically, the most alone Charlie and I have ever been, but we don't have long until Libby will be here, and there are, ostensibly, more important things to focus on than the places that sweat has his shirt clinging to him.

"You can get started out back," I say, and head for the stairs to gather the rest of what we'll need.

By the time I kick open the back door, arms loaded with bedding, Charlie's already got the tent set up.

"Well," I say. "You've done it. You've surprised me."

"And here I thought that if you needed to stun a shark, you were supposed to just smack it between the eyes."

"No," I say. "Competency with portable shelters is the way to do it."

He crouches inside the tent and starts unrolling the air mattress we bought at Target—because, sure, Libby and I are going to camp, but we're still Stephens women. "How are you such a pro at this?" I ask.

"I camped a lot with my dad, growing up." The intense daylight has every sharp line of his face shadowed to black, his eyes more molasses than honey.

"Have you gone since you've been back?" I ask.

Charlie shakes his head. After a few seconds, he says, "He doesn't want me here."

His tone, his brow, his mouth—everything about him has taken on that stony quality, like he's just reciting facts, objective truths that don't affect him. "They weren't thrilled when I decided to stay in the city instead of coming back to work for one of them."

I wonder if people fall for that. If, every time Charlie talks about the things that mean the most to him, the world sees a cold man with a clinical view of things, rather than someone grappling for under-standing and control in a world where those rarely appear.

I swallow the aching knot in my throat. "I'm sure they want you here, Charlie. It sounds like that's what they wanted from the beginning."

He tips his chin toward the patio table, on which the extension cords we bought sit. "Mind plugging in the air pump?"

For the next couple of minutes, we're silent as the pump howls. I set up the fans we pulled from the closet and plug them into the power strip. Charlie puts the bedding onto the mattress, and I hang the paper-lantern lights, arranging the mosquito-repelling candles at regular intervals.

We're quiet until I can't take it anymore. "Charlie," I say, and he looks over his shoulder at me, then turns to sit on the edge of the air mattress.

"I'm sure he's grateful you're here," I say. "They both must be."

He uses the back of his hand to catch the sweat on his brow. "When I told him I was staying for a while, his exact words were, *Son, just what do you think you can do?* The emphasis on *you* was his, not mine."

I sit on the deck in front of him, cross-legged. "But aren't you two close?"

"We were," he says. "We are. He's the best person I know. And he's right, there's not a lot I can do to help him. I mean, Shepherd's the one keeping the business going, keeping up with the work their house always needs. All I can do is run the bookstore."

My heart stings. I remember that feeling, of not being enough. Of wanting so badly to be what Libby needed after we lost Mom and failing, over and over again. I couldn't be tender for her. I couldn't bring the magic back into our life. All I had on my side was brute force and desperation.

But I was trying to live up to a memory, the phantom of someone we'd both loved.

Now I see what I missed before. Not just that Charlie never felt like he fit, but that he saw what it would've looked like if he *did*. I didn't make much of it at the time, but seeing Shepherd standing with Clint at the salon—it isn't just that they are comparable heights and builds, or the same trope. They look alike. The green eyes, the blond hair, the beard.

I climb into the tent beside him, the mattress dipping under my weight. "*You're* his son, Charlie."

He runs his hands down his thighs, sighing. "I'm not good at this shit." He kneads his eyebrow, then leans back on the mattress, staring up through the mosquito-netted roof, a Charlie-suggested compromise that still counts as Libby and me sleeping under the stars. "I've never felt so useless in my life. Things are falling apart for them, and the best I can do is open the store every day at the same time."

"Which, from what you've told me, is a vast improvement." I move closer, his warm smell curling around me, the sun coaxing it from his skin. Overhead, spun-sugar clouds drift across the cornflower blue sky. "You're not useless, Charlie. I mean, look at all this."

He gives me a look. "I know how to set up a tent, Nora. It's not Nobel-worthy."

I shake my head. "*Not that.* You're . . ." I search for the right word. It's rare that my vocabulary fails me like this. "Organized."

His eyes crackle with light as he laughs. "Organized?"

"*Extremely,*" I deadpan. "Not to mention thorough."

"You make me sound like a contract," he says, amused.

"And you *know* how I feel about a good contract," I say.

His smirk pulls higher. "Actually, I only know how you feel about a bad one, written on a damp napkin." He lies back fully on the mattress, and I do too, leaving a healthy gap between us.

"A good contract is . . ." I think for a moment.

"Adorable?" Charlie supplies, teasing.

"No."

"Comely?"

"At bare minimum," I say.

"Charming?"

"Sexy as hell," I reply. "Irresistible. It's a list of great traits and working compromises that watch out for all parties involved. It's . . . satisfying, even when it's not what you expected, because you work for it. You go back and forth until every detail is just how it needs to be."

I look sidelong at Charlie. He's already looking at me. The healthy gap has developed a fever. "What's the deal with Amaya?" It's out before I can second-guess it.

The corners of his mouth turn downward. "What do you mean?"

"I mean," I say, "you almost married her. What went wrong?"

"A lot of things," he says.

"Oh, like you were too forthcoming?" I tease.

His lips draw into their smirk-pout. "Or maybe she just wasn't enough of a smart-ass for my taste."

After a beat, we turn our gazes back to the cotton-candy-soft clouds and he says, "We started dating in high school. And then she went to NYU, and after some time at community college, I followed her."

"Your first love?" I guess.

He nods. "When we finished school, she wanted to look at places back in Asheville. It had never occurred to me that she'd want to move back, and it had never occurred to her that I wouldn't, and we were so bad at communicating that it didn't come up much."

"Did you try long distance?" I ask.

"For a year," he says. "Worst year of my life."

"It never works," I agree.

"Every day feels like a breakup," he says. "You're constantly letting each other down, or holding each other back. When we finally ended things, my mom was pretty brokenhearted. She told me I was making all the same mistakes she did and I was going to end up alone if I didn't figure out my priorities."

"She just wanted you to come back," I say. "And Amaya was the fastest path."

"Maybe." He lets out a breath, like he's resigned himself to something. "We barely spoke for a few months, and then . . ." He hesitates. "I came home for the holidays, and I found out Amaya had been dating my cousin since a few weeks after we split. That's what she wanted to clear the air about, the other night."

I sit up on my forearms, surprised. "Wait. Your *ex-fiancée* dated *your cousin? Shepherd?*"

He nods. "My family basically agreed not to tell me, but I found out anyway, and we had another rough stretch after that."

And there it is, another little piece of Charlie popped into place.

"There aren't a ton of prospects here," he goes on, "so I didn't exactly blame them, but at the same time . . ."

"Fuck that?" I guess.

He runs a hand up the backside of his head, then tucks it there. "I don't know, she deserves to be happy. Shepherd had a better chance of giving her that."

"Why?" I ask. He looks at me, brow pinched, like he doesn't understand the question. "Why does he have any better chance at making someone happy than you do?"

"Oh, come on, Stephens," he says wryly. "You of all people know what I mean."

"I definitely don't," I insist.

"Your *archetypes*," he says. "The tropes. He's the guy every woman falls for. The son my parents wanted, working full-time at the job my dad wanted *me* to have, all while making, like, fucking rocking chairs in his spare time. He even went to my top choice for school."

"Cornell?" I say.

"Went there to play football," Charlie says, "but he's fucking smart too. You went out with him—you know what he's like."

"I did go out with him," I say, "which is why I'm qualified to say, you're wrong. I mean, not about him being smart. But the other thing, that he's more qualified to make someone happy."

His smile fades. He looks back to the sky. "Yeah, well," he murmurs. "At least for Amaya, it made sense. During our breakup, one of the last things she said to me was, *If we stay together, every single day for the rest of our lives is going to be the same.* Wasn't even the last time I heard that in a breakup speech." He shakes his head. "Anyway, that's why she wanted to meet up. To apologize for how things ended."

I feel my cheeks coloring. "It's cute of you to think that, Charlie," I say. "But based on how she looks at you, I'm pretty sure all that sameness isn't so unappealing to her anymore."

"It wasn't just that I was too boring for her. She also decided she wanted kids—or, I guess, *admitted* she did, and was just waiting for me to change my mind."

I turn onto my side and face him. "You don't?"

"I hated *being* a kid." He folds his arm beneath his head and looks almost furtively in my direction. "I'd have no idea how to get someone else through it, and I definitely wouldn't enjoy it. I like them, but I don't want to be responsible for any."

"Agreed," I say. "I love my nieces more than anything on the planet, but every time Tala falls asleep in my lap, her dad gets all teary-eyed and is like, *Doesn't it just make you want to have some of your own, Nora?* But when you have kids, they count on you. Forever. Any mistake you make, any failure—and if something happens to you . . ."

My throat twists.

"People like to remember childhood as all magic and no responsibilities, but that's not really how it is. You have absolutely no control over your environment. It all comes down to the adults in your life, and . . . I don't know. Every time Libby has a new kid, it's like there's this magic house in my heart that rearranges to make a new room for the baby.

"And it always hurts. It's terrifying. One more person who needs you."

One more tiny hand with your heart in its grip.

I draw a breath, steeling myself. "Can I tell you something? Another secret?"

He turns onto his side, peering at me through the light. "Are we back on who killed JFK?"

I shake my head. "I think Libby's getting a divorce."

His brow creases. "You think?"

"She hasn't told me yet," I explain. "But she's not answering Brendan's calls, and she's not sleeping well. She hasn't had trouble with that since—" Charlie's presence has once again uncorked me. He wraps my focus around him in a way that makes it hard to think forward, to be on guard against every possible scenario.

Or maybe it's because he really *is* so organized and thorough, it's easy to believe that he could fix anything with the sheer force of his will, so it feels safe to unbolt all these chaotic feelings.

"Since your mom passed away?" he finishes my sentence for me.

I nod, run my fingers over the cool pillow between us. "The only thing that's ever really mattered to me is being sure she has what she needs. And now she's going through something life-changing and—I can't do anything. I mean, she hasn't even told me about it. So if anyone's useless . . ."

His hand glides up my back, a light, soothing trail over my spine, and settles beneath my hair. "Maybe," he says, "you're already doing what she needs you to do. Just by being here with her."

I cut him a look, feeling a lift and swell in my heart. "Maybe that's all your dad needs from you too."

He gently squeezes my neck, then lets his hand fall away. "The difference," he says, "is Libby asked you to be here. He asked me not to."

"Well, if that's all you need," I say quietly, like it's a secret, "Charlie, will you please be here?"

He leans forward, softly kissing me, his fingers fluttering over my jaw as I breathe in his minty breath and warm skin. When he draws back, his eyes are melted gold, my nerve endings quivering under them.

"Yes," he says, and pulls me into him, his arm coiling around me and chin tucking against my shoulder. "I already told you, Nora," he murmurs, his fingers splaying on my stomach, just beneath my shirt. "I'll go anywhere with you."

Sometimes, even when you start with the last page and you think you know everything, a book finds a way to surprise you.

25

WHY DO YOUR hands smell like that?" Libby demands as I guide her through the back door, palms pressed over her eyes.

"My hands do *not* smell," I say.

"It's, like, New TV Smell," she says.

"That's not a thing," I tell her.

"Yeah it is. New TV Smell."

"You mean New Car Smell."

"No," she says. "It's like, when you open the TV box and pull the Styrofoam packing sheet out, and it smells like a swimming pool inside."

"Then why wouldn't you just say I smell like a swimming pool?"

"Did you buy us a big-ass TV?"

"You know what, forget the grand reveal." I release my hold on her, and she screams.

Charlie jolts like she just chucked a priceless vase his way. "Sissy!"

she yelps, spinning toward me, then back. "Charlie!" Then to me again. "We're camping?!"

I shrug. "It's on the list."

She throws her arms around me and lets out another high-pitched shriek. "Thank you, Sissy," she murmurs. "Thank you."

"Anything for you," I tell her. Over her shoulder, I lock eyes with Charlie.

Thank you, I mouth. His chin dips as he smiles. *Anything for you,* he mouths. In my chest, something heavy turns over.

⌒

I wake up twice, gasping for breath. The second time, Libby rolls over, flopping her arm around me in her sleep, her leg twitching so that she's kind of kicking me.

Even with the strategically positioned fans, it's uncomfortably warm, but I don't shake her off. Instead I lay my hand over hers and squeeze her to me.

I will take care of you, I promise her.

I won't let anything hurt you.

For once, I get up first. I skip my run and head straight for a shower, then preheat the oven.

The corn-lime cookies are ready by the time Libby's up, and we eat them for breakfast with coffee.

"You are just *full* of surprises," Libby says, and pretends not to notice that the cookies are lumpy and burnt at the edges. In this scenario, my cookies are definitely the bad drawing with the penis hat, but I don't care. She's happy about them.

On my walk into Goode Books, *Frigid*'s final pages arrive. The last stretch has officially begun.

When Charlie and I aren't in the same room, we're emailing

about the manuscript. When we're not emailing about the manuscript, we're texting about everything else.

On Tuesday when I bite the bullet and order a salad from Poppa Squat's, I send him a picture of the cubed ham monstrosity Amaya drops in front of me.

I think I underestimated your sadomasochistic streak, Stephens, he says.

The next day, he sends me a blurry shot of the bickering geriatric couple from town hall caught in a passionate embrace outside the new Dunkin' Donuts. Love conquers all, I guess, he writes.

I reply, or she's found a discreet way to suffocate him.

What a beautiful, twisted brain you have, Nora.

He stops by one night with the wood Sally promised us, along with s'mores supplies, and helps us build a fire the night is technically too hot for. While we sit around the deck roasting marshmallows, Libby announces, "I've decided I like you, Charlie."

"I'm honored," he says.

"Don't be," I tell him. "She likes everyone."

She reaches into the bag of marshmallows and flings one at me. "Not true," she cries. "What about my vendetta against the guy in the Trivago commercials?"

"One unpleasant sex dream does not a vendetta make," I say.

"I once had a sex dream about the green M&M," Charlie says bluntly, and Libby and I descend into snorting laughter.

"Okay," Libby says when she recovers. "But she can get it. She's fucking gorgeous."

"Fucking gorgeous," Charlie agrees, locking eyes with me over the flames. "So much better than adorable."

We make plans to finish our notes on the final portion of the book on Saturday. Every moment until then feels like part of a countdown. Sometimes all I want is to run down the clock. Sometimes I want to stuff sand back up through the hourglass's neck.

He texts me things like holy shit, page 340.

And she's on fire.

And the cat!

I write back things like I SCREAMED.

Her best yet.

And the cat stays.

To which he replies, agreed.

Sometimes he sends me texts that just say, Nora.

Charlie, I type back.

Then he'll say, this book.

And I'll say, This book.

It's killing me not knowing how it ends, I tell him.

It's killing me that it's going to end, he writes back. If I weren't editing it, I wouldn't finish it.

Really? I write. You have that level of self-control?

Sometimes. After a moment, he sends another message. There are full series I love whose last chapter I've never read. I hate the feeling of something ending.

Instantly, my heart feels raw, rug-burned, every inch of it stinging.

This book, this job, this trip, this never-ending, days-spanning conversation. I want to make it all last, and I need to know how it ends. I want to finish it, and I need it to go on forever.

If I thought I was sleeping badly our first two weeks here, week three obliterates the notion. Charlie and I text until at least midnight each night, sometimes interspersed with quick calls to talk through plot points that leave me so energized that I have to walk a loop in the meadow to cool down.

All these years spent thinking that I had superhuman self-control, and now I realize I just never put anything I wanted too badly in front of myself.

But I've made it to Thursday night, which means there's only two days until we finish the edit letter. A week and some change until I go back to the city, where The Future We've Agreed Not to Discuss will begin. This interlude will be over. The future will be the present, and this will become the past.

But not yet.

26

~

LIBBY AND I walk to the fence line with celery, carrots, and sugar cubes, but even with our best baby talk, we can't coax the horses over.

"You think they know we're city people?" I say.

"They can still smell Drybar all over you," she replies.

I cup my hands around my mouth and shout out across the dusky pasture, "This isn't the end! We'll be back!" We hike back to the cottage, then decide we're too hungry to cook and instead trek into town, destined for Poppa Squat's loaded fries and cauliflower wings.

On the whole walk, Libby's a little shaky. Beneath the streetlamps, she's past the realm of peaked and into the territory of Straight-Up Ghostly.

Behind the glow of Goode Books' windows, Charlie's closing up. "Let's invite him to dinner," she cries, unlatching herself from me and leading the charge across the street.

Despite our early efforts at discretion, I'm positive she's noticed the vibe between us, but she's kept any disapproval to herself ever since Charlie helped with the surprise campout.

She pounds on the shop door with the ferocity of an FBI agent on TV until Charlie reappears, looking exactly how he always looks: tidy, overworked, well dressed, and like he wants to bite my thigh.

"We came to invite you to dinner." Libby pushes inside, beelining toward the bathroom, as she is wont to do these days, calling, "We're going to Poppa Squat's."

"Maybe you've heard of it," I say. "It was on a *very* exclusive BuzzFeed list."

Slow nod. Dark, gut-melting eyes. Holding his gaze *feels like* public indecency. " 'Places That Sound Like They'll Definitely Give You Diarrhea While Really They Only Just *Might* Give You Diarrhea.' "

"That's the one," I agree.

He widens the door for me, but just then my phone rings. On instinct, I check it. Sharon's calling. While on maternity leave. "I should take this."

Libby does a cartoon screech-to-halt and turns back to me. "No work calls after five," she reminds me.

"This is different," I say, the ringing scritching against my nerves like fingernails on a chalkboard. "It might be important."

Libby's lips fall into a straight line. "Nora."

"Just give me a minute, Libby," I say. Her eyes go wide at the sharp edge to my voice. "I'm sorry—I just—I have to do this."

I take off down the dark block, heart thudding as I answer the call. "Sharon? Is everything okay?"

"Hi, yes!" she says brightly. "Everything's fine—sorry to worry you. I just had a question."

The tension in my shoulders dissolves. "Sure. How can I help?"

"I can't give too many concrete details," she starts. "But . . . Loggia might be hiring a new editor soon."

"Oh?" The floor of my stomach sinks. I've gotten enough of these calls over the years to know where this is going. Sharon's leaving—or, rather, not coming back from parental leave.

"Yeah," she goes on. "Looks that way. And hey, I know you're doing great at the agency, so this might not be interesting to you at all, but I've been talking with Charlie, and he says you're *really* helping get Dusty's book into shape."

"He makes it easy," I say. "And she does too."

"Of course," Sharon says. "But you've also always had a knack for this kind of thing. I guess I'm wondering if there's any chance you'd be interested."

"Interested?"

"In editing," she says. "For Loggia."

I must be stunned into silence for longer than I realize, because Sharon says, "Hello? Did I lose you?"

My mouth's gone dry. It comes out small. "Here."

This must be how people feel when their water breaks. Like they've been carrying a new future around inside themself and suddenly it's gushing out, ready or not.

"You want me to be an editor?"

"I'd like you to interview, yes," she says. "But I totally understand if you're not interested. You've made a name for yourself as an agent—and you're great at it. This might not make sense for you."

I open my mouth. No sound comes out.

I'm stumped.

"I don't need a concrete answer yet," she says, "but if you're at all interested . . ."

I expect to have to swim through the soup of my thoughts and feelings, to have to give a hacking cough to get out some words.

Instead, I hear my voice as if through a tunnel: "Yes."

"Yes?" Sharon says. "You'll meet with us?"

I squeeze the bridge of my nose as pressure rushes into my skull. This isn't the kind of decision you just make. Least of all when your sister's in the middle of a potentially very expensive crisis.

"I'd like to think about it," I backtrack. "Can I call you in a couple days?"

"Of course," she says. "Of *course*! This would be a big decision. But I'll admit, when Charlie said you might be interested, I was *very* excited."

I barely hear the rest. My mind has become one of those FBI corkboards with zigzagging red string between every pushpin it can find, trying to make things add up, to make all of it fit into one uninterrupted pattern, proof that this can work, that I can have this, that it's not too good to be true.

When I hang up, I sit on a bench beneath a streetlamp, waiting for the daze to fade. After six full minutes, I still feel like I'm inside a fishbowl, everything surreally bent and distorted around me. When I finally walk back, the bells over the shop door seem to chime from miles off, but Libby's voice is close and jarring. "*There* you are, *finally*." With obvious annoyance, she adds, "Can we go to dinner now, or do you have a board meeting to get to?"

I feel brittle, stretched too far in too many directions, and when she rolls her eyes, something in me finally snaps: "Can you *not* do that, Libby? Not right now."

"Do *what*?" she says. "You said you'd be fully present after five, and—"

"*Stop.*" I lift a hand, trying to hold off the fresh onslaught of red string and pushpins raining down on me, reality crashing in from every direction.

Because even if I want this job, I can't have it.

Just like I couldn't last time. But at least then, Libby *told* me what she was going through. At least I wasn't throwing darts in the dark, hoping they'd plug up the holes of a sinking ship.

"What's going *on* with you?" she demands, brow lifted, face torqued with dismay.

An unstoppable wave rises through me. "Me?" I repeat. "I'm not the one sneaking around, disappearing, not answering her husband's texts, keeping secrets. I've *been* fully present, Libby, all month, and you're *still* keeping me in the dark." My pulse feels erratic. My fingers tingle. "I can't help if you don't tell me!"

"I don't want your help, Nora!" She pales at the thought, sways between her feet. "I know I used to rely on you a lot, and I'm sorry for that, but I don't want to be another excuse for you not to have a life—"

"Oh, right," I fume. "I don't have a life! 'The only thing that matters to me is my career.' Guess what, Libby? If that were true, I'd be an editor right now! I wouldn't have passed on the job I *actually* wanted to make sure you could afford the best fucking doula in Manhattan!"

Her face is white now, her brow damp. "Wait . . . y-you . . . you . . ." Her breath is shallow. She turns, setting one palm on the counter. Her other hand rises to her forehead, eyes fluttering closed. She shakes her head, gathering herself.

"Libby?" I take a half step toward her, my heart in my throat.

That's when she collapses.

27

CATCH HER, BUT I'm not strong enough to hold her up. "Help!" I scream as we slump to the ground, the worst of her fall softened.

The door to the office flings open, but I'm still shrieking *Help*, screaming like it's doing anything, as if just shouting the word has power. Action over inaction. Movement over stagnation. An illusion of control.

Charlie comes running, crouches beside us. "What happened?"

"I don't know!" I say. "Libby. *Libby*."

Her eyes slit open, flutter closed again. God, she's pale. Was she that pale all afternoon? And her heart is racing. I can feel it shivering through her. Her hands are icy. I take one between mine, rubbing it. "Libby. *Libby*?"

Her eyes open again, and this time she looks more alert.

"Let's get her to the hospital," Charlie says.

"I'm okay," she insists, but her voice is shaky. She tries to sit up. I pull her back into my lap. "Don't move. Just take a second."

She nods, settles into my arms.

Charlie's on his feet already, headed for the door. "I'll pull my car up."

~

Charlie is the one who talks to the receptionist in complete sentences when we arrive.

Charlie is the one who pulls me away when I start half shouting at the nurse who tells us we're not allowed through the doors Libby's ushered through. He's the one who pushes me into a chair in the waiting room, takes hold of my face, and promises it'll be okay.

You can't know that, I think, but he's so sure that I almost believe him.

"Just sit right here," he says. "I'll figure this out."

Seven minutes later, he returns with decaf, a prepackaged apple fritter, and the number of the room Libby's been moved into. "They're running tests. It shouldn't take long."

"How did you do that?" I ask, voice hoarse.

"I was on the high school paper with one of the doctors here," he says. "She says we can go and wait in her hall until the tests are over."

I've never felt so useless, or so grateful not to be in charge. "Thank you," I croak.

Charlie nudges the fritter toward me. "You should eat something."

He ferries me through the hospital, stopping by another vending machine for a bottle of water, then to a pair of hideously outdated chairs in a hellishly lit hallway that smells like antiseptic.

"She's in there. If they're not out in five minutes, I'll find someone to talk to, okay?" he says gently. "Just give them five minutes."

Within twenty seconds I'm pacing. My chest hurts. My eyes burn, but no tears come.

Charlie grabs me, pulls me in around his chest, and wraps a hand around the back of my head. I feel small, vulnerable, helpless in a way I haven't for years.

Even before Mom died, I wasn't much of a crier. But when Libby and I were kids and I was upset, there was nothing that could make me tear up faster than having Mom's arms wrapped around me. Because then—and only then—I knew it was safe to come apart.

My sweet girl, she'd coo. That's what she always called me.

She never did the *You're okay, don't cry* thing. Always *My sweet girl. Let it out.*

At her funeral, I remember tears glossing my eyes, the pinprick sensation at the back of my nose, and then, beside me, the sound of Libby breaking, descending into sobs.

I remember catching myself holding my breath, like I was waiting.

And then I realized I *was* waiting.

For her.

For Mom to put her arms around us.

Libby was crumbling, and Mom wasn't coming.

It was like a collapsed sandcastle leapt back into place inside me, rearranging my heart into something passably sturdy. I wrapped my arms around my sister and tried to whisper, *Let it out.* I couldn't get the words past my lips.

So instead I dropped my mouth beside Libby's ear and whispered, "Hey."

She gave a stuttering breath, like, *What?*

"If Mom had known how hot the reverend here is," I said, "she probably would've made it down here sooner."

Libby's saucer eyes looked up at me, glazed with tears, and my chest felt like a can being crushed until she let out a scratchy jolt of laughter loud enough that Hot Reverend stumbled over his next few words.

She lay her head on my shoulder, turned her face into my jacket, and shook her head. "That is so fucked up," she said, but she was shaking with teary laughter.

For that second, she was okay. Now, though, when she really needs me, I'm useless.

"Why couldn't we be in the room for *tests*?" I get out.

Charlie inhales, shifting between his feet. "Maybe they think you'll give her the answers."

There is absolutely no conviction in his joke. When I draw back, I realize he's not doing so hot himself.

"Are you okay? You look like you're going to be sick."

"Just don't like hospitals," he says. "I'm fine."

"You don't have to stay."

He takes my hands, holds them between our chests. "I'm not leaving you here."

"I can handle it."

His mouth shrinks, the crease beneath it deepening. "I know. I want to be here."

A group of nurses pass with a gurney, and an ashen cast seeps onto Charlie's face.

I scrounge around for something to say, anything else to think about. "Sharon called me."

His lips press into a knot.

"She told me you put me up for a job."

After a beat, he murmurs, "If I overstepped, I'm sorry."

"It's not that." My face prickles. "It's just . . . what if I'm bad at it?"

His hands skim up my arms until he's cradling my jaw. "Impossible."

My brow arches of its own volition. "Because I helped edit one book?"

He shakes his head. "Because you're smart and intuitive. And good at getting the best writing out of people, and you put the work before your ego. You know when to push and when to let something go. You're trustworthy—partly because you're so bad at lying—and you take care of the things that matter to you.

"If I had to pick one person to be in my corner, it'd be you. Every time. You take care of shit."

With a sharp throb in my chest, my gaze falls to the floor. "Not always."

"Hey." Charlie's rough fingers come back to mine. He lifts my hand, brushing his mouth over my knuckles. "We'll figure out what's wrong and do everything we can to fix it."

"That fucking list." My chest is too tight to let anything out but a whisper. "She's been doing too much. I shouldn't have let her. We slept out in the heat and—we've been working on this fundraiser. She should've been resting."

Charlie sits, drawing me into his lap, every thought of discretion, of avoiding complication gone in an instant. I need him, and he's here, I realize. Fully, not with caveats or stipulations. His hand slides up the back of my neck, tucked beneath my hair, and I'm wrapped up in him like he's my personal stone fortress. Like even if I came apart, nothing could get to me.

"Libby makes Libby's decisions," he says. "Imagine how you'd react if someone tried to stop *you* from doing what you want, Stephens." A hint of a smile tugs at his pout. "Actually, don't imagine it. It's inappropriate to get turned on in a hospital."

I laugh weakly into his chest, another knot unwinding in my own. "I missed something. I'm here with her, and Brendan isn't, and—" My voice catches. The rest tumbles out painfully: "It's my job to watch out for her."

"I know it's scary, being here," he says. "But this is a good hospital. They know what they're doing." His fingers move in soothing, rhythmic circles against the nape of my neck. "This is where my dad came."

The words *sweet guy* sear through my mind, like the afterimage left behind by the pop of a camera's bulb.

That's what Charlie called his father. *A sweet guy. The best person I know.*

"What happened?" I ask.

After a protracted silence, he says, "The first stroke wasn't bad. But this last one . . . he was in a coma for six days." He watches the progress of his thumb running back and forth over mine. His brow tightens. The day we met, I mistook this expression for surliness, brooding, proof he was as warm and human as a block of marble.

Now all it does is bring out the lost look in his eyes. "This huge, handy guy who can fix anything, build anything. And in that hospital bed, he looked—" He breaks off. I twine my free hand into the hair at the base of his neck.

"He looked *old*," Charlie says, then, after a fraught silence, "When I was a kid, all I ever wanted was to be like him, and I wasn't. But he always made me feel like it was okay to be the way I am."

I cup his jaw and lift his gaze. I wonder if he can see every word in my expression, because I feel them tunneling up from the lowest part of my gut. *You're more than okay.*

He clears his throat. "My dad's alive because of what they were able to do for him here. Between them and you, Libby's going to be all right. She has to be."

As if on cue, the doctor, a balding man with a Salman Rushdie goatee and brow, walks out of the exam room. "Is she okay?" I lurch to my feet.

"She's resting," he says. "But she gave me permission to speak with both of you." He nods toward Charlie, who stands, tightening his grip on my hand, anchoring me.

"What happened?" I ask.

In an instant, my mind cycles through every ailment it knows of.

Heart attack.

Stroke.

Miscarriage.

And then it snags: *PULMONARY EMBOLISM.*

The words repeat. They echo. They reach back to the beginning of my life and forward to the end of it, this outstretched Slinky of a phrase, looping through time, fucking with everything, warping my life in places, ripping through it in others. *Pulmonary embolism.*

The doctor says, "Your sister is anemic."

The words slam into a wall. Or maybe run off a cliff—that's how it feels, like I've stepped off a ledge and am hovering before the drop.

"Her body is lacking in iron and B12," he explains. "So she's not manufacturing enough healthy red blood cells. It's not uncommon during pregnancy, and especially unsurprising for someone who's already dealt with this issue in a previous pregnancy."

"Libby hasn't had this before."

He studies the clipboard in his hands. "Well, it wasn't as severe, but her levels were definitely low. I spoke with her ob-gyn, and apparently your sister was a bit more stable in her first trimester, but they've been keeping an eye on this since the beginning."

My fingers are tingling again. My brain works to clear the smoke and start a checklist, but it's just not happening.

"What do we need to do?" Charlie asks.

"It's pretty simple," the doctor says. "She'll need to take an iron supplement, and eat more meat and eggs, if possible. She'll also want to do the same with B12. We'll get you a printout on the best sources for those, though I assume she'll remember from last time."

Last time.

This has already happened. I didn't just miss it once, but twice.

"She'll possibly have to deal with nausea, but having more, smaller meals throughout the day should help. I'd like to see her next week, to make sure she's doing better, and then after that, she'll need to have regular checkups with her doctor until delivery."

That's manageable. It's fixable. List-able.

"Thank you." I shake his hand. "Thank you so much."

"My pleasure." He smiles, a remarkably warm, patient smile. "Just give her time to rest. The nurse will let you know when you can see her."

As soon as he's gone, I feel exhausted, like a thousand-pound weight just lifted off me, but only after hours of carrying it.

"You okay?"

When I look at Charlie, he's blurry; my vision is distorted.

"Breathe, Nora." He grips my shoulders, taking an exaggerated inhale. I match it. We stay in sync for a few breaths until the pressure releases. "She's okay."

I nod, let him pull me into his chest, wrapping me up tight against him.

I try to tell him I'm just relieved, but there's no room for words—for logic, reason, arguments. My body's decided what to do, and it's this: nothing, in Charlie's arms.

He buries his mouth against my temple. I close my eyes, letting the waves of relief crash over me.

Gradually, they draw back, and I'm left floating, drifting in a current of Charlie: his faintly spiced scent, the heat of his skin, the fine wool of his light sweater.

A picture of my apartment flickers across my mind. The yellowy-red streetlights catching raindrops on my windowpane, the sound of cars slushing past, the radiator hissing against my socked feet. The smell of old books and crisp new ones, and the cologne whose cedar-wood and amber notes are meant to conjure up the image of sun-soaked libraries. The creak of old floorboards, the shuffle of footsteps, half-drunken singing as revelers make their way home from the tequila bar across the street, stopping for dollar slices of pizza dripping with oil.

I can almost believe I'm there. In my home, where it's safe enough to relax, to undo the brackets of steel in my spine and slip out of my harsh outline to—*settle*.

"You're not useless, Charlie," I whisper against his steady heartbeat. "You're . . ."

His hand is still in my hair. "Organized?"

I smile into his chest. "Something like that," I say. "It'll come to me."

At the creak of Libby's door, my eyes open.

The nurse smiles. "Your sister's ready for you."

28

~

LIBBY PERCHES ON the bed, already changed back into her purple polka-dotted sundress and looking thoroughly chastened. A meek smile tugs at her lips. "Hi."

"Hi." I close the door and go to sit beside her.

After a moment, she says, "Are you okay?"

I balk. "Libby, I'm not the one who passed out and nearly cracked her skull on an old-timey cash register."

Her teeth sink into her lip. "You're mad." She wrings her hands in her lap. "That I didn't tell you this happened before."

"I'm . . . confused."

Her eyes dart furtively toward mine. "I'm confused why you didn't tell me you had a chance at an editing job."

"It was years ago," I say. "On the bottom rung, and the pay was shit. It wasn't all about you. There were a lot of reasons to stay at the agency."

She looks at me with watery sapphire eyes, a wrinkle between her brows. "You should've told me."

"I should have," I agree quietly. "And you should've told me about all this."

Libby heaves a sigh. "No one knew except Brendan. And he wanted me to tell you, but I knew it would freak you out. And it's super common. I mean, my doctor was pretty sure everything would be fine. I didn't want to burden you."

I reach for her hand. "Libby, you're not a burden. You're *it*. You come first." I add lightly, "Even before my career. *And* my Peloton."

Huffing, she pulls her hand from mine. "Do you know what kind of guilt that comes with, Sissy? Knowing you'll drop everything to manage *my* life? That you'd give up on your *dream* job to—to mother me? It makes me feel . . . incapable."

"I just want to be there for you," I reason.

"I shouldn't always come first, Nora," she says softly. "And neither should your clients."

"Fine," I say. "From now on my bagel guy comes first, but you're a close second."

"I'm being serious. Mom expected too much from you."

"What does Mom have to do with this?" I say.

"Everything." Before I can argue, Libby continues, "I'm not saying I blame her—she was in an impossible situation and she did a fairly amazing job with us. But that doesn't change the fact that sometimes, she forgot whose job it was to take care of us."

"Lib, what are—"

"You're not my dad," she says.

"Since when has that been on the table?"

She huffs again, grabbing my hands. "She treated you like her partner, Nora. She treated you like you were—like it was *your* job to take care of me. And I let you, after she died, but you're still doing it. And it's too much. For both of us."

"That's not true," I say.

"It is," she replies. "I have my own daughters now, and let me fucking tell you, Nora, there are days I get into the shower and sob into a loofah because I'm so overwhelmed, and maybe keeping it hidden from them isn't the answer either, but I can't *imagine* putting my worries on Tala or Bea like Mom did to us. Especially you.

"She had it really hard, but she was our only parent, and there were times she forgot that. There were times she treated you like you were an adult."

An icy pang lances through me. Guilt or hurt or run-of-the-mill homesickness for Mom, or all of it braided into one icicle right through my heart, burning like only cold can.

Like the most precious thing—the only precious thing—in my life has frozen over so deeply that there are spiderwebs of ice veining through me.

"I wanted to help," I say. "I wanted to take care of you."

"I know." She lifts my hands between hers, holding them against her heart. "You always do, and I love you for that. But I don't want you to be Mom—and I definitely don't want you to be my dad. When I tell you something's going on, sometimes I just want you to be my sister and say, *That sucks.* Instead of trying to fix it."

The distance between us. The trip, the list, the secrets. I've seen all of these as little challenges to overcome, or maybe tests to prove I can be the sister Libby wants, but Charlie is right. All she really wants is a sister. Nothing more, nothing less.

"It's hard for me," I admit. "I hate feeling like I can't protect you."

"I know. But . . ." Her eyes close, and when they open again, she struggles to keep her voice from splintering, our hands trembling in a tightly gripped mass between us. "You *can't*. And I need to know I can be okay without you.

"When we lost Mom, I was gutted, but I was never scared about how we'd get by. I knew you'd make sure we did, and—Sissy, I appreciate it more than I could ever put into words."

"You could try," I joke quietly. "Maybe get me a card or something."

She laughs tearily, pulls one hand free to swipe at her eyes. "At some point, I have to know I can do things on my own. Not with Brendan's help, not with yours. And you need to make room in your life for other things, other *people* to matter."

I swallow hard. "No one will ever matter like you do, Lib."

"No one will ever matter like you do either," she whispers. "Other than my bagel guy."

I wrap my arms around her neck and drag her into a hug. "Please tell me the next time you find out you have an illness or vitamin deficiency," I say into her wispy pink-blond hair. "Even if all I'm allowed to do is say, *That sucks.* And then ship six cartons of supplements to your house."

"Deal." She draws back, her smile shifting into a wince. "There's something else you should know."

Here it is, I think, *what she's been keeping from me.*

She takes a deep breath.

"I eat meat."

My instant reaction is to jump off the bed like she's just told me she personally slaughtered a baby cow here moments ago and drank blood straight from its veins.

"I know!" she cries through her hands. "It started when I was pregnant with Tala! Because of the anemia. And, frankly, this bizarre and constant craving for Whoppers."

"Ew!" I say.

"I stopped as soon as she was born!" Libby says. "But then I started again when I found out about Number Three, and I didn't think a couple weeks off would make a difference for my levels, but I wasn't being conscientious enough about filling in the gaps. So. Whoops! Or . . . *whops?*"

"I can't believe you tricked me into being a vegetarian, for a decade, then caved for a *Whopper*!"

"How dare you," she says. "Whoppers are amazing."

"Okay, you're getting too good at lying."

She guffaws. "Okay, not amazing, but the heart wants what it wants."

"Your heart needs therapy."

"Can we get some on the way home?" She pushes off the bed. "Whoppers, not therapy."

"Whopp*ers? Plural?*"

"They have veggie burgers, you know," she says. "And we're already so close to Asheville, and there's a BK there."

I stare at her. "So not only did you just call it 'BK' without a hint of irony, but you're telling me you *checked* where the nearest one is."

"My sister taught me to be prepared. I scouted it out when Sally and I went to hang fliers for the Blue Moon Ball."

"That's not 'prepared,'" I say. "It's disturbed." At her laugh, I cave. "Whoppers it is."

~

"Are you *sure* you're up for this?"

Libby gives me a look. "Congratulations. You went a full twelve hours."

"Right," I say. "You're in charge of yourself. Who even cares if you're up for it? Not me."

She grins and jogs her huge purple purse. "I've got beef jerky in here, and almonds, and one of those peanut butter dipping cup things. Plus I'll be with Gertie and Sally and Amaya. You go get those edits done so you can take time off next week and *party*." Her phone buzzes, and she checks it. "Gertie's here. Looks like it might rain—want us to drop you at the bookstore?"

Charlie agreed to take over Sally's shift so she could focus on next weekend's ball, which means we'll be hammering out the final notes in the shop. We'd planned to finish reading pages last night, but that was shot to hell when Libby passed out, so we'll be finishing our reads today too.

"Why not."

Gertie's muddy hatchback sits at the bottom of the hill, even more covered in bumper stickers than when she drove us home from the salon, and she's burning incense on her dashboard. I have to literally bite my tongue to keep from momming her about how dangerous this is, not that she'd even hear it over the dissonant industrial music she's blasting.

The thrumming mostly drowns out the rumble of thunder approaching as I climb out in front of Goode's. Overhead, frothy black clouds are clumping up, and there's a bite to the air as the hatchback peels away from the curb.

Through the yellowy glare on the windowpanes, I spot Charlie reshelving at the nearest bookcase, cast in reds and golds.

His lips and jaw are shadowed to perfection, his dark hair haloed by the soft light. At the sight of him, my stomach flips and something blooms like a time-lapse flower behind my rib cage. Now that I'm here, so close to the end of this book, this edit, this trip, a not-small part of me wants to turn and run.

But then he catches sight of me, and his mouth splits into a full, sensual Charlie smile, and my fear blows away, like dust swept from a book jacket.

He opens the door, leaning out as the first fat droplets of rain splat the cobblestones. "You ready to finish this, Stephens?"

"Ready." It's true and a lie. Does anyone ever want to finish a good book?

The back office looks irresistibly cozy in the gloom of the storm, the scarred mahogany desk covered in papers and knickknacks but meticulously arranged in Charlie's signature style. Beside the lumpy sofa, the fireplace's mantel and its three-deep rows of family pictures are freshly dusted, and vacuum streaks are still visible on the antique rugs. The bulky air-conditioning unit hangs silent in the window, put out of work by the false-autumn cold snap.

He moves a stack of hardcovers off the sofa, then crosses the room to take the chair behind the desk. His expression seems to tease, *See? I'm perfectly harmless over here.*

Except nothing about him looks harmless to me. He looks like a Swiss Army knife. A man with six different means to undo me.

This Charlie, for making you spill your secrets.

This one for making you laugh.

This one can turn you on.

This is the one who will convince you you're capable of anything.

Here is the Charlie who will pull you into his lap to form your human barricade at a hospital.

And the one with the power to take you apart brick by brick.

"How's Libby?" he asks.

"Well," I say, "she has a beef jerky purse now."

"So I guess you're saying it's a mixed bag."

My head tips back, a veritable chortle leaping out of me. "What is it with this town and wordplay?"

"I have no idea what you're talking about," he deadpans.

"Settle a bet for me and Libby." I hunch forward over my laptop, the screen folding half closed.

"That's not really fair to Libby," Charlie says. "I'm always biased toward a shark."

Warmth fills my chest, but I press on, undeterred, a hammerhead to my core. "Is *Spaaaahhh* meant to be said as a sigh or a scream?"

Charlie runs a hand over his eyes as he laughs. "Well, I hate to muddy things even further for you, but back when I lived here, it was called G Spa. So I guess the pronunciation depends on how you think an orgasm sounds."

"You're making this up," I say.

"My imagination is good," he says, "but not *that* good."

"What goes *on* in those hallowed halls," I marvel, "and is it legal?"

"Honestly," Charlie says, "I think it was just a fortuitous mistake. The owner's name is Gladys Gladbury, so I think *that* was the reference she was aiming for."

"She might've been aiming for that, but she definitely hit the G Spa."

He smothers his face with his hand. "Your nightmare brain," he says, "is my absolute favorite, Stephens."

My blood starts to simmer as our gazes hold. "I guess we should read."

"I guess we should," I say.

This time he looks away first, moves the cursor on his laptop. "Let me know when you've finished," he says.

With some effort, I pivot my attention to *Frigid*. Within a few paragraphs, Dusty's hooked me. I've sunk into her words, engulfed head to toe by her story.

Nadine and Lola, the perky physical therapist, rush Josephine to the hospital, but after twenty-two hours, the swelling on Jo's brain still hasn't gone down. Nadine has to run home to feed the feral cat she's been housing, and by then, the storm is amping up.

Here, in Goode Books, the walls shiver with our real-life thunder in agreement.

Nadine calls the cat as she walks through her dark apartment, but the usual nonstop yowling doesn't answer. She sees the window over the sink; she'd left it cracked, and now it's wide open.

She runs out into the rain, wishing she'd given the cat a name, because screaming *You asshole, come back* into the wind doesn't do the trick. Finally, she spots the mangy tabby cowering, halfway in the storm drain.

Nadine starts across the street, hears the peal of rubber over wet asphalt, sees the car barreling toward her.

And then—the air rushes from her lungs.

Her eyes snap closed, pain shooting through her ribs. When she opens her eyes, she's on the grassy shoulder, Lola sprawled over her. As they catch their breath, the cat scrambles out of the storm drain, looks at her warily, and trots off.

"Shit," Lola says, scrambling up to chase the cat.

Nadine catches her arm. "Let him go," she says. "I can't help him."

The hospital calls.

My chest aches as I scroll to the first page of the last chapter, taking a breath in preparation before I keep reading.

Nadine and Lola stand together in the sunlit cemetery. No one else has come, apart from the priest. Jo had no one except, over these last months, them. Lola reaches for Nadine's hand, and though surprised, she lets her take it.

Later, at home, Nadine finds a floral arrangement on her step, a card from her former assistant: *I'm sorry for your loss.* She carries it inside and gets a vase down. Light streams in from the open window, making the water sparkle as it sluices from the faucet.

From the other room, she hears a feral yowl. Her heart lifts.

White space stretches out down the screen, room to sit and breathe within.

I stare at the blank page, emptied out.

In my favorite books, it's never quite the ending I want. There's always a price to be paid.

Mom and Libby liked the love stories where everything turned out perfectly, wrapped in a bow, and I've always wondered why I gravitate toward something else.

I used to think it was because people like me don't get *those* endings. And asking for it, hoping for it, is a way to lose something you've never even had.

The ones that speak to me are those whose final pages admit there is no going back. That every good thing must end. That every bad thing does too, that *everything* does.

That is what I'm looking for every time I flip to the back of a book, compulsively checking for proof that in a life where so many things have gone wrong, there can be beauty too. That there is always hope, no matter what.

After losing Mom, those were the endings I found solace in. The ones that said, *Yes, you have lost something, but maybe, someday, you'll find something too.*

For a decade, I've known I will never again have everything, and so all I've wanted is to believe that, someday, again, I'll have enough. The ache won't always be so bad. People like me aren't broken beyond repair. No ice ever freezes too thick to thaw and no thorns ever grow too dense to be cut away.

This book has crushed me with its weight and dazzled me with its tiny bright spots. Some books you don't *read* so much as *live*, and finishing one of those always makes me think of ascending from a scuba dive. Like if I surface too fast I might get the bends.

I take my time, letting each roll of thunder usher me closer, closer to the surface. When I finally look up, Charlie's watching me. "Finished?" he asks softly.

I nod.

Neither of us speaks for a moment.

Finally, quietly, he says, "Perfect."

"Perfect," I agree. That's the word. I clear my throat, try to think critically when all I want to do is bask in this moment. *Settle.* "Would the cat really come back?"

Without hesitation, Charlie says, "Yes."

"It's not her cat," I say. It's Nadine's constant refrain throughout the book, the reason she never names the little stowaway.

"She understands it," he says. "Everyone looks at that cat and sees it as a little monster. It doesn't know how to be a pet, but she doesn't care. That's why she says it isn't hers. Because it's not about what the cat can give her. It can't offer her anything.

"It's a mean, feral, hungry, socially unintelligent little bloodsucker." The sky is black beyond the window, the rain thick as a sheet every time the lightning slashes through it. "But it *is* her cat. It's never belonged to anybody, but it belongs to her."

I feel an uncanny ache. This is what looking at Charlie is like sometimes. Like a gut-punch of a sentence, like a line so sharp you have to set the book aside to catch your breath.

He opens his mouth to speak, and another earthshaking crack of thunder rends the rooms. The lights sputter out.

In the dark, Charlie clatters out from behind the desk. "You okay?"

I find his hand and cling to it. "Mm-hmm."

"I should lock the front door," he says, "until the power's back up."

At the edge to his voice, I say, "I'll come with you."

We creep out of the office. With the shop in the dark, the emptiness takes on a slight chill, and the hair along my arms pricks up as I wait for Charlie to flip the sign and lock the door. "There are flashlights in the office," he tells me afterward, and we shuffle back the way we came. He releases his hold on me to riffle through the desk drawers. "You cold?"

"A little." My teeth are chattering, but I'm not sure that's why.

He hands me a flashlight, flicks on the emergency lantern in his other hand, and carries it to the hearth. His face and shoulders are rigid as he piles logs in the hearth, the same way he showed me and Libby the other night: a nest of logs, its nooks filled with crumpled newspaper.

"You really don't like the dark," I say, kneeling on the rug beside him.

"It's not the dark, exactly." It takes a minute, but the kindling catches, warmth and light rippling over us. "It's just so quiet here, and when it's dark too, it's always made me feel sort of . . . alone, I guess."

This close, I can see all the fine details of his face, the darker brown ring in the middle of his gold irises, the crease under his lip and the individual curves of his lashes.

I push myself onto my feet and walk toward the desk. "I need to say something."

When I turn, he's standing again, his brow grooved, his hands in his pockets.

"Maybe, for whatever reason, you just don't want to date right now," I say, "and that's fine. People feel that way all the time. But if it's something else—if you're afraid you're too rigid, or whatever your exes might've thought about you—none of that's true. Maybe every day with you *would* be more or less the same, but so what? That actually sounds kind of great.

"And maybe I'm misreading all of this, but I don't think I am, because I've never met anyone so much like me. And—if any part of all this is that you think, in the end, I'll want a golden retriever instead of a mean little cat, you're wrong."

"Everyone wants a golden retriever," he says in a low voice. As ridiculous a statement as it is, he looks serious, concerned.

I shake my head. "I don't."

Charlie's hands settle on the edge of the desk on either side of me, his gaze melting back into honey, caramel, maple. *"Nora."* My heart trips at his rough, halting tone: the voice of a man letting someone down easy.

"Never mind." I avert my gaze but I'm unable to remove him from it entirely, not with him so close, his hands on either side of my hips. "I understand. I just wanted to say something, in case—"

"I'm not going back to New York," he interrupts.

My eyes rebound to his. Every sharp edge of his expression takes on new meaning. "That's why," he says. "The reason I can't . . ."

"I don't . . ." I shake my head. "For how long?"

His throat bobs as he swallows. "My sister was supposed to come back in December to take over the store. But she met someone in Italy. She's staying there."

My heart has gone from feeling like an over-caffeinated hummingbird to an anvil, each beat a heavy, aching thud.

"I already emailed Libby about the apartment," he goes on. "It's hers if she wants it. It was always going to be."

My eyes sting. My heart feels like a phone book whose pages have all come loose, and I'm trying to stuff them into an order that makes sense, that fixes this.

"That first night I ran into you in town," Charlie says, "I'd just found out Carina was staying awhile longer. I wasn't sure how long, but . . . she and her boyfriend eloped. She's not moving back."

His words wash over me in a buzzing, distant way.

"I've been trying to find a way out. But there isn't one. My dad's the one who held everything together. Their house is old—it *constantly* needs work that *I'm* trying to figure out how to do, because he won't let me hire someone, and the store's worse than ever—my mom's trying, but she can't do it.

"The way we're going, the shop has maybe six months left. Some-one needs to be there, every day, and my mom didn't even manage that *before* she had to help my dad get around. And fuck, he's *terrible* at relying on people, so even if we could afford to hire a nurse, he wouldn't let us. And if we could afford to hire a store manager, my mom wouldn't allow it. It's always been in her family. She says it would break her heart to have someone else running things."

The muscles in his jaw work, shadows flickering against his skin. "And they weren't perfect, but my parents gave up a lot for me. So I could go to the school I wanted and have the job I wanted and—I can't keep this up. Loggia wants someone local, and my family needs me. They need someone *better* than me, but I'm what they've got. I'm leaving after *Frigid*'s done. That's the job opening, the one I put you up for."

His job. *His* apartment. Like he's just handing over the life he's worked so hard for, wholesale. Giving up the city where he belongs. Where he feels like himself. Where he doesn't feel wrong or useless.

"What about what *you* want?" I demand. He looks at me like he believes I could give it to him, and I want to, so badly. "Who's mak-ing sure *you're* happy, Charlie? What about *your* heart?"

He tries to smile; he's too bad at lying. "Do people like us have those?"

I touch his face, tipping his eyes up to mine. It takes me a beat to swallow down the jumble of emotion rising through me, to tuck the shrapnel of my thoughts away and accept this new reality. I'm trying to make a list, a plan, a plotline that takes us from A to B, but it's only this one bullet point, this cliff-hanger of a chapter.

"Tonight," I say, "can I just have you, Charlie? Even if it can't last. Even if we already know how it ends."

He holds my jaw so gingerly. Like I'm something delicate. Or maybe like he is. Like with one wrong move we could crack each other open. My chest squeezes with that heart-crushing final-chapter feeling, only now I know the word for it. I know it even if I can't bring myself to think it. "You do have me, Nora. I never stood a chance."

For the first time in my life, I know what the hell Cathy was talking about when she said *I am Heathcliff*. Not just because Charlie and I are so similar, but because he's right: we belong. In a way I don't understand, he's mine, and I'm his. It doesn't matter what the last page says. That's the truth. Here, now.

His lips brush mine, light, careful, warm. I open to him, knowing how it will feel when I turn the page but unwilling not to turn it at all.

29

His FINGERS SNAKE into my hair, his tongue dipping between my lips. A sound rises out of me, and he eases me onto the desk. In the past, our connection has been frantic, mindless, but now he's so careful and tender it makes me ache.

His fingers brush one of my dress's shoulder ties, tugging the knot loose before moving to the other one. My hands are under his shirt, feeling his smooth, warm skin until it's alive with goose bumps.

He tastes like coffee, with a wintergreen edge. His tongue skates over my bottom lip and his hand trails down my side.

I pull him closer, and he jerks me to the edge of the desk, his mouth more urgent now, his teeth sinking and releasing as we pull together and draw apart, each breathy gap making the next kiss more needful. His palm rakes up to my chest, his thumb stroking over my nipple, and I shiver. His heart hammers against me, and mine matches its pace, two metronomes falling into sync.

Lightning screams across the sky, followed by a low boom. The fire gutters, then flares. Little by little, Charlie kisses away the ache of these past three weeks. His lips skim my jaw, my throat, his hands moving back to finish unknotting the ties at my shoulders. The bodice of my dress gapes, and my heart spins like a pinwheel beneath his warm breath as his mouth moves down me.

I tip my head back, my lungs catching when his tongue brushes the inner curve of my breast. Charlie pushes the fabric lower until warm air meets my skin. His eyes lift to mine as he drops his lips to me, watching me as he draws my nipple into his mouth. When I start to arch, his tongue and teeth carefully skim across my skin.

His name slips out of me. Our mouths collide again, deeper, surer. His hand finds the hem of my dress and slips up the inside of my thigh. I widen my knees, his palm grazing higher until it reaches the lacy band at my hips. His other hand does the same, and I lean back, lifting myself so he can gather the fabric and slip it down my legs.

His eyes lock with mine, his grip tightening on the creases of my bare hips, as he kneels and brings his lips to the inside of my knee, kissing higher until his mouth sinks between my thighs. I lean back onto my hands, breath going shallow as the heat of his tongue melts against me.

I roll my hips into the pressure and he groans, his hand sliding up over my stomach, pressing me back until I'm lying on the desk.

I think about suggesting we move. I think about asking if doing this, here, is disrespectful. But then I'm unable to think at all, because his tongue has found a breaker switch in my body, cutting power to my brain entirely.

"Nora," he rasps. A small sound of acknowledgment hums out of me. "We shouldn't have waited. We should have been doing this since we met."

My hands tangle in his hair. His are under me, cupping me, angling me up to his mouth.

Slow, hungry, purposeful. For once nothing between us is happening by accident.

The pressure grows until I'm shuddering under him, my hands twisting into his hair as I arch, crying out. He straightens and pulls me back to the edge of the desk, our mouths sliding together, our hands in each other's clothes. I get his shirt off, undo his pants. He peels off my dress, then lifts me and turns to lay me on the couch, his tongue under my bra.

"This is the one," he says, almost reverently, "you wore the night we swam."

I rake my hands down his back, taking in every firm curve and hard line: my first chance to have as much of him as I want, and also possibly my last.

He kisses the base of my throat. "I remember exactly how you feel, Nora. Like fucking silk."

My mouth softens against the side of his neck, his pulse against my tongue. My hands raze down him, pushing past his loosened pants and briefs, my nails biting into his skin as I rock into him. I reach between us, and when I wrap my fingers around him, a burst of too-bright light flashes through me, turning everything to dark, shimmering spots for a second. "I remember how *you* feel too."

He groans as he moves himself within my hand. I push his pants below his hips. He goes on moving slowly, heavily against me, getting closer and closer to me. No matter how I shift beneath him, he seems always just barely out of reach.

Until he's not. Until his mouth is running urgently over me, and his hands are tearing my bra straps down my arms, and the whole thing winds up bunched around my waist. Then we're both half-crazed for each other, his hands on my thighs, my mouth on his shoulder, his tongue in my mouth, his erection moving against me until my insides are violin-string taut.

"Birth control?" he asks.

"Obviously, but—"

"Got it," he says. Of course he does. He's just like me: even when we're both out-of-control obsessed with each other there are still a few (dozen) threads holding reason in place. Charlie moves off me, finds his wallet, and comes back with a condom, no further questions asked, no huffing, no hint at frustration, no implied *uptight*, *nag*, or *bore*. He tucks his hand against my jaw and kisses me with a tenderness I feel all through my body, all these little pockets of warmth nestled between bones and muscle and cartilage: Charlie, diffused into my bloodstream. And then finally, he's pushing into me.

Slowly. Carefully. He draws back before I've gotten any relief, and a laugh rattles out of him at the sound I make. "I had no idea it was possible," he says, "for you to want me as much as I want you."

"More," I say, too deep into this now to second-guess admitting something like that.

"Now, that," Charlie says, pushing deeper this time, "I *know* is impossible." I lift myself up, drawing him closer. His head tips back and a groan rises in his throat. As we move together, the world goes soft and dark, everything shrinking to the points where our bodies meet. His hands massaging me, his mouth unraveling mine, my nails digging into the contours of him to urge him closer than our bodies let us get.

I'm already sad at the thought of this ending. If I could make the feeling last for days, I would. If the world was ending in twenty minutes, this is how I'd want to go out. He thrusts deeper, harder.

"Fuck," Charlie."

"Too hard?" he asks, slowing.

I shake my head. He understands. No more caution or restraint.

"I thought about you everywhere," he says. "There's nowhere in this town we haven't done this."

Half laughing even as I'm wrapped around him, ravenous, I ask, "How was it?"

"My imagination's not as good as I thought."

My brain feels like fireworks across a black sky. Charlie sits up and pulls me into his lap, pushing back into me. I brace my hands on the back of the couch, working myself against him harder, until every tilt and roll of my hips has him swearing into my skin. One of his hands winds into my hair, the other flattens on my back, holding me where he wants me.

"I want more of you," I gasp into his mouth, feeling each beat of his heart surging through me. Harder, faster, more, all.

"You're perfect," he rasps. "That's the word, Nora. You're fucking perfect."

Oh, God. Oh, God. Charlie, on repeat in my mind. "*Please*," I say.

After that, there is no more talking. I have never been so glad for someone to see straight through me, to read me like a book, as he brings me to the edge again, and again, and—yes, the romance gods would be proud—again.

30

~

WHEN I SIT up, Charlie catches my arm, his eyes heavy and warm. "Stay," he whispers.

My heart flutters. "Why?"

He tucks my hair behind my ear, mouth quirking. "So many reasons."

"I just need one."

He sits up, his hand settling between my thighs, his mouth pressing to my shoulder tenderly as the pressure of his thumb moves in a slow circle. "One."

"In that case," I say, "maybe two."

He leans in and kisses me deeply, his hand gentle at my throat, thumb nestling into the dip at its base. "Because," he says, "I want you to."

"I don't stay over at strange men's places," I say, blood fizzing.

"Then it's lucky this isn't my place."

"Yes, because if it *were*, your parents would come running in, bleary-eyed with a shotgun, thinking you were being burglarized."

"But at least we'd already be inside a getaway car," he says.

I laugh, and the corner of his mouth hitches higher.

"*Stay*, Nora."

I feel that blooming in my chest again, like petals uncurling to leave something delicate exposed in its center. And then a stab of panic, a needle in my unprotected heart.

"I can't," I barely whisper.

His disappointment is visible, only for a moment. Then I watch it dissolve as he accepts it, and it feels like some of those healed-over stitches in my heart open back up. He sits up, searching for his discarded clothes, and I touch his arm, stilling him. More than anyone I've ever met, Charlie craves honesty, and he doesn't punish anyone for it. He takes it as immutable and synthesizes it into his world, and I don't want to be another person dealing in half-truths with him.

"I was staying at my boyfriend's place." It actually hurts to say the words. I've never had to before. Libby already knows, and I don't talk about this with anyone else. I've never wanted to make myself that vulnerable, to see the pitying looks, to feel weak.

Charlie's eyes hold mine.

"Jakob," I say. "I was with him the night my mom died."

His brow softens.

I haven't weighed out pros against cons, costs versus benefits of telling him. I just want it out. Want to hand it—this thing I've never been able to fix—to him and see what happens.

"He was my first serious boyfriend. Maybe my only serious one, in a way. I mean, I dated other men for longer, but he was the only one I ever *chose* like that." Over everything else. Or maybe it was that I *didn't* choose him. Just fell headfirst into my feelings for him, without any caution.

"I was twenty, and I was always over at his place, so we decided I should move in. And my mom—she was such a romantic, she wasn't even trying to talk me out of it. She wanted me to marry him. I did too."

Charlie says nothing, just watches me, leaving space for me to go on, or to stop.

"My phone died at some point in the night." My voice is hoarse now, like my throat is closing off to keep the rest in. But I can't stop. I need him to know. I need to not be alone with this for another second.

"When I was with him, I'd just . . . get so swept up. When we woke up, I didn't even plug my phone in until after we'd made breakfast." Eaten. Had sex. Made more coffee.

The back of my nose burns. "Libby had been calling me for four hours. She was alone at the hospital, and . . ." Nothing comes out after that. My mouth is moving, but there's no sound.

Charlie sits forward, pulls me in against his chest. His mouth presses hard against the top of my head, his thumb brushing over my shoulder.

"I can't imagine." He pulls my legs over his lap, crushes me to his chest again, smoothing my hair and kissing it.

I close my eyes, focusing on *these* sensations, in *this* moment. *I'm here,* I promise myself. *It's over. It can't hurt me anymore.*

"Libby would wake up screaming." My voice is wet now, thin. "For months after Mom died. And I couldn't sleep at all. I was too scared I wouldn't be there if she needed me."

I learned to wait until she woke in a panic, to throw my blankets aside and scoot to the far side of my bed so she could slip in beside me under the quilt. I'd wrap my arms around her until she cried herself back to sleep.

I never told her it would be okay. I knew it wouldn't. Instead I took up Mom's old refrain for comforting us: *Let it out, sweet girl.*

"Jakob was great at first," I say. "I barely saw him, but he understood. And then he got the chance to go to this residency, out in Wyoming—he was a writer."

"He left you?" Charlie says.

"I told him to go," I admit weakly. "I felt like . . . I didn't have the time or the energy for him anyway, and I didn't want to hold him back."

"Nora." His chin nudges my temple as he shakes his head. "You shouldn't have been alone through that."

"He couldn't have done anything," I whisper.

"He could've *been* there," he says. "He should've."

"Maybe," I say. "But it wasn't just him failing me. I kept making plans to visit and then canceling. I couldn't leave Libby. And then . . ."

He brushes my sweat-dampened bangs out of my eyes. "You don't have to tell me."

I shake my head.

All this time, deep in the pit of my stomach, the shadowy monster of grief and fear and anger has been in the corner where I locked it, but it's been growing, new ropes of angry black lashing out in every direction, starving, mad with hunger.

A demon that's going to devour me from the inside out.

"I planned a surprise visit. Got Xanax, took a bus out because that's all I could afford, left Libby alone. I could tell as soon as I saw him that things had changed. And then, the first night I was there, I woke up in a panic. I didn't know where I was, and I couldn't find my phone. All I could think was—that something had happened to Libby. I was . . . hallucinating, almost. My chest hurt so badly I thought I was dying.

"Jakob thought I was having a heart attack. He took me to the ER, and they sent me home a couple hours later with a huge bill and some breathing exercises. It happened again the next night, and the next. I told Jakob I needed to go home early. He bought me a plane ticket and told me he wasn't coming back. He'd decided to stay.

"I wanted to figure something out. Libby only had a year of high school left, but I thought maybe I could move her out there with us. A week after I got home, he told me he'd met someone else."

Like the universe was punishing me, for wanting too much, for even considering putting Libby through that when she was at her breaking point. It still makes me sick to think about.

Charlie's fingers glide up and down my arm. "I'm so sorry."

"It's not that I am sure he was 'the one' or something." I close my eyes, heart racing. "It's just . . . ever since then, it's been hard to imagine letting anyone close like that. Not when I'm so fucking broken I can't sleep anywhere but my own bed. Even here it's hard, with Libby right next to me. I've just never trusted myself since then." I press my face into his warm skin as that ache yawns wide in my chest. "I'm sorry. I'm just . . ."

"Don't be sorry," he says roughly. "Please don't apologize for letting me know you."

"It's embarrassing," I say. "To be so obsessed with being in control that *sleeping* makes me panic. I'm a fucking mess."

He turns me to face him, his hands laced against my lower back. "Everyone's a mess," he says.

"You're not."

He smiles faintly, the reflection of the embers in the fireplace catching the flecks of gold in his irises. "I'm living in my childhood bedroom."

"Because you're helping your family," I say. "I threw mine under the bus the first chance I got."

"Hey." He touches my chin, lifts it. "Your ex left you in the fucking wilderness, Nora, on your own, and you did your best. You're not the villain in his story. He is—and not because he fell for someone else, but because he exited your relationship the second *you* were the one who needed something."

He cradles my face between his hands. "I'll take you home whenever you want," he says. "But if you want to stay, and you wake up screaming, it's okay. I'll make sure you're okay. And if you want to stay, and then change your mind, I don't mind driving you back at four a.m."

I read once that not everyone thinks in words. I was shocked, imagining these other people who don't use language to make sense of everyone and everything, who don't automatically organize the world into chapters, pages, sentences.

Looking into Charlie's face, I understand it. The way a crush of feeling and feathery impressions can move through your body, bypassing your mind. How a person can know there's something worth saying but have no concept of what exactly that is. I'm not thinking in words.

It's a feeling of not quite *Thank you*, not just *You make me feel safe*, but something that dances in between those.

"I want to stay," I say. "But I don't think I can."

He nods. "Then I'll take you home."

"Not yet."

He smooths my hair, tucks it behind my ear. "Not yet."

We lie down together, my back pressed against his warm stomach, his arm draped over my hip, fingers brushing along my ribs like tiny skiers following the gentle slopes, until he's hard again, and I'm drunk on the way he's touching me. We have slow, dreamy sex, and when it's over, I settle against his chest, feeling his heartbeat thudding softly against me, as calming as the lights and hums of the city blurring past my apartment window, a whole world that keeps spinning while you sleep.

If I don't say it aloud, I think, it doesn't count. Maybe it won't even be true.

But it is true, and I'm not sure I'd want to stop it, even if I knew how: I am falling in love with Charlie Lastra.

In the morning, I skip my run. Libby and I sit on a blanket spread in the meadow, coffee in hand, and I tell her everything.

Eyes lit up from within, she says, "He's *staying*?" and my heart crumples in on itself.

"Why don't you tell me how you really feel?"

She tucks her nose into the steam rising from her mug. "Sorry, I didn't mean it like that."

"Like you would love nothing more than to put Charlie Lastra on a ship bound to permanently circle the earth?"

"It's not that! It's just . . ." She scoots around in her chair. "I guess it changes how I see him. He qualifies for the list now."

"How helpful."

"Nora." She sets her mug in the grass. "If you're really this excited about him, you should explore it. I can't remember the last time you actually *were* excited about someone. No, wait, I can. It was a full ten years ago."

The deep pain, like a pulsing phantom limb, doesn't feel quite so severe as it usually does when I think about Jakob. I meant what I told Charlie—that it wasn't about missing my ex so much as the loneliness of being unable to trust myself with anyone.

"It doesn't matter what we 'explore,'" I say. "We know how this ends."

Libby squeezes my arm. "You *don't* know. You can't, until you try."

"This isn't a movie, Libby," I say. "Love isn't enough to change the details of a person's life, or—or their needs. It doesn't make every-thing fall into place. I don't *want* to give up everything."

I can't let myself do that.

There's still no happy ending for a woman who wants it all, the kind who lies awake aching with furious hunger, unspent ambition making her bones rattle in her body.

My cozy West Village apartment with its huge windows. The café on the corner that knows my order. All four seasons on the Central Park mall.

The job at Loggia, I think, the image of their gallery-white offices and balsa wood floors burning bright in my mind.

Knowing my sister is okay. Waking every night believing to my core that I'm safe. That nothing can get me.

How does a vast, uncontrollable feeling like love fit into that?

It's a loose cog in a delicate machine.

When I look back to Libby, her lips are parted, her brows knit together. *"Love?"* She repeats the word in a small voice.

I look back toward the cottage, gleaming in the sun, surrounded by lazily twirling butterflies. "Hypothetically." I lie to my sister. She lets me.

~

In the early afternoon, Bea and Tala come bounding up the hillside—Bea in frilly pink and Tala in navy overalls. My heart soars, and to no one's surprise, tears rush to Libby's eyes as I help her off the blanket. They scream *Mommy* in their impossibly high voices and hurl themselves at her legs, where she peppers their tangled hair with kisses.

"I missed you so, so, so much," she tells them. Tala looks grumpy and resentful as she wraps her arms around Libby's leg, and Bea, of course, immediately starts crying like she's in bad need of a nap, and then Brendan comes huffing up behind them, looking roughly twenty-three times as tired as Charlie Lastra ever has.

When his and Libby's eyes catch, their smiles are calm. Not over-joyed, but relieved: like they've slipped back into the current and don't have to work quite so hard.

The final ounces of anxiety I've been carrying around dissipate in an instant. These two people love each other. Whatever I *thought* was going on between them, they're okay.

They *belong* together, in some mysterious way, and they both seem to know it.

While Libby finishes her penance with the girls, Brendan pulls me into one of his famously awkward and excruciatingly earnest side hugs. "Good flight?" I ask.

"There were some tears," he says warily.

"Oh, were they showing *Mamma Mia!* on the plane again?" I say. "You *know* you can't handle anything with Meryl in it at that alti-tude."

Right then, the girls pry themselves from Libby and barrel at me, screaming, not quite in unison, "Nono!"

"My favorite girls in the whole world!" I say, catching them.

Tala screeches, "We flew on the airplane!"

"You did?" I sweep her onto my hip and squeeze Bea's hand. "Who drove? You or Bea?"

Bea giggles. It is, very likely, the sound that the earth made the first time it saw the sun come up.

"Noooo." Tala shakes her head, irritated by my incompetence. Honestly, when she's grumpy, it's the cutest thing in the world. May all our sour moods be so adorable.

I guide them across the grass, away from Libby and Brendan so they can have a second alone. Brendan looks like he could use a few years in a cryogenic chamber, whereas Libby is grabbing his ass like that is not at *all* what she needs.

"Hey. I forget," I say, leading the girls toward the flowers nestled around the footbridge. "How do you feel about butterflies?"

They have a lot of thoughts, and they're sure to scream them all.

31

LIBBY CHOOSES A dinner spot in downtown Asheville, a chic Cuban restaurant with a rooftop patio. Yesterday's storm left the air cool and breezy, a huge relief after the last three sweaty weeks.

The city is lit up below us, halfway between quaint village and bustling metropolis, and the food is divine. Brendan and I split a bottle of wine and Libby even has a couple sips, moaning as she swishes them around in her mouth.

"It kind of feels like we're in New York, doesn't it?" she says, eyes misty. "If you close your eyes, just the sounds of all these people, and that feeling in the air."

Brendan's mouth screws up like he's considering disagreeing with her, but I just nod along. It doesn't feel like New York, but with all of us together, it almost feels like home.

I feel an improbable wave of nostalgia at the thought of running up or down the stairs to a train platform, hearing that metallic shriek, feeling the wind gust through the stairwell, and not knowing if I've arrived in the nick of time or if my train just went screaming past.

What's the weirdest thing you miss about the city? I text Charlie.

He writes back, It used to be having access to a Dunkin' Donuts within three blocks at all times.

I smile at my phone. The DD-to-person ratio there has to be like one to five. What else?

I miss Eataly, he says, but I wouldn't call it weird.

If you didn't miss Eataly, we could never speak again. Because you'd be in prison, where you'd belong.

Relieved to have dodged that bullet, he says. Also not weird but I think a lot about the first day in spring that's actually kind of warm. How everyone's out at once, and it feels like we're all almost drunk from the sun. People in the park in shorts and bikini tops, eating Popsicles, even though it's like fifty degrees out.

Charlie, I reply. Those things are all objectively amazing.

He takes a while on his next reply. Early-morning commute maria-chi bands, he says, or opera singers, or any singing group really. I know it's not a popular stance, but I fucking love when I'm almost asleep on the train, and suddenly five guys are singing their hearts out.

I love watching everyone's reactions. There are always some people who are kind of feeling it, and some who look like they're plotting mur-der, and then the ones who pretend it's not happening. I always tip be-cause I don't want to live in a world where no one's doing that.

I can't think of a greater symbol of hope than a person who's willing to drag themselves out of bed and sing at the top of their lungs to a group of strangers trapped on a train. That tenacity should be re-warded.

I love, I write, your nightmare brain.

And here I thought you were using me for my nightmare body.

And then, a minute later, I love your brain too. And your body. All of it.

I've spent ten years guiding my life away from this feeling, this terrible want. All it took was three weeks and a fictional woman named Nadine Winters to pull me right back.

"Don't make any plans for tomorrow afternoon," Libby says, kicking my sandal under the table. "I've got a surprise for you."

Brendan's looking at the table, almost guiltily. Either he's not convinced I'll like my "surprise," or Libby's threatened him with murder if he gives it away.

"Brendan," I say, fishing, "tell your wife she can't go skydiving while pregnant."

He laughs and lifts his hands, but still avoids my gaze. "Never tell a Stephens what she can and cannot do."

The editing job at Loggia flutters across my mind, and Charlie's voice saying, *If I had to pick one person to be in my corner, it'd be you. Every time.*

~

Once again, Libby has me tie a silk scarf over my eyes for the length of our cab ride—driven, unfortunately, by Hardy, but luckily it only lasts five minutes, and then Libby's wrenching me from the car, singing, "We're heeeere!"

"*Once* Unofficial Town Tour?" I guess.

"Nope!" Hardy says, chuckling. "Though y'all really gotta do one! You're missing out."

"Funeral for Old Man Whittaker's fictional dog," I guess next.

Libby shuts the car door behind me. "Colder."

"Funeral for the iguana that played Old Man Whittaker's fictional dog in the community theater play?" I listen for clues as to our location, but the only sound is the breeze through some trees, which could put us approximately . . . anywhere.

"There are two stairs, okay?" She prods me forward. "Now straight ahead, there's a small ledge."

I stretch my foot out, feeling through space until I find it. A blast of cold air hits me, and my shoes click onto hardwood floors as we take a few more steps.

"Now." Libby stops. "Give me a drumroll."

I slap my palms against my thighs while she unties the scarf and yanks it away.

We're standing in an empty room. One with dark wooden floors and white shiplap walls. A large window overlooks a thicket of blue-green pine trees, and Libby steps in front of it, vibrating with anxious energy despite her grin.

"Imagine a huge wooden table right here," she says. "And some wicker plant stands under this window. And a Scandinavian chandelier. Something sleek and modern, you know?"

"Okayyyy," I say, following her into the next room.

"A dark blue velvet couch," she says, "and, like, a small canvas tent in one corner for the girls. Something we can leave up, string some lights inside." She leads me down a narrow hall and then I follow her through another doorway as she flicks on the lights to reveal a butter-yellow bathroom: yellow fifties tile, yellow wallpaper, yellow tub, yellow sink.

"This . . . needs some work," she says. "But look how *huge* it is! I mean, there's a *tub*, and there's a whole other bathroom with a walk-in shower. That one's already been redone."

She looks to me for some sort of confirmation that I'm hearing her.

And I am, but there's a dull buzzing rising in my skull, like a horde of bees growing more and more agitated by the uncanny sense of wrongness creeping up my spine.

"There's an en suite. Three *whole* baths—can you imagine?" She gestures toward a smear of lipstick on the carpet, beside a full-pot-of-coffee-sized stain. "Ignore that. I already checked and there's hardwood under it. There will be some damage from the spills, probably, but I've always loved a good rug."

She stops in the middle of the room and holds her arms aloft at her sides. "What do you think?"

"About you loving rugs?"

Her smile wavers. "About the house."

The blood rushing through my eardrums dims my voice. "This house? In the middle of Sunshine Falls?"

Her smile shrinks.

The buzzing swells. It sounds like *No*, like a million miniature Noras humming, *This isn't happening. This can't be happening. You're misunderstanding.*

Libby's hands cradle her stomach, her frown lines firming up between her brows. "You wouldn't believe how cheap it is."

I'm sure I wouldn't. I'd probably fall down dead, and then my ghost would haunt this place, and every night when I rose out of the floorboards, I'd scare the shit out of the owners by asking, *Now,* how many *closets did you say it has?*

But I don't see how that's important.

I shake my head. "Lib, you couldn't live somewhere like this."

Her face goes slack. "I couldn't?"

"Your life's in New York," I say. "Brendan's job is in New York. The girls' school—our favorite restaurants, our favorite parks."

Me.

Mom.

Every last bit of her. Every memory. Every spot where she stood, in some other life, a decade ago. Every window we looked into, our mittened hands folded together, the three of us in a row as we watched Santa's animatronic sleigh arc over a miniature Manhattan skyline.

Every step across the Brooklyn Bridge on the first day of spring, or the last of summer.

Freeman Books, the Strand, Books Are Magic, McNally Jackson, the Fifth Avenue Barnes & Noble.

"You've loved it here," Libby sounds uncertain, young.

All those veins of ice holding my cracked heart together thaw too fast, broken pieces sliding off like melting glaciers, leaving raw spots exposed. "It's been a great break, but Libby—in a week, I want to go *home*."

She turns away. Right before she speaks, I feel this throb in my gut, a warning, a change in barometric pressure. The buzzing drops out.

Her voice is clear. "Brendan got a new job. In Asheville."

I felt something coming, but it didn't prepare me for this missed-step weightlessness, the sensation of falling from a great height, hitting every stair on the way down.

Libby's looking at me again, waiting.

I don't know what for. I don't know what to say.

What is the correct course of action when the planet's been punted off its axis?

I have no plan, no *fix-it* checklist. I'm standing in an empty house, watching the world unravel.

"This is what Brendan kept checking in about," I whisper, the roar of blood in my ears starting anew. "He was waiting for you to tell me."

The muscles in Libby's jaw flex, an admission of guilt.

"The list," I choke out. "This trip. That's what this was all about? You're *leaving* and this whole elaborate game of Simon Says was some fucked-up goodbye?"

"It's not like that," she murmurs.

"What about the lawyer?" I say. "How does she fit into this?"

"The what?"

The world sways. "The divorce attorney, the one Sally gave you the number for."

Understanding dawns across her face. "A friend of hers," she says feebly, "who knew about a good preschool here."

I press my hands to the sides of my head.

They're looking at *schools*.

They're looking at *houses*.

"How long have you known?" I ask.

"It happened fast," she says.

"How long, Libby?"

Breath rushes out between her lips. "Since a few days before we made the plans to come here."

"And there's no way out of it?" I rub my forehead. "I mean, if it's money—"

"I don't want out of it, Nora." She crosses her arms over her chest. "I made this decision."

"But you just said it happened fast. You haven't had time to think about this."

"As soon as we decided Brendan would apply for the job, it felt right," she says. "We're tired of being on top of each other. We're tired of sharing one bathroom—we're tired of being *tired*. We want to spread out. We want our kids to be able to play in the woods!"

"Because *Lyme disease* is such a blast?" I demand.

"I want to know that if something goes wrong, we're not trapped on an island with millions of other people, all trying to get away."

"I'm on that island, Libby!"

Her face goes white, her voice shattering. "I know that."

"New York's our home. Those millions of other people are—are our *family*. And the museums, and the galleries, and the High Line, skating at Rockefeller Center—the Broadway shows? You're fine just giving all that up?"

Giving *me* up.

"It's not like that, Nora," she says. "We just started looking at houses and everything came together—"

"Holy shit." I turn away, dizzy. My arms are heavy and numb, but my heart is clattering around like a bowling ball on a roller coaster. "Do you already own this house?"

She doesn't reply.

I spin back. "Libby, did you buy a house without even telling me?"

She says softly, "We don't close until the end of the week."

I step backward, swallowing, like I can force everything that's already been said back down, reverse time. "I have to go."

"Where?" she demands.

"I don't know." I shake my head. "Anywhere else."

❧

I recognize this street: a row of fifties-style ranches with well-tended gardens, pine-covered mountains jutting up at their backs.

The sun's melting into the horizon like peach ice cream, and the smell of roses drifts over the breeze. A few yards over, a half dozen kids run, shrieking and laughing, through a sprinkler.

It's beautiful.

I want to be anywhere else.

Libby doesn't follow me. I didn't expect her to.

In thirty years, I've never walked away from a fight with her—*she's* been the one I've had to chase, when things were bad at school or she'd gone through a particularly rough breakup in those dark, endless years after we lost Mom.

I'm the one who follows.

I just never thought I'd have to follow her so far, or lose her entirely.

It's happening again. The stinging in my nose, the spasms in my chest. My vision blurs until the flower bushes go bleary and the kids' laughter warbles.

I head toward home.

Not home, I think.

My next thought is so much worse: *What home?*

It reverberates through me, rings of panic rippling outward. Home has always been Mom and Libby and me.

Home is striped blue-and-white towels on the hot sand at Coney Island. It's the tequila bar where I took Libby after her exams, to dance all night. Coffee and croissants in Prospect Park.

It's falling asleep on the train despite the mariachi band playing ten feet away, Charlie Lastra digging through his wallet across the car.

Only it's not that anymore. Because without Mom and Libby, there is no home.

So I'm not running toward anything. Just away.

Until I see Goode Books down the block, lights glowing against the bruised purple sky.

The bells chime as I step inside, and Charlie looks up from the *LOCAL BESTSELLERS*, his surprise morphing into concern.

"I know you're working." My voice comes out throttled. "I just wanted to be somewhere . . ."

Safe?

Familiar?

Comfortable?

"Near you."

He crosses to me in two strides. "What happened?"

I try to answer. It feels like fishing line's wound around my airway.

Charlie pulls me into his chest, arms coiling around me.

"Libby's moving." I have to whisper to get the words out. "She's moving here. That's what this was all about." The rest wrenches upward: "I'm going to be alone."

"You're not alone." He draws back, touching my jaw, his eyes almost vicious in their intensity. "You're not, and you won't be."

Libby. Bea. Tala. Brendan.

It knocks the wind out of me.

Christmas.

New Year's.

Field trips to the natural history museum.

Sitting in front of a huge Jackson Pollock at the Met, asking the girls to please make us rich beyond our wildest dreams with their finger painting.

Laughing at Serendipity until whipped cream comes out our noses. All the memories, and all those future moments, all together, with Mom's memory hovering close.

It's slipping away.

The stinging in my nose. The weight in my chest. The pressure behind my eyes.

Charlie tugs me back into the office. "I've got you, Nora," he promises quietly. "I've got you, okay?"

It's like a dam has broken. I hear the strangled sound in my throat and my shoulders start to shake, and then I'm crying.

Tidal waves hitting me, every word obliterated under a current so powerful there's no fighting it.

I'm dragged under.

"It's okay," he whispers, rocking me back and forth. "You're not alone," he promises, and beneath it I hear the unsaid rest: *I'm here.*

For now, I think.

Because nothing—not the beautiful and not the terrible—lasts.

32

NOW I UNDERSTAND why I didn't cry for all those years. I want it to stop. I want the pain tamped down, divided into manageable pockets.

All this time I thought being seen as monstrous was the worst thing that could happen to me.

Now I realize I'd rather be frigid than what I *really* am, deep down, every second of every day: weak, helpless, so fucking scared it's going to come apart.

Scared of losing everything. Scared of *crying*. That once I start, I'll never be able to stop, and everything I've built will crumble under the weight of my unruly emotions.

And for a long time, I don't stop.

I cry until my throat hurts. Until my eyes hurt. Until there aren't any tears left and my sobs settle into hiccups.

Until I'm numb and exhausted. By then, the office has gone dark except for the old banker-style lamp on the desk.

When I close my eyes, the roaring in my ears has faded, leaving behind the steady thud of Charlie's heartbeat.

"She's leaving," I whisper, testing it out, practicing accepting it as truth.

"Did she say why?" he asks.

I shrug within his arms. "All the normal reasons people leave. I just—I always thought . . ."

His thumb hooks my jaw again and he angles my eyes to his.

"All my exes, all my friends—half the people I work with," I say. "They've all moved on. And every time, it was okay, because I *love* the city, and my job, and because I had Libby." My voice wobbles. "And now she's moving on too."

When Mom died and we lost the apartment, it was like our whole history got swallowed up. The city and each other, that's all Libby and I have left of her.

Charlie gives one firm shake of his head. "She's your sister, Nora. She's never going to leave you behind."

I'm not out of tears after all: my eyes flood again.

His hands run over my shoulders, squeezing the back of my neck. "It's not you she doesn't want, Nora."

"It is," I say. "It's me, it's our life. It's everything I tried to build for her. It wasn't enough."

"Look," he says, "whenever I'm here, it feels like the walls are closing in on me. I love my family, I do. But I've spent fifteen years coming home as rarely as possible because it's fucking lonely to feel like you don't fit somewhere. I never wanted to run this store. I never wanted this town. And whenever I'm here it's all I think about. I get so fucking claustrophobic from it all.

"Not from *them*. But from feeling like I don't know how to be myself here. From—getting in my head about who I'm supposed to be, or all the ways I haven't turned out how they wanted me to. And then you showed up."

His eyes flare, flashlights racing over the dark, searching. "And I could finally breathe."

His voice trembles, skates down my backbone, and my heart flips like it's inside a bingo cage. "There's nothing wrong about you. I wouldn't change anything." It's almost a whisper, and after a pause, he says, "You've never needed to. Not for your shithead exes and not for Blake Carlisle, and definitely not for your sister, who loves you more than fucking anything."

Fresh tears sting my eyes. He just barely smiles. "I honestly think you're perfect, Nora."

"Even though I'm too tall," I whisper tearily. "And I sleep with my phone volume all the way up?"

"Believe it or not," he murmurs, "I didn't mean perfect for Blake Carlisle. I meant, to me, you're perfect."

It feels like heavy machinery is excavating my chest. I knot my hands into his shirt and whisper, "Did you just quote *Love, Actually*?"

"Not intentionally."

"You are too, you know." I think about my dreamy apartment, sun pooling on the armchair under the window, the summer breeze wafting in with the smell of baking bread. I think about schlepping off the train, sticky with heat, paperbacks and towels tucked into a bag, or freshly printed manuscripts and brand-new Pilot G2s.

My city. My sister. My dream job. Charlie. All of it, exactly right. The life I would build if it *was* possible to have everything.

"Exactly right," I tell him. "Perfect."

His eyes are dark, sheening as he studies me.

My heart feels like a cracked egg, nothing to protect it or hold it in place. "I could stay."

He looks away. "Nora," he says quietly, apologetically.

Just like that, the tears are back. Charlie brushes the hair from my damp cheek. "You can't make this decision for me, or for Libby," he says, voice thick and rattling.

"Why not?"

"Because," he says, "you've spent your life making sure she has everything she needs, and it's time someone made sure you did. You want that job at Loggia. And you fucking love the city. And if you need to save money, take my apartment. It's probably half the price of yours. If that's what you want, *that's* what you should have. Nothing less."

I try to blink the tears back, instead loosing them down my cheeks.

"You should have everything," he says again.

"What if it's not possible?"

He tips my jaw up, whispers almost against my lips. "If anyone can negotiate a happy ending, it's Nora Stephens."

Despite—or maybe because of—the sensation of my chest cracking clear in half, I whisper back, "I think one of those only costs forty dollars at Spaaaahhh."

He laughs, kisses the corner of my mouth. "That brain."

Neither of us leaves the shop that night. I don't want to leave him, and I don't want him to feel alone in the dark and quiet. Even if it can't last, even if it's just for tonight, I want him to know that I've got him, the way he's had me. The way he *has* me.

For once, I sleep like a rock.

⌒

In the morning, I stir awake and piece together the night. The fight, finding Charlie at the bookstore, falling into each other again.

Afterward, we talked for hours. Books, takeout, family. I told him about how Mom's nose used to crinkle just like Libby's when she laughed. How they wore the same perfume, but it smells different on Libby than it did on her.

I tell him about Mom's birthday routine. How every December twelfth at noon, we'd go to Freeman Books and browse for hours, until she picked out one perfect book to buy at full price.

"Libby and I still go," I said. "Or we used to. Every December twelfth, at noon—*twelve, twelve*, at twelve o'clock. Mom used to make a big deal of that."

"Twelve's a great number," Charlie said. "Every other number can go to hell."

"*Thank* you," I agreed.

At some point, we drifted off, and I wake now to the realization that, in our sleep, we've begun to move together again. I kiss him awake, and in a heady fog, we give in to each other, time grinding to a halt, the world fading to black around us.

Afterward, I lay my head on his chest and listen to his blood move through his veins, the current of Charlie, as he plays with my hair. His voice is thick and scratchy when he says, "Maybe we can figure it out."

Like it's an answer to a question, like the conversation never stopped. All night, all morning, every touch and kiss, all of it was a back-and-forth, a push and pull, a negotiation or a revision. Like everything is between us. *Maybe this could work.*

"Maybe," I whisper in agreement. We're not looking into each other's faces, and I can't help but think that's purposeful: like if we looked, we couldn't pretend any longer, and we're not ready to give up the game.

Charlie threads his fingers through mine and lifts the back of my hand to his lips. "For what it's worth," he says, "I doubt I will ever like anyone else in the world as much as I like you."

I slip my arms around his neck and climb into his lap, kissing his temples, his jaw, his mouth. *Love,* I think, a tremor in my hands as they move into his hair, as he kisses me.

The last-page ache.

The deep breath in after you've set the book aside.

When he walks me to the door sometime later, he takes my face in his hands and says, "You, Nora Stephens, will always be okay."

33

LIBBY SITS ON the front steps, wrapped in one of Brendan's old sweatshirts, two cups of coffee steaming on the step beside her.

Neither of us speaks as I close the distance, but I can tell she's spent the night crying, and I doubt I look any better.

She holds out a mug. "Might be cold by now."

I take it and, after another strained second, perch on the step, dew seeping into my jeans.

"Should I go first?" she asks.

I shrug. We've never been this angry with each other—I don't know what comes next.

"I'm sorry I didn't tell you sooner," she says, like she's trying to shove the words through a too-narrow doorway.

All the way over here, I wondered if laying into her would give me some sense of control. But there's no outcome to force here. What I want is slippery, uncatchable: those days when there was nothing between us, when we belonged together more than we belonged anywhere else. When it felt like *I* belonged.

"When did we start keeping things from each other?"

She looks surprised and hurt, almost impossibly small. "You've *always* kept things from me, Nora," she says. "And I know you were trying to protect me, but it still counts when you pretend things are okay and they're not. Or when you try to fix things without me knowing."

"So is that what you're doing?" I ask. "You kept the fact that you were moving away from me so that—what? It wouldn't hurt until the last possible second?"

"That's not what I was doing." Fresh tears spring into her eyes. She burrows her fists against them, shoulders twitching.

"I'm sorry." I touch her arm. "I'm not trying to be mean."

She looks up, wiping her tears away. "I was trying," she says, through a shuddering breath, "to win you over."

"Libby, in what universe do you need to *win* me over? I'm sorry for making you feel incapable. I was trying to help, but I *never* thought you needed to be fixed. *Never.*"

"That's not what I mean," she says. "I wanted to win you over to . . ." She waves toward the meadow and the sun-dappled footbridges, the flowering bushes swaying in the breeze and the thick piney forest covering the rolling hills.

And then the rest of it clicks. The list wasn't about Libby trying on her new life, and it wasn't about saying some spectacular goodbye or making a last-ditch effort to save me from a life of sleeping alone with my laptop.

It was a sales pitch.

"Brendan wanted me to tell you right away," she goes on. "But I thought that maybe—if you *came* here, if you saw what it could be like . . . I wanted you to come with us." Her voice cracks. "And I thought if you realized what life could be here, maybe even met someone, you would want that too. But then you started spending time with Charlie, and—god, it's been so long since I've seen you like that, Nora. I was going to let the whole thing go, but then you said he was staying . . . and it just seemed like . . . like you could want this too. Like I could have all this—*and* you."

I feel so empty, wrung out, like I've been treading water for weeks only to realize the shore was a mirage.

This is Libby, who never asked for anything until a month ago, admitting what she really wants.

For me to follow her.

And I want to give her what she wants. I always want her to have everything she wants.

All the organized compartments in my mind came crashing down last night, and for the first time I see it all clearly. Not the tidy, controlled version of things, but the mess of it, when it all spills loose.

Libby and I have been caught in a slow boil of change for a long time, one path splitting into two. There's no less room in my heart for her than the day she first came screaming into the world.

But there *is* less time. Less space in our daily lives. *Other* people. *Other* priorities. We're a Venn diagram now, instead of a circle. I might've made all my decisions for her, but now that I'm here, I *love* my life.

"I was asked to apply for another editing job," I get out.

Libby blinks rapidly, tears clinging to her sparkly blue eyes. "Wh-what?"

I stare at the tree line beyond the meadow. "Charlie's job at Loggia," I say. "They want someone local, and he's staying here. So he mentioned it to Dusty's editor. I'd be taking over some of his list, and then I'd start acquiring my own too."

"It's your dream," Libby says breathlessly.

Something about that word sets off fireworks through my body. "I . . ." Nothing else comes out.

She reaches for my hands, squeezing them hard, her voice cracking: "You have to do it."

My chest cramps as I study her, the only face I know better than mine.

"You have to," she says through tears. "It's what you want. It's what you've always wanted, and—don't put it off again, Nora. It's your dream."

"It's not something I've . . ." I wave my hand in a vague spiral.

"Done before?" she says.

"And if it didn't work out . . ."

"You can do it," she tells me. "You can do it, Nora. And if you fail, who cares?"

"Well," I say. "Me."

Her arms coil around my neck. She shakes with something halfway between more sobs and giggles. "You're going to have the world's best guest room here," she cries. "And if everything goes to shit there, you'll come stay with us. I'll take care of you, okay? I'll take care of you how you've always, always taken care of me, Nora."

I want to tell her how perfect these last three weeks have been.

I want to tell her this is the happiest I can remember being in so long, and it's also the worst pain I've ever felt.

Because all those gaps between us are finally gone, but the impact of the collision has shaken every last remnant of the ice loose, leaving nothing but a soft, pulpy tenderness.

So all I can do is cry with her.

Somehow, it never occurred to me that this was an option: that two people, in the same hug, could both be allowed to fall apart. That maybe it's neither of our jobs to keep a steel spine.

That we can both survive this pain without the other shouldering it.

"I don't know how to be without you, Nora," Libby squeaks. "I never thought I would be. And I know this is right for me and Brendan, but—fuck, I thought you and I would always be together. How is it possible for two people who belong *together* to belong in two different places?"

"Maybe I won't even get the job," I say.

"No," Libby replies with force. "Don't try to fix it. Don't choose me over you, okay? We've done this for years, and it's almost broken us. It's time to just be sisters, Nora. Don't fix it. Just be here with me, and say it fucking sucks."

"It does." I scrunch my eyes tight. "It fucking sucks."

I didn't know the power of those words. They fix nothing, *do* nothing, but just saying them feels like planting a stake into the ground, pinning us together at least for this moment.

It sucks, and I can't change that, but I'm here, with my sister, and somehow we'll get through it.

You can take the city person out of the city, but the city will always be in them. I think it's the same for sisters. Anywhere we go, we won't leave each other. We couldn't even if we wanted to. And we don't. We never will.

~

Brendan meets the home inspector at the house, but Libby and the girls stay back with me, giving him some much-needed quiet after his weeks as a solo parent.

They're not moving in earnest until November, a month before Number Three's due date. Until then, Brendan will be back and forth, getting the house ready.

Two and a half months. That's how long we have left together, and it's going to count.

We spend the morning wandering the woods, trying to keep the girls on the trail and googling "what does poison ivy look like" every forty-five seconds, never getting any closer to a concrete answer.

We take them to the fence, and the horses clomp over eagerly to be petted, despite our lack of bait. "I guess we know where *you and I* stand," Libby jokes as the girls' little fingers swipe down a chestnut mare's pink snout.

Afterward, we take the tin buckets from the cottage's cabinet out to the blackberry thicket at the edge of the meadow and pick and eat plump berries until our fingers and lips are stained purple and our shoulders are sunburnt.

By the time we arrive home, our knees smudged with dirt, Tala is fully asleep in my arms, sticky and warm, and we pour her onto the couch to keep napping. Bea leads us into the kitchen to explain the art of blind baking a pie crust for the blackberries—she and Brendan have watched a *lot* of *Great British Baking Show* this month—and I still feel like a city person, through and through, but maybe it's possible to have more than one home. Maybe it's possible to belong in a hundred different ways to a hundred different people and places.

34

THE GIRLS ARE tucked into the air mattress in the upstairs bedroom (I've been relocated to the foldout couch), but Brendan, Libby, and I stay up late, picking over the leftovers of Bea's blackberry pie.

Someone knocks on the door, and Brendan kisses Libby's forehead on his way to answer it. "Nora?" he calls. "For you."

Charlie's standing in the doorway, his hair damp and his clothes perfectly wrinkle-free. He looks like a million bucks. Actually, more like six hundred, but six hundred *very* well-appointed dollars.

"Up for a walk?" he asks.

Libby shoves me out of my chair. "She sure is!"

Outside, we wander across the meadow, our hands catching and holding. It's been years since I've held anyone's hand other than Libby's or Bea's or Tala's. It makes me feel young, but not in a bad way. Less like I'm powerless in an uncaring world and more like . . . like everything is new, shiny, undiscovered. The way Mom saw New York—that's how I see Charlie.

When we reach the moonlit gazebo, he faces me. "I think we need to consider an alternate ending."

I balk. "We already sent the notes. Dusty's been working on edits all week. She's—"

"Not for *Frigid*." He lifts our hands, holds them against his chest, where I can feel his heart speeding. His eyes bore into me. Black-hole eyes. Sticky-trap eyes. Decadent dessert eyes.

"We take turns visiting each other," he says seriously. "Once a month, maybe. And when you're able, you come here for holidays. And when you can't, I get my sister and her husband to fly out and be with my parents so I can get up to New York. We video call and text and email as much as we're able—or if that's too much, I don't know, maybe we skip all of that. When you're in the city, you're working, and when we're together, we're together."

My stomach feels like it's overstuffed with drunken, glittering fireflies. "Like an open relationship?"

"No." He shakes his head. "But if that's what you'd prefer . . . I don't know. We could try it. I don't want to, but I will."

"I don't want that either," I tell him, smiling.

He releases a breath. "Thank fuck."

My heart twists. "Charlie . . ."

"Just consider it," he presses quietly.

It didn't work for Sally and Clint. For me and Jakob. Charlie and Amaya. Even if I can overcome my travel anxiety, even if Charlie doesn't mind talking me down in the dead of night, how am I supposed to deal with the constant fear of losing him? The anxiety every time he cancels a call or a visit falls through? Waiting for the other shoe to drop, for the day he finally says, *I want something different.*

It's not you.

I want someone different.

A slow, excruciating heartbreak unfolding bit by bit for weeks.

I'd take a swift beheading over that death by a thousand paper cuts, every time.

"Long distance never works," I say. "You said that yourself."

"I know," he says. "But it's never been *us*, Nora."

"So we're the exception?" I say, skeptical. "The people it just works out for."

"Yes," he says. "Maybe. I don't know."

His eyes rove over me as he regroups. "What else can we do, Nora? I'm open to notes. Tell me what you'd change. Get out your fucking pen, and shred it all up, and tell me how it's supposed to end."

It actually hurts to smile. My voice sounds like it's scraping over broken glass. "We enjoy this week. We spend as much time together as we want, and we don't talk about after, and then I leave, and I don't say goodbye. Because I'm not good at them. I've never really said one, and I don't want to start with you. So instead when I kiss you for the last time, neither of us draws attention to it. And then . . . I get on a plane and go home, incredibly grateful for the life-ruiningly hot man I once spent a month with in North Carolina."

He stares at me, his eyes focused and brow furrowed as he absorbs what I said, his lips pouting. It's his Editing Expression, and when it clears, he shakes his head and says, "No."

I laugh, surprised. "What?"

He straightens, steps in close. "I said, *no*."

"Charlie. What's that even mean?"

"It means," he says, eyes glinting, "you'll have to do better than that."

I smile despite myself, hope thrashing around in my belly like a very determined baby bird with a broken wing.

"I'll expect notes by Friday," he says.

~

The rest of the week, we're running. Libby's working on the fund-raiser ball. Brendan's finishing the final phases of the mortgage pro-cess. Charlie's at the register, and Sally's in and out nonstop, getting everything ready for the virtual book club with Dusty.

There's a new sign in the window, reading *MAKE GOOD CHOICES, BUY GOODE BOOKS*, and a poster of Dusty's face ad-vertises both the book club and the *Once in a Lifetime Blue Moon Ball*.

Volunteers transform the town square, and technically I've called off for the week, but some things won't wait, so I do my best to squeeze in bits of work in between giving the girls piggyback rides and cleaning up my résumé for Loggia.

I've always thought of myself as a creature of survival, but lately I've been daydreaming. About a new job. About Charlie. About hav-ing everything, all at once.

So in that way, maybe this place did transform me. Just not into a girl who loves flannel and pigtail braids.

When we're together, Charlie and I don't keep our distance or circle each other warily. We give in to every moment we can, but we don't talk about the future. When we're apart, though, we keep the story going over calls and texts.

You'll spend Christmas in Sunshine Falls and I'll spend New Year's Eve in the city, he says.

We'll get up early and train hop until we find a mariachi band, I say.

We'll go to town hall meetings and involve ourselves in public feuds, then go back to the cottage and have sex all night, he says. And, We'll do a taste test of all the dollar slices in the city.

We'll get to the bottom of the cubed-ham salad at P.S., I say.

I believe in you so deeply, Nora, he says, but not even you can unlock the secret of that great mystery.

I'll be so busy, I remind him. For the first couple months when I get back, I'll be cramming in time with Libby and the girls—and, if I get the Loggia job, tapering off my agency work, off-loading my clients to another agent. Then there will be the learning curve of stepping into a new role.

Busy doesn't scare me, Charlie says.

This, I think, *is what it is to dream,* and I finally understand why Mom could never give it up, why my authors can't give it up, and I'm happy for them, because this *wanting*, it feels good, like a bruise you need to press on, a reminder that there are things in life so valuable that you *must* risk the pain of losing them for the joy of briefly having them.

Sometimes, I write to Charlie, the first act is the fun part, and then everything gets too complicated.

Stephens, he replies, for us, it's all the fun part.

It hurts, but I let the dream go on awhile longer.

~

No one will ever convince me that time moves at a steady pace. Sure, your clock follows some invisible command, but it feels like it's randomly spouting off minutes at whatever intervals suit it, because this week is a blip, and then Friday night arrives.

Another heat wave breaks, ushering in fall weather, and we set up the tent and air mattress again. While Libby and Brendan walk into town to pick up quattro stagioni pizza, the girls and I lie on our backs, watching the sky darken.

Bea tells me about everything she and Brendan have baked over the last few weeks. Tala regales us with a tale that is either the nonsense ramblings of a toddler or a faithful retelling of a Kafka novel.

After we've eaten, Libby suggests Brendan take the king bed to himself tonight, and he says, mid-yawn, "Oh, thank God."

When he kisses the girls good night, they're so sleepy they hardly react, except for Tala reaching her little arms up toward his face for a second before letting them flop down on her tummy.

He kisses Libby last, then gives me a side hug (world's worst hugger), and I feel a bigger crush of love for him than I did the day he married my sister.

"What the hell," Libby whispers, laughing. "Are you *crying*?"

"Shut up!" I toss a pillow at her. "You broke my eye muscles. I can't stop it now."

"You're crying because you love Brendan so much," she teases. "Admit it."

"I love Brendan so much," I say, laughing through the tears. "He's *nice*!"

Libby's laughter escalates. "Dude, I *know*."

Tala grumbles and rolls over, her arm flinging across her eyes.

Libby and I lie back side by side and hold each other's hands as we study the improbable number of constellations.

"You know what?" Libby whispers.

"Probably," I say, "but try me."

"Even if you can't see them back in Manhattan, all of those stars will be over you too. Maybe every night, we look up at the sky at the same time."

"Every night?" I say, dubious.

"Or once a week," she says. "We get on the phone, and we look up at the sky, and then we'll know we're still together. Wherever we go."

I swallow a rising lump. "Mom will be with you too," I say. "Just because you're leaving New York, it doesn't mean you're leaving her behind."

Libby snuggles closer, resting her head on the divot of my shoulder, the smell of crushed blackberries still lingering in her hair. "Thank you."

"For what?"

"Just," she says, "thank you."

For once, I don't dream about Mom.

35

~

THE CENTER OF town is a wonderland of string lights and bunting, long tables covered in pretty gingham cloths and loaded with pies. A dance floor sits in the square, and a branded Coors truck sells beer behind the gazebo. Next to it, Amaya and Mrs. Struthers hawk donated wine, every glass poured with a heavy hand. I doubt they have the permits for most of this stuff, but then again, Libby made it sound like just about everyone at that town hall meeting was involved in one way or another in making this happen, so there's a small chance this is all aboveboard.

Brendan, Libby, the girls, and I stop by Goode Books to catch Dusty's event, but the place is packed and we don't linger long. Charlie and Sally arranged all the new furniture—along with the old folding chairs—into rows in the café, with Dusty's videoconference projected onto the far wall and her audio playing through the shop's speakers so that even the overflow of visitors could hear while they shopped.

The girls are bouncing off the walls, so we take them over to Mug + Shot's pop-up soda shoppe for frothy pink cows.

"This is a huge mistake," Libby notes as she passes the red-soda-and-ice-cream-plus-whipped-cream concoctions to Bea and Tala.

"A delicious one, though," I point out.

"*And*," Brendan adds, dropping his voice, "they always crash after a sugar blitz."

Back in the town square, we gorge ourselves: on popcorn, on chocolate pie and rhubarb, on sugar-dusted pecans that make me think of cold mornings in Central Park, and on one local wine that has to be the worst I've ever had, along with another that's actually pretty good.

We dance with the girls to pop songs Bea somehow knows better than Libby or I, and as the night wears on and total darkness falls, bringing a slight chill with it, Tala falls asleep in Brendan's arms while he and Clint Lastra are talking about catch-and-release fishing spots.

Brendan's never fished in his life, but he's determined to try, and Clint's happy to get him started.

Libby's going to be happy here, I think as I watch them from a distance. She's going to be so fucking happy, and that will make the distance bearable, almost.

She and Bea slip off to see if they can find some sweatshirts or blankets in Brendan's rental car, but I hang back, watching Gertie and her girlfriend, the bickering couple from town hall, and a dozen other pairings sleepily sway on the dance floor.

I spot Shepherd in a gap in the crowd, and he gives me a sheepish smile and wave before ambling over. "Hey there," he says.

"Hey," I say. After an awkward moment, I begin, "I'm sorry about—" right as he's saying, "Just wanted to say—"

He smiles again, that handsome, leading-man smile. "You go first."

"I'm sorry if I misled you," I say. "You're a great guy."

He gives another warm, albeit vaguely disappointed smile. "Just not *your kind* of great guy."

"No," I admit. "I guess not. But if you're ever in New York and you need a tour guide—or a wingman . . ."

"I'll look you up." He stifles a yawn with the back of his hand. "Not used to being up this late," he says apologetically. "I should turn in."

Of course he's a morning person. Life with Shepherd would be a lot of slow, romantic sex with intensely loving eye contact, followed by watching the sunrise over the valley. He will, no doubt, be part of someone's happy ending. Maybe he belongs to someone already, in a way that can't be explained.

For someone else, he will be *easy* in the best way.

As if the thought has conjured him, Charlie appears a few yards behind Shepherd, and my heart lifts, warm and reliable as Old Faithful.

Shepherd catches me looking away, a sunflower finding its light source. He follows my gaze straight to Charlie and smiles knowingly. "Have a good flight, Nora."

"Thanks," I say, blushing a little at my own transparency. "Take care, Shepherd."

He walks off, pausing for a moment to talk to Charlie on his way to the edge of the town square. Smiles are exchanged, Charlie's a bit wary but not so guarded as that day outside Goode Books. Shepherd claps him on the shoulder as he says something, and Charlie looks toward me, that geyser of affection erupting in my chest again at his faint smile.

With a few more words, they part ways, Shepherd making his way to the fringes of the crowd and Charlie coming toward me with his smile tugging wider.

"I heard you might be cold," he says quietly. He holds out a bundled-up flannel shirt I hadn't noticed him carrying. I glance toward where Libby and Bea have rejoined Brendan, and Libby flashes me a quick smile.

"Wow," I say. "Word *does* travel fast here."

"Once, in high school," he says, "I went to a barber on a whim and got my head shaved. My parents knew before I got home."

"Impressive," I say.

"Demented." He holds the flannel up and I turn, feeling like a delicate socialite in an old black-and-white movie as he slips it over my arms, then turns me back to him and starts buttoning it.

"Is this yours?" I ask.

"Absolutely not," he says. "I bought it for you." At my surprise, he laughs. "It was on your list. I got Libby one too. She screamed when I handed it to her. I thought she was going into labor."

For a few moments, we just smile at each other. It's the least awkward extended eye contact of my life. It feels like we've both signed on for the same activity, and this is it: existing, *at* each other.

"How do I look?" I say.

"Like a very hot woman," he says, "in a very unimpressive shirt."

"All I heard was *hot*."

His mouth splits into, quite possibly, my favorite of his various smiles, the one that makes it look like there's a secret tucked up in one corner of his mouth. "Do you want to dance, Stephens?"

"Do you?" I ask, surprised.

"No," he says, "but I want to touch you, and it's a good cover."

I take his hand and pull him out onto the dance floor, beneath the twinkling lights, while James Taylor's "Carolina in My Mind" plays like the universe just wants to tease me.

Charlie folds my hand up in his warm palm and I rest my cheek against his sweater, closing my eyes to focus on how this feels. I imprint every detail of him on my mind: the scent of BOOK and citrus, with the almost spicy note that's all his own; the soft, fine wool and firm chest underneath it; the eager, pulpy thud of his heart; his cheek brushing my temple; the indescribable shivery feeling when he nestles his mouth into my hair and breathes me in.

"Are you excited to eat?" he says quietly.

I open my eyes to study his thick, serious brows. "I already ate. I had Pie Dinner."

He half shakes his head. "I mean when you get back to the city."

"Oh." I press my cheek into his shoulder, fingers curling in, trying to keep him, or me, here awhile longer. "We don't have to talk about that."

His hands gently increase their pressure for a moment. "I don't mind."

I close my eyes against tears, and after a pause say, "I've been craving Thai."

"There's a great Thai restaurant around the corner from my apartment," he says. "I'll take you someday."

I let myself picture it again: Charlie in my apartment, his laptop in front of him, his face stern as he reads on my sofa. Ice hiding in the corners of the windowpane behind him, snowflakes melting across the glass, Christmas lights wrapped around the lampposts on the street below, people carrying oversized shopping bags past.

I let myself imagine this feeling lasting. I imagine a world within a world just for Charlie and me, moving the stone walls back a few feet to fit him inside them, and not spending every second looking for the cracks.

This, I think again, *is what it is to dream.*

And then, because I have to—because if anyone deserves honesty, it's Charlie—I invite the truth forward to replace the story.

Me working twelve-hour days, trying to off-load my clients, then settle into a new job. Charlie exhausted from long days at the bookstore, weekends at physical therapy appointments with his dad, hours' worth of googling how to fix leaky sinks and replace loose shingles.

Missed calls. Unanswered texts piling up. Hurt. Grief. Missing each other. Visits canceled for work or family emergencies. Both of us stretched too thin, our hearts spanning too many states, the tension unbearable.

My chest squeezes so tight it hurts. He told me someone needed to make sure I have what I need, but he deserves that too.

My heart races and my body feels like it's on the verge of coming apart. *"Charlie."*

There's a long silence. His throat bobs as he swallows. His voice is a hoarse, growly whisper. "I know. But don't say it yet."

We don't look at each other. If we look, we'll know this game of make-believe is over, so we just hold on to each other.

His long-distance relationship was the worst year of his life. Mine almost broke me. He's right that it's different, that it's *us* and we understand each other, but that's why I can't do it.

"A week ago," I say, "I liked you so much I would have wanted to try to make this work." I swallow a jagged, fist-sized lump, but still my voice has to scrape by to get out. "But now I think I might love you too much for that."

I'm surprised to hear myself say it. Not because I was unaware of how I felt—but because I've never been the first person to say the L-word. Not even with Jakob. "You don't have to say anything," I hurry to add.

His jaw flexes against my temple. "Of course I love you, Nora. If I loved you any less, I'd be trying to convince you that you could be happy here. You have no idea how badly I wish I could be enough."

"Charlie—" I begin.

"I'm not being self-deprecating," he promises softly against my ear. "I just don't think that's how it works in real life."

"If anyone could be enough," I say, "I think it might be you."

His arms squeeze around me, his voice dropping to a soft scratch. "I'm glad we had our moment. Even if it didn't last as long as we wanted it to."

The tears are so thick in my eyes that the dance floor dissolves into streaks of color and light.

"But," I finally get out, my eyes scrunching shut, "it really was fucking perfect."

"You're going to be okay, Nora," he whispers against my temple, his hands loosening. "You're going to be better than okay."

Just like I asked, there's no goodbye. When the song ends, he presses one last kiss against the curve of my jaw. My eyes flutter closed.

When I open them, he's gone.

But I still feel him everywhere.

I *am* Heathcliff.

~

As I escape toward the dark edge of the town square, I fire off a text to Libby and Brendan, telling them that I'll meet them at home.

"You taking off?"

I not only yelp in surprise but throw my purse. It crashes into a planter.

"Didn't mean to scare you." Clint Lastra sits on a bench, his walker beside him, a few stray moths circling overhead.

I retrieve my purse, wiping at my eyes as discreetly as I can. "Early flight tomorrow."

He nods. "I wouldn't mind getting to bed either, but Sal won't let me out of her sight." He casts me a wry look. "It's hard getting old. Everyone treats you like a kid again."

"I would've given anything to see my mom get old." It's out before I realize it wasn't just a note in my brain.

"You're right," Clint says. "I'm lucky. Still, can't help but feel like I'm failing him."

I feel my brows flick up. "Who? Charlie?"

The corner of his mouth flinches downward. "It wasn't supposed to be like this. He shouldn't be here."

I balk, torn for a moment about how much, if anything, to say. I've barely spoken to Clint in the weeks I've been here.

"Maybe not," I say tightly. "But it means a lot to him, to get to be here for you. It's important to him."

Clint gazes wistfully toward the crowd on the dance floor, where Charlie and I stood together moments ago. "He won't be happy."

I'm not sure it's that simple. It's not like I wouldn't be happy if I were here with Libby. It's more that it would feel like I was borrowing someone's jeans. Or like I was taking a break from my own life, like this was a period of time when I'd sidestepped out of my own path for a while.

I've done that before, and I've never had regrets, exactly. There've always been things to be grateful for.

That's life. You're always making decisions, taking paths that lead you away from the rest before you can see where they end. Maybe that's why we as a species love stories so much. All those chances for do-overs, opportunities to live the lives we'll never have. "He wants to be here for you and Sally," I say. "He's working so hard to be what he thinks you need."

Confirmed Sweet Guy Clint Lastra wipes at his cheek. His hands shake a little when they rest against his leg.

"He's always been special," Clint says. "Like his mom. But sometimes . . . well, I think Sally's always enjoyed standing out a bit."

His mouth twists. "I think my son has spent most of his life feeling lonely." Clint glances sidelong at me, appraising, that same X-ray sensation his son's so good at evoking. "He's been different these last few weeks."

Clint laughs to himself. "You know, I used to try to read a book a month with him. Did it all through high school, and college too. I'd ask for recommendations—the last thing he'd read and loved, so we'd always have something to talk about, that mattered to him. He was probably fourteen years old the first time I read one of his books and thought, *Shit. This kid's outgrown me.*"

When I start to argue, Clint lifts a hand. "I don't mean that in a self-deprecating way. I'm a smart enough man, in my way. But I'm amazed by my son. I could listen to that kid talk for way longer than he ever would, about pretty much anything. The first time Sal and I visited him in New York, it all made perfect sense. It was like he'd been living at half volume until that moment. That's not what a parent wants for their kid."

Half volume.

"He's been different these last few weeks." In the twitch of his mouth, I see shades of his son, biological or not. "More comfortable. More himself."

I've been different too.

I wonder if I've been living at half volume too. With agenting. With dating. Tamping myself into a shape that felt sturdy and safe instead of right.

"You know," I say cautiously, not wanting to out Charlie in any way but also *needing* to be in his corner, to not choose politeness or likability or winning over anyone over him, "maybe you're trying to prove you don't need him, because you think he doesn't want to be here. But don't act like he's not doing any good, or like he can't help. This place already gave him enough reason to feel like he was the wrong kind of person, and the very last person he needs to get that from is you."

White rings his eyes. He opens his mouth to object.

"It doesn't matter whether that's how you feel or not, if that's how it looks to him," I say. "And if you *do* let him help you, he'll do it. Better than you ever expected."

With that, I turn and walk away before any more tears can fall.

~

36

WHEN I STEP out of the building into the crisp September afternoon, a flurry of pink and orange hurls itself at me. Libby's lemon-lavender scent wraps around my shoulders as she squeals, "You did it!"

"If by *it*," I say, "you mean 'completed the first step of an interview process that might go nowhere,' then I sure did."

She pulls back, beaming. Her hair has faded almost entirely back to blond, but her clothes are as colorful as ever. "What'd they say?"

"They'll be in touch," I reply.

She threads her arm through mine and turns me up the sidewalk. "You've got it."

Nerves jostle in my stomach. "I feel like it's the first day of school, I'm naked, *and* I forgot my locker combination. Wait—no, it's the *last* day of school, and I never went to math, plus all those other things."

"The uncertainty is good for you," she says. "You really want this, Sissy. That's a good thing. Now let's go, I'm famished. Do you have the list?"

"Oh, do you mean *this list*?" I say, producing the laminated sheet she made of everything we need to eat, drink, and do before she leaves.

Most days, I see her. For lunch, or a walk to the playground by her place, or to sit on the living room floor packing stuffed animals and tiny overalls into cardboard boxes. (Sometimes I cry over particularly tiny onesies that used to belong to Bea, then to Tala, and will soon be inherited by Number Three.)

One Saturday, we take the girls to the Museum of Natural History and spend two and a half hours in the room with the huge whale. Another night, Brendan and Libby and I meet at our favorite pizza place in Dumbo and we stay out on the patio talking until the staff is cleaning up for the night.

We overpay to have our caricatures drawn at Central Park. We ask a tourist to take our family picture at Bethesda Fountain. We meet for crepes, Sunday after Sunday, at Libby's favorite spot in Williamsburg.

And then November comes.

They leave on a Thursday, bright and early. The girls are so sleepy that we're able to plop them into the U-Haul without much fanfare, and secretly I'm disappointed. It kills me to hear them crying over the words *Aunt Nono*, but to *not* hear them might be worse.

Brendan and I hug goodbye, and then he climbs into the rental truck to give me and Libby some privacy.

"Run!" I stage-whisper to Libby, and he shoots me a smile before pulling the door shut.

Libby's already crying. She said she woke up crying. I didn't, but then again, I'm not sure I slept.

The third time I jolted awake, I got online and made appointments with both a therapist and a sleep specialist, then ordered four books that promised to have "helped millions in [my] exact situation!"

It was almost nice to have something else to focus on in the dead of night.

"We'll talk all the time," Libby promises. "You're going to be sick of me." There's an iciness to the wind, and I lift her chilly fingertips to breathe warmth into them.

She rolls her eyes, laughing tearily. "Still such an utter Mom."

"You're one to talk." I bend down to kiss her belly. "Be good, Number Three, and Auntie Nono will bring you a present when she visits. A motorcycle, maybe, or some party drugs."

"I don't know what to say." Libby's voice cracks.

I pull her into a hug. "This sucks."

She relaxes in my arms. "This does indeed suck."

"But it also rules," I point out. "You're going to have a big-ass house, and windows that don't face that old guy who never wears pants, and you're going to have a garden and you'll wear those overpriced prairie dresses when you host dinner parties with fresh floral arrangements on every surface, and your kids are going to stay out late catching fireflies with the neighbor kids, and Brendan's probably going to learn how to, like, chop wood and get ripped and carry you around like you're in a romance novel."

"And then *you're* going to visit," Libby cuts in. "And we're going to stay up all night talking. We're going to drink one too many gin and tonics, and I'm going to convince you to sing Sheryl Crow with me at Poppa Squat's karaoke night, and we're going to go to a *real* Christmas tree farm, not just a tent in an alleyway, and we're going to show the girls *Philadelphia Story*, and they're going to say, *Hey, am I mistaken, or is Cary Grant kind of being an asshole? Why wouldn't she end up with Jimmy Stewart?*"

"And we'll have to tell them that some people simply have bad taste," I agree solemnly.

"Or that sometimes, there are not one but two hot men vying for your heart, and you have to spin in a circle and choose one at random, then marry the other off to his coworker."

"Babe?" Brendan calls from the truck, grimacing apologetically.

Libby nods in understanding and we draw apart, still gripping each other's forearms like we're preparing to spin in circles at full speed and don't want inertia to pull us apart. Pretty accurate, actually.

"This isn't goodbye," she says.

"Of course not," I say. "Nadine Winters never remembers to say hello or goodbye."

"Also we're sisters," she says. "We're stuck together."

"That too."

She lets go of me and climbs up into the truck.

As they pull away, my eyes fill up. At least the tears held off this long. At least I earned them.

The white and orange of the U-Haul melt together until it's like I'm looking at a watercolor painting that's been left out in the rain, my family disintegrating into colorful streaks. I watch the blur of them shrink away. One block. Then two. Then three. Then they turn, and they're gone, and it feels like I'm a concrete slab that's just been cracked in half, only to realize my insides never quite set.

I'm mush.

I'm crying hard now. Not cute little sniffs. Ugly gasping breaths. People walk by on the sidewalk. Some give me a wide berth. Others shoot me sympathetic looks. As one woman around my age passes, she holds out a tissue to me without so much as slowing her pace and I clutch it like a baby blanket, unable to do anything but cry harder *and* laugh, my abdomen ricocheting between the two.

It's like Mom used to say: You're not a true New Yorker until you're willing to feel your emotions out in the open, and only now, having made a firm decision to stay, have I crossed that last threshold.

I drop onto Libby's stoop—her *former* stoop—laughing and crying so hysterically I can no longer discern one from the other. Only once my phone starts to ring do I manage to get any kind of hold on myself.

I sniff, clearing out some of my tears, as I free my phone from my pocket and read the screen. "Libby?" I answer. "Is everything okay?"

"What's up?" she says.

"Nothing?" I smear the backs of my hands across my eyes. "You?"

"Not a lot," she sighs. "I just missed you. Thought I'd call and say hi."

Warmth fills my chest. It creeps into my fingers and toes, until there is so much of it, it hurts. I'm overfilled. No one person should ever have quite so much love in their body at one time.

"What's New York look like right now?" she asks.

They've been gone eight minutes. "Did Brendan's foot fall off onto the gas pedal or something?"

"Just tell me," she says. "I want to hear *you* describe it."

I look around at the hustle and bustle, the trees pushing out their first spurts of reds and yellows across their leaves. A man unloading crates of fruit at the bodega across the street. An old lady with jet-black hair under a white rhinestoned cowboy hat picking through the DVDs for sale on some guy's folding table. (Libby and I took a glance before we parted ways and realized eighty-five percent of the collection featured Keanu Reeves, which begs the question: did this man and Keanu Reeves have some great falling-out?)

I smell kebab cooking down the street, and in the distance car horns blare, and a woman who may or may not be an actress I've seen on *SVU* hurries past in huge sunglasses, walking a tiny, prancing Boston terrier.

"Well?" Libby says.

It looks like home. "Same old, same old."

"I knew it." I can hear her smiling.

She wanted me to go with her, but she's happy that I'm getting what I want.

I wanted her to stay, but I hope she finds everything she's looking for and more.

Maybe love shouldn't be built on a foundation of compromises, but maybe it can't exist without them either.

Not the kind that forces two people into shapes they don't fit in, but the kind that loosens their grips, always leaves room to grow. Compromises that say, there will be a you-shaped space in my heart, and if your shape changes, I will adapt.

No matter where we go, our love will stretch out to hold us, and that makes me feel like . . . like everything will be okay.

37

ON DECEMBER TWELFTH at eleven twenty, I make my way over to Freeman Books.

It's the one day a year I've always taken off at the agency, and as soon as I started at Loggia Publishing, I requested the twelfth off there too.

The learning curve is brutal, but after so many years of knowing exactly how to do my job, the challenge is exhilarating. I comb through each of my newly inherited authors' manuscripts like an archaeologist at a newly discovered dig site.

Is it possible to be a zealot for editing books?

If so, that's what I am.

I almost hated to miss work today, but if I'm going to be out of the office, at least I'll still be surrounded by words.

I take my time walking, enjoying a surprise bout of sunshine that melts the snow into slushy lumps on the sidewalk, the feeble warmth seeping into my favorite herringbone coat.

At the diner where Mom used to work, I buy a cup of coffee and a danish. It's been a long time since anyone recognized me here, but I'm pretty sure the same cashier rang up Libby and me *last* December twelfth, and that's enough to fill me with a pleasant sense of belonging.

And then the sharp ache, like I've brushed up against the blistered part of my heart: *Charlie should be here.* I don't avoid thinking about him, like I used to do with Jakob. Even if it hurts, when he shimmers across my mind, it's like remembering a favorite book. One that left you gutted, sure, but also one that changed you forever.

I pass a flower shop with a heated plastic tent propped up around its storefront and duck in to buy a bouquet of deep red petals sprinkled with silvery green leaves and tiny white blossoms. I don't know flower types, but for these to be blooming in winter, they must be hardy, and I respect them for that.

At eleven forty-five, I'm still two blocks away, and my phone vibrates in my coat pocket. Shifting the bouquet into the crook of my arm, I fish around in my pocket, then tug my glove off with my teeth to swipe the phone unlocked and read Libby's message.

Happy birthday! she writes, like she's sending the text straight to Mom.

Happy birthday, I write back, my chest stinging. It's hard to be apart today. It's the first time I've had to do this without her.

FaceTime later? she writes.

Of course, I say.

She types for a minute as I hurry across the last block. Did you get my present yet?

Since when do we do presents for Mom's birthday? I write.

Since we have to be apart for it, she says.

Well, I didn't get you anything.

That's fine, she says. You can owe me. But you haven't gotten yours yet?

No, I write. I'm out.

Ah, she says. At Freeman's already?

In about three seconds. I shoulder the door open and step into the familiar dusty warmth.

I'll let you go, she says. But send a pic when the present gets there, okay?

I reply with a thumbs-up and a heart, then drop my phone and gloves into my pockets, freeing my hands to browse.

I head straight for the romance shelves. This year, I'll buy two copies of whatever I choose and mail one to Libby. Or, better yet, take it with me when I visit her for the holidays and Number Three's birth.

As I wander along the hundreds of pristine spines, time unspools around me, the current slowing. I have nowhere to be. Nothing to do but peruse summaries and pull quotes on dust jackets, skimming some last pages and leaving others unread. Again and again, I ask, *What about this one, Mom? Would you like this?*

And then, *Would* I *like this?* Because that matters too.

Whenever I'm in front of a row of books, it's like I can hear Mom's loud yelp of a laugh, smell her warm lavender scent. On one occasion, Libby and I were so absorbed in our December twelfth process that, for like ten minutes, we failed to notice the man in the trench coat next to us doing his level best to expose himself.

(When this happened, and I finally noticed, I heard myself calmly, disinterestedly, say—a book still in my hand—*No.* The look on his face gave me the greatest surge of power I've had to date, and Libby and I laughed for weeks about what otherwise might've been a fairly traumatizing experience.)

So though I'm aware a couple of other people are milling around in my periphery, I don't exactly acknowledge any of them until I reach for January Andrews's novel *Curmudgeon*, only to find someone else reaching for it at the same moment.

Most people, I guess, would blurt, *Sorry!* What comes out of *my* mouth is, "Agh!"

Neither of us lets go of the book—typical city people—and I spin toward my rival, unwilling to back down.

My heart stops.

Okay, I'm sure it doesn't.

I'm alive still.

But this, I realize, is what they mean, all those thousands of writers who've tried to describe the sensation of following the trail of your life for years, only to smack into something that changes it forever.

The way the sensation jars through you, from the center out. How you feel it in your mouth and toes all at once, a dozen tiny explosions.

And then an unfurling of warmth from your collarbone to your ribs, to thighs, to palms, like just seeing him has triggered some kind of chrysalis.

My body has moved from winter into spring, all those scraggly little sprouts pushing up through a crush of snow. Spring, alive and awake in my bloodstream.

"Stephens," Charlie says softly, like a swear, or a prayer, or a mantra.

"What are you doing here?" I breathe.

"I'm not sure which answer to start with."

"Libby." The realization vaults up through me. "You're—you're my gift?"

His mouth curves, teasing, but his eyes stay soft, almost hesitant. "In a way."

"In what way?"

"Goode Books," he says carefully, "is under new management."

I shake my head, trying to clear the fog. "Your sister came through?"

He shakes his head. "Yours did."

My mouth opens but no sound comes out. When I shut it again, tears cloud my eyes. "I don't understand."

But some part of me does.

Or wants to believe it does.

It *hopes*. And that hope registers like a burning knot of golden, glowing thread, too tangled up to make sense of.

Charlie slides the book caught between our hands back onto the shelf, then steps in close, his hands taking mine.

"Three weeks ago," he says, "I was at the shop, and our family showed up."

"Our family?" I repeat.

"Sally, Clint, Libby," he says. "They brought a PowerPoint."

"A PowerPoint?" I say, my brow wrinkling.

The corner of his mouth curves. "It was very organized," he says. "You would've fucking loved it. Maybe they'll email you a copy."

"I don't understand," I say. "How are you here?"

"They put together a list," he says. " 'Twelve Steps to Reunite Soul Mates'—*which*, by the way, involved multiple Jane Austen quotes. Not sure if that was Libby or Dad. But what I'm getting at is, they made some compelling points."

Tears flood into my eyes, my nose, my chest. "Such as?"

A full, bright smile; an electrical storm behind his eyes. "Such as I'm desperate to see your Peloton in real life," he says. "And I need to know if your mattress deserves the hype. And most importantly, I'm so fucking in love with you, Nora."

"But—but your dad . . ."

"Graduated early from physical therapy," he says. "The Power-Point said 'with honors,' but I'm eighty-eight percent sure that's not a real thing. And Libby took over the store. The girls run wild there every day, and Tala arm wrestles anyone who tries to leave without buying anything. It's beautiful. Libby also said to tell you that she and Brendan are 'Manhattan Destitute but North Carolina Rich,' so after the baby comes, Principal Schroeder's going to help out while Libby takes a leave, then when she's ready to come back to work, she'll hire a nanny, so you should stop worrying before you even start."

I laugh wetly, shake my head again. "You said your mom would never let someone outside the family run the store."

His eyes settle on my face, his expression going serious. "I think she's hopeful Libby won't be outside the family forever."

That's it. The dam breaks, and I burst into sniffling, happy tears as Charlie frames my face with his hands. "I told my parents I couldn't leave them if they needed me, and you know what they said?"

"What?" My voice cracks about four times on that one syllable.

"They said *they're* the parents." His voice is damp, throttled. "Apparently they don't need 'jack shit' from me except for me to be happy. And they wouldn't mind a hot, sexy daughter-in-law."

I don't know whether to laugh or cry some more, or maybe just scream at the top of my lungs. Excited scream, not scared scream. (Is *that* how you're supposed to say *Spaaaahhh*?)

"Exact quote from Sally?" I say.

He grins. "Paraphrasing."

The knot is unbraiding, unsnarling in me, reaching upward through my throat and rooting down through my stomach as he goes on.

"Nora Stephens," he says, "I've racked my brain and this is the best I can come up with, so I really hope you like it."

His gaze lifts, everything about it, about his face, about his posture, about *him* made up of sharp edges and jagged bits and shadows, all of it familiar, all of it perfect. Not for someone else, maybe, but for me.

"I move back to New York," he says. "I get another editing job, or maybe take up agenting, or try writing again. You work your way up at Loggia, and we're both busy all the time, and down in Sunshine Falls, Libby runs the local business she saved, and my parents spoil your nieces like the grandkids they so desperately want, and Brendan probably doesn't get much better at fishing, but he gets to relax and even take paid vacations with your sister and their kids. And you and I—we go out to dinner.

"Wherever you want, whenever you want. We have a lot of fun being city people, and we're happy. You let me love you as much as I know I can, for as long as I know I can, and you have it fucking all. That's it. That's the best I could come up with, and I really fucking hope you say—"

I kiss him then, like there isn't someone reading one of the Bridgerton novels five feet away, like we've just found each other on a deserted island after months apart. My hands in his hair, my tongue catching on his teeth, his palms sliding around behind me and squeezing me to him in the most thoroughly public groping we've managed yet.

"I love you, Nora," he says when we pull apart a few inches to breathe. "I think I love everything about you."

"Even my Peloton?" I ask.

"Great piece of equipment," he says.

"The fact that I check my email after work hours?"

"Just makes it easier to share Bigfoot erotica without having to walk across the room," he says.

"Sometimes I wear *very* impractical shoes," I add.

"Nothing impractical about looking hot," he says.

"And what about my bloodlust?"

His eyes go heavy as he smiles. "That," he says, "might be my favorite thing. Be my shark, Stephens."

"Already was," I say. "Always have been."

"I love you," he says again.

"I love you too." I don't have to force it past a knot or through the vise of a tight throat. It's simply the truth, and it breathes out of me, a wisp of smoke, a sigh, another floating blossom on a current carrying billions of them.

"I know," he says. "I can read you like a book."

EPILOGUE

~

SIX MONTHS LATER

T HERE ARE BALLOONS in the window, a chalkboard sign out front. Through the soft glare on the glass, you can see the crowd milling around, toasting with champagne flutes, talking, laughing, browsing.

To the uninitiated, it might look like a birthday party. There is, after all, a little girl with strawberry blond waves—newly four years old—who has stolen a cupcake from the tower of them at the back of the shop, and now runs in dizzying figure eights around the legs of the adults, knocking into chairs and shelves, purple icing smeared around her lips.

Or the crowd could be celebrating her lanky older sister, with the straight, ashy bangs, who has finally, after some struggle, learned to read. (Now she spends almost every day folded up in the green bean-bag chair inside the children's book room with a book in her lap.) Or it could all be for the baby on the pink-haired woman's hip. She crawled for the first time just nine days ago (albeit backward, and only for a second), and you'd think she'd won the Nobel Prize, from the screaming on her mom and aunt's video call. ("Do it again, Kitty! Show Auntie Nono how you're the most agile, athletic baby of all time!")

There's cause to celebrate the pink-haired woman's husband too. After *weeks* of trailing along with the local Catch-and-Release Club, he finally caught something early that morning, while the mist was still thick across the river—even if it *was* just a very large bra.

The cupcake-thieving four-year-old darts through his legs and runs smack into the tall older man using the cane. She giggles as he rustles her hair. Someone pats his arm and congratulates him on finally retiring. "More time to clean the gutters at home," he says.

Maybe everyone's here to honor the woman with the sweet, crinkly eyes, who moves in a cloud of weedy jasmine—two of her paintings have just been accepted into a group show.

Or they could be celebrating that the shop hosting the party just had its most profitable month in eight years.

It could be that, after months of working freelance, the thick-browed man with a pout of a smile has just accepted a job offer at Wharton House Books, a position several rungs higher than when he worked there the first time. Or this could all have something to do with the small velvet box he can't stop turning over in his jacket pocket. (There's nothing inside it; she mentioned once that if she ever got married, she'd choose the ring herself.) Or that the ice-blond woman leaning against him has known for weeks already what she's going to say. (She made a pro-con list, but only ended up writing his name under *pro* and *possibly wear a piece of jewelry I didn't pick out for life????* under *con*.)

The party in question might also be for the woman in the Coke-bottle glasses, clutching a champagne flute as she approaches the microphone in the center of the bookstore, a stack of slate-gray books arranged on a table beside her, a room of readers falling quiet, rapt, waiting for her to speak, to introduce this new story to a world that has been waiting for it.

"For anyone who wants it all," she begins, "may you find something that is more than enough."

She wonders whether what comes next could ever live up to the expectations.

She doesn't know. You never can.

She turns the page anyway.

ACKNOWLEDGMENTS

~

Every time I write a book, the list of people I need to thank grows while the odds of me hitting everyone who deserves a heartfelt mention shrinks. But I'm going to try anyway, because the truth is, I wouldn't be here in this book you're holding without the essential help of so many people.

Thank you first and foremost to my beloved Berkley family: Amanda, Sareer, Dache', Danielle, Jessica, Craig, Christine, Jeanne-Marie, Claire, Ivan, Cindy, and everyone else. I love being a part of this team so much, and genuinely feel like the luckiest writer on the planet to have landed among such smart, talented, passionate, driven book lovers like you. Huge appreciation also to Sandra Chiu, Alison Cnockaert, Nicole Wayland, Martha Cipolla, Jessica McDonnell, and Lindsey Tulloch.

I also have to thank my incredible UK team over at Viking, especially Vikki, Georgia, Rosie, and Poppy.

Immense gratitude to Taylor and the whole Root Literary team—including but not limited to Holly, Melanie, Jasmine, and

Molly. You all are the more organized, more savvy, more pragmatic half of my brain, and I would be lost in this business without you. Huge thanks also to Heather and the rest of Baror International for getting my work into the hands of readers all over the world, and to my tireless film agent, Mary, as well as Orly, Nia, and the rest of the UTA team.

Publishing has a lot of fairy godparents, and I want to thank a few of mine from the past handful of years: Robin Kall, Vilma Iris, Zibby Owens, Ashley Spivey, Becca Freeman, Grace Atwood, and Sarah True.

Additionally, I wouldn't be where I am today without Book of the Month Club *and* my local independent bookstore Joseph-Beth Booksellers, not to mention all the other indie shops across the US and beyond who've so graciously supported me and hosted virtual events over these last two strange years. You've worked so hard to find ways to connect authors and readers in the midst of a global pandemic, and I couldn't be more grateful.

One of my absolute favorite things about getting to publish in this space is how many kind, generous, funny, smart, empathetic people I've been lucky enough to cross paths with. Some (but certainly not all) of those include Brittany Cavallaro, Jeff Zentner, Parker Peevyhouse, Riley Redgate, Kerry Kletter, David Arnold, Isabel Ibañez, Justin Reynolds, Tehlor Kay Mejia, Cam Montgomery, Jodi Picoult, Colleen Hoover, Sarah MacLean, Jennifer Niven, Lana Popović Harper, Meg Leder, Austin Siegmund-Broka, Emily Wibberley, Sophie Cousens, Laura Hankin, Kennedy Ryan, Jane L. Rosen, Evie Dunmore, Roshani Chokshi, Sally Thorne, Christina (and) Lauren, Laura Jane Williams, Jasmine Guillory, Josie Silver, Sonali Dev, Casey McQuiston, Lizzy Dent, Amy Reichert, Abby Jimenez, Debbie Macomber, Laura Zigman, Bethany Morrow, Adriana Mather,

Katie Cotugno, Heather Cocks, Jessica Morgan, Victoria Schwab, Eric Smith, Adriana Trigiani, and (my absolutely perfect audiobook narrator, friend, and fellow author) Julia Whelan.

The rest of my friends and my family: You know who you are, and I love you so much. Thank you for your love, support, and patience. There's no one I'd rather be quarantined with.

And lastly, the biggest thank-you ever to everyone who's read, reviewed, bought, borrowed, lent, and posted about my books. You have given me an incredible gift, and I will never stop appreciating it.

**NEED ANOTHER LAUGH-OUT-LOUD
LOVE STORY TO SWEEP YOU OFF YOUR FEET?**

Beach Read

EMILY HENRY

*TWO WRITERS, ONE HOLIDAY.
A ROM-COM WAITING TO HAPPEN...*

January is a hopeless romantic who narrates her life like
she's the lead in a blockbuster movie. Gus is a serious literary
type who thinks true love is a fairy tale.

But January and Gus have more in common than you'd think.

They're both broke.
They've got crippling writer's block.
And they need to write bestsellers before summer ends.

The result? A bet to swap genres and see who gets published first.
The risk? In telling each other's stories, their worlds might be
changed entirely...

**Set over one sizzling summer, *Beach Read* is a witty love story
that will make you laugh a lot, cry a little and fall head over heels.
For fans of *The Flatshare* and *If I Never Met You*.**

'The hottest book of the summer' **JOSIE SILVER**

'One of the most perfect love stories of the year' ***PRIMA***

'The perfect escapist romp' **LAURA JANE WILLIAMS**

'Funny, and seriously sizzling' ***BEST***